WANDRESS

A NOVEL

BY

BECKI ALFSEN

KISMET PRESS, LLC.

Cover art by Michelle Marman (micannmarman@hotmail.com). Michelle, thank you for your wonderful work.

Manuscript and cover edited and produced by Jeff Ludwig | Editing, Writing (jeffrey.ludwig76@gmail.com).

Author photo by Jack Ratliff.

For Jack and Milo, who began calling me an author from the first words I put on paper.

WANDRESS

CHAPTER ONE

T *his isn't coming out of the blue. It's been months in the making.* Ruby glanced away from the plastic bag that was flitting by outside her window. She watched Scott, silent in his anger, sharpen a knife. The scraping of metal along the honing steel may as well have been a buzz saw in their fourth story apartment. Doubt had turned into hairline fissures that were now gaped as wide as canyons. The words that kept repeating in Ruby's head were, "I can't stand the person I am with you."

Outside the glass, the March wind had caught the bag on a bare branch, ending its short journey. Somehow the sight put an exclamation mark on what she needed to do. *I need more than this*, she thought.

Ruby's throat tightened. She found it nearly impossible to swallow around the ball of sawdust that choked her throat. When she locked eyes with Scott, she willed herself not to turn away and realized that after six months, she had no idea who he was. Sure, they lived together and ate together. They slept together and did things. But a favorite color? Does he like a certain time of year? Is he scared of anything? Ruby couldn't answer any of these questions, and was sure he couldn't answer for her either.

Her entire life she had heard that relationships were work, but relationships were supposed to be enjoyable work, not the rip-your-hair-out dread she felt with Scott. A relationship was meant to be interesting and that you want the very best for that person and them for you. Listening, debating, laughing, arguing, and making up—and wanting all of it. This, with Scott, had sucked every living cell in her body.

What do I want? I don't want someone who makes me feel less than I am. I want more. I want to stretch who I am and what I do. I want life to happen on a whim. I want magic. I want – No, I need . . . more. More than this.

"What Ruby? What kind of look is that? Are you fucking not talking to me now?" Scott tossed the knife, causing it to skate across the kitchen counter and clatter into the sink. He left the uncut carrots marooned on the cutting board.

She looked at him to study him, to think. What did it take, a few months? It seemed such a short time to strip a person down. Yet, the time stretched like a taffy pull – over and over in never ending twists.

"I swear to God, you better say something or I'm going to lose it." His voice was quiet with danger. Ruby had never before heard the venom that poured out of him now. Scott kept everything in check. This, whatever this was he was doing, was new. She might have just opened a door that should have stayed closed. Maybe she had guessed at the person he kept out of sight on some level, but she never wanted to look too closely, never rock the boat, perhaps for exactly this reason.

When they began dating in October 1991, she had wanted passionate feelings, to feel her breath catch, to experience anticipation of a searing touch and of someone that wanted to listen to her thoughts, and she to his. She wanted a man that was valiant. She pretended that those sensations were there, but she would have had better luck squeezing a lemon to make orange juice. It wasn't going to happen. She had settled, and tonight she was through.

Though her body trembled with anxiety, Ruby's voice came out flat and even. "I'm not going to do this. I am not going to hang from strings for a puppet master." She began walking toward the short hallway that led to the bedroom they shared. Her legs were rubber, but somehow they kept moving.

Scott slid over and blocked her way. He didn't tower over her, but he may as well have been ten feet tall. He was livid with heat, and alarm bells went off in Ruby's head. *I need to get out of here. Now.*

"Strings? Puppet master? I don't know what the hell you're talking about. You're nuts. Fucking crazy! What are you going to do, leave me?" An ugly snort came out of his mouth. Droplets of spit hit her face.

Anger began building in her chest. The emotion was red hot and alive. Her teeth clenched together as she spoke through them. "Yeah, I'm leaving. Either get out of my way, or I will scream so loud someone will call the police."

Scott stood still as a stone. She stared at the Claddagh ring on his hand, which grasped the doorframe. *What is he doing? Testing me? Waiting to see what I'll do?*

He turned, and she would never know if it was accidental or intentional, but the back of his hand was as quick as a cobra strike when it hit Ruby's cheek and right eye. Stars fell from the sky as she leaned against the wall. The shock of what happened numbed the pain that was sure to come.

"Ruby." His voice sounded displeased, like a father scolding a naughty child.

"What did I do?" almost made it out of her mouth before she pounded it down with a virtual sledgehammer.

She touched a finger to her cheek and saw a trace of blood. "Get out of my way." Her voice sounded raspy and foreign. As tears stung her light blue eyes, she had the sensation of looking through a glass Coke bottle. "Move."

Her voice was louder this time.

Acting the part of complete asshole, Scott backed against the wall and held up his hands in mock surrender. "Christ, Ruby. It was an accident." He reached out and slid his fingers down a long strand of her blonde hair.

Confusion flooded her mind, not sure if his gesture was an attempt at an apology or to bully her. She slapped his hand away and walked to the bedroom. Her suitcase was under the bed, and any piece of clothing she could find was thrown inside and zipped up. She turned to leave.

Scott grabbed her arm in a vice grip. "You're making a huge mistake. Enough with the drama. If you walk out the door, you'll never see me again."

Ruby looked down at her arm, looked at Scott, and then kneed him in the balls as hard as she could. He crumpled like a crushed can. The only sound that made it out of his twisted mouth was a froggish croak.

Her lips curved as she skirted past him out the door, slamming it as an exclamation point. She knew she'd never see him again, she was banking on it. His macho Jersey-boy self would never beg for a woman's forgiveness. Oddly enough, given the scenario, she had not felt this good in a long time.

* * *

Ruby stood in the dark parking lot of the apartment complex and surveyed the remnants of the latest snowstorm. Glassy patches of ice coated the asphalt after the sun had set behind the Colorado Mountains. Her hair whipped around, giving the illusion of flaxen snakes dancing in the wind. The suitcase dropped from her hand with a thunk.

I don't have a car. Of course I don't have a car. He has the car. A scream came up her throat, muffled behind tightly closed lips. *Poppy, I'll call Poppy.* There was not a doubt in her mind that her sister would come.

Every few seconds, Ruby glanced up at the sliding glass door of the apartment. *Strange, I have never called it "my apartment" or "our apartment." That should have been a sign. It's a box—a ceiling, a floor, and four walls. That's all.*

She wrapped shivering arms around herself and hopped up and down to keep warm. The wind sliced right through her black turtleneck sweater. She thought about her puffy winter jacket that hung from a hook—four stories up. Her teeth gritted together. "Eehh."

Headlights swung into the parking lot fifteen minutes later, causing Ruby to shield her eyes. Poppy's 1981 BMW slid a few inches on the ice before it came to a stop alongside her. Poppy had her hands on her sister's shoulders before Ruby's had even touched the door handle. "Are you okay? It sounded like you were crying on the phone. Are you crying?"

Thankfully, shadows from windblown branches played across her face. The bruise would be difficult to see. "Yeah, I'm fine. Can we go?"

The tension she held in her shoulders eased when she relaxed against the headrest of the warm car. After one more glance up at the balcony, not even a ripple from the vertical blinds met her gaze. *Huh.*

The drive was mostly silent. Ruby knew that Poppy had never approved of Scott; thankfully, she didn't mention it now. It was only a matter of time, though, given the fact that she would be powerless to conceal her cheek behind her hair once they reached her sister's house.

Ruby left her suitcase in the car—she would get it later. The sisters leaned into the wind as they made their way up Poppy's cracked concrete walkway. Now, in the bright light of Poppy's living room, there was no hiding her face. "Oh, my God, Ruby. What happened?" She brushed Ruby's hair over one shoulder, gently touching the cut and bruise that had sprouted.

Embarrassment filled Ruby as she looked past her sister, unable to make eye contact. Then, a lightning bolt hit her. *I am not going to play the victim.* She ignored her sister's question. Instead, she said, "I've got to get out of Boulder, out of Colorado. I don't know what happened." It was not an answer to Poppy's question, but a query she made to herself.

"We need to call the police. Has he done this before?" She had turned to lawyer mode.

"Why do you think it was Scott?"

"Are you kidding? It was bad enough when you were dating him, but since you moved in together, you've become a different person." Poppy walked to the kitchen. Ruby heard the freezer open and things being shoved around. She wanted to be angry and tell her sister that she was full of crap, but Ruby couldn't form the words.

Poppy returned to the living room. She was still in a dark, tailored suit, and her blond hair was up in a perfect twist. "Here, put this on your face." She handed Ruby a frozen bag of peas. "We hardly ever do anything together anymore. You never call. You used to be optimistic and funny. In fact, I don't remember the last time I've heard you laugh." Poppy sat next to Ruby on the couch. "He is always around. But this," she touched her sister's knee, "I never thought he would do something like this, or I would have pulled you out of there myself."

"I'm not calling the police and, no, he's never laid a hand on me before. But you're right. It is a scary thing when you think you're one thing and then realize you're not. I thought I was strong and independent." The shake of her head was nearly imperceptible.

"Ruby, you are an amazing woman. You just lost you're way for a bit."

Ruby was thankful. Her sister could yell or demand that she go to the police. Poppy was the one person she could always count on to be exactly what she needed. "I've got to find myself again, and I can't do it here. I don't want to be anywhere near him."

Poppy tapped manicured nail against her bottom lip. "Yeah, you do." She seemed lost in thought. "Come here." She wrapped a blanket over both their shoulders, and they sat quietly for so long that Ruby drifted off. Her eyes flung open when Poppy tore the blanket away.

"Ruby, I've got it." Her deep blue eyes met her younger sister's. "Leave. Go somewhere, do something. This is your time. You can do anything."

"Go where? What would I do?" Ruby took the peas, which had slipped onto her lap, and set the bag on the coffee table. In contrast to the doubt she verbalized, her heart began racing with the possibilities.

Two beats passed. "Europe. Go to Europe. It's perfect. It's safe, beautiful, and not so foreign that you'll feel completely out of place. You already graduated." Ruby had graduated from the University of Colorado at Boulder winter semester. Her sister gestured to Ruby's face, "After this, Margie would probably buy a ticket for you."

Margie owned Whimsy, and had become one of Ruby's closest friends.

"You can use the money Nita left you." Poppy grinned.

Nita was an eccentric relative who had traveled the globe and had a soft spot for Ruby and Poppy. When she died, never having married, the sisters were each bequeathed ten thousand dollars. Ruby had used a large chunk on school, but had a few thousand left.

Ruby's front teeth grasped onto her thumb nail. Her head nodded. "Yeah, I could do that." She felt life seep into her pores. A smile—albeit a nervous one—spread across her face. It made sense to use the money to travel. Nita would beam down on her from above. The weight that had been dragging her down for months lifted—maybe not completely, but she felt lighter, freer.

"Let's find out how much tickets are."

After that, everything came together.

CHAPTER TWO

*W*hat a difference a few days make. Colorado is a perfect place to re-discover life. It is always in a state of flux: the seasons, the temperature, and the landscape are always shifting. Sixteen days ago it was cold, snowy, and dreary. Now five days into April, the sky was blue, the sun was out, and Ruby could taste spring in the air—sweet and fresh on her tongue.

Sliding her bicycle up to Whimsy, Ruby lightly tapped an orange bucket of bright yellow and purple tulips with her tire. She was right on time for an impromptu going away party that Margie had insisted on. She could see Poppy through the Tudor window, waving a champagne bottle over Margie's grey, curly hair. Huge smiles were on both of their faces.

The tinkle of the brass bell above the door, followed by a loud pop, sounded as Ruby walked into the shop. "Bon Voyage!" Both women cried in unison. Foamy bubbles ran down the sides of the bottle as Poppy poured the champagne into cups held by Margie. Margie passed the cups around and offered a toast. "Here's to the beginning of finding your true self." Everyone raised their cups and drank. "You look better, and I'm not only talking about your face. Your whole body looks different—more like you did when you first started working here, young and sprightly."

"I feel really good." Ruby reflexively touched her cheek. "Sam went and got the rest of my stuff from the apartment so I wouldn't have to go back. By the way, I don't know if I thanked him, Poppy."

Sam was Poppy's long-time boyfriend. Ruby always

thought they looked like siblings with their blonde hair and piercing blue eyes, which was nice, given that she often treated him like a brother. She guessed that the inverse was true as well. After he had dropped her things at Poppy's house, Sam told Ruby that she didn't need to worry about Scott bothering her. A protective big brother.

"I'm sure you did, but I'll tell him again. Better yet, you can tell him when we go to Nostimo tonight." Nostimo was Ruby's favorite Greek restaurant in Boulder, the one that the three of them would go to before she left for Europe.

Margie cleared her throat. "Alright. That sounds good and all, but let's get this party started." The lines around her brown eyes crinkled as she smiled. "You two sit down, and I'll get the gifts."

The two sisters sat on iron chairs around a salvaged mosaic table. Ruby ran her fingers over the jagged pieces of tile. "I'm getting gifts?" She grinned. "I cannot believe I'm leaving tomorrow. I should be frantic, but I'm completely relaxed, I have some weird mellow vibe going." Ruby drank from her cup. "Maybe it's the champagne."

Margie walked back to the table holding two marvelously wrapped boxes. "No, sweetie. You feel that way because this is exactly the place and time you are destined for." Margie took her cup and tipped it toward Ruby, emphasizing her point. "You've made the perfect decision. You're young and need to find out who you are without anyone telling you this, that, and the other."

"Although I'm not as hippie as you," Ruby winked at Poppy, "it does feel like destiny, kismet, or some other cosmic force leading me in the right direction." She watched the effervescence dance around the cup. "I feel resilient. More like the person I was before the whole Scott debacle."

"That's your past. Let's toast to the future and the

journey we're all on, and to timeless friendships." Margie said. They lifted their cups and drank them down.

Ruby shivered as the sharp taste made its way down her throat. The sides of her mouth pulled up with anticipation as she looked at the gifts. "These look so pretty." She held up the first package, which was the size of a shoebox and was wrapped in tangerine orange paper with a blue hydrangea tucked under a wide, multi-colored grosgrain ribbon.

"That one is from me." With a mischievous gleam in her eyes, Margie raised her eyebrows.

Ruby put the box to her ear and shook it. There was no sound, and it weighed nothing. "I don't have a guess." She lifted the lid and reached down into orange tissue paper. Both sisters gaped at the red, foil-wrapped condom in Ruby's hand.

Ruby turned the box over, and a rainbow of assorted rubbers skittered across the table. "What do you think I'm going to do, screw my way through Europe?" Ruby laughed. The thought was ridiculous. She hadn't even considered the possibility of sex overseas. In reflecting on the mess of her one and only relationship, she didn't think she'd be in the market anytime soon.

"Hey, you never know. Don't let some ass stymie you from your future." Margie danced her fingertips over the condoms. "And with that thought in mind, you can pick and choose flavors, colors, and textures. I want you to be well protected, but also enjoy yourself."

Poppy rifled through the assortment. "What is this?" Her voiced squeaked. One package was embossed with the words "Nubby Love." They all hooted and, before long, Poppy took the foil off and stared at a limp rubber with bumps that ran its length. "Wow. Do you mind if I take one of these?"

Ruby had only enough time to scrunch her slightly turned up, Scandinavian nose before Margie chimed in. "Yum, 'Monkey Business' tastes like bananas." She licked the smooth surface.

"Okay, everyone drop the happy hats," Ruby laughed. "I want to open Poppy's gift." This gift was smaller and intricately wrapped in glossy, light pink paper. Three delicate silver butterflies floated above its surface. "It's lovely Poppy," she said, and proceeded to tear into the wrapping with gusto. Inside the box was a beautiful necklace lying on a creamy satin pillow. Ruby lifted it out and draped it over her two middle fingers, resting it on her inner wrist. The necklace was made of tiny round stones with an old Chinese coin in the center.

"It has special meaning," Poppy said. "The onyx is supposed to calm and empower you to have the strength to transform. The amethyst is to remind you that you can achieve whatever you set your mind to, and the coin attracts luck and opportunity. The way I see it, you should be covered." She smiled at her younger sister.

Ruby admired the beads and then nodded to Poppy. "Very fortune cookie-esque of you. I absolutely love it." She handed it to Poppy, lifted her hair, and said, "Here, put it on for me." Poppy came up behind her sister and fastened the toggle clasp. Ruby dropped her hair and turned. The coin lay at the indentation between her collarbones, and the beads felt soft and cool as they encircled her neck. Ruby spread out her arms, "What do you think?"

"Perfect," Poppy and Margie said in unison.

"I'm going to go see what it looks like. I'll be right back," Ruby said as she started walking to the back of the store.

She zigzagged through an array of potted plants spaced throughout Whimsy, past a glass cooler that was jammed with roses. As she moved through the store, Ruby slid her hand along the cool, stainless steel garden table where they made arrangements and snatched up a pair of scissors lying next to discarded daisy stems. Without thinking, she kept them in her hand as she made her way to the bathroom.

An artist friend of Margie's had transformed the closet-sized room into the most magnificent bathroom Ruby had ever seen. She created a world where the forest touched the sea, both giving the illusion that they went on until the eye could see no further. Sitting on top of a thick tree stump was a glacier-blue glass bowl and a faucet that resembled a waterfall. It was as if she were washing her hands in a natural pond. Ruby looked at herself in what Margie coined "The Looking Glass." One hand curled around her neck, and the other clenched the cool metal of the scissors.

Her fingers left her neck and slowly grabbed a bundle of hair. The sound the blades of the scissors as they made their way through each strand transported her back to when she was six. She could hear her mom: *"Ruby, don't wiggle. Keep your head still while I put the tape on your bangs."* Her mom stood back from the kitchen counter Ruby sat on and tilted her head. *"I think that looks straight."* With Scotch tape in place, she commenced cutting. Each time, one side ended up shorter than the other. Ruby breathed in with the memory.

The scissors made their way through another fist-full of hair. By the time she was done, the sink was full of golden silk, and her eyes sparkled with life. She looked into the mirror. Hysterical giggles came in spurts from her opened mouth. Her previously long, wavy hair was now cut at the jaw. Without the weight, waves became loose curls. It looked messy and carefree. She scooped the hair from the sink, shoved it into the trashcan, and returned to the shop.

Poppy and Margie were cleaning up the wrapping paper

when they saw Ruby. "Oh my God, what did you do?" Poppy screeched, her voice was octaves above its usual warm tone.

"You sloughed your skin like a snake!" Margie bounced on her toes, her palms together.

Ruby ran her fingers through her hair, letting loose strands fall to the floor. "I don't know. It was like the sheers had a mind of their own. Am I crazy? Holy shit."

"No, no. You're in the middle of your catharsis. Changing is exactly what you should be doing. How do you feel?" Margie asked. She watched Ruby with excited anticipation.

"It feels lighter." A laugh bubbled up from her throat.

"I love it. It suits you." The older woman nodded her head in approval.

"It's all choppy and uneven," Poppy said. She walked in a circle around Ruby, her face scrunched up as if she was viewing a sculpture she didn't quite understand.

"Sit, sit. We'll do some trimming up, and it will look fabulous. You really didn't do that bad of a job," Margie said. She reached for the scissors Ruby had dropped onto the table.

Twenty minutes later, her hair was trimmed, the wrapping was thrown away, the condoms were back in the box tucked underneath Ruby's arm, and strong hugs were being given.

"I'll send you a postcard of the tulip fields," Ruby said as she and Poppy made their way to the front of the store.

Ruby smiled over her shoulder. Margie had once told her that it was fate that brought Ruby through her door two years ago, "like a breath of fresh air." As Ruby looked at the older woman, she had a feeling she couldn't deny: some things in life are serendipitous and, as people, we are simply along for the ride.

Margie turned her "Come and Smell the Flowers" sign over. Whimsy didn't open for another ten minutes, but Ruby knew she had never been one to be ruled by the clock.

As Ruby got on her bike, Margie touched her hand gently. "You are an amazing woman, Ruby Larsen. The world is waiting for you. Go show them." She stepped back as Ruby blew her a kiss and started rolling down the street.

* * *

Ruby breathed in the air. It was calming, a balm that traveled through her blood. She sat on the porch of Poppy's house, her feet planted on the wooden step. It was a perfect evening, crisp and cool. The Big Dipper twinkled through the tree branches. It was a habit from childhood to find the constellation, for no other reason than to see where it hung in the sky on any given night.

Poppy put Carole King on her ancient turntable. "Home Again" floated through the mesh of the screen door and drifted off into the night. Ruby was humming when Poppy came through the door with two mugs of coffee. Ruby took one and coiled her hands around the hot pottery. She had been mentally going through her list of things to pack in the hours before she was to leave. *Small towel, extra socks, foot scrub...*

Poppy ruffled Ruby's hair and sat down. "I'm getting used to it. Who knew we had so much curl?"

Her sister had changed into a pair of sweatpants and an old law hoodie. She crossed her legs in front of her, leaned against the wooden post, and took a slurp of coffee. "I thought we were going to have to surgically close mom's mouth when she saw your hair," she said, laughing.

"Maybe my hair thwarted the tears. I don't think I could have taken crying." The sisters had spent the afternoon at their parents' house, with Ruby listening to last-minute advice that she only half paid attention to. Before they left to return to Boulder, her dad hugged her and pressed a hundred-dollar bill into her hand. Two things were funny about being given money: one was that, at twenty-three, he still thought he was responsible for her cash flow; and two was that she gladly accepted it.

Ruby pulled her knees up and hugged them to her chest. The sisters, who were more like best friends, sat and talked easily about inconsequential topics, like how they were meeting Sam in an hour, if Ruby had packed enough underwear, and the hair that stuck out of the nose of one of Poppy's co-workers. It was easy, comfortable, and exactly how it had always been between them.

CHAPTER THREE

Ruby stood outside the terminal at the Denver airport, heaved her backpack out of the trunk of Poppy's car, and leaned it up against the door. Her nerves were stretched and she found it difficult to breathe normally. Her fear of flying had reared its head. As a result, she continually wiped her clammy hands on her pants and kept touching the necklace Poppy had given her, as if it was a talisman that would keep disaster at bay.

Poppy took Ruby into her arms and hugged her in a protective embrace. "I love you," she said into her sister's hair. "You call me when you get there. I don't care what time it is." She then handed Ruby an envelope. "Open it when you get on the plane."

Sam had given Ruby a fifty-minute international phone card at the restaurant the night before. It was more a token for Poppy than for herself. Ruby's fondness for Sam had grown the longer he dated her sister.

* * *

Ruby laid her head back on the seat and watched the clouds hang in the sky outside the scratched oval window of the 747. Her emotions were all encompassing—fatigue, excitement, fear, and a sense of being completely alone. All of these sensations mingled in a tight butterfly dance that was centered in the pit of her stomach. She opened the envelope and saw her sister's writing:

> *Ruby,*
> *I know you think this trip is something that anyone*

*would do, but I'm here to tell you they wouldn't. It takes guts
to pack up and do this on your own. Don't roll your eyes. It's
true. You are one of the strongest, most daring people I know.
You and I, for some reason, devalue the accomplishments we
make. Do not let this be one of those times for you. I love you
so much. Have a great time. I'll be thinking of you every day.*
    P. xo

As uncomfortable as it was to admit, Poppy was right:
she did feel strong. She would use this trip to experience and
live exactly how she wanted. Ruby closed her wet eyes and
took a deep breath through her nose to loosen up her
muscles—something Margie had told her always helps
center one's self. She slowly released the breath from her
mouth, opened her eyes, and glanced up and down the
aisles.

Ruby surveyed the rows of seats. She found what she
was looking for in 10B—a girl who was a year or two
younger than her, wearing airline headphones and reading a
magazine. From her age and clothing, she had the look of a
fellow backpacker. After they had been in the air for a while,
the girl got up. Ruby followed and stood outside the
bathroom. When the girl came out, rather than doing what
her instincts told her, which was to skirt around and go into
the bathroom, Ruby didn't let the fact that she was a born
introvert get the best of her.

"Hi. I saw you sitting a few rows up from me. Are you
going to Amsterdam?" Ruby asked. It felt like plaster was
drying in her mouth. *Is having a conversation so hard? Maybe
it's the vulnerability of it. Well, get over it.*

"Yeah, are you staying there too, or going on?" the girl
asked. She pitched forward as the plane hit an air pocket.
"Woo, I love that feeling. My stomach is in my throat."

Ruby felt something else in her throat and grabbed the

coin around her neck. "I'm staying outside Amsterdam, a town called Leiden."

"Oh yeah? What's there? Do you know someone, or just visiting?" she asked. The girl had a pursed mouth, her lips the same color as her skin, which made them fade into the background. That fact drew more attention to her near black, almond-shaped eyes. It was hard to distinguish what her nationality might be—Asian, or maybe eastern European.

The "Fasten Seatbelt" sign came on, and the male flight attendant told them they would have to take their seats. With another jolt of the plane, Ruby was ready to jump onto the nearest person's lap and ask them to hold her tight.

"There's an empty seat next to me if you want to sit there. By the way, my name is Retta—short for Henrietta— but, to me, that sounds like a nineteenth century spinster." Retta continued talking as she walked back to her seat, most of the chatter lost over the sound of the engine.

Ruby was nearly flung into the seat, and she proceeded to strap herself in, tightening the belt like a vise over her lap—for all the good it would do when the plane fell like a meteor from the sky. Her palms left puddles on the arm rest, and her hand returned again to the coin at her neck. Retta was somewhere in the middle of a sentence, and Ruby decided to pay attention to her rather than her heartbeat that was comparable to a herd of buffalo stampeding through her chest.

". . . But they were pretty cool about it. I figure I can finish in about a year. Now I'm going between biology and journalism. I know they're really different, but I like both, so this should give me time to think about it. Or maybe . . . "

Perhaps she doesn't need my undivided attention. Ruby did discover that the drone of Retta's voice was like a tonic to her panic. Pretty soon, she was able to pry her hands off the armrest, her breathing came more naturally, and she could actually participate in the conversation.

She asked Retta where she was from. After that, all she to do was sit back and nod her head every now and again. Retta grew up in Niagara, Canada, an only child, two cats, one dog, and a hamster whose ear was bitten off by one of the cats before she left, and was not expected to make it. Ruby felt like part of the workings of an hourglass. As each grain of sand fell, she gathered more information about Retta. It was hypnotic, and the time passed. She now knew more about this near stranger than she did about some of her long-time acquaintances.

Retta's talking didn't seem to be about nerves. She was a book that was wide open—she did not try hiding anything from anyone. She was so unlike Ruby, not that she had secrets that she hid away but, for her, words had never come easily.

She watched Retta and studied her face and the way she held herself, her various mannerisms. Retta was animated with her hands and her face—she wrinkled her nose at distasteful memories, lifted one raven-winged brow to allude to some mystery, and threw her head back, her mouth wide open, and laughed at the many things that struck her as funny. With every new story, Retta neatly tucked her chin-length, black, silken hair behind her ears. All the while, her hands moved like a maestro conducting a symphony. She was different than anyone Ruby had ever known and, rather than being annoyed, Ruby enjoyed her company. Ruby became a ticketholder to a theater production.

When the attendants requested the lights to be turned off, Ruby and Retta sat and whispered as if they were long-lost friends. Ruby gave away tidbits of herself and her family whenever Retta asked. It was much easier to talk about her family and Margie; so, when Retta asked about siblings, the flood gates opened.

Ruby told about growing up with Poppy and how her older sister had taught her to jump rope and ride a bike. Poppy sneaked Ruby into her first R-rated movie through a side door and, together, they pushed their dad's car out of a ditch when Poppy was giving Ruby driving lessons.

Neither of them slept, which was fine with Ruby. The past few months, she often got by on little rest, instead spending hours on an old Adirondack chair reading under a blanket on the apartment balcony. She now knew that it was an exercise in avoidance—avoiding a roommate that had made her very unhappy.

And so, they chased the sun across the Atlantic.

* * *

It was eleven-thirty in the morning when the plane landed in Amsterdam. Ruby's eyelids had turned to sandpaper and her body floated in some netherworld. Not having anywhere to go until the end of the week, Retta hinted that she wouldn't mind seeing the tulip fields in Leiden. She was to meet two friends in Greece, on the island of Santorini, where they had rented a small house for a month. Ruby welcomed the company. She had no schedule, and didn't know where she was going exactly.

While they waited for their backpacks to slide down the chute, they exchanged money and Ruby got an espresso. The droves of people filling the terminal reminded Ruby of worker ants scuttling around. Some were sure of their route, while others followed the line of people, trying to look like they knew where they were going. Ruby chose to stand still and, although her mind raced, her body did not. The opposing forces threw her slightly off balance.

With a grunt, they both hoisted padded straps over their shoulders and left baggage claim. Out of nowhere, Ruby heard her mother's words from when she stood in her parent's living room the day before she left: "You should carry your bag around and get used to the weight." Ruby distinctly remembered rolling her eyes. She wasn't eighty. More the fool her! She wondered if the pressure in the luggage hold had somehow caused a freak occurrence, making her bag expand and, in so doing, adding extra pounds. She now coined her backpack "The Beast."

Ruby and Retta joined the rest of the ants and made their way through Customs and into the main terminal. Ruby had experienced Customs before, and always felt like a criminal. She was positive someone had dropped coke into her bag. Heck, this was Amsterdam, it could happen. As luck would have it, the agent was all business. He looked at the passport, looked at Ruby, looked again at the passport, asked business or pleasure, and stamped the third page. No muss, no fuss, and no smile.

Welcome to Amsterdam.

Retta followed in Ruby's wake similar to a baby duckling who will not venture too far from its mother. As Ruby glanced back, she saw Retta's head swivel back and forth. It became apparent that Retta was more interested in the shops that lined either side of the terminal than a need to find the train to Leiden.

Ruby looked up at the glass and metal that made up Schiphol airport. The sky was grey, and the tower in the distance was cloaked in fog. The airport was spotless. The entire building was laid out in a grid pattern. Potted plants were spaced every twenty feet, the walls where white, and the only vibrant color came from the duty-free shops they walked by. The perfumeries, smoke shops, and clothing shops added splashes of blues, reds, browns, and greens.

In her attempt to find a restroom, Ruby saw the train sign with an arrow that pointed down from where they had just come. *Damn.* "I need to go to the bathroom, and then we'll go back down and see about the train," Ruby said.

"This place is amazing." Retta reminded Ruby of a ballerina in a jewelry box as she did a pirouette turned round and round, her head tilted back, with a glowing smile. "Hey, I'll be in the perfume shop."

"Okay, I'll be right back." Ruby headed to the women's room. An attendant inside the door pointed to an empty stall. The sight of her conjured up pictures Ruby had seen of old babushkas. Wizened, piercing blue eyes peeked out of her brown, leathery scrunched face, which held a roadmap of wrinkles. She came up to Ruby's shoulder, and wore a black skirt that covered her thick sturdy legs and a white shirt that could never camouflage her heavy, sagging breasts. Her grey hair was in a tight bun that Ruby would bet money on had been in the same style for at least fifty years.

Ruby made her way to the stall. Even the bathroom was clean. The sinks and the floors gleamed. She took her pack off her shoulders. The door swung out, which left plenty of room to maneuver. *I love this place.* She made an obligatory stop at the sink on the way out, and was handed a thick paper towel by the kindly attendant. *I mean, I love, love this place.* The attendant cocked her tight, smiling face at the basket that sat on the counter. A couple of coins lay in the bottom. A light bulb went on in Ruby's head. *Oh, of course there's a price to pay. Do they put old grandmotherly ladies at these posts knowing no one with a conscience could walk by and not toss in a coin?*

Ruby washed her face in cold water and looked in the

mirror. Her eyes were red, and she had shadows underneath them. The lady nodded. Ruby reached into her pocket, put the change from her espresso into the basket, and walked out the door.

She found Retta exactly where she said she would be, winding through the glass shelves, spraying herself with various scents, and coming perilously close to knocking entire displays down with her pack, which looked like a bloated seal hanging from her shoulders.

Ruby waved and then shut her eyes tightly. She pictured the glass—which was sure to shatter—behind her black lids. She knew Retta was close, not because her premonition came true, but because of the aroma that snaked its way to her nose. Ruby opened her eyes to slits, her lashes created a lacy screen as the fuzzy image of her odiferous travel companion walked toward her.

"My God, you smell like a simmering pot of spiced rose petals." Ruby opened her eyes to the sight of a giddy young girl who had the guilty look of trying on all her mother's makeup when she knew it was against the rules.

A huge sneeze escaped Retta's mouth. She tucked a strand of hair behind her ear. "I know. I don't usually wear perfume. I think I got carried away with all the different bottles and names. But seriously, tell me you could resist Conquest. It's on my wrist." She held her left wrist up to Ruby, "or Enchantment. I think it's on my shirt." She stretched onto her toes and pulled her t-shirt out.

"Maybe it's the mixture of all of them together that's turning my stomach. By themselves, of course, men would fall at your feet."

Retta's cheeks took on the shade of red apples as she screwed up her features. "Okay, I'm going to run to the bathroom and try and wash off some of it." She dropped her bag into a heap at Ruby's feet and skipped off to the loo.

Ruby put her own pack down and rubbed her hands over her face. As she circled her neck around, there was the sound of ice scooting around in a glass. Making a couch of her luggage, she lowered herself against the wall. Weirdly, she almost wished she could stay in the airport. It felt safe, and she wouldn't have to look for schedules and platforms, or hoist a heavy weight onto her back.

She closed her eyes and drifted off. She dreamed that a flock of redwing blackbirds took flight over her head, and then Poppy ripped a newspaper in half. She jerked awake to find Retta sitting cross-legged next to her, shuffling a new stack of playing cards. *The ripping sound.*

"I thought I would let you sleep for a while, and then I remembered that I brought cards with me. Hey, did you see the lady in the bathroom? How old was she?" Retta asked. The words spewed out of her, leaving no room for Ruby to reply, which was all the better. Her head felt fuzzy, as if she was still in her dream.

"Do you still want to sleep? I could go get us something to eat. Are you hungry? There's a Food Village with sandwiches and stuff." Retta stated. Her eyebrows arched up, expectantly.

"Yeah, that does sound good. Do you want me to go with you?" Ruby crossed her fingers for the answer she wanted. Hunger and fatigue pulled her in opposite directions.

"No, I'll get it. What do you want?" She bounced up and looked over her shoulder as she made her way down the concourse.

"Anything is good, and another coffee. Wait, here's some money." Ruby dug into the pocket of her wrinkled, grey tencel pants.

"Don't worry about it. I'll be back in a sec," Retta said.

Ruby watched the girl walk away with a bounce in her step, as if she had come from a spa day. Ruby reached up and felt her hair. It was matted down in the back where she had rested her head. She already knew her eyes were red and puffy, and now she took inventory of the rest of her.

Her pants were not the 100% wrinkle free that was promised, but looked okay considering the long day. Her robin's egg blue, long-sleeved shirt had droplets of coffee down her left boob—the result of hiking her backpack higher onto her shoulder and trying to drink at the same time. The mint gum she popped into her mouth took care of the coffee breath, but she still felt fuzz growing on her teeth. Overall, she considered herself quite the pretty girl. She wanted a hot shower, a comfortable bed, and maybe a toothbrush, depending on how comfortable the bed was.

Twenty minutes later, Retta swung a bag and held a cup carrier with two paper cups. "Everything looked so good, so I got a little of a lot," she said. She hunkered down next to Ruby and started to pull items from the bag. There were two pre-made sandwiches on French bread, an egg, two apples, a square of cheese, a box of cookies, and about seven bars of chocolate.

"I figured we could take some of it with us when we left. I didn't know about the egg, so I only bought one and, well, the chocolate speaks for itself. I am so hungry."

Retta tried to unwrap the sandwich with one hand and lift the cup up to her mouth with the other. Ruby wondered which would win out. Soon enough, Retta gave a piglet-sized grunt and put down the cup. She tore at the tight plastic, which seemed to require all of her attention. In a very short time, the bread was opened and the meat was rolled up and shoved into her open mouth. The slice of cheese was then folded into smaller squares and gobbled up. Apparently satisfied, she began leisurely picking at the bread and chewing.

Ruby had opened a Belcolade bar and swirled it around her mouth. The chocolate was thick and creamy as she held it on her tongue, not willing to give it over to her stomach. Sweets always held a soft spot for Ruby. She broke off another square and licked the melted chocolate off her fingers.

Retta had an amused look on her face. "Maybe I should try some of that. She snatched a bar from the bag. "Who needs a lover when there's Belgium chocolate to be had?" She plopped a piece into her mouth. "Oh, man, you're right to have that orgasmic look on your face. This is amazing. So, do you have a lover?" The casualness of the question caught Ruby by surprise.

Unblinking, her eyes stared like a deer caught in the headlights of an oncoming semi-truck. The once smooth chocolate was now stuck halfway down her throat like a thorny chicken bone. Ruby reached for the coffee and gulped, searing the inside of her mouth. For the life of her, she could not figure out why such a simple, common question had caught her so off guard.

During her coughing respite, she realized that they had not spoken about boyfriends, love, or anything related. It seemed odd. Women were usually hunting dogs on a rabbit's scent for intimate tidbits from one another.

"A lover?" Ruby asked. That is not how she would describe Scott. A lover held so much emotion, a promise of the feelings she wanted to have and never did. *What had he been? A companion and bed partner? In the end, he was someone who nearly swallowed me whole. Nearly, but not quite.* She had put him out of her mind for the last few days, but now she was forced to describe a point in time she only wanted to forget.

A good amount of time must have gone by in silence. Retta's frozen brows were arched questioningly, like black caterpillars in mid crunch. Ruby noticed that she did not take the question back, which would have given her a way to laugh it off.

"I had a boyfriend, but now I don't." There, that was easy enough. Did she really want to confide in this girl, whom she had known for only hours, when she could barely form reasons and decisions she had made in her own head? "We dated for some months, but broke it off a little bit ago," Ruby said, her voice flat.

"Do you think you had to leave to make sure you don't want to go back to him?" Retta asked. Her words struck Ruby as odd, and the meaning behind them—maybe by choice—was out of her reach. Ruby also realized that Retta's flighty persona might hide a more intuitive soul. "Well anyway, I think I've had enough, shall we?" Retta asked, picking up the leftovers from their impromptu picnic.

Ruby gathered the trash and went a few steps to throw it away. They both looked at their backpacks with heavy sighs and lifted them up. "We need to go back down to get the train." She moved on autopilot toward the escalator.

Finding their way to the correct train platform wasn't as difficult as Ruby had anticipated. After they activated their Eurail passes, asked a few people for directions, and waited forty minutes for the train to arrive, they were situated in the second-class car for the twenty-two minute trip to Leiden.

Ruby leaned her head against the headrest and watched the airport disappear from her vision. At two-o'clock in the afternoon, the sky still held the promise of rain. The deep grey clouds were heavy, and dipped down to graze the green rolling hills. Field after field flew by, dotted every so often with grazing cattle.

CHAPTER FOUR

They sat in silence, which Ruby thought peculiar given that Retta usually ran her mouth. Ruby turned to ask if she was okay, and found Retta asleep. She looked young and peaceful. Dark, spider-leg lashes rested on the tops of her cheeks. The animation was gone from her face, which left the defined lines of her brows and aristocratic straight nose reminiscent of a Michelangelo painting. She had yet to acquire a crease between her brows or laugh lines around the corners of her lips. Her mouth was parted, revealing the edges of her white teeth.

Ruby's gaze returned to the landscape outside the window. They passed two small stations, but did not stop to pick up any passengers. The villages were nothing more than fields with two or three wooden houses. The intercom crackled through the car, and Ruby heard what she thought could be the word "Leiden." It fit with the timetable they had been given. She nudged Retta on the shoulder. Rather than stir like a waking kitten, easing into the present with a slow stretch, her eyes popped open as if they had never been closed. Ruby should have anticipated that Retta did not need time to get her bearings, but would awake like a soldier coming to attention.

"Are we there?" Retta asked, craning her neck. "Oh, what did I miss?" The life was back into her, and played along her features.

"I can easily and happily say, not much. Not a castle, not a lake, not even a town, but you did miss a cow or two." Ruby stretched her arms over her head and arched her back.

Now that is how one is supposed to wake up.

The train began to slow, so that the blur of the foreground became clearer. Where there had once been different degrees of greens, browns, and whites, Ruby could now make out individual trees and houses. The screech of metal on metal as the brakes began to catch made Ruby's teeth clench together. The vibrations started at her feet and moved to her chest.

The tracks skirted along a canal that led to the city. There were two stations in Leiden: a central one and another on the outskirts. Because they didn't know where they would stay, Ruby opted for the center of town with the thought that there would be more options for lodging.

Other passengers started to get up, so the girls took their cue from them and made their way to the rack near the door, where they had stored their packs. The anticipation of a quiet room with a shower and a bed was an anecdote to the dread she felt about having to don The Beast, which rested innocently among the haphazard luggage. They grabbed their respective bags and made a grunting sound that Ruby knew she would become intimate with over the next few months.

A break in the clouds met them as they exited the station, but the fog that followed most of the way left the air heavy with moisture. The April afternoon was cool, yet Ruby's t-shirt stuck to her back between the sheen of sweat caused by the humidity and the heat generated from her bag. Ruby had taken out her guidebook before they got off the train, and now flipped through it as they walked across the brickwork in front of the station. Without realizing, she had lit a flame in a lighthouse window, beckoning all those who made a living by finding accommodations for tourists. Within seconds, they had a small gathering of foreign men around them, all promising safe, cheap rooms to let.

Retta stood apart and looked at her surroundings. She had left Ruby to the hustlers, but Ruby didn't fault her. She wanted to do the same thing. Between fatigue and the need to escape, she followed an older man who broke away from the crowd. He swung his arm like a backhoe, gesturing for the girls to come with him. Ruby pulled on Retta's arm, and they soon trotted behind the man. The rest of the men broke away like bees seeking sweeter nectar.

"I am Anek. You need a room, I have a room. It is very nice." His heavy Indian accent was a song that rose and fell in a soothing cadence. Now that he had put space between them and his competition, Anek smiled at the girls. He had a pleasant face, the color of roasted almonds with dark, deep set eyes and a wide mouth that lay in a straight line across his tight-skinned, boney jaw. The hair he had was silver and settled in two brillowy bushes above his ears.

Now it was Ruby that held back. Retta swung her arms like a school girl on a field trip. She asked Anek questions: Where was he from? Did he miss his home? Was he married? From him, she won toothy smiles and deep laughs. It was impossible to deny her these things when she was so sincere and enthusiastic. Ruby would not have been surprised if she reached out and grabbed his hand to swing along with hers and, she thought, he would gladly take it.

They walked along a cobbled street crowded with narrow, grey brick buildings that housed shops, restaurants, and second-story apartments. Many of the windows were opened to the welcome change in the weather. It was a picturesque town.

The canal was home to several moored boats, and bicycles leaned arbitrarily against black lamp posts that lined the waterway. Anek pointed out various sights of interest, always saying, "Soon we will to be at Jeug Hotel?" He phrased everything as a question, and had a peculiar side wobble of his head that paired perfectly with his charming inflections.

After forty minutes, Anek made a turn down a narrow side street. The buildings blocked the sun that had started to descend. He stopped in front of a shiny, red lacquered door. It was on a corner, the door on an angle. "We are here. Please to go?" He held out his thin, wrinkled arm the way a host welcomes a royal guest.

When Ruby's eyes adjusted to the dim interior, she realized that the Jeug Hotel was no castle. In fact, it was more accurately a deserted bar. The smell of stale beer, cigarettes, and fried food assailed her nose. Ruby raised her hand instinctively to cover her nostrils. There was a single patron who appeared to have spent the majority of the day on a well-worn stool. He was hunched over a mug filled with dark liquid, staring at it with unfocused eyes.

Anek walked to the bar and began to talk with a woman who leaned against heavy wooden shelves of liquor that were behind her. She was tall and wore a black, sleeveless t-shirt that exposed lean, muscled arms. Her chestnut hair was pulled up in a lazily wrapped knot that was secured with a pencil. She snapped a cloth over her shoulder as she pushed away from the shelves, looked at both of the girls, and continued to talk to Anek. She leaned her forearms on the bar and wiped a wisp of hair from her forehead.

Retta inched close to Ruby and talked through smiling, clenched teeth. "I don't want to stay here. Let's go," she said, keeping her eyes on the bar and pulling on Ruby's arm.

Ruby looked at her and almost laughed. Retta's eyes were saucers, and she kept tucking her hair behind her ears like an Olympic backstroker. It was probably a nervous habit. "Anek wouldn't lead us wrong and, really, I don't know where we are," Ruby said.

The bartender hailed them over. Anek scooted up to them and, in turn, took each of their hands in his. "Good-bye Ruby. Good-bye Miss Retta." *Indeed we are in good hands,* Ruby sighed. He shuffled past them and out the door to gather more lucky travelers.

"How many nights do you want?" The bartender asked.

When they got closer, Ruby saw that her skin was an unflawed ivory and her face housed wide-set eyes that were the color of the sky in the seconds before the sun dips below the horizon. In youth, the woman must have been pretty, but now, beautiful was more fitting. The subtle lines around her eyes and mouth added character, and her voice was low and raw, most likely from years of smoking. The evidence sat propped against a soot-smudged, misshaped pottery bowl next to her. The smoke that drifted from the cigarette added to the city's underbelly vibe the "hotel" gave off.

"It's twenty for a room. Two singles in the room. The toilet is down the hall, and there is a sink in the room," the bartender said. She did not try for idle chit-chat and looked bored, as if she could care less if they got a room or not. She started to rinse the glass that the barfly had slid down the counter.

At this point, after the flight, the train, and the hike here, Ruby was almost willing to curl up on the floor. "Yeah, we want one room." She didn't chance a look at Retta, but heard a small squeal breach her mouth. Now the question was, what does a person get for twenty Francs? Ruby handed her the money and, in turn, was given a generic silver key with a metal-plated #102 that dangled from the ring.

"Go up the stairs, and the room is on your right, two down. If you need anything, my name is Cat."

"Thanks. Is there a phone I could make an international call on?" Ruby asked.

"By the front door." Cat had already turned her attention from them and filled the patron's mug for what appeared to be one too many times.

* * *

"Do you want to go up and check out the room?" Ruby displayed a mischievous grin. She sensed what Retta might say.

"No, I think I'll wait with you. Are you calling Poppy?" Retta asked.

Weird that a practical stranger is so familiar with Poppy. "I promised her I would call, no matter what time it is. What time is it? We're eight hours ahead, so a little after seven in the morning? That should be okay." Ruby reached for the neck pouch that carried her passport, Eurail pass, exchanged money, one credit card, and a calling card. She pulled it out and looked at the directions. The backpack bit into her shoulders, but she didn't want to have to reach down and pick it up again, so she kept it on and took the discomfort.

The telephone rang the instant she punched in the last number. After initial hellos, Ruby filled Poppy in on all the high points—how she met Retta on the plane at which point, said girl bellowed "Hello!" to Poppy, getting the train, the countryside, and of course, the weather. Ruby told her to call their parents and relay the information. They said their good-byes, and that was that. The connection had been so clear, as if her sister were actually there, so that there was no homesickness when the call disconnected. She looked over at Retta. "Okay. You ready?"

They did not have to return through the main bar. The stairs that led up to their room were beside the door by the telephone. The carpet was threadbare, and occasional holes revealed brown linoleum underneath the shorn, grey-blue covering. Stains from years of use made it seem polished and slick. The stairway was dark, but there was dim light coming from what must have been windows above them.

When they reached the top, there were three doors on the right and two on the left. A large, wooden, grid window at the end of the long, narrow hall looked out the front of the building. Now setting, the sun cast a warm glow onto what were usually white stark walls. Above each of the rooms were thick, opaque plastic sconces that lit the black plastic numbers attached to each door.

There were only four rooms. The middle door on the opposite side was marked "Toilet" in the same plastic. The door hung slightly open, and Ruby glanced at the white tile before moving on to their room. Number 102 was near the window, on the left. She slipped the key into the hole and swung the door open. The room was larger than she thought it would be, with well-worn wooden floors, dulled in the paths that most guests must walk. The walls were made of white stucco and completely bare—only occasional dark areas gave the hint of pictures that may have hung inside the rectangular patches. Ruby walked over to a white pedestal sink and ran her finger over a chip in the basin. She looked in the mirror at the reflection of the two beds that were staggered on opposite sides of other. They were covered with thin, striped cotton, brown and pink coverlets that did little to hide the sag in the middle of each mattress. A single light fixture hung from the center of the ceiling, leaving the room just dim enough to miss other imperfections—not that Ruby wanted to look closer.

"What is that smell?" Retta's turned slowly back and forth, her nose scrunched up, trying to find the source.

Ruby dropped her pack from her shoulders, opting for

the floor rather than the bed, which looked more like an old camping cot. She made her way to the partially opened window that looked out onto an alley. There was a slight breeze blowing into the room. "I think I found the smell," Ruby laughed. "I don't know what it is, but it's funky."

Retta came over, opened the window the rest of the way, and leaned out. "It smells like cat urine or trash."

"Well, given the location, it's probably a mixture of both. Window up or down?" Ruby had both hands on the frame.

"Let's keep it open." Retta sat down on the bed by the window and fell back with a heavy sigh, not bothering to remove her bag. The mattress springs creaked underneath her slight weight. For the first time, Ruby saw a weary look cloud the usually bright eyes of the girl across the room, and her once fond feelings toward Anek headed out the window to mate with the stink. Ruby took a mental step back. Maybe their spoiled standards were higher than what he knew. It was definitely utilitarian, but it wasn't dirty—it was just old. He promised cheap. She had wondered what twenty Francs bought. Well, this was it.

Ruby walked over and shut the door, which closed with a heavy *clunk*. She stood above the other bed, closed her eyes, and snapped the cover back. *"Please let them be clean, please let them be clean,"* she chanted to herself. She peeled one eyelid back and smiled. The sheets were bright white— not a stain to be seen. *Well, there. Things aren't so bad after all.*

Ruby checked the time: three-thirty-one. The greasy feeling from the day was too much. She rifled through her bag for new clothes and toiletries. Bare bones apparently meant no towels, soap, or a washcloth. Luckily, in a last-minute decision during packing, Ruby had thrown in a small towel, just in case. Ruby grabbed new clothes, the towel, and a combination body soap and shampoo. "I'm going to take a shower." Retta grunted, looking like a turtle that had flipped onto its back after giving up in righting itself. Ruby went down the hall.

The bathroom door was still ajar. It opened with a creak that must have been years in the making. The room was small, but seemed clean enough. The walls and the floors were covered with white tile, and the smell of bleach lingered in the air. Though she had to push it with her whole body, Ruby closed the door. It was slightly warped, as old wood often is, especially given the damp climate.

Ruby measured the bathroom with critical eyes. No shower. Instead, six feet up from the floor, there was a small tank and nozzle with two handles centered between the sink and toilet. The floor had a slight dip in the middle where a drain was placed. "Okay, this isn't terrible," she said to the empty room. She stripped off her shirt and bra and hung them on the chrome double hook by the door. She then added her pants and underwear, and hung the neck pouch last. She left her necklace on, running slow fingers over the smooth bumps—a piece of home she would not part with. Her Teva sandals stayed on because, even though the floor looked clean, she didn't need some exotic foot fungus.

It felt strange to stand naked without a curtain to shower behind. Luckily, Ruby had never felt particularly modest about her body. The openness and chill of the room suddenly made her need to go to the bathroom desperately. She put her forearms on her thighs and held herself over the seat, vowing never to touch a public toilet. Finished, she watched the slow flush of the water.

She stood in front of the sink and reached over to turn the shower handles on, not knowing if the water would be cold or hot. She turned both handles, held a hand underneath, and waited for a good temperature. The water was so cold it felt like a mountain river. She turned off one side and left the other one on. *Still cold.* She switched. It got a little warmer, which was most likely wishful thinking. *Crap. Nothing is changing.* At this point, pretending that a shower could come later was out of the question, especially with the bologna smell wafting upward from sweaty travel pits. Ruby leaned further over the sink and put her hair under the water. It was so cold that it made her head feel like it had been zapped with an electric paddle. The jolt travelled to her toes.

Without getting anything else wet, Ruby put shampoo on her hair and scrubbed, moving desperate hands like pistons of an engine. She grabbed the sink with her left hand so as not to fall, and rinsed the soap out with the right. Enough water splashed onto her body so that she could suds up and rub the soap into lather. Now there was no choice but to stand under the spigot to rinse off. She took a deep breath and held it, tensing her whole body. A breathless scream made it past quivering lips as she jumped under the water.

Visions of mindlessly cannonballing into a lake during summer camp flooded her mind. The air was sucked out of her, and she couldn't get it back. As soon as was possible, she frantically turned off the water. She clasped her hands and arms to her chest in a pose that resembled a desperate prayer. Her body was shaking, and errant suds still held onto the goose bumps that covered her body.

The water was slow to drain, so she was standing in a pool of freezing water. Skirting to the side, she grabbed the small towel from the hook and started rubbing to dry off and warm up. Soon, another long sleeved t-shirt was pulled over her wet head, this one a plain white. Ruby carefully stepped into clean underwear, trying not to get them wet.

The tile was slick under her sandals, so she made sure she was within reach of something to grab easily.

Getting the inside of each leg wet was unavoidable as she put on her tencel pants, and the hem turned black from being dipped into the water, but her goose bumps started to smooth out. She rubbed her towel on the mirror, and could almost make out her reflection through the droplets of water smeared by the material. Ruby pulled out her toothbrush and squeezed a generous amount of paste onto the bristles. It felt familiar and somehow comforting to circle her brush around every tooth in the mundane motion. She closed her eyes, propped a closed fist on her left hip, and hummed a random song. She had started this ritual as a kid, and still followed it today. Then she shook her head, letting the excess water sprinkle the white tiles. The curl sprang into place, as if she had gone to a salon. *Not bad.*

She remembered her coffee-stained shirt and, given the limited supply of clothing, she grabbed it, ran it under the water and squeezed some soap onto it. After scrubbing the stain, she rinsed it out and held it up for inspection. She took a look around, swung the neck pouch over her shoulder, and was out the door, heading to their room.

There was a bounce in her step as she made her way down the hall. Imperfections in the glass panes from the window cast waves of light from the sun along the narrow walls of the hallway. Although the shower was not ideal, Ruby felt refreshed and reenergized.

What should we do? Walk around the neighborhood? Ask Cat good places to go? These thoughts ran through her head as she opened the door. Retta still had her backpack on, but had rolled onto her side, her hands tucked under her cheek. Ruby quietly shut the door, trying not to make any noise.

"How was the shower?" Retta's eyes slowly opened and

looked expectantly at Ruby.

"Well, on the bright side, I'm squeaky clean, and I got the coffee out of my shirt."

"And on the not so bright side?" Retta was doing some kind of weird roll off the bed, trying to stand up.

"It was a bit cold. Think of swimming in the Pacific Ocean without the sun or the sand, and that was my shower experience."

"No, no, no I can't take that." Her voice took on a desperate tone. "I'm going to go ask Cat if there is some way to get hot water." With that, she was out the door.

Ruby went to the window and looked out over the alley. She opened the window the rest of the way and leaned onto the brick sill. It was still warm from the day, and felt rough under her palms. The sun had dipped below the rooftops, bathing the entire backstreet in shadow. Groups of people had started milling about, and Ruby craned her neck to watch the movement on the sidewalk.

On their way to the hotel, Ruby had noticed several cafes and shops lining the street outside the hotel. Now, she could hear laughter and music drifting through the open doorways. She took a deep breath in through her nose and, rather than being offended by the noxious smells, she took it in as another experience. She was somewhere different, somewhere she chose—the sky was the limit, and destiny was calling.

She slid the backs of her fingers slowly over her cheek as she recalled the night Scott hit her. Her breath caught in her chest when she tried to push the memory out of her head. If it hadn't happened, would she be here right now? As Ruby looked down at the cobbles below, she heard the sound of his hand as it met her skin. She closed her eyes, rested her chin on her raised shoulder, and the thought disappeared.

Ruby sat on the sill, hugging one knee and letting the other leg hang over the side into the room. The air was cool and damp and hung heavily over the city. To change the course of her thoughts, she began to watch the people below. There was a mix of cultures and languages, and Ruby tried to guess the various countries different people were from. She discovered that shoes and pants often gave away someone's ethnicity: A European man could pull off wearing white jeans and look sexy. Americans just didn't have the style. It was how the person walked and held themselves — an air of self-assuredness. As they ambled, Ruby could sense that they enjoyed the smallest bits of life. Germans tended to wear socks with sandals. Americans had jeans and running shoes. Europeans wore leather jackets, and the women wore skirts and had scarves artfully wrapped around their necks. Ruby's game was going quite well, having no way to prove her guesses as incorrect, all became right. Her mouth turned up in a small smile.

Retta sprang into the room swinging a white towel over her head like a cowboy's lasso. "There is hot water! There's a button or handle on the side of the tank above the knobs, and Cat had towels behind the bar. She seems pretty nice. There are more people in the bar now, and she said there's a band coming later. Are you hungry? I think I'm going to take a shower." Her *One Flew Over the Cuckoo's Nest* mania was coming through loud and clear.

Ruby cocked her head in thought. "Okay, let me go through these. I wish I would have known. Great, yes she does. Maybe . . . never mind, I have no idea. I hope it's not really loud. Yes, and I hope you have a good one." Ruby put a finger on her lip and nodded. "I think that covers it. What do you think? On second thought, don't tell me and go take a shower. I'm starving." Still sitting in the window, Ruby turned her face back to the street below and listened to Retta paw through her bag and gather bathroom essentials. Soon enough, the door swung open and closed.

Ruby returned to watching people and gathering her thoughts about the next few days. Before she left, she had written an outline of places and things she wanted to see in the next months. At the top of the list was to see the tulip fields and the big windmill they passed on the way here. After Leiden, she was headed to the town of Brugge, described as an ideal Belgian village. Visiting relatives in Norway was an obligation, and she wanted to touch all the countries in the bulk of Europe.

Retta came back in the room all scrubbed and shiny. Her hair was dripping on her shirt the same way a pesky faucet that won't turn off all the way does. "The shower felt great! You should go take another one. I think the bar downstairs has food. Do you just want to go there?" Retta was bent over, drying her hair with the towel and trying to step into her shoes at the same time.

"Yeah, let's try the bar. I just want to eat and go to sleep." Ruby's body felt numb and sluggish, but her stomach would not be put off much longer. As Retta brushed her hair, it fell in a perfect black veil that didn't quite brush her shoulders. Other than her eyes being a little red, she seemed like she was starting her day rather than ending it.

Ruby pulled her neck pouch over her head, grabbed the key from the bed, and walked to the door. By the time they made it downstairs it was already six-fifteen. Ruby wanted to make it to at least nine before she went to bed, which would have been nearly twenty-four hours of being awake.

CHAPTER FIVE

Cat was still behind the counter, and the barfly who had been there when they arrived was replaced by two American college-aged boys. Ruby continued playing her game, guessing what country people were from. The American boys both dressed in new jeans meant to look worn and t-shirts that clung to well-muscled arms, one with a university emblem and the other in a fraternity t-shirt. Their hair was messy, and probably took some time to get that way. The one with brown, wavy hair had his sunglasses propped on the back of his head. Their backpacks were resting on the floor beside their stools. *Another couple of Anek's suckers*, Ruby thought. They turned around when they saw Ruby and Retta come down the stairs and did a cool, non-committal nod of their heads.

There were ten tables that filled the room, and Ruby and Retta plopped down at one closest to the bar. Cat came around the side and set two menus in front of them. They were in English, which annoyed Ruby, but she couldn't deny the convenience of being able to read familiar words. When she started her European tour, she wanted to try something authentic, but opted for a hamburger and a local cherry beer. She considered herself halfway there.

After they looked at the menu and had sat for a while, Retta waved to Cat. "I read that is how it is done over the pond," Retta said with what Ruby guessed was her best English accent. It was funny, and they both giggled, Retta with her mouth open and Ruby squeezing her lips together and shaking her head at her companion.

Cat made her way over slowly. "What will you have?" She had taken a pencil from her hair and left another in its place. Her arms were toned, and she wore a loose, grey skirt that came just below her knees. With her height and body type, she looked like she could have once been a dancer. Her walk was fluid and unhurried. Ruby wondered how she ended up here—not that it was terrible, but it just seemed like her presence and that of the bar were at odds.

"I'll have a burger and a Kriek." Ruby leaned back into the chair.

Retta nodded her head. "I'll do the same, thanks." Cat wrote down their orders and turned back to the bar.

Ruby looked around the room. A set of windows with trim the same cherry red as the door they had come through faced the street outside. The ceiling was low and had beams that ran its entire length. She touched a heavy wooden post next to her, and felt the dips and grooves that had smoothed over with time. The floor looked oiled from years of people gathering—the imperfections, bows, and dips gave it an authentic pub feeling.

Cat returned to the table and put two big glass mugs down in front of them. She looked at Ruby. "How's the room?"

"It's good. I'll take a hot shower later." Ruby smiled, trying to make light of the cold water.

"Yeah." Cat looked at three people walk in the door and head back to the bar.

Ruby tilted her head toward Cat. "A woman of few words, I guess." She picked up the mug and took a big swallow. She hadn't realized how thirsty she was. She took another gulp and rolled it around her mouth, it was both bitter and sweet. The cherry taste was definitely present. It was an unusual combination, but one welcomed in her throat. She propped an elbow on the thick wooden table and rested her chin in her palm. Her head felt heavy and relaxed. She closed her eyes and listened to the sounds around her.

The trio that had come in looked like local students and had slid two small tables together to make room for their party. She heard glass clang against glass, and figured it must be Cat filling two mugs from the tap. Retta chimed in. Ruby slowly opened her eyes, but kept them half closed.

"What do you want to do tomorrow?" Retta had turned halfway around in her chair and was craning her neck, with one arm draped over the back. She seemed intent on glancing around the bar, but talking was something she did without thinking, like breathing.

Ruby decided not to answer because, first, she didn't want to and second, she thought it would go unnoticed. Her eyes slid shut again, and everything around her became white noise, lulling her into a waking sleep state. She didn't know how much time had passed, but her eyes snapped open when her chin slipped off her hand.

Cat walked to their table with two plates in one hand and two more mugs in the other. Ruby looked across the table and saw an empty space. She scanned the room and saw Retta propped up on a stool at the bar. Her hands moved with her typical animation as the two boys from earlier, one sitting on a stool and the other leaning on the bar, listened to whatever yarn she was vividly weaving. She must have seen Cat coming to their table, because she slipped off the stool and skipped her way back toward Ruby.

"Thanks, Cat. This looks great. I decided to get you another beer, too. The first one was so good. Did you know that Belgium is famous for its beer?" Cat cast a blank look at Retta and produced the nearest thing to a smile Ruby had seen from her yet. She blew out a quick breath of air and turned from them.

"As a matter of fact, I did Retta. Belgium is also known for their windmills, lace, chocolate, and, of course, the diamond." She took the tone of a sarcastic English professor, and Retta grinned and saluted her with a raised mug, before gulping half of it down.

Ruby picked up her burger, saluted in kind, and took a huge bite. What she didn't know was that Belgium was not known for hamburgers. Whatever was making its way around her mouth resembled nothing of the juicy, tender beef she was used to. No, this was the bottom of a well-worn shoe. It took a full minute to chew it enough to get it down her throat, and even then it went down only with a hearty swig from her glass.

Retta hadn't noticed the incessant chomping Ruby had gone through just to get a hunk of burger down her gullet without choking, so she was completely caught by surprise when she took her own first bite. She looked utterly befuddled. Her face scrunched up like a Cabbage Patch doll, but her jaw kept working. To Ruby, the scene was so funny that the beer still in her mouth came spraying out like a fire hose. Even if she had tried, there was no way to stop the spray. The droplets looked like splash-back from a bus and the shock on Retta's face made her laugh even harder. Fortunately, her face had received most of the impact, leaving her clothes relatively dry.

Ruby held her palms up to Retta as an apology. She was unable to talk because she was laughing so hard. In defeat, Retta spit out the half-chewed meat and chuckled as she wiped the beer off her face. "Retta, I am so sorry. I was going to warn you, and then the look on your face—" Ruby started laughing again. She grabbed the edge of the table to regain her composure. "Oh, my God. Okay, okay. Here, take my napkin." She took a huge calming breath.

Retta dried off and started picking at her bun. It was a good thing she was with someone like Retta, who didn't hold a grudge or get mad at a little thing like beer being spewed at them. In mid-thought, Ruby was smacked in the face with a charcoaled piece of meat. Retta pumped a fist in a weird Canadian victory dance. Now it was Retta's time to laugh, and she was roaring. Her head was tilted back, and her fist pounded on the table.

Ruby felt the smear of grease on her cheek, but didn't particularly care. Retta's laugh was infectious, and soon they both howled, holding their sides. Somewhere in the far reaches of Ruby's mind, she thought perhaps no sleep or food and two mugs of beer may have not been the best idea, but she was having too much fun to care.

By the time they made it back to their room, it was completely dark outside and the band was rolling their things in to get ready for their set. The bar became crowded—it looked to be a popular place for foreigners and for locals. Ruby was never a fan of crowds, so she was not disappointed when Retta apologetically told her that she couldn't stay up until the band started.

Ruby brushed her teeth at the sink in the room while Retta sat with her legs crossed on her bed and ran a brush through her hair. *Maybe that's why it looks like spun silk.* After Ruby had brushed her teeth, she could do little more than pull her pants off and crawl under the stiff sheets. She could hear Retta walking around the room by the creaking floorboards. Ruby started to get the "floaty" feeling that always happened right before she fell asleep, when the walls started shaking like a subway was passing right underneath their room. Thinking a train was underneath her, she sat up and looked around. Then she heard the music downstairs.

"Oh my God. Tell me I'm having a nightmare and that it's not the band that just started."

"I'm afraid it is the band, but…" Retta whipped a small baggy out of her toiletry bag. "I have ear plugs. I always take them with me. I have a hard time sleeping in new places, so I take a supply of these and a sleep mask. Sorry, I only have one, and my alarm clock makes ocean noises. Maybe that would be too much."

"Do you have anything in there that will make the room stop shaking?" Ruby sat up, bent weary knees underneath the sheets, and crossed tired arms to rest her chin on them. As fatigued as she was, booming bass would not stop her from sleeping. Perhaps she could pretend she was on a boat lifting up and down with the waves, though loud base was not close to gentle waves. She could pretend it was an artificial heartbeat that lulls dogs and babies to sleep. Yep, that's it. The ear plugs might mute the music, leaving her with a comforting heartbeat.

"Hand over some earplugs." She held her palm open to Retta, who seemed to not hear her. Her head was half-way out the window, and then she hit the floor.

While crouched on the floor, Retta motioned with her arm for Ruby and whispered, "Hurry, hurry, hurry."

Following Retta's lead, Ruby got down on all fours and crawled across the floor to the window. "What?" she whispered in kind.

Both girls peeked over the sill. There were two men standing in the alley. One faced the wall, and the other faced into the alley with little regard to modesty. They both had their pants down at their knees. *Why all the way to the knees?* Ruby wondered. The man facing the wall had his forehead pressed against the brick as though he was trying to hold up the building. Either that or the building was keeping him from falling flat. It was anyone's guess.

The one facing their window seemed to be having a little fun with the novelty of public urination. He reminded Ruby of a sprinkler her grandparents used to have, waving one way and then back the other, covering a large arc of ground. Ruby and Retta squatted in silence until said sprinkler was finished and tugged at his penis like it was a rubber band. Ruby hoped it wouldn't snap. She couldn't help herself from guessing where these two were from. They both had baggie hoodies, and "sprinkler" wore obligatory jeans and running shoes. *American.*

At once, Ruby and Retta let out a howl that caused the men to "drop everything" and look up to the window. Now the girls were flat on their stomachs as the yahoos below yelled up to them.

"Hey, you like what you see? Come on down!" *Yeah, definitely American.*

The two women covered their mouths as tears popped out of their eyes. Ruby crawled on her belly across the floor to her bed, thinking that she would have made a good soldier. Retta, on the other hand, leaped up, flew to the light switch, put out the light, jumped into her bed, and pulled the sheet over her head. From under her little igloo, she panted, "Well, now we know without a doubt what the smell is, and I cannot stay here another night. How important is it for you to see the tulips?"

Ruby replied, "I'm thinking that if the train goes by them that would be sufficient, and on the way to the station, we can take a picture of the windmill. That, my friend, should do it for Leiden." It was unspoken, but Ruby had the feeling that she would be with Retta until she made her way to Greece.

Ruby patted a hand along the sheets trying to feel for the ear plugs. She found them toward the foot of the bed, rolled them in her fingers, and pushed them into her ears. They slowly expanded, muffling the sounds. She couldn't make out the words, but the base from below was still causing the room vibrate to the beat.

With the window still open, the night breeze caused her sheet to flutter slightly. It felt good. "Good night, Retta." There was no reply, maybe because of the plugs, or maybe Retta was already asleep. After that, there was only darkness.

* * *

Ruby was lying in a field of soft green grass. Her arm was draped over blue eyes, blocking the sun. The fingers of her other hand were gently stroking the necklace at her throat. She was not alone. There was laughter in the distance. She lifted her arm slightly and squinted. Two figures—one small and the other large—were running together. They were familiar, but not focused. She stretched to get a better look and woke herself up, blinked to see the banal room and tried get her bearings. The sunlight was bright and coming in the window. The sheet was pulled up to her chin, just like it had been at her last memory. She felt stiff, as if she had not changed positions all night. Ruby tried to remember the dream. For some reason, it felt important, but she couldn't she put faces or meaning to the figures. She heard a door slam from the hall, and looked over to see Retta's bed empty.

The dream was gone.

* * *

Ruby could not move out of bed. She looked out the window and saw high, billowy clouds between the buildings. The sky was light blue—different from the blue skies of Colorado, which spread forever—so blue that she always felt she could taste the freshness.

Europe seemed different. It was as if a haze lay over the town, maybe from the sea. It was not better or worse, just different. She braided both hands behind her head and let her mind wander. It felt weird not having an agenda or anywhere she needed to be.

A door opened somewhere down the hall but, other than that, it was quiet. Looking over to the other side of the room, she saw an earplug on the floor. She had no idea where the other one went, but it was not in her ear. It was probably somewhere in the sheets. Thirty minutes later, Retta swung open the door to the room, bright as sunshine.

"I feel so much better today. I think we slept for over twelve hours, it's already eleven. Man, the shower felt good. You're going to have to give it another try." Retta widened her eyes and nodded. "I peeked down the stairs, and I think they still have some breakfast stuff out. We have to leave by one o'clock, or they'll charge us for an extra night. Did you change your mind? Do you want to stay another night?"

Every time Retta talked, it reminded Ruby of buzzing bees—busy, busy, buzzing bees. "No, I don't want to stay. Let me go shower, and then I guess I'm ready to go. She reluctantly rolled out of bed to a rhapsody of squeaky springs. "These little cots were more comfortable than I imagined they would be. Did you sleep well?"

"Like the dead, I don't remember anything after my head hit the pillow. Hey, your plug is on the floor. You might want to keep them. You never know when a band will be playing underneath you, or if drunkards will be yelling for your attention in an alley." She raised her winged brows, looking like an exaggerated silent movie actress. "I got an extra towel for you. It's over there." She waved her hand in the direction of the chipped sink.

Ruby fished around for her toiletries. "Thanks, I'll be right back." Before she left, she grabbed the towel and swung it over her shoulder.

The shower felt like heaven. She should have seen the button yesterday. It was red and stuck out from the tank. The water ran over her in a soothing stream. She closed her eyes and let the soap bubbles skim over parted lips and down the rest of her. Ruby could not remember the last time she stood under the shower just because she wanted to. It felt as indulgent as ordering a pizza at midnight. As good as the shower felt, she still couldn't last a whole five minutes. It was the Scandinavian blood in her, reminding her to never be too extravagant.

Toweling off, she wrapped her hair and put on the same grey tencel pants and white shirt from the day before. Over that, she pulled on a slate blue, half-zippered pullover. She brushed her teeth, applied a generous coat of Chap Stick, and was out the door, feeling happy and re-energized after all the travel yesterday.

When she walked into the room, Retta was packed and gently bouncing on her bed, looking out the window. Her mouth was moving, and Ruby could only guess that there was a song going along with the bouncing.

"Let me just shove this stuff into my pack and we can go see about something to eat." Ruby unwrapped the towel from her head and pulled a brush through her hair. She felt looser and more carefree in the new doo. The towel and shirt from last night were still damp, so she hung them from a strap on the outside of her backpack and put the brush into an outside pocket. Remembering the missing earplug, Ruby looked around the room. She ran her hand under the sheet and found it toward the bottom. She put the earplugs in her toiletry kit and clamped the pack closed.

"Do you have a train schedule? Mine's in my bag somewhere, but I thought if yours was handy, we could look at it while we were eating," Retta was walking a step behind Ruby, the hallway too narrow for them to walk side by side.

"Yeah, mine is in one of these outside pockets." Ruby made her way down the stairs. The bar was pretty much empty, except for Cat, who was behind the counter reading the newspaper. There was a coffee carafe set up on the bar, and a tray with some hard rolls and two pieces of white cheese. The rest of the tray was full of crumbs from people who had actually woken up in the morning, rather than close to noon. Ruby wondered what else had been on the tray.

"Morning. There are eggs if you want." Without looking up, Cat nodded her head in the direction of a basket that contained three eggs covered with a cloth white napkin.

"Thanks," said Retta. Both women put their packs down against one of the posts and grabbed a plate.

Ruby plucked an egg out of the basket, along with a roll and one piece of cheese. She went to the table, put the plate down, grabbed a mug, and filled it with dark coffee. Retta was at the table picking at her roll and drinking a glass of milk.

Ruby sat down and took a sip of the coffee. It was perfect, strong and dark. She reached down, unzipped one of the front pockets of her bag, took out the condensed version of the train schedule that came with her Eurail Pass, and set it on the table.

She put both thumbs against her roll and tore it apart. It was soft inside, and she ripped the cheese in half, putting a piece on each half. After that, she peeled the egg, tore off a chunk, and put the yolk on top of the cheese, making two open-faced sandwiches. When her stomach made a growling sound, she realized that last night she had drunk most of her dinner and spewed the rest onto Retta. At the memory, a quick, hard laugh made it up her throat, but not quite past her lips.

With her mouth full, she bent her head over the schedule and started thumbing through it. First finding Leiden and then Brugge, she ran her finger along the train lines, looking at times and routes. "Let's see." It looked like they would have to connect twice, Leiden to Antwerp and Antwerp to Brussels, and then to Brugge. She hadn't noticed that Retta had flown the coop, so that she was left talking to empty space. "Three and a half hours, maybe a little more, but about that." She kept on with the one-sided dialogue.

Miss social butterfly was making what could only be called "the rounds." She had been up at the bar, talking to Cat a few minutes ago, and now she sat at a table close to the window with three other girls. Casual conversation with anyone, stranger or not, came effortlessly to Retta. Ruby wasn't sure she would like that quality or not, it was such a foreign concept.

Ruby remembered that she was the one who had approached Retta on the plane, so there. The three girls Retta talked with looked to be just out of high school. Their hair was long, layered, and straight, with bangs swishing to the side. Each had on jeans and tight, low-cut shirts. Though they were in different colors, they were clones of one another. *American. I'd bet my house on it.* Their tittering laughter reached Ruby and rubbed like sandpaper.

Ruby put her eyes back on the map. Maps had always been a hobby of Ruby's, and she imagined the history that went along with the ancient names of various cities: Barnstaple, Ferrimaroc, Helsingborg. What would the food taste like? Would the streets wind aimlessly? Would there be a castle on a hill? Although she was sitting in a bar hotel in Belgium, and it was a long way from her usual life in Boulder, she felt as if she were walking around the edge of a beautiful lake, dipping her toes in the water, but not diving in. She was also completely unaware of what it would take to slide in below the surface, giving everything over to the fates. Retta sat down and wrenched her from her thoughts.

"Those girls over there live about twenty miles from my home town. Can you believe it?"

"Good thing I don't have a house." Ruby did not know she had spoken aloud, but Retta asked her what she was talking about. "Nothing. Did they just get here?"

"They were on March break and decided to extend it a little. They're hung over from spending two days in Amsterdam."

"Sounds like fun." Ruby couldn't quite keep the aloofness out of her voice. She wrinkled her nose at the memory of her own escapades last night, but that was purely situational, and not the norm. "Are they in high school?"

"First year of university."

Now, if I did have a house, I could keep it, Ruby thought.

"Yeah, they're going to Germany next to party in some of the pubs. They asked if I wanted to go, but I said that we were going to stay around here." Retta scrunched up her face. "Really, bar hopping isn't my cup of tea, so I kind of used you as an excuse. I didn't think you'd mind. Hey, did you figure out our schedule? I'm actually excited to get back on the train. I think I missed most of the scenery on the way here." Retta finished off the last of her roll. The poor thing had lost the battle, and was torn to shreds.

Ruby had her jaw cupped in her palm and was tapping

her cheek to the beat of an old Eagles song that Cat played from hidden speakers. She couldn't help but sway to the tune. "Well, we have about fifty minutes to get to the train station, and there are two stops from what I can make of the train times." Ruby calculated if there was time for one more cup of coffee. *Maybe I could do a European tour of coffee rather than beer.*

She pushed up from the chair and went to fill her mug. People were trickling in. With the door open, she heard cars and street noise. It was odd how the same things could sound so different in different places. There were cars and people in Boulder, but these sounded foreign. She wasn't sure what the dissimilarity was; maybe it was the narrow streets and the sound bouncing off the old stone. The city pulsed with life.

Ruby decided that there was no time to savor the coffee, so she chugged it, searing her throat as it made its way down. Somehow it felt good, as if burning one's throat could cause excitement. She was doing something, living the dream she had for herself, no longer just daydreaming about it and, like the city, she felt alive.

"Well, Retta, it looks like you have sufficiently killed your breakfast. Are you ready to go?" Standing next to her chair, Ruby hitched her backpack onto her shoulder. Retta held a piece of cheese an inch from her mouth and smiled up at Ruby.

Retta looked at her plate. "It seems I have a nasty habit of bad table manners. My mom always told me I did, but I thought she was exaggerating." Her eyebrows squeezed together, and she cast a guilty look at Ruby. "I don't like my food touching," she said, as if that was a perfectly reasonable answer. She then lifted one shoulder in resignation, picked her plate up, and went to set it in the tub placed at the end of the bar for dishes.

At least she had manners enough to clear her own plate, unlike many people who had left their cups on the table for someone else. In Ruby's mind, Retta's behavior was a much better quality.

Retta had already talked to Cat and given her the key. On the way out, Ruby raised her hand to signal their departure. Cat lifted her chin slightly. Ruby wondered how many people Cat saw come and go from behind her bar, a revolving door of strangers. No wonder she seemed detached. No one stayed long enough to exert the effort to find out more than how many nights they wanted.

Chapter Six

The sun was directly above them as they made their way to the station. Although it was not particularly hot outside, Ruby stopped and took off her blue pull-over, leaving her comfortable in her long sleeved t-shirt.

It has taken forty minutes to wind their way back through the city. They stopped and took a picture of the Valk Windmill listed in their "Things to See in Leiden." *Check one thing off the list*, Ruby thought. If Ruby could find even one misplaced tulip from the train compartment, her reason for coming to Holland would be complete.

They arrived at the train station ten minutes before the departure time, so Ruby sat down on a small bench positioned between two metal poles holding up the Leiden sign. Retta laid her bag beside Ruby and trotted to the facilities before the train arrived. The day was beautiful, and Ruby turned her face up to the sun and closed her eyes. The air was cool on her skin, but the warmth of the sun kissed her.

Clouds started to form, slowly skittering across the light blue of the sky, creating light and dark underneath her lids every few seconds. A shadow fell over her, and when it didn't move, Ruby cupped her hand over her brow and peered out. Retta stood in front of her, holding up a map to shade the sun.

"What are you doing?" Ruby asked, squinting to see her better.

"Didn't I tell you my mom is a dermatologist? It's second nature to protect those who won't protect themselves."

Ruby rolled her eyes and sat up. "I don't think five minutes in the sun is going to do irrevocable damage. Anyway, it feels so nice." She couldn't help but remember her early teenage years, when she and Poppy spent hours at the pool getting tan. Even if suntan lotion had been available, it was never used; consequently, by the end of a week in the sun, she and Poppy were pulling hunks of skin from their very red Scandinavian noses. What a carefree life before skin cancer alerts took hold. "So that's the reason behind your peaches and cream, oh-so-pretty face?" Ruby asked.

"I do take care of my skin." Retta raised her dark brows, touched her index finger to her cheek, and then plunked Ruby on the nose with the same finger. "Train," she said, turning on her heel and moving to stand with the rest of the crowd that had gathered along the platform.

Ruby rose from the bench and grabbed her backpack from the top strap, not bothering to put it on her shoulders. She slid beside Retta, her backpack similar to a cane resting between her legs, holding her up. So far it had been a couch, a cane, a pillow, and one must not forget, her nemesis.

The train screeched to a stop. People got on and got off, trying to wedge by each other to capture a seat to their opposing destinations. On the way to a seat, Ruby and Retta crammed their bags into the luggage rack by the door and continued up the aisle. This train had rows of three seats on both sides of the aisle, and then pods with four chairs facing each other and a small square table between them. Ruby slid into a chair closest to the window, and Retta followed suit on the opposite side.

The seats were similar to an airline but, unlike an airline, there was plenty of room and there was a foot rest that could be pulled down. Ruby watched the remaining passengers make their way into the cars. Noise from the walkway outside the train, and the rise and fall of voices around her, were comforting. She felt safely cocooned away from the jostling and stress of getting on, hoisting bags, or getting a seat. She could sit back and watch everyone else struggle their way on board.

A couple making their way down the car made eye contact with Ruby and asked if anyone was sitting in the two empty seats. Retta chimed in that they should sit there (of course; not that Ruby would have said otherwise). She might have thought about saying it, but never actually say so. *Okay, I wouldn't say it, but it may be written on my face, so, it's good that Retta spoke up.* It wasn't that she didn't want people sitting there, just they would want a conversation, and she was expected to ask questions that she may or may not even care about just to fill space.

My God, what am I doing? I came here to find out who I am, and I am playing duck-duck-goose and filling the part of both duck and goose. "Enjoy every part of this adventure, she told herself, "and, for Christ sake, relax." She took a cleansing breath in through her nose and blew out of her mouth. Margie would be so proud.

The said couple was Alex and Kerry from Ann Arbor, Michigan, who were taking some time off from their doctorate program from the university. Both were studying Roman history and had decided to create their own field trip. They started in Naples, where they went to castles and cathedrals, and then to Pompeii. They talked about the structure of the Coliseum in Rome and the ruins of the Forum. What they did not mention were the smells, colors, or feelings they got when standing at these important sites. It was like hitting play on a sound recording of an audio history book but, to their credit, their eyes lit up and they talked with such enthusiasm that it was difficult not to get caught up in their fervor.

If Ruby had to picture historians in her head, these two would be poster children. She doubted even a bullet could penetrate the amount of glass they had between them in their thick frames. They were definitely nerdy, but they were nice nerds with a wealth of knowledge had she or Retta known what to ask.

The couple was headed back to Naples, on their way home after two weeks of time off. Kerry had always wanted to see Ann Frank's house, so Alex made it his mission to get her there. It was such a nice gesture, and all the women looked at each other with lopsided grins and sighed with puppy dog eyes. Oh, love.

After a while, Alex got up, saying he needed to stretch his legs. Ruby had her suspicions that he needed a break from the female running of the tongues. Between Retta and Kerry, Ruby could not have squeezed a word in, even if she wanted to. Ironically, she actually did want to.

During a lull in the conversation—something about how Kerry had taken a school group to a snow sculpture competition of ancient wonders, and Retta had volunteered at a camp for blind skiers two winters ago—Ruby chimed in with a tubing story. It had nothing to do with academics or selfless acts of volunteering, but someone could have been blinded (namely herself or Poppy), and they did learn something: Don't take ski poles down the tubing lane as a breaking mechanism.

All three women had tears in their eyes from laughing at Ruby's description of Poppy's face when she realized that Ruby was out of control and was heading straight at her, her pole finding no purchase in the glazed-over snow, and looking more like a lance coming to "unhorse" Poppy from her tube. In the end, the tube had been the only fatality; and the girls were reprimanded for their dangerous shenanigans and were made to pay for the ruined equipment.

Thinking of Poppy, Ruby reached under her collar and absently ran the necklace through her fingers. For having an uneventful childhood, she had tons of memories that popped into her head, reminding her of how much she cherished her family. She looked over at Kerry, who was looking somewhere below Ruby's eyes. She rubbed at her nose, thinking she may have an embarrassing, wayward booger.

"That is a beautiful necklace, Ruby. Can I see it?" Kerry asked.

Dropping her hand from her nose, Ruby arched herself forward and tilted her head back, looking somewhat like an egret during mating season.

The first few days after Scott had hit her she tried to discretely cover the mark he had left. Although the bruise was long gone, close scrutiny of her face brought back the memory. Now, even though she knew it wasn't noticeable, in her mind it was there—an odd reminder and an inspiration of all that she could do.

"My sister gave it to me before I came on this trip." Wanting to describe the necklace in more detail, she added, "The stones mean different things. Empowerment, contentment, and inspiration, something like that anyway. The coin is for luck. But then, I live in Boulder. I'm sure they make up half the stuff. No matter; I love it anyway."

"Actually, there is historical significance in various stones going back to the writings of Homer all the way to Biblical times. I've read some on historical gemology and mythology. The ruby for instance," she looked pointedly at Ruby, "is Latin for "ruber," and was thought of as an inextinguishable internal flame; therefore, it was often given as a token of love." Kerry pursed her lips together and raised her head and eyes to the ceiling. She seemed about to go on about another gem when Alex bent down and kissed her on the forehead.

"Let me guess, she's going on about some historical this or that. I've seen that look many times." He held four tall, narrow cans of Coca-Cola and smiled down at all of them.

"I didn't bring it up." Kerry squished her face up and hiked her glasses higher up her slight nose. "Okay, so I brought it up, but it had to do with Ruby's necklace, and really it is very interesting." She looked at Ruby and then at Retta for support, which both were truly able to do without a second of hesitation, nodding their heads in unison.

"Your wife is a treasure-trove of information. Is there anything she doesn't know?" Retta moved her foot she had been resting on his seat.

Alex's eyes opened wider, and a strange look crossed his face. "I'd venture to guess she doesn't know that she is my wife." A funny laugh escaped as Alex added, "Well, because she's not."

Ruby wasn't sure if he looked plucky or panicked. His cheeks were stained red, and he was bringing his occupied hands up in an attempt to move his dark cowlick from his brow. For a full ten seconds (which, until now, was unheard of in this group) they all stared at Alex.

"Well," Retta said in her breezy way, "you seem to be meant for each other, and if you aren't now, I have a feeling marriage is in your future. See, I can be mythical and new-agey too."

With that last comment, Alex let out a mix of grunts and laughs. "I should be so lucky."

Smart man, Ruby thought. Alex handed the sodas around

and sat down with a *thunk*. They all thanked him for the drinks and cracked them open. Retta held up her hand, stilling all of their half-raised arms. "Here's to ancient history and the history we have yet to make. Cheers!" They gathered their cans together, clanked, and drank.

Ruby couldn't help but notice the small smile that passed between Kerry and Alex. She felt an unexpected tug on her own heart. What is this feeling? She had come to Europe to find out who she was on her own, and now craved the look that moved so easily between Alex and Kerry. Surely it was just the talk of the ruby and Retta's faux pas. She gave herself a mental shake and thought of something other than the fact she didn't have someone looking at her in that way.

Ruby went down the list of sights to see while in Europe: *Windmill (check), tulips (check), the Eifel Tower, Trevi fountain . . .* She began to feel better. Also on her list were the fjords of Norway and the Leaning Tower of Pisa. *Okay.* She took a deep breath. The weird tingly sensation that happened when she got excited buzzed under her skin; she was back on track. Ruby had been so caught up in her own thoughts that she hadn't noticed Alex and Kerry gathering their things, or the announcement for Antwerp.

Retta finally broke through Ruby's reverie. "Hello, hello." She was fanning her hand in front of Ruby's face. "What are you thinking about? You seem a million miles away."

Ruby tilted her head to the side. "Just how much I'm enjoying your company," she said smiling innocently.

"Okay, you don't need to tell me." Retta snorted. "Anyway we're getting close to Antwerp."

Ruby had glanced at the train schedule before boarding, and remembered Alex saying he and Kerry were heading back to Naples to fly home. Ruby looked up at him as he stood, with his hand on the seat. "Don't you need to catch the train from Amsterdam to make it down to Naples?" she asked.

His glare seemed to pierce her. "Well, there are a lot of routes to get there. Why don't you help me get the bags?" If Ruby thought it an odd request, she didn't show any puzzlement on her face.

As they walked down the aisle, Alex turned to her with the look of a conspirator. "I'm making a detour to Antwerp to buy Kerry a ring before we go back to Naples. What better place to buy a diamond?" He sounded like a boy going to see Santa Claus when he still believed in magic.

"Oh, my God, I am so sorry! I hope I didn't ruin it." Ruby's jaw clenched together like a vice as she spoke through her teeth.

Alex was completely relaxed. "Nah. As smart as she is, maps and schedules aren't her forte. We could be heading to Finland and I don't think she'd know. However, I must say when Retta mentioned her being my wife, I could have fallen to the floor. No harm done. Kerry seemed dumbstruck by the thought." He looked at Ruby sheepishly. "Do you think it's a crazy idea?" He nervously fluttered his first two fingers against his lips as his other arm encircled his slightly pudgy waist.

Ruby began feeling agitated just watching his fingers. Her instinct was to clamp down on them; instead, she touched his arm, which distracted him enough to stop his pattering. "I can't think of a better plan. Very romantic. She's going to be so surprised."

Ruby glanced back up the aisle and saw smiles on Kerry's and Retta's faces as they spoke to each other. She didn't know why, but there was both a sense of melancholy and deep happiness that went beyond Alex's news or watching both women look so happy. Ruby stood at the precipice of her life, and she had the overwhelming feeling that the decisions she made in the next few months would either see her to the top of the cliff or plunge her into an abyss. She couldn't help but laugh out loud at the seriousness of her thoughts. *My God Ruby*, she reprimanded herself, *this is a pleasure trip, not life or death*. The laugh must have been louder than she thought, because Alex looked uneasily at Ruby.

"So, you do think I'm crazy?" He shoved his hands into his pockets and looked over her shoulder at Kerry.

Ruby held her palms forward. "No, I swear I was honestly thinking of something else." Not wanting to go into her own neurosis, she brought the topic back to his plan. "Are you going to have her pick it out with you, or surprise her?"

It worked like a charm. Alex soon rattled off his plan and, again, looked happy rather than the odd shade of green he had been minutes before. They had to continue the ruse, so Alex and Ruby lugged the backpacks up the aisle to their seats. It wasn't far, but Ruby had one on her back and one on her front, making a very clumsy show on the way back to Retta and Kerry.

"Wow, thanks sweetums, you really shouldn't have." Retta gave her best smile and bat of her eyelashes.

Ruby grunted, heaving Retta's bag onto her lap, dropping it with a bit more force than necessary. "You're welcome." She returned Retta's sweet smile. All she heard from Retta was a satisfying "humph." Ruby left her bag on and grabbed for the rail that ran above the seats to keep her balance. With the extra weight on her back she felt like she was a Weeble Wobble when the rails made any sort of turn and, at the moment, it felt like the train was going down

Lombard Street in San Francisco.

The sign for Antwerp came into view, and half of the passengers started gathering their things and heading to the doors on either end of the car. Because she was more in the way than not, Ruby said she would meet them at the door. She joined the people, who looked like spawning salmon going upstream.

The engineer, Ruby found out, had a heavy foot—or whatever it was they did for breaking—because, before she could brace her feet, she plowed into the person in front of her. It would have been funny had said passenger seen the humor, but instead Ruby was shoved backward with a butt bump. Given the girth of the person in front of her, there was quite a bit of oomph behind that bottom. Ruby had never thought of herself as clumsy, but so far on this trip she felt half smashed most of the time. At least she didn't fall, but her knee would have a bruise from where it clipped the seat on her way into the rude large man. She seriously hoped the damp spot on her shirt was not butt sweat. He didn't even spare her a glance as he made his way further up the aisle. The doors opened, and everyone streamed out.

Ruby caught up to Retta, Kerry, and Alex, who had all gone out the other side of the car. When she got closer, they looked like they were at the end of a good laugh. Kerry was taking a steadying breath, Alex was wiping his eyes, and Retta had the hiccups and held her stomach.

"What's so funny?" Ruby asked as she smoothed out her shirt and hiked her pack higher on her shoulders.

"You," Retta said with another hiccup. "You looked like the ball in a pinball machine bouncing from peg to peg. That guy was three of you, and you smashed into him and then bounced back." Hiccup. "It looked so funny."

Ruby plastered an exaggerated smile on her face and

cocked her head. "Yeah, it was hilarious." Her tone was less than sincere. "Especially the sweat smear on my shirt." She held her shirt out from the hem so they could get a closer look. Not that there was anything to see, but she felt it, and it was making her shiver as if a slimy worm had been thrown down her shirt. "Anyway, if you're all done getting a good laugh, I figured out a quicker way to Brugge." She actually wasn't too offended. Had it been Retta, she probably would have been doubled over. "Rather than going to Brussels, we can go through Gent and not have to change trains. That will save some time." She looked over at Alex and Kerry and formed an "O" with her mouth. It had slipped her mind that they were separating in Antwerp.

Alex piped up. "Kerry and I need to make a quick stop before our next train leaves, so…" He had taken Kerry's hand as she started to question him, thinking their train was going to Naples.

"It was great to meet both of you." Retta threw her arms around Kerry, which was awkward since they were both loaded down and because Alex had not let go of Kerry's hand. "I have your address, so I'll write. Have a good trip back."

Ruby had not thought about getting addresses and, because she was not super affectionate, she held back and looked at Alex. He tugged on Kerry's hand, trying to get her to move. Ruby decided to help the guy out. "Our train leaves in ten minutes, so we'd better go. Good to meet you." She flicked her hand up in a haphazard wave.

Alex winked at her as Kerry tried to get out. "Nice to meet you, too," but her words ended up, "Nice to oohhhh." Alex's final yank had her trotting alongside her soon-to-be fiancé and looking back at the two women with a perplexed look on her face.

CHAPTER SEVEN

"What was that all about?" Retta's mouth hung open.

Ruby stood smiling, not sure at what—maybe the funny look on Kerry's face, but more likely that she felt happy for both of them.

"Alex is buying an engagement ring in Antwerp. He wanted to surprise Kerry, and I think he was freaking out," she said absently. Ruby watched the crowd swallow up the couple as they snaked their way out of the station. "Shall we?" After five steps, Ruby realized she was not being followed. Retta stood motionless, gawking at the thinning crowd surrounding her.

"I wish I would have known." Retta hooked her hair behind her ear. "I would have asked more questions. What she thought, what kind of ring she liked…"

"You couldn't have asked any questions regardless," Ruby replied. "It was a surprise."

"Oh my gosh. And I called her his 'wife.' Was he just dying?" Her dark eyes questioned Ruby.

"Yeah, he did mention wanting to throttle you."

"No…" her shoulders sagged, and Ruby decided she couldn't be cruel to Retta, even if it was in jest.

"Oh, of course he didn't say that. He was just surprised, and actually rather happy that you could see they were meant to be." Ruby got the result she thought she would. Retta kept her lips together, but her little mouth stretched as wide as it could.

She gave a bob of her head and put her arm through Ruby's. "See, I knew it. I told them. Do you remember me saying it?" She glanced sideways at Ruby and then bounced into motion down the lane. Without missing a stride, she added, "Where are we going?"

Ruby had to laugh. What would Retta be doing if she did not have someone pointing her in the right direction? Surely enjoying herself and walking aimlessly through one city or another. "We just need to get over to the next platform." Ruby finally looked around.

The station was actually a work of art; it felt like they were in a crystal cathedral. The panes of glass rose up in diamond arches, supported by beautiful marble and colorful stone. Levels of tracks seemed connected by escalators and walkways. If they had more time, it would have been fun just to walk around but, as it was, they had five minutes before their train left. They went up one escalator, walked the short distance to an escalator going down, and made it to the platform just as the doors were opening. A conductor stood to the side of one of the cars, and Ruby pointed at the car. "Brugge?" Not wanting to end up in Barcelona, she thought it best to confirm.

He cocked his head toward the train and took a sip from the paper cup he held in his hand, putting a stop to any conversation. She looked at the number next to the door and saw a "1," meaning First Class. They kept walking down to the next car, and then the next. She began to think that they would never find a second-class car and, by the time they did it, would be difficult to find a seat. She heard Retta chattering on about something, but Ruby was on a mission and infinitesimally nodded her head a few times and gave affirmative sighs.

Ruby thought she was placating her until she heard Retta's affronted voice. "I knew it! You're not listening to me."

"I am, too, listening to you," Ruby tried saying with conviction while, at the same time, racking her brain to remember even a nibble of what Retta had been talking about. "You love the color of the stones of the train station. See?"

"Not even close. I was telling you about the terrible dye job my mom once got."

"Oops. Here we are, second class." Ruby walked onto the train, leaving Retta piercing her back with a glare. Not that there was much punch behind it; she looked too much like a doll to have the effect she was going for.

The train pulled out to the minute of its scheduled time. Ruby reflected on how she loved punctuality. She had never understood people who were not punctual, and there were no words for those that did it purposefully. For her, the stress of being tardy far outweighed the fashion statement. It was one thing that had always stuck in her craw about her pre-living together experience. If they planned to go out somewhere, she could count on Scott being fifteen or even thirty minutes late. When they first started dating, she waited with an anxious, acid stomach, thinking he was mysterious and so above everything. Eventually, the tardiness was only irritating. She became done with thinking that he was coolly detached. His lack of regard was plain rude, and she was worth more than being an afterthought.

Yes. That's it. I felt like an afterthought in the relationship. Is it too much to want a man that can't wait to see me, or think that I am the highlight of his day? Is it too much to want his face to glow when I walk into a room, to think that I am both the sun and the moon? Oh, why not go for broke—that I am the center of the universe?

Maybe I went a little overboard, Ruby thought wispily. *Heck, they are my thoughts.* She could think up crazy things if she wanted. It wasn't like anyone knew her irrational flights of fancy. Really though, if she had to be painfully honest, she had had only one boyfriend, and there had never even been a close call of a man using a catchy pick-up line on her. It was enough to make her think she had bloomed into a perfect wallflower.

The wheels of the train bumped along as they pulled out of the station. The jarring movement brought Ruby back to reality. A bank of heavy clouds wrapped around the buildings in misty shawls. Raindrops began to hit the window, dancing their way to the other end of the large panes. Ruby touched her finger to the cool glass and traced one jerky line that a drop had made. *A catchy pick-up line. Ha!*

"Do you have a place in Brugge that you want to stay?" Retta asked. "Those two guys at Urine Hotel said there was a good hostel that the bus goes to. I can't remember the name, but they said most backpackers stay there, so it shouldn't be that hard to find." Retta was digging in her bag for something as she spoke, trying in vain to keep her shiny locks behind her ear. Every time she looked in her pack, her hair fell forward like a pesky shirt that doesn't stay on the hanger.

"Urine Hotel, that's clever and pretty funny. If my stomach wasn't grumbling, I'd probably even laugh."

The train to Brugge was older and had compartments with six seats—three facing forward and three facing backward. A sliding glass door separated the coach from the walkway. As of now, they had seats to themselves, so Ruby had her backpack sitting next to her on the seat. A couple people had walked by and looked in the window, but they kept going, probably trying to find an unoccupied car of their own.

"Was the hostel called Prima Facie? And what are you

looking for?" Retta's bag looked like it had thrown up. She
had shirts, socks, a pair of sandals, and underwear in a pile
in her seat and the one next to it.

"I know I put a bar of chocolate in here somewhere." Her
head snapped up, and Ruby could practically see the light
bulb brighten over her head. "Aaah, it's in the front pocket."
She reached down, unzipped a small pocket in her pack, and
pulled out a large chocolate bar, holding it up as if it were
the Hope Diamond. Her smile lit up what was previously a
gloomy day. She threw the chocolate in an arch over to
Ruby. "You open this while I put all my stuff back. And
yeah, I think that is the name. It did sound Italian."

"Latin, actually. 'At First View.'" Ruby was quickly, if
not frantically, ripping at the foil. Even as a kid, whenever
she got too hungry, her body felt like what she could only
describe as fuzzy inside, and she would get shaky. Her mom
learned to throw her a piece of Wonder bread, and disaster
was averted. She popped four squares into her mouth and
laid her head on the back of the seat with a long sigh.

Retta clipped her bag shut and sat across from Ruby. She
took the bar from Ruby's lap. "I don't think I'll ever be able
to eat a Hershey bar again. I wonder why we can't make
chocolate like this? Do you think it's going to keep raining? I
wonder where the bus will drop us off?" She sat, inspecting
the clouds that seemed to have gotten denser the further
west they went.

Ruby got out her travel book, which, after Leiden she
was reluctant to do; but since it was only the two of them,
she didn't think they would get mobbed. She started reading
about the hostel. "I think it stops three blocks away. The
rooms are co-ed, with three bunk beds or private rooms for
double the cost. I say the bunk room. It looks like it has a
restaurant and bar, and one toilet per floor and two shower

rooms." The rain was coming in fast bursts against the window and, because it was only an hour until they got there, Ruby had a feeling that it would keep raining.

When the train pulled into the station, Ruby and Retta were already standing by the door. It was not the elaborate depot that Antwerp was, and the majority of it was not covered. So, when the door slid open, both women made a dash to the inner lobby. It reminded Ruby more of a small airport.

The depot had a ticket counter with an electronic arrival and departure board, a few shops, and a restaurant. There was also an information booth, which Ruby made her way toward. She was like a homing pigeon to the white "i" on the blue background. After figuring out which bus to take to get to the hostel, they bought a couple of waffles at a small counter and ate them as they walked to the exit.

The rain was coming down as if a stagehand on a movie set was standing with a hose and spraying it straight down. Ruby had already put her yellow, water-resistant jacket on and shoved the last of the waffle in her mouth as the bus pulled up. The ride took fifteen minutes and wound its way to the old section of Brugge.

Canals crisscrossed stone bridges, and small parks were tucked into hidden nooks and crannies. The buildings had subtle variations of tan brick, and were accented with step-gabled roofs the color of paprika. It was charming, and if Ruby had to think of a classic European village, this one would be it. Even though the rain was immune to her windshield-wiper swipes, she kept rubbing her hand along the window, trying to get a better view.

When they stopped, she asked the driver the direction of Prima Facie. He pointed across the narrow street to the left and said, "Straight, three streets." It was right on target with the book. She gave him a lopsided smile and squinted her eyes up at the murky sky. She looked over her shoulder at Retta.

"Are you ready?" Mist coated her face as she stood on the steps of the bus. "Go, go, go!"

The driver saluted with his hand. "Veel geluk!" Whatever the saying meant (probably "So long, sucker!), he said it with a huge, crooked, toothy grin. At least that's what Ruby would say. The bus let them cross before it continued its route.

Both girls ran and looked for the hostel sign. "Running" would have been stretch, because with each clumsy stride, Ruby's backpack bumped her forward. Maybe it was more of a trot-lunge. Spray stung her face as they raced down the street. Retta overtook Ruby after the first block and, by the time the third block came into view, they had slowed to a hunched hustle. They were both laughing so hard that they nearly collapsed through the bright blue entrance to the hostel.

CHAPTER EIGHT

Finley sat with his back to the door, swirled the amber liquid in his glass, and listened to the others at the table talk. It could be said he was shirking responsibilities. It could also be said that he was hiding from his family. Whereas some people wanted to find themselves on their walkabouts, he wanted to lose himself, duty be damned.

Finley was the youngest of three and the second son of the Sinclair family. In being the second son, he received the benefits of their privileged life without the accountability that was shouldered by his older brother, Ian. On the northern shores of Scotland, the family went back multiple generations. It began with whiskey, and had expanded over the years to horses—a brief dabble with mining, some investments in art, and extensive land ownership. Finley was lost in thought over the Scottish shores when he was interrupted.

"Finey, can we?" The voice of his sister, Anne, sounded different somehow, and he tried to find his own voice to ask her what she was talking about. He ran his finger over his bottom lip that had somehow lost all feeling, and peeled back his eyelids, which he had closed for a quick rest. He looked at Anne. The Sinclair eyes, slate-grey and piercing, looked back at him. Fin smiled as his sister flipped her waterfall of ebony hair over one shoulder. It was something she never did, and he thought she must be imitating one of the women in her circle of friends.

"How did you know where I was?" His speech came out in a slow, raspy whisper. He squinted, trying to bring her into focus. Maybe he was dreaming. A warm hand touched his face. *Okay, I'm not dreaming.*

A giggle made it to his ears. "You told me to sit down with you, Finey."

Fin blinked once, twice, and a third time. Coming into view was a different person, not Anne, and that giggle—it was squeaky and grating, not the rich tone of his sister's.

"Finey…"

Before another word escaped, he placed his hand over the one still on his cheek.

"Don't." Anne called him Finey. Only Anne.

The nickname brought a flood of memories, wonderful, fun, and heart-wrenching memories. His eyes closed again. He saw a young Ian, Anne, and himself as they raced colorful kites across a field of high, wild grass. He saw them as adults the last time they had been together, Anne had teased him about the need to find a wife and was triumphant when their mother became inspired by the thought of a perfect suit for him. Ian smiled subtly as he bounced his son on his lap and their father hid behind his paper. His eyes stung. *Happy times.*

That was three months ago, before everything changed.

The Sinclairs had gathered at their family home in Stonehaven for their annual winter party. Anne and her new husband, Thomas, had a home on the property. Fin had been back for two days. He chose to skirt back and forth between Stonehaven and the more entertaining city of Glasgow. Ian and his family were coming from their country estate ten miles away. A winter storm had blanketed the eastern coast in snow and ice. On a narrow, windswept road, Ian and his family were hit head-on by a delivery truck, killing everyone in their vehicle.

Finley's world imploded in that instant. At twenty-seven, he had thought that the world was his. He was handsome, privileged, and unhindered by responsibilities. The call came that there had been an accident involving Ian. That was all.

Finley left the house, sped down the lane, and saw emergency lights in the distance. When he arrived, an officer tried to pull him aside as he rushed to the familiar, overturned car. He wrenched his whole body away from the officer's grip and got to the car as rescue paramedics took his nephew, his beloved five-year-old nephew, through the back window. Fin knelt in the snow, taking the boy into his arms and rocking his still body back and forth.

The smell of gasoline was everywhere. It seemed like hours and, at the same time, seconds, before someone touched his shoulder, saying that he needed to release the boy. Fin's face was wet, mixed with tears and sleet. He pressed his forehead to the icy road and screamed, clawing at nothing, trying to get back the things he loved.

At the funeral, Fin stoically gave the eulogy that left those present wondering if there wasn't more to the man than his rakish, devil-may-care ways—even if he himself did not realize it. Without a word written down, Fin spoke of Ian, Ian's wife, and their son from the heart, of the remarkable impact they made within the family and to those in the tight-knit community. He stood tall next to his mother, answering questions she could not. He held Anne as she cried what should have been a lifetime of tears, soaking through his jacket and shirt, reaching his skin. After the service, after the condolences were given, and when it was quiet, he felt as if he were Atlas being crushed by the weight of what had been disastrously thrust upon him.

Sequestered with his father days later, going over the estate, the assets, and the mind-boggling amount of investments, Fin left the office with a new appreciation of the overwhelming task that Ian had shouldered. He also left the family home, stuffing a rucksack with a few changes of clothes, other essentials, and a note on the fireplace mantel simply stating, "Give me some time - F."

His mother had his father, and Anne had Thomas. Fin felt completely alone. He had never been jealous, nor had he wanted the power that Ian had. Now there was no choice, and he was floundering. He did not want his brother's legacy to be in vain, but he wasn't sure he was capable, and he was scared to death. Even as a child, Fin exuded confidence. All the Sinclairs did—they just had differing goals. Ian had a passion for numbers and an unwavering dedication to seeing the family prosper. Anne was tenacious in her pursuit of the arts. She was a self-taught painter and spoke three languages. Her love of meddling only made her more endearing, if said meddling was not directed at one of her brothers. Then there was Finley, who could illuminate a room. He did not live on the fringes of life; he lived in the center. If he tried something, he would eventually master whatever he put his mind to.

Fin currently sat in a youth hostel in Brugge, Belgium, trying to forget what he knew he should be doing and tactfully ignoring the woman who was, for some reason, still trying to touch his face. She had quit calling him Finey, so, perhaps there would be a use for her later on. He tried to smile, but it didn't quite reach his lips.

A few weeks ago, Fin hadn't even known that such places existed. Now he was friends with the Dutch owner, Hans, and he lived over his shop, which was behind the hostel. The name Sinclair was well-known in Scotland but, outside the country, he was just like everyone else, and he enjoyed the anonymity. He had gone through several bottles of whiskey and numerous women who had come through the doors of the hostel.

He had let himself fall into a disheveled mess. His hair looked like he had just rolled out of bed, as it hung below his strong brow. His square jaw was rarely clean shaven, and his clothing, although well cut, hung on his athletic frame in wrinkled disarray. Even with the untidiness, women were drawn to his masculine, self-assured presence. Although he projected an air of unapproachability, they were still flies to honey. His eyes, bloodshot from lack of sleep and too much drinking, could penetrate to a person's soul, leaving many women in his company wanting more. Unfortunately, he had nothing to give except emotionless trysts that briefly shrunk the hole in his gut. He had faithfully written short missives to his mother every week, saying that he was fine, but he could not work up to calling or telling the Sinclairs when he would return to take his place.

* * *

Fin had happened upon Prima Facie quite by accident, while idly walking around the streets of Brugge. He remembered the town from a family vacation in his teens, and had fond memories of running along the low stone walls that bordered the canals with his siblings. He was daydreaming as he walked, wondering how he had gotten to the burg. He remembered driving in his car, but he did not remember making a conscious decision to make this his destination.

"Aahh! Hold the rung. Damn man, hold the rung!"

"Holy Christ, I've got it," Fin said as he got hold of the wooden step, righting the man who was trying not to fall. In his reverie, he almost tripped over the ladder that the pudgy man had climbed to fix a loose shingle.

"I don't know where my head was. Are you okay?" He

watched as the man made it to solid ground. Fin wore a
pullover in the cool weather, but the man had rings of sweat
that reached around his thick arms and the grease-smeared
t-shirt held tight to his generous girth.

"My back has a twinge. Good thing you caught me." The
man was touching right below his ribcage, stopping mid-
squeeze. "Well, it's your bloody fault now, isn't it?" He eyed
Fin up and down. "Tell you what. Can you work?" He had
returned to massaging his ribs, perhaps with more
exaggeration than he had before.

Fin rubbed his stubbled jaw with a hint of a smile behind
his eyes. "What do you have in mind?"

Fin didn't know if it was because he looked worse than
he thought, or if Hans was just crazy but, in the end, he
offered Fin room and board in exchange for odd jobs that
needed to be done around the hostel. On top of that, the
Dutchman had made Fin come as close to a true laugh as he
could remember since the accident.

He was given the space above the shop that Hans had
purchased with the hostel. The garret was twenty yards
from the rear of the main lodge and in need of repair. The
outside looked like a ramshackle barn with peeling white
paint and a sliding wooden door on rails. Inside were five
thick, wooden work tables littered with tools, paint cans,
and tarps. The floor was fine dirt to soak up spills, leaving
dark areas over the places that were visible underneath the
piles of junk that covered most of the interior. Three rusty
bicycles hung from the rafters, and a push lawn mower, five-
gallon drums of used paint, and various other oddities had
accumulated in the space over the years.

Square wooden posts held up what was to become Fin's
temporary quarters, and an open set of rickety stairs led up
to the attic. The stairs looked like they could hold his weight,

but Finn waited for Hans to do the honors first. This ended up a good thing, for when the older man stood at the top step, he slammed his head into the metal roof that sloped down above him.

"Ah shit, man. I forgot how low this bloody roof was. God, my damn head feels like it split open." Hans touched his greasy flop of brown hair like he was playing piano, searching for gashes.

Rather than ask the man if he was okay, Fin quipped, "If your paunchy, puny self can't stand up there, how am I expected to?"

"Just get your arse up here and bend down. Don't think that you're going to sue me if you whack yourself, because I just warned you."

After only five steps, Fin poked his head up to see where he'd be staying. He ran his fingers through his hair and raised his brows. Wide wood planks ran the length of the attic, a half inch of space between them so that he could see down to the workshop. More castoffs littered the makeshift floor, and the whole thing was covered with a rusty metal roof that sloped at a pitched angle to the floor. "What do you suggest I sleep on, or am I to just drag a tarp up here? Maybe you have a wheelbarrow I could curl up in?" He shook his head and feigned a scowl.

"Well, it's not a throne room but, then again, you aren't a bloody king, are you?" Given he was hunched over and looked no more daunting than an ill-dressed hobbit, Hans's speech did not have the intended effect. Both men looked at each other for a full thirty seconds, and then burst into laughter. "This is what you get for trade but, on the bright side, you can get your exercise—there's no plumbing in the garage."

Fin groaned. He decided to try and spend most of his

time in the main hostel.

Hans had waddled down the ladder and, at the bottom, he said, "Why don't you pretty yourself up, and I'll have one of the crew help me schlep a mattress over here. Then we can get a drink. Toodleoo." With his last comment, Hans wiggled his sausage fingers in front of his face and walked out the barn door.

That's how Finn came to be in Brugge. Now, five weeks later, Fin tried filling up his days hammering, sawing, and climbing. He used anything he could to keep his mind and hands busy. In the times he was idle, memories of Ian, his beautiful wife, and the nephew he had doted on flooded his mind. When it got too dark to work, he moved inside and kept company with the nine other employees of the hostel, drinking in the back booth and debauching with the faceless women who all but threw themselves at him.

Fin had always been the center of attention—not because of vanity, but because people were simply drawn to him. He was gregarious and sincere, and whomever he spoke to felt like the only person on earth, their opinion mattered. Finn could mesmerize with the tilt of his head and his steady gaze. In Brugge, though, he was detached. If something got too personal, his eyes became hard and he'd shut down. That was why he liked Hans and tinkering at the hostel: No one asked many questions, and those who did soon realized that Fin would not be forthcoming, so they quickly moved on to other topics.

It had been raining off and on all day, and Fin had quit work early. He had started patching the metal roofing to his humble abode, and had told Hans that with the amount of leaks the roof had, Hans would lose most of the tools and other junk he had. Fin also preferred to not be soaked when he slept.

Hans grumbled, "At least fucking paint the inside of the hostel, where paying customers spend time."

Fin crossed his arms over his chest and, with a hint of a smile, said, "The only way to patch is in the rain. Then I know where the bloody leaks are." Hans threw up his hands and stalked off with a "humph" in response.

After hours of going in and out of the rain, looking for the leaks and repairing them, Fin was tired, cold, and wet. He took a shower to warm up and put some clean clothes on. He now sat gracefully slouched on a wooden chair, facing the large booth drumming a finger on the table to the beat of the music. His half-lidded eyes tried paying attention to the chestnut-haired college student next to him, knowing that later she'd invite him to do more than talk. She had quit using his name altogether, and had moved from his face to his leg. Both were preferable in his hazy mind. Luckily, there was a small group at the table, so he didn't have to concentrate on her babbling. Instead, he focused on the tawny colored liquid rolling around in his glass.

The girl—Lori, Laura, or some version of that—blathered on about her escapades through Italy. She stole sideways glances at Fin. He could only guess it was her attempt at flirting. Occasionally he made eye contact for her troubles, which caused her to stumble over her words. He was not the only staff member going through the all-too-eager tourists. There were wagers made—not that Fin showed interest in the ill-mannered game, but it was nearly impossible for him to remain completely sanctimonious. He just didn't kiss and tell. Maybe it was that he had a sister, and had it been *her* that bets were being made on with this shameless group of heathens…well, he could not even think about what he would do. Still, it made him smile every time Hans howled out the Dutch rhyme, "Neuken in de Keuken," when a hint of an indiscretion was about to take place.

"I don't want you sounding like a complete cocker while you're in my village," Hans had said. "You are representing the hostel, after all. So, when you meet these fine people for the first time, the formal greeting is 'Neucken in de Keuken.' Then, when you get to know them, a simple 'Hallo' will do." Han's face was a mask of innocence.

Fin thought back to the day he met the owner of the hardware store. He had gone to buy a paint scraper, and had greeted the older woman behind the counter with his new Dutch saying. She gasped open-mouthed and clutched a clenched fist to her bosom, fleeing to the back room without a word.

That was when the woman's husband came to help Fin instead. "What in the name of God did you say to my wife?"

"Hans told me the Dutch greeting. Did I mispronounce something?"

The man shook his head and gave an oath under his breath, mentioning Hans's name somewhere in an unflattering light. He then explained that Fin had been going around town saying that he wanted to have sexual relations in the kitchen—and that was the polite version. *Well, the joke is on him. Point for Hans,* Fin had thought, but it did give him something to chew over. How could he repay Hans in kind? Thus, he had one more thing to occupy his thoughts.

Lisa, Lindsey, droned on. A clap of thunder and the door banging into the wall behind him brought him out of his reverie. Fin lifted his head and glanced over his shoulder. A cold gust of wind whipped in, causing a shiver to ripple up his back. It took a full three seconds for him to turn his head and for his eyes to close and open. He focused his gaze on two women tumbling through the door, bursting in with laughter and so drenched that they could have just jumped into a canal. To Fin, they were nothing but a blur—black hair and blonde, a streak of absolute joy and life streaming into the crowded room. The blonde's eyes scanned the room.

Something changed in Fin. His breath was physically taken from his lungs, as if he had been poleaxed. His knuckles turned white from clenching onto the table. The world moved in slow-motion. The noise in the bar became muffled, as if he was submerged under water. Then it was gone. She was gone, tripping into the reception room of Prima Facie. Everything in him screamed to run after the girl, but he felt a tug on his shirt. "Have you seen the Leaning Tower of Pisa? It is sooo much smaller than I thought it would be." Giggle, giggle.

Fin's first instinct was to tell Lauren or Lucy that he didn't give a flying fuck about the tower, but good breeding took over, and he agreed. "Much smaller." He scanned the others around the table. No one else seemed to be affected by the whirlwind that had just swept through the room. Fin shook his head to clear it. *Maybe it's time to cut back on the drinking.*

Lily or Leah ran her fingers through Fin's hair. "Hey, do you want to go up and see my room? It's private." She ran a perfectly shaped nail along her shiny lip.

This time, a very different shiver ran through Fin. He felt numb and weary as he walked behind her, on autopilot. Through the rectangular window that led to the kitchen, he heard Hans's thundering voice, "Neuken in de Keuken!"

As he ascended the stairs, he did not smile.

* * *

When he felt he had given it enough time—frankly, he could not have stayed a minute more—he rolled over and began picking up his clothes, which were strewn about the floor. He was a thoughtful lover; he made sure that the women were satiated before he gave in to his own needs. However, being thorough in bed was completely different than wanting a conversation or any form of relationship.

Fin was introduced to dozens of suitable candidates, as his mother often pointed out. He was sick of making small talk and watching bedroom eyes look at him as if he were a prized stallion, one with looks and a purse. He was satisfied with having an occasional liaison with no strings. He easily skirted those who tried to get him to the altar, and he left them thinking it was their decision. It was a win-win for both.

A crushing reality hit him as he tried gracefully extricating himself from another meaningless night of indiscretion. Ian and his son were gone, and now the pressure for Finley to produce an heir to carry on the Sinclair name and fortune would be thrust upon him. Although his family held to modern thinking in many things, they were very traditional as far as lineage and inheritance. The eldest son was to produce an heir to take over for the father. Thinking about it now it seemed archaic, but the tradition of patrimony was something they all grew up with and never questioned.

Fin's hands dangled between his thighs as he sat at the edge of Lea's or Libby's bed. His mouth felt like he had eaten chalk, and his head began to pound. He let his head fall forward, and he ran his fingers through his thick, black mane. He pushed the wave of hair back, holding it to his crown for a moment before releasing it, letting it tumble in a perfect disarray over his equally dark brows.

The lady behind him lay tangled in a bed sheet and was circling a long finger nail along his back. "You can stay. I wouldn't mind a second round."

He could almost hear her purr. Bile stung his throat. He

wanted to run back to his shack and pull the covers over his head. *Bloody hell, now even sex can't get rid of the ghosts hovering around me.* "As much as I would love to, Hans has me doing a crazy amount of work tomorrow. I need to wake up early." He dropped a kiss on her pouting lips and decided to carry his shoes instead of taking the time to put them on so he did not have to listen to her go on about meeting him later. She was to be in Brugge for one more day.

He mumbled on his way out the door. The lady behind him piped up. "Oh, good. I hope we can get together again, too. I don't remember anything quite like that."

Hell, lady, I was saying God help me. Language barriers. Fin grunted as he looked back at her rolling over, a huge smile on her face.

Fin descended the back stairs to avoid seeing anyone. He was met with stars and illuminated, billowy clouds that squeezed out what was left of the rain. He slipped his shoes on and walked the short distance to the garage, enjoying the sound of the gravel crunching underneath his feet, reminding him of the family home in Stonehaven.

The house was surrounded by a pea-gravel drive and was lined with sweet briar roses that were his mother's favorite. He could see Ian, Anne, and himself chasing after one another in a game of tag, their mother laughing as they tried hiding behind her skirt. Thinking back, he realized how much he had taken for granted. His throat tightened as he tugged on the sliding door, making his way inside, hopefully to a dreamless sleep.

CHAPTER NINE

R uby and Retta were told at the reception that the hostel would be close to capacity, but when they got to the room, the only thing they saw was an array of backpacks leaning against two of the three unoccupied bunk bed frames. Retta shook her head, a perfect imitation of a black lab spraying droplets of water throughout the room. "I don't think I've ever been so wet. Well, in the shower, but not clothed," she tilted her head to the side. "Oh, there was this time I jumped into our community pool, but that was a dare."

Ruby sat cross-legged on the floor and went through her backpack. She decided that nothing had gotten wet and congratulated herself for forking out the extra money for the water-resistant bag. "Retta, my clothes are stuck to me like plastic wrap. I'm going to go take a hot shower, and then I would be happy to listen to more of your tomfooleries."

She never saw the wet sock coming, and then it hit her in the back of the head. "Ack," Ruby cried and flung the sock off her shoulder. "Tell me that was clean and just got wet in your bag." She looked and saw Retta, a grin spread across her puckish face, waggle a white, wrinkly un-socked foot in the air. Ruby shook her head and thanked the gods that she did not have a younger sister as Retta's trilling laughter followed her down the hall and to the shower.

The shower room was a pleasant, unexpected surprise. It was small but clean, and had an actual stall with a curtain. The dandelion yellow walls breathed cheerful life into the space. Ruby quickly found out that scalding herself was a viable option. So far she loved Brugge: Prima Facie was much busier than the hotel in Leiden, and Ruby heard people walking around on the other side of the door. She took the noise as a good sign. If people wanted to be here, it must be okay. She actually hummed as she walked back to the room, and ran smooth fingers over the textured lavender hallway wall. Swinging the door open, Ruby nearly ran head-on into what co-ed meant. For her, scant clothing was never a huge deal, but she came up short seeing a man lean over his bed in a very tight pair of white underwear. Her eyes became two blue marbles, and her mouth gaped open like a fish about to gulp a worm. She diverted her gaze, but instead met Retta's as she peered over the cover of a book she was pretending to read. Rather than her mouth being open, Retta chewed the inside of her cheek like it was a piece of Hubba Bubba.

Something in between a snort and a croak made its way out of Ruby's still opened mouth. The young man's head swiveled around, catching Ruby in mid-snort.

"Hey, I'm Brian. You must be Ruby. Retta was just telling me about you." He turned and pulled on a black turtleneck in one fluid movement.

Had it been Ruby, pants would have been the first priority, but who was she to give her opinion to a stranger? "Yeah, I was just taking a shower," she said in response. His white underwear kept drawing her attention. She tried keeping her eyes on his face, which was like being told not to stare at the sun. His thick, kinky hair was the color of a copper penny. Long and unruly on the top and shorter on the sides, the epitome of an eighties rocker as it popped through the top of his sweater. A cough that sounded suspiciously like a muffled laugh came from the top bunk, reminding Ruby that Retta was up there. Ruby looked up to the bunk and rolled her eyes at Retta, who still hid behind her book.

"What are you reading?" she challenged, thinking to catch Retta not quite knowing what she was reading.

"Brian had a book on Brugge he let me look at. Very informative." Her face was the picture of innocence. Ruby squinted at her, and would have stuck out her tongue had Brian not been watching. Humor played in his chocolate brown eyes.

"Retta said you ladies only had a day to spend here, so I thought you could pick out the most interesting places to visit. I have some suggestions, if you want." He pulled on his jeans, zipped them, and slid into a pair of black flip-flops. "I'm going to the bar. They have decent food and great beer. I'll save a spot for you." He walked out the door without closing it.

Ruby turned to Retta, "I don't think I've heard you this speechless since we met. How and when did you get changed?"

"I had just put on dry underthings when the door swung open. It scared me to death. They really need to put locks on these doors." Her hand fluttered toward the door. "As you can imagine, Brian didn't even bat an eyelash, which I guess I should take offense to. I sputtered like an idiot, and I think I set the speed record for fastest dresser. Hang your clothes up so we can go eat. How was the shower, I was going to take one, but maybe I'll wait until after we're done eating." She jumped down off her bunk and started putting Ruby's clothes over the rails of the bed.

Ruby didn't stop her, figuring it gave her something to do. Instead, Ruby plopped the sopping mess into her hands and unwound her towel from her head. She grabbed her brush and ran it through her hair. "Margie would love this place. The paint colors make it feel like one giant bouquet."

Their room was the color of blue hydrangea, and the white of the bed sheets made it look crisp and airy. A large window that started a foot from the floor faced an open space behind the hostel. Beyond was an old garage. Ruby cranked open the window and held her hand out. The downpour was now a drizzle, and she glimpsed the setting sun between the billowy, grey and white clouds. She closed the window and put her brush away. "I'm ready."

The two women wound their way to the large rectangular restaurant. Vibrant geranium-red walls had become the canvas for a very bohemian conglomeration of bric-a-brac, including a five-inch golden Buddha, a bronze Eiffel tower, and a string of faded peace flags. Everything looked like items that could easily have been left by travelers passing through.

The front of the restaurant was made up of windows, and had a thick wooden bar that was the color of maple syrup—it was probably as sticky. Booths flanked the long walls with a large, half-circled booth that took up the back corner. A few square, miss-matched tables were spaced throughout the center of the room, with Chinese lanterns hanging over each. Out of the corner of her eye, Ruby saw two people going up the stairs to private rooms. At the same time, a man bellowed some foreign rhyme from the pass-through of the kitchen.

Retta waved to Brian who had, unfortunately, planted himself at the circular booth in the back corner. She thought it unfortunate because it was crowded with people, she was trying to ease herself into the new Ruby, the one that wants to approach people rather than avoid them. Ruby took in a large lung full of air and looked to the stairway where the couple had disappeared. When they got to the table, she let out the air and eased into a vacant chair that faced the booth. The wood underneath her was still warm. A musky scent hung in the air, sending a shiver up her spine. Slightly shaky fingers unconsciously touched the beads around her neck.

She wondered what Poppy was doing. *She's probably snuggled down under her puffy feather tic, her mouth slightly open, drooling onto her pillow.* A snicker spewed out and, drat, eyes swivel her direction. *So much for blending in.*

Because no one else laughed, she assumed that she couldn't use their discussion to mask her silly gaffe. She waved her hand the way one does to get rid of a pesky fly saying, "I was just thinking of something my sister does. It's really nothing."

Retta merely looked at her and, thankfully, came to the rescue. "Brian was saying we need to go to the top of the Belfry and take a cycling tour. There's a tour company right across the street. In the morning we should do that first, then walk around some, and then do the bell tower. The town hall is in the square, so we can go there and eat at one of the cafés. What do you think?"

The four others looked to Ruby expectantly. She felt her cheeks warm and, with a tight smile, nodded her head. "Sounds good." That was all it took. The backpackers around the table started in on what they would do with one day in Brugge. Retta couldn't help but put in her two cents, even though she'd never been here.

A pizza and a round of Belgium beers arrived for everybody. Ruby guessed that the ordering happened during her reverie, but it was perfect timing, as she heard her stomach rumble. The waitress squeezed into the booth and picked up one of the mugs. She introduced herself as, "OliviafromAustralia" to Ruby and Retta. Everybody grabbed for a slice and continued on about Brugge and other places they had traveled to or heard about.

"Last call for food." It was the same voice from before, but now she saw a flop of brown hair and chubby fingers waving from the kitchen.

Her body felt drained; she craved solitude. "Hey, I'm so tired. I think I'll just go back to the room and crash."

"Yeah, you look tired. See you tomorrow." Retta raised a hand, barely missing a beat of the discussion around her.

* * *

The room was empty, and Ruby changed into a grey, long-sleeved CU t-shirt and multi-colored leggings she always slept in before a stranger plowed into the room. The bunk was close to the window, so she cranked it open and started flipping through Brian's book.

The night air smelled like freshly mowed grass and dirt. It was cold as it came through the window, so she wiggled under the crisp sheets and blanket to enjoy the quiet. Her eyes started to close after thirty minutes, but opened with a jerk when she heard the door on the shed behind the hostel slide open. She couldn't see who it was, but a few minutes after it closed with a clank, a light came on in a top window and a bent, shadowed figure walked across the room.

Surely no one lived there. It looked as if even a car would be putting itself in peril if it were parked in the dilapidated shack. *It must be someone tinkering with something or other*, she told herself. She turned her head into the soft pillow and lay on her side, looking out the window and watching the shadows play on the walls across the lane.

* * *

Finley locked the large farm door with the padlock that Hans had given him when he moved in. He had not thought it necessary, but to stop Hans from barking at him, he gave in and used the lock. He breathed in the now familiar smell of gasoline and musty tarps, mixed with turpentine and oil. He had been surprised at how comfortable, if not content, he had become with his present surroundings, which were so different from what he knew but so vital to what he needed at this precise time in his life.

A cloud hid the little light from the moon as it streamed through the opening, and he ran into a paint drum making his way to his bed. "Shit. Damn," he cursed to the empty room. Fin found the stair railing—something he installed two weeks ago—and climbed the steps, feeling for the lantern he had hung on a rope from a wooden beam. He switched it on and watched it swing back and forth. The effect of the light reminded him of an engineer swinging his oil lamp to signal an oncoming train.

He felt too weary for a virile man of twenty-seven. He ached for even a modicum of the happiness he had before Ian's death. Fin had always enjoyed listening to people, learning, and experiencing all that was possible. Now, thinking of this evening, he couldn't recall a single conversation or even if he had participated in any. Christ, he couldn't even remember the name of the woman he just had sex with, if he ever knew it.

He bent at the waist, being careful not to bump his head (as he had done when he first arrived), and made his way to the thick futon. He lay on his back with his arms behind his head and stared out small gable window above him. In that instant, with the stars peeking between the clouds and the lantern stilling, Fin decided that he needed to change. The women and the drinking were not making him happy or helping him to forget. Although he was not quite ready to go home, something had to change. He barely remembered who he was before the god-dammed delivery truck fucked everything up. Fin pulled at his hair, a scream just behind his lips. He needed even an ounce of the enthusiasm and pleasure he once had. Spinning ideas like a manic spider creating a web, he forced himself to fall asleep, stamping down his racing mind.

CHAPTER TEN

R uby woke up when, beneath her eyelids, the room began to lighten. She had always loved mornings, and she often lay with her face to the sun, feeling its warmth rather than watching it rise. Her skin glowed under the dawn. She stayed still for a while, not opening her eyes, trying to remember the dream she had had during the night. It came to her like an old photo that was fuzzy around the edges and, like an old photo, it was faded—she couldn't quite see it clearly. It reminded her of a dream she had before. There was a field, and she knew that there were people. She could feel the sunshine on her face, but that could have been the light from the window. Then the vision was gone.

She opened her eyes slowly and knew it was quite early—the magical time between night and day when things were shrouded in misty grey and had a golden shimmer that sang with anticipation. Ruby was still on her side, in the exact position she had been when she closed her eyes. Retta must have shut the window when she returned to the room the night before, but the air was still pleasantly cool on her face and warm under her covers. She heard no movement around her, and turned from the window to look around. In the dimness, she still saw faint outlines of the bunks that were occupied by an array sleeping people.

Brian's bare leg was on top of his sheet and, given his lack of modesty yesterday, she could just imagine that the rest of him was probably bare underneath his covers. His head was hidden, except for a crazy, curling shock of hair that poked out.

The bed above him held a waif of a girl. Her body looked to be that of a young teenager, but her face looked older. Everything was black. The contrast was dramatic against the white of the sheet. Her short, spikey hair was the exact color of the soot that clung to the inside of Poppy's fireplace, and her thin, black t-shirt and leggings looked as if she'd worn them every night for years. The only color came from the coral pink toenails on her dainty feet. Although her eyes were closed, Ruby thought they would be the color of a forest acorn, perhaps because it seemed like she could be a wood nymph prancing around in the dappled light of a fairytale glen. Ruby made a mental note to seek her out later to see if her guess was correct.

The next bunk over held two young men from Japan: Genji and Haruki. In the top bed, Genji had been at the booth the night before and had said that he and his friend had come from a trek in Nepal. They had made their way from Greece across to Italy, and then skipped over to the Netherlands. Retta had quizzed them on their time in Greece, and asked if they had, by chance, met her friend, whom she was to meet in three days' time. She gave the names and what they looked like but, sadly, they had not met up with anyone fitting her description. She let out a puff of air and slouched down rather dejectedly. Ruby smiled at her complete innocence.

The boys looked like clones of one another—each was flat on his back, left arms at right angles above their heads, with right arms across their stomachs. Their legs looked like two sets of sturdy wooden bats beneath the sheets, as neither had even a slight bend. They wore their straight hair long, ending below their ears. The only difference was that Genji had a slight reddish tinge to his hereditary midnight black, as if he were letting a dye job fade. Ruby could not see Retta in the bed above hers, but she did see her limp hand dangle over the side of the bed.

Ruby rotated her shoulder and pointed and flexed her toes. She itched to get up. Reception had said that breakfast was from seven to nine and included coffee or tea, rolls with jam, and hard boiled eggs. *Perfect.* She could nearly smell the coffee. *Surely it's near seven. Well, maybe not, but maybe they have the pot out early.* Quietly, Ruby peeled her sheet back and sat up. She didn't want to scavenge through her bag for clothes, so she decided that her nightwear was acceptable. She had draped her yellow rain jacket and socks over the rail at the end of the bed last night, hoping they would dry. The jacket was dry and the socks were still slightly damp, but wearable. She sat down on the carpeted floor, pulled on her socks, and put on her Tevas.

She stood and was pushing her arms through her jacket when she glanced over at the top bed of Brian's bunk. Two moss green eyes stared at her. Her arms flailed and got caught up in her left sleeve. Luckily, she was breathing in, because she sucked in a lungful of air rather than letting it out in what assuredly would have been a scream. She finished getting her jacket on and closed her eyes for a full three seconds to let her heart return to normal. Her eyes looked like those of a doll in a horror movie, when the doll comes to life and kills unsuspecting campers. Ruby tried being as quiet as possible while getting ready to leave the room.

The girl put up one finger, indicating that she wanted Ruby to wait. She then crawled down to the end of the bed. She sat with her legs over the edge before she sprang to the floor. In the back of her mind, Ruby noticed that there was no sound when she hit the floor, exactly what one would expect from a flittering nymph. She slipped on a pair of grey high-top All-Stars, and they both tip-toed out the door.

"Why don't you go to the restaurant and I'll catch up with you," Ruby whispered in the quiet of the hallway. The girl nodded and kept walking.

Ruby walked to the bathroom, splashed some cold water on her face, and shook her fingers through her hair. "It could be worse," she said to the empty room. She had some weird bedhead thing going on, but there wasn't much she could do about that right now. She used the toilet and washed her hands, wondering what on earth she would talk about with the girl. Humming a random tune and making a mental list of potential topics of conversation, she wound her way to the quiet of the restaurant.

There were three people in the room. A short, pudgy man with at least two and, most probably, three chins underneath his thin red lips, stood behind the bar. His eyes were dark and a tad too close together. He wore thick, black reading glasses perched low on his wide nose—all of which was covered by the bushiest eyebrows Ruby had ever seen. She tried snuffing her urge to get out her tweezers and start plucking. He wore a red and navy striped rugby shirt, with none of the buttons buttoned. A tuft of dark curls sprang from the opening. It now occurred to her why larger people should not wear horizontal stripes.

The other person at the bar had his back to her. He was the opposite of the man behind the bar. Standing with his arms folded, and resting on the wooden counter, he exuded an air of confident masculinity. He wore worn leather work boots, a perfectly fitting pair of faded jeans, and a grey, long-sleeved t-shirt that clung to his wide shoulders. His hair was the color of ravens' feathers—it touched his collar in waves and looked as soft as silk. Ruby couldn't tell if it was wet from a shower or dry and naturally shiny. He was talking to the man behind the counter, and nodded at something the man had said.

Ruby wasn't close enough to hear their conversation, but suddenly the older man let out a deep hoot. Ruby realized it must have been the man in the kitchen the night before. He looked over at Ruby and met her eyes before she could look away. Her head swiveled to meet the wisp of a girl in front of her, and she was thankful that she had brought two mugs of coffee to the table. There was a carafe on the bar but, frankly, the little man was a bit intimidating. The Adonis keeping him company was even more so. Her booth was the farthest from the bar, and Ruby slid into the seat across from the girl.

"Sorry I startled you earlier. I'm Chloris." She had a sing-song lilt to her voice that reminded Ruby of a pretty song bird. Her accent sounded like a mixture of Dutch and French, with something else mixed in.

"I got you some coffee," Chloris said.

"Thanks, I'm Ruby. You didn't really scare me. I just didn't know anyone was awake." She surrounded the mug with her hands and absorbed the heat.

"No, I know you weren't scared. It would take more than that, I would think?" There was a question at the end of her sentence that Ruby inwardly smiled at. *Yes, it would take more than that.* "How long have you been traveling?" Her green eyes were intent on Ruby's face.

"Well, let's see. It feels like months, but I believe it has been a whole three days, this being the third. I flew into Amsterdam and took the train to Leiden, quickly left, and came to Brugge," Ruby replied.

"Why do you think that is?" Chloris took a sip of coffee and continued looking at Ruby.

"Why did I come to Brugge? I guess it was on my list of places to visit." Ruby blew on her coffee.

"No, why do you think it feels like months?" Chloris cradled her chin in her hands in a gesture of curiosity that seemed much older than she looked. As an afterthought she asked, "Do you really have a list?"

Ruby leaned back in her seat. "It was just a lot to do in two days," she said. "I guess I thought I'd spend more time in Leiden. I wanted to see the tulip fields, but I couldn't wait to get out of there. It smelled like pee. It was dirty, I couldn't get the shower to work, and the food was bad. I'm usually not a complainer." She scrunched up her face and bit down on her thumb nail.

Chloris nodded her head slightly to the side and drummed her index finger against her lips. "It didn't start out great, did it? What else is on your list?" Her eyes shined expectantly.

"Let's see . . . The only thing I need to do is visit family in Norway. I do want to see Finale Ligure in Italy and Hallstatt in Austria. I want to go to Prague, but just the places I've read about." Ruby took a large swallow of coffee. Thankfully, it was strong.

There was a large smack, like a hand hitting still water. Both their eyes moved to the counter, where they saw the fat man bent over, slapping his thick hand on the wooden bar. Ruby turned back to Chloris; she leaned in and lowered her voice.

"That guy is crazy. He reminds me of a deranged carnival worker."

"That's Hans. He's my dad." Chloris watched Hans, and looked both resigned and amused.

Ruby choked on her sip of coffee, trying not to spray it all over the table while pounding on her chest. "I meant crazy in a good way. I don't even know him. You know what, he seems like he has a lot of energy. It's good to have energy. Who doesn't love a carnival?" She babbled, unable to stop herself. "He's your dad?" Her voice was unnaturally high and squeaky.

"Crazy is a good adjective to use." She laughed. "He's a lot to take in. He seems pretty rough, but really he's very genuine."

Ruby looked at the girl across from her. She observed a resemblance in height, and maybe if she gained fifty pounds and he lost as much. He had dark hair, what was left of it—a kind of brown that she thought was closer to Chloris's more natural color. She caught him smile at his daughter—there it was, in the smile.

Ruby's world dropped away when the other man turned their direction. His eyes glided past Chloris and held Ruby's for a beat too long. She wanted to be part of the bench she sat on. She felt like lead—her face warmed as if the unnaturally quick pounding in her chest had sent blood directly to her cheeks. Her feet tingled. *My feet are tingling? That only happens before I throw up. Oh, my. Oh please, please, do not throw up now.*

Ruby looked down at her lap and nervously wiped her hands on her pants. Taking a deep breath through her nose to give herself a moment, she slowly looked back up. He still looked in their direction, but with what can only be described as a baffled expression. He seemed intent on something above Ruby's head. Without seeming too obvious, Ruby pretended to stretch her neck in a wide circle to see what he looked at above her and to the side. From the corner of her eye, she caught sight a wooden chalet cuckoo clock, complete with a water wheel and German dancers. Ruby blinked. *Of course, he isn't looking at me. He did look, right?* He had locked eyes with hers. She felt a jolt strike her, all the way to her toes. She stared at the table so long that the wood grains began to form into pictures. Y*ep, there's a man's face with a big hook nose, or it could be a dinosaur.* She raised her head slowly and met Chloris's eyes, which now bore into hers. How could she have forgotten that there was someone else sitting with her? Annoyingly, the little fairy had a wide grin and laughing, knowing eyes.

"That's Fin. He's been here for, uh, maybe a month. I'm not really sure. I've only been back for a couple of weeks. He's staying in the garage behind Prima Facie." Chloris shrugged her shoulders and smiled as she lifted her mug.

The light that Ruby had seen last night now meant something to her. She wanted to act casually, pretending that she had no idea who Chloris was talking about, but what was the point? She had never been a good liar. Poppy was forever saying she could tell a whole story just by the expressions on Ruby's face.

"What is he doing here?" she asked because, when mythology became reality, one wants to know the hows and whys.

"My dad kind of found him, I guess. He's been doing odd jobs since then. He doesn't put up with my dad's crap, and he gives as much as he gets." Chloris glanced back, over at the men.

"Usually people are intimidated by Dad," she continued, "but I think he gets a secret kick that Fin isn't. It's almost like I have a big brother. He's a really nice guy. He taught me how to juggle, and I am proud to say that I can now throw four lemons at once." Her face lit up like she had discovered the secret behind the legend of the Hanging Gardens of Babylon.

"Where were you before two weeks ago?" Ruby asked,

mainly wanting the earth to shift back onto its axis by changing the topic.

"My mom and I were in South America. She's doing some volunteer work at an animal habitat for illegal trafficking. They rehabilitate injured animals and make sure they have a safe environment." She twisted a black spike of hair. "It was really amazing. Of course, I wasn't old enough to do anything with the animals, but I helped repair a shelter for a parrot with a broken wing."

"How old are you Chloris? Do you go to school here?" The little wood nymph amazed her at every turn.

"I'm sixteen as of three-and-a-half weeks ago. I guess you'd call it homeschooling. I just do it in a variety of homes. My parents work better when they see each other only a few times a year. It's like they're newlyweds when they get back together. It's pretty gross and a little embarrassing." Her brows came together and her eyes squinted, but her smile said that although she might be embarrassed, she didn't mind it. In that moment, she looked as young as her age.

"So, you go back and forth? Do you like it?" Ruby stole a glance over to the bar, telling herself it was to look at Hans. A soft puff of air escaped her lips, and her shoulders fell slightly when she saw that neither man was there.

"He'll be back," Chloris went on, as if she hadn't spoken. This left Ruby wondering if Chloris had actually made the comment at all.

"I do like it. Like my mom says, 'The world is going to give you your best education.' We've had this place for four years, it's where my dad stays, and it's my home base." She moved to another spike and began twirling.

"Mom likes to see the world, so she works for a while or volunteers and then moves on. It's always interesting getting her post cards telling us where she is. She'll come back here for a month, maybe two, and then she starts getting itchy. She'll be gone until she comes back again. Sometimes I go with her, or I meet her for a while. I didn't used to like it as much as I do now." She looked up at the clock and started sliding across the bench.

"I told my dad I would help him in the kitchen this morning. What are you going to do today?" She now stood next to the booth, looking at Ruby with complete ease.

"I have a full day planned with a girl I met on the plane ride to Amsterdam." Ruby looked at the clock. It was a few minutes till seven. She didn't know when Retta had gotten in last night, but she assumed she would still be sleeping.

"Well, have fun. I'll get some food out here in just a bit. Get some more coffee while you wait." With an open, breezy smile, she cocked her head over to the bar.

* * *

Finley was hiding out in the kitchen, which was completely foreign to him. Never one to back down from a challenge, he was in unfamiliar territory without really knowing the reason why. He only knew that he had been telling Hans that he was turning over a new leaf. In return, Hans gave his signature, guttural hoot. Then the air seemed to shimmer. That was how he would describe it. It was like driving down an open road on a hot day, and the air, well, it just shimmered. He watched Hans watch who he thought was Chloris behind him, and turned to say "Good morning" when he was struck dumb with the same awareness that came over him last night.

She has to be the same girl. It was too coincidental. This time she was right there. He would have sucked in his breath, but found that he had none to grab, which left him feeling weightless and muddled. He almost laughed; she looked exactly like a cornered animal.

When their eyes locked, he was transported back to an earlier time in Stonehaven. Her eyes were bright and clear. They reminded Fin of a small, blue Wedgewood jewelry box that had sat next to his mother's bed since he was a child. The two figures on the front were dressed in white, and one held a harp. Around the sides where fat cherubs in flight. His childhood curiosity often got the best of him, and he would often hold up a favorite pin or ring to catch the light from the window that streamed into his parents' room.

The color of the box was an exact match to that of her eyes. Her nose had a slight tilt that fit her face, and her lips were light pink, the color of the inside of a seashell. They were slightly parted, and he glimpsed her white teeth inside. He ached to trace his finger along the rise and fall of the smooth lines, dipping into the moist heat within.

The girl tore her gaze from him and looked down at her lap. She leaned back in the booth, and it looked as if she had just woken up. Her hair was tousled, with one loose curl springing at an odd angle above her ear. He wondered if she slept on her side or if the curls were naturally unruly.

When she raised her head again, Fin gave himself a mental shake to clear his head. He then found a point above her head to focus on. He felt her eyes on him, and it took some strength to not meet her gaze. Her shoulders drop slightly when she looked away. He felt a niggling guilt that he was the cause of her dejected look, but he needed to breathe and figure out what he would do. He would find out more about her later, which wasn't even the question; but, not two minutes before, he had been talking about cleaning up his act. In his bones he knew that meeting the girl who sat twenty feet from him would be different from his usual dallying.

Fin had relished the rotating door of backpackers. There

was nothing permanent, and that was exactly what he could give. What he felt now was different. It was a clap of thunder, a tempest. He needed to decide if he wanted to watch the storm from a safe distance or go into its eye. Something about this girl made him think he was on a precipice, and he eluded the feelings by escaping into the kitchen. *Coward.*

* * *

The dancers and the water wheel started turning for the second time in as long as she had been sitting. It was eight o'clock. Several people had come down. Some stayed, while others drifted here and there. Ruby was on her third cup of coffee, and had another roll and a hardboiled egg in front of her. Genji had sat with her for a while, but he and Haruki were to leave on the 9:07 train. He grabbed an egg and a roll for Haruki, and was on his way to bowl him out of bed. Ruby told him to shake Retta while he was at it. He gave a windy laugh between his teeth and bid her good-bye. Fifteen minutes later, a disheveled Retta bounded around the corner and planted her hands on the tabletop. She was bent over at the waist and her breath came in fast spurts, like she had just finished a 5k sprint.

"What are you doing?" Ruby looked up from peeling her egg.

Retta's head was pointed at the floor. "Genji said you were leaving," she panted. "I thought the bike tour already started. Oh my gosh, I got up so quick I hit my knee jumping off the bed. What time is it anyway? The tour is at nine. Do I have time to eat, or should I get dressed?" Retta had lifted her head, but she still leaned on the table, her breath coming more normally.

"What I think you should do is go get some coffee, although maybe that's not the best avenue for you." Retta looked at Ruby and rolled her eyes. "All right, get some coffee and an egg. The rolls are really good. Then come and sit down. It just turned eight."

Retta turned and made her way to the bar, where breakfast was set up in a line of tightly woven straw baskets that Chloris kept refilling. Ruby watched as she walked away, glancing for the hundredth time toward the kitchen. She had not seen Fin since he walked through the door an hour ago. Maybe there was a back door. She knew he wasn't avoiding her because, for one, he didn't know her, and two, if he did know her, surely she did not need to be avoided. More in the realm of reality, he likely never gave her a thought.

"I can't wait for the bike tour. It's actually sunny outside. I had the best sleep. I hope we didn't wake you when we got back to the room last night. I didn't see you move. Did you sleep well?" Retta tore her roll apart and pancaked it between her fingers before placing it into her mouth.

"I did. I couldn't keep my eyes open. I don't even think I changed position." She remembered looking at the light from the upstairs window in the garage. Knowing now that the shadow she had seen was Fin made her shudder. This was not something she wanted to share with Retta. Who knew what crazy fit that information would throw her into? Ruby laced her fingers together and pressed them to the ceiling in a long stretch. "I'm going to go change and get ready for the tour."

Retta slid errant crumbs into her open palm. "I'm ready, too. I think I'll take an egg for the road."

As she made her way to the basket of eggs, Ruby waited in the reception area. She leaned her back against the wooden railing going up the stairs and crossed her arms over her chest. It was fun to watch Retta. She stopped at a table after getting her egg and began her patented puppet animation. Retta looked over and pointed at Ruby, and the two occupants of the table turned toward her. Ruby unwound her arms and gave a little wave. Retta waved back, tucked her hair behind her ears, and waltzed back to where Ruby stood.

Chloris was coming out of the kitchen carrying another basket of rolls and a coffee pot. She caught Ruby's eye, tilted her head back, and raised her voice. "Have fun today. I'll try and catch up with you later and see how your day was." Ruby raised her hand in acknowledgment and turned around the corner to walk back to their room.

Retta was at her side. "Who was that?"

"Her name's Chloris. She's the owner's daughter. She came down with me this morning." Ruby stopped outside their room and peeked in. Genji's and Haruki's bags were gone. Strange how people came and went without a goodbye. She made her way into the room and saw movement underneath Brian's white sheet. Then, two feet stuck out from the material and stretched, toes pointing just like a gymnast. She looked at Retta, and they both started laughing. Retta tiptoed over and tickled the bottom of his foot, sending sheets into a veritable popcorn popping flurry. The covers came down with a cacophony of croaks and crows, allowing Ruby to see that indeed she was correct in her guess at his night-time attire. Both women's eyes were glued to his soldier, at full salute.

When Ruby was able to stop ogling—which wasn't more than a few seconds—she looked up to see a lopsided grin on Brian's face, with no attempt to cover up. A spurt of laughter came out of her mouth, and she flipped the sheet over Mr. Woody. "Get some clothes on. You're going to cause Retta to have a fit of apoplexy."

Brian threw his head back and howled with laughter. He sat up, but kept the covers over his lap. "This little thing? Oh, come on. It's not that scary." If he weren't so funny, she would have gotten sick. They both laughed and turned to Retta, who was not laughing. She was shaking her hand like she was trying to get gum off her fingers.

"I'm going to get changed. I'll be right back. Are you ready to go?" Retta was already in the hall, heading to the shower.

"Put your head under the covers. I want to change, and I can honestly say that I have nothing as impressive as your soldier, so no looking." Ruby placed her hand on her hip and stared at him.

Brian stuck his bottom lip out in a feigned pout and pulled the bedding over his head. "Really Ruby, I think you're selling yourself short. Let me peek and I'll give you my honest evaluation. Think of me as your private connoisseur."

"There is something wrong with you." She smiled as she spoke. Heck, who doesn't like a potential complement. She had already slipped on her comfy jeans and was working on her bra when Brian's sheet started dipping down. A high pitched squeal came out of her mouth. "I said no looking!" In her panic, she had somehow gotten both her arms tangled in one strap and could not right the mistake without having to start over.

"But Ruby, my arms are getting tired. I'm going to have to drop the sheet." There was humor behind his serious tone. She snapped the straps in place as he poked his head out.

Her back was to him, so when she heard his disappointed humph, she looked over her shoulder with a victorious smile and slipped her arms through her white, long-sleeved t-shirt and twirled around. "Ta-da."

* * *

Fin had finished tinkering with a knob that had come off a drawer in the kitchen. He told himself that it was on some mental list that needed to be done. He glanced through the pass-through five times while going to retrieve a screwdriver, another screwdriver, and a towel to wipe some grease off his hand. Once, he forgot what he was getting and turned back around to get a wrench to hold the screw. Each time, his eyes were drawn to Ruby. He discovered her name upon his third pass, when Chloris walked by and said, "That's Ruby." She said it with her sing-song voice and an annoying secret grin.

He wanted to tell her that he had no idea what she was talking about, but he thought better of it. He ached to know something about her, and she and Ruby *had* been sitting together. "What do you know about her?" He ruffled Chloris's short, spiky hair.

"This and that." Chloris raised her chin and went out the door to the restaurant, giggling.

Everybody loves to have a secret, Fin thought. Anyway, he would find out; Chloris wouldn't be able to last long. Fin smiled to himself and took another look before he finished up the handle and headed out the back door of the kitchen. He needed to go get his coat. Even though it didn't look like rain, he was used to weather changing on a dime. He made his way up the creaking stairs of the garage, thinking that those should be next on his list of jobs. His jacket was by his pillow, where he always left it just in case there was a leak in the roof he had missed.

He was on his knees on his futon, reaching for it when movement below him caught his attention. She was there in the window, Ruby. Her hand was on her hip and she was looking at something he could not see. After a moment, she turned and faced the window, wiggling out of her clothes. He froze. He knew he should look away, but he realized that the sun had a better chance of setting in the east. She took quick looks over her shoulder, probably to make sure that no one came in while she was undressing. *Little does she know,* he thought, surreptitiously. She had shimmied into her pants and was working on her bra when something must have happened, because her arms started flailing and she got tangled. He found himself shaking his head and smiling, completely entranced by her.

He could not remember a time that he had been so aware of another person. His skin was warm, not so much his skin, but his blood. He felt tight, as if he were a teenage boy again and lacked the discipline to keep his body parts under control. Thank goodness he was alone, or he would have embarrassed himself. Her skin looked so smooth, and the light made her glow. Her breasts were like ripe fruit. His breath hitched—he could almost feel them under his hands, soft and supple, like silk on his palm. He wanted to feel her hair against his face, his chest. He took in a ragged breath, looked down, closed his eyes, and tried to regain his equilibrium. When he couldn't look away any longer, his gaze met an empty window. She was gone, and he was left hungry.

* * *

"Ta-da." Ruby twirled back to the center of the room.

"Did I miss a magic show?" Retta quickly averted her eyes from Brian's bed.

"Of sorts." Brian raised his eyebrows at Ruby. "Oh, for God's sake Retta, throw me those jeans and I'll dress under the cloak of darkness."

She threw the jeans that hung over the end of the bunk

and pretended not to notice as he shimmied them on under his sheet. Retta stood by Ruby. "Do you think we need to bring anything? Did they say how long the bike tour was? Maybe I should bring some water." She looked Ruby up and down. "Hey, are you bringing a jacket?"

"No, I'm not bringing a jacket, just a pullover, and it's two hours." She was at the door and looking at Brian. "Are you staying today?"

Brian sat with his legs over the bed. "Yeah, I think I will. You both staying the one day?"

"I need to be in Greece in a few days to meet some friends. I'm trying to get Ruby to come with me. I think I almost have her." She smiled her biggest smile at Ruby.

In return, Ruby looked up at the ceiling. "We need to go. See you later. She gave an exaggerated wink to Brian and giggled. Maybe down at the restaurant tonight?" Ruby put her head into her pullover.

Brian laughed, "Crazy girl. Yeah, okay. Sounds cool." Brian ran his fingers through his springy red hair.

CHAPTER ELEVEN

Ruby and Retta made their way across the street to the bicycle tour company. Five people were already there. A man that looked to be in his thirties walked up at the same time. It was a nice mix. There were three younger girls Ruby recognized from the hostel and an older couple in their fifties. When Ruby, Retta, and the man walked up, everyone introduced themselves. Ruby, who had never been good with names, smiled and quickly forgot what she was told. Retta, on the other hand, began asking questions and telling stories, at which point Ruby stepped away and looked around.

The narrow street forked just after the bike shop, and the building that sat on it created a "v" that followed the lines of the road on either side. Cars zoomed down one street, but the other was quiet and met up with a canal further along. The brilliant blue sky and crisp air reminded Ruby of a fall day in Colorado. She lifted her face to the sun that peeked between buildings and was instantly warmed. A garage door opened in front of the group, and Ruby saw who she guessed was their guide walk out.

"Hi. I'm Jon. I'll be your guide today. Have you all made introductions?" Jon looked to be in his forties. He was tan and cheerful, with a heavy Dutch accent. He wore camouflage cargo shorts and a tan, fisherman's knit sweater that hung loosely on his build. He also wore a red knit cap, with a light brown braid that came out from beneath, ending at the middle of his back.

"How are you all enjoying Brugge?" Jon asked. It must

have been a rhetorical question, because he kept talking without a pause. "The tour will take you some places you can't get to by car, and I would guess you have not seen on foot. We will be out close to two hours; there are bottles of water inside." He motioned with his head toward the open door. "Each of you will have a holder on your bicycle. There's also a toilet if you need it." As Jon talked, he walked through them to gauge what size bikes were needed and to make his way to the racks that held the cycles in the garage.

"Why don't you tell me your names and where you are from, and I'll get you all set." He looked at the older couple, Janet and Dick from California. Ruby and Retta introduced themselves to Jon, as did the single man, Stefan from France, and the three girls, Hillary, Brook, and Rose, two from Vermont and one from Spain. Ten minutes later they were all peddling across the busy street and across another street that headed toward a dirt path that ran parallel to a narrow canal.

Once they made it to the trail, Jon gave some history of the area, sprinkled in with funny tales of growing up in the West Flanders capital. One story was about the time some of his chums were riding along the canal after a night at the pub and, rather than turn with the path, he went straight into the water. They got his bike out, but it never rode the same again.

The group stopped at a windmill that was dated at 1770 and which still operated in the summer. It stood on a perfect setting: atop a green knoll with whitewash paint against the blue of the sky. The riding was relaxing rather than strenuous. Because the terrain was so flat, a person could put down a level and the bubble would be dead center. Wispy trees lined both sides of the path and were just beginning to leaf, giving a hint of the approaching summer.

Just then, Ruby saw a large shape in the distance on the trail ahead of them, and Jon held his hand up for them to stop. "This is something quite unique on the tour. You are all very lucky. There's a shepherd bringing his sheep to pasture. We'll move aside while he passes."

Everyone moved off to the side, leaving it clear for the man to maneuver the sheep. Ruby felt her insides tingle. Brugge continued to give off a magical aura. The man and his flock had surely just walked off the pages of a Mother Goose tale. They were a well-honed unit, moving as one. In the lead, the shepherd wore a black bowler hat and a black duster. His face looked round and soft, except for the shadow on his unshaven skin. Most of this was lost under the brim pulled low over his head. He kept his eyes pointed down, toward the sheep, and not on the cyclists who tried not to block his way. Light wood made up most of the staff he held, which came to his shoulder and had a dark iron hook at the top. Busy with close to seventy sheep in his care, a border collie trotted close to the man's side, having no interest in the bikes that had congregated along the trail. Fifteen lambs trotted in front, their ears flopping as they moved. Older, rounded sheep weighed down with full wool coats brought up the rear. It only took minutes for the flock to move past the conglomeration of bikes and bodies. Once past, the tour group did not move, as if they were in a trance. They all seemed to know a very unique moment had occurred, and each wanted to remember it in their own way.

Jon looked at his own flock with a large toothy grin. "Well, that is one for the memory, aye? I say we need to partake of a fine Belgium pint. I know it is early for imbibing, but the place I will take you to is not to be missed." He tilted his head at the same time that he nodded, and started pedaling toward a small cluster of brick buildings fifty yards away.

"This medieval monastery has been brewing beer for three hundred years. I believe they have perfected it. Let's see what you think." Jon smiled. "We cannot go into the abbey today, but they have a small café next to it that sells their beer and the bread and cheese they make on premises."

They parked the bikes and walked into a small courtyard between the buildings, where cobalt blue bistro tables with three chairs around each were located. They crunched their way over the pea gravel and sat down while Jon went into the café. Retta waved for Stefan to join them. She put her elbows on the table and intertwined her fingers. "I love Belgium. After Leiden, I didn't hold out much hope, but doesn't it make you happy being here? Can you believe we saw an actual shepherd? I honestly didn't know shepherds really existed. I don't know who I thought took care of sheep. I figured they just roamed around."

Stefan had joined them. "In France, we drink wine. I do not know beer." He leaned back in the wobbly chair and crossed one leg over the other.

"I'm sure it will be great. Lord, they've had three hundred years of practice." Retta laughed, Ruby smiled, and Stefan sat stone-faced. Ruby and Retta looked at each other and could read the "Oh, great. This should be fun" expression each held.

A slender man followed Jon out. Both carried round metal trays laden with un-labeled bottles and globe glasses. As they set them down, another man held a tray with plates of cheese and baskets of bread. Each table received two bottles made of thick glass that looked as if they could have come from a sunken ship. They were clouded by years of use and had a different look than glass made today. The second man put cheese and bread at each table, and the disappeared back inside.

"This is Thomas. He has become a friend of mine over the years, and he is one of the monks responsible for the fine beer you will drink. The beers made at Belgium monasteries are called Trappist, and there are only six Trappist breweries in the country; so, again, you are lucky to be here, eh? This is a malt that is both dark and rich in flavor. The bread was made this morning. It's delicious. I already had a bite." He looked right at Ruby, impishly. "Enjoy! We will be leaving in thirty minutes. You are welcome to walk the grounds, if you choose." He and Thomas began speaking in Flemish as they walked back into the café.

Ruby had to give points to Stefan for being a gentleman. He took the glasses, filled them, and handed them each bread and cheese. Other than these thoughtful gestures, he had few redeeming qualities. He wrinkled his nose at the beer (which was excellent; it was smooth and dark), the cheese (which didn't compare to French versions), and the warm bread (which melted in Ruby's mouth) got a "hrf."

Ruby took Stefan's last complaint as a cue to stand with her glass and bid them adieu. Retta looked panicked, but was stuck until Stefan quit talking about how he missed France. Frankly, Ruby did not feel like listening. She wound her way through the atrium, looking at the vine-covered brick and the arched wooden doors. Everything was simple but functional. Maybe it was the quiet, or maybe it was because she knew it was a spiritual place, but a wave of calm enveloped Ruby as she meandered through the yard. Her life was changing. She could feel it in the in the air and under her skin.

Ruby felt giddy, as if old skin was sloughing off and new skin was replacing it. She then remembered Margie's words—which felt like a lifetime ago—of beginning a journey to find her true self, catharsis, and destiny. She felt them all. She ran her fingers along her necklace and remembered the morning with Poppy and Margie, smells of the shop, the sunlight, and of people she loved dearly. She was brought back from her musing when she heard Jon rounding everyone up to go. Making her way back to the café, she set her glass back on the table, and they all returned to their bicycles. Thomas and Jon gave each other a heartfelt hug, and Thomas sent greetings to Jon's family.

Everyone laughed and joked as they continued on the tour (except Stefan, but they were all ignoring him, so he didn't count). They made a large loop around the outskirts of Brugge and were heading back to the city. Jon kept them entertained with histories and stories of the legend of the swans and the ghost of the clock tower. He pointed out places they might want to return to, all of which included the stops on Ruby and Retta's list. After a wonderful morning, they came back to where they had started, parked their bikes in the racks, and milled about, idly talking about the day ahead. Ruby and Retta thanked Jon and decided to return to Prima Facie to regroup before heading out again.

CHAPTER TWELVE

The hostel was close to empty when they walked in. After a few days of being overcast and rainy, most people were out enjoying the seasonable weather. It was still cool, but the sidewalks were crowded with pedestrians making their way to the assortment of shops and eateries that lined the streets.

Chloris stood atop a short, wooden step stool, holding an arabesque stance and cleaning the shelves behind the bar with a feather duster. She was quite the little dancer. She turned when she heard them come in and jumped the short distance to the floor. "How was your bike tour? Did you have Jon or Samuel as your guide?"

Ruby sat on one of the bar stools and rested her feet on the rung. "We had Jon. He was great. Really funny."

"Then you met Thomas. Wasn't the monastery lovely?" She looked over at Retta. "Hi. I'm Chloris. I saw you earlier, but didn't have time for introductions. Did you like the tour?"

Retta touched her hand to her chest and said, "Retta, and it was amazing. We saw a shepherd with a bunch of sheep, and the monastery was fantastic, although Ruby left me with Stefan who, to put it mildly, was a stick in the mud." She looked pointedly at Ruby. "By the way, I cannot believe you bailed on me. He didn't stop talking about all the ways France is superior to everyone and everything. My head felt like it would explode."

"I can't imagine someone talking non-stop." Ruby's voice was flat, and she pretended to find interest in something on the wall behind the bar.

Retta narrowed her eyes and stared at her until Ruby looked back. "Okay, I may talk a lot, but at least I am not such a downer. He was really annoying."

Chloris looked from one to the other. "Well, can I get you some water or tea before you two go out again?" She went behind the bar, pulled out two bottles of Spa water and three glasses, and placed them on the bar.

Retta sat next to Ruby. "Ruby said your family owns the hostel. You must love that. Weren't you sleeping in our room last night?"

"Yeah, if we're not full, I sometimes flit around to different rooms, but I have my own room on the top floor. It's a small, two-bedroom apartment my mom and dad stay in. I guess I like to move around." She looked over at the window and waved. Ruby and Retta followed her gaze to see who she waved to and found Hans and Fin looking at the roof line above them. Hans was pointing with a sweeping motion.

Retta's mouth gaped. "Who is that?"

Ruby quickly glanced down. *Why do I keep doing that?* If she could have, she would have kicked herself. *It's nothing, but why do I feel so dazed when I see him? The sensation is so stupid. I'll have to give myself a good talking to later, but right now I need to breathe.*

"That's Fin. He's the handyman for Prima Facie," Chloris said with nonchalance, but she didn't take her eyes off of Ruby. Ruby felt her face warm. She wiped her hands on her jeans, betrayed by her own traitorous body. *Merde.*

"Did you meet him this morning? It's Galahad or Lancelot come to life. Are you friends with him, Chloris? Maybe I should hold off my trip for a while." Retta kept her eyes glued to the men outside.

"Fin's really nice. He doesn't really talk about himself a lot, but having seen him around, I can tell you he does like company. I'm not saying he is a libertine, but it does seem like he doesn't want to get too close to any one person." Then, as if it occurred to her that she had insulted a person she was really very fond of, she said, "He's a complete gentleman, clever and decent. He just seems detached." To Ruby's ears, she sounded like a protective sibling and, for some reason she couldn't guess at, she was glad Chloris had championed him.

"Did you meet him?" Retta asked again.

Ruby felt agitated. "I think I saw him earlier." She didn't know where to look. To cover, she took a breath and blew it out. "Well, we should go."

"You think you saw him. You *think* you saw him? He is not someone you would forget. Are you okay? You look a little red. Do you feel sick? You could go lay down for a while." Her face was a mixture of concern and befuddlement.

"No. What? I look sick? No, no. You know, it must have been the bike ride. Maybe I got a burn." She felt her cheeks. "That happens at the beginning of summer to me. It is a little hot. Here, let me drink some more water. I'm really fine." She then made the mistake of looking at Chloris. She knew she hadn't wanted to, and then it happened anyway. The girl's head was tilted slightly to the side, and she was looking at Ruby. Her green eyes narrowed and bore into Ruby. Her lips were pursed, like she was working a puzzle. Ruby didn't think she could get hotter. Suddenly, all she wanted was to get away.

"Ruby, you're babbling. Maybe you need something to eat. You must have low blood sugar," Retta said, looking around like she would find a cake lying around.

"You know what? I'm fine. Let's go and I can get a waffle at one of the shops." She got off the stool and wondered how they could go out the door without having to see Hans and Fin.

She was saved from planning an alternate route by Retta. "Oh, shoot. He's gone. Maybe we can meet him later."

"Yeah. Later. Bye Chloris." She tried to sound breezy, but thought she may have missed the mark and sounded deranged.

"Bye, Ruby," Chloris' voice was a little too innocent. Ruby stopped and cocked her head. She didn't have time for contemplation—she needed some air.

* * *

Fin was outside with Hans, looking at a section of rotting fascia. They discussed replacing the ten-foot section when Hans looked through the window and raised his chubby hand. Chloris was behind the bar, talking to someone sitting on the stool. It looked like there may have been another person with them, but with the glare on the window, it was hard to see. Fin was saying that he would paint the wood first in the garage, remove the rotted section, attach the new one, and then give it a second coat. He guessed the whole thing would take two days.

Hans rubbed his face. "Christ, I worry about her sometimes. She seems happy, right?"

Fin turned his head to Hans at the change of subject. They rarely spoke of anything personal, but he felt they had a friendship of sorts, and he took the role seriously. He looked back at Chloris and the other girl, who looked frighteningly like a china doll. She and Chloris still were watching them.

"I mean, with her mother across the globe and me busy here, she's back and forth all the bloody time. Shit, she doesn't even go to school, and she likes to sleep in the dorm rooms. Is that normal?"

Fin took some time to think. He felt Hans deserved his contemplation. "Chloris is one of the most well-rounded people I know. She has a great head on her shoulders, and she knows more than most kids her age, I'm sure." He cocked his head toward the concerned father. "She seems to cherish her times with you and Evie. She would let you know if she didn't. She's a special girl. There's something about her, a grace." He then turned back to the window and lowered his voice. "How she got that from you, I have no idea. It had to be Evie." He shook his head, mystified.

"Okay, you bloody cocker. Why don't you start doing some work." He clapped Fin on the back. His eyes had a spark that let Fin know that he had said what he needed to hear. Fin headed to the garage to see if there might be a piece of wood that would be appropriate for the job and would also help clear more space to the accumulating piles. Chuckling, Hans headed back into the hostel.

CHAPTER THIRTEEN

Retta and Ruby passed Hans before they walked out to the street again. The sky had become cloudy, but did not look like rain. The clouds floated like fluffy pieces of cotton across the deep blue of the sky. Ruby slipped her pullover off and wrapped it around her waist. She looked up and down the street. It was clear. She let out the breath she didn't know she had been holding onto and looked to Retta. "Where to?"

"Let's make our way back to the main square. We can climb up the tower. Oh, but wait. You need something to eat. I'm sure there will be some place along the way. I found a small street map in our room. I think someone left it. Let me see." Retta unfolded the map, turned it, and then turned it again and again.

"Where are we?" She handed the map to Ruby and tucked her hair behind her ears, which immediately unhooked when a breeze blew through the narrow street, making it look like spider legs wiggling from her head.

Ruby folded the map and gave it back. "Let's be crazy and just make our way to the center with no map to guide us—just a couple women throwing caution to the wind."

"Ruby, you know what I've discovered about you?" Without waiting for a reply, Retta charged on. "You are funny. Not super funny and not clown funny, but in a dry sort of way." She linked her arm through Ruby's and began walking.

With anyone else, Ruby would have tried to extricate her arm but, with Retta, the closeness felt natural. They walked through the cobbled streets, stopping every now and again to look into shop windows or on a bridge that crossed over a canal. The shops were filled with the things the region was famous for: lace, chocolate, and statuary. The door they stood in front of now had everything for a bath. Without even walking in, floral smells wrapped around them, teasing them to enter. It was a small, well-decorated space that was crammed with oils, candles, and bath paraphernalia. Each picked up and smelled dozens of bars of soap and scented flakes that went into the water. Chloris had said that she had a tub in their apartment that Ruby could use if she wanted. Upon further thinking, she did want. When would be the next time she could take a bath in Brugge? She grabbed a packet of one that smelled like a garden without being too frilly: bergamot, ginger, and something woodsy.

They left the shop and stopped at a waffle window next door. The waffle was warm and was wrapped in paper. Ruby tore it and plopped a large chunk in her mouth. "Retta, if I didn't believe in heaven before, I think I do now." She held her satchel up to her nose. "I cannot get enough of this smell."

She then held it to Retta, who closed her eyes and took in a long, luxurious breath through her nose. "You're right, it's amazing. Maybe we should stop on the way back and get some more. This whole town is amazing. It reminds me of the Pied Piper without the rats and the mass exodus of children." To punctuate her point, chimes from the belfry began to pealing over the village.

Walking parallel to a canal, they looked at the charcoal and watercolors lining the pedestrian street that were being displayed by local artists. Most of the pictures were the main sights of Brugge: the belfry, the swans majestically gliding over the lake, Town Hall, and (of course) the churches.

Buildings on the other side of the water seemed to grow right out of the canal like lilies in a pond, marked with green moss and water lines.

Retta crossed her arms over her chest and looked across the canal. "How do you think they built these houses? Some of the windows are so close to the water that a person could dunk their hand in to catch dinner. What do they do if it floods? That would be horrible. I bet no one lives on the bottom floors, but someone must have at one time. There are doors and windows."

Ruby didn't have any answers, so she didn't feel the need to say anything. They walked around a curve in the road, and the belfry soared in front of them.

"Oh, I cannot wait to climb to the top." Retta shielded her eyes from the sun that peeked out from the clouds and stared upward at the top octagonal tower that housed the bells. It took them five minutes to navigate the streets that opened up to the square, and another fifteen to climb the 366 steps to the summit. Even with the crowds of people, it was worth it. The views were magnificent. Red tiled roofs spanned the city and, beyond that, the green of the countryside. Ruby thought that she could see the sea to the west. Surely it was too far, and maybe it was the shadows of the fields creating the illusion of water. It was cooler 272 feet above the ground, and the breeze whipped their hair around their faces. They made three trips around the bell tower, stopping and discovering something new to look at each time.

They then made their way to the Town Hall. It was amazing from the outside, but when they stepped in they were awed by the murals on the walls and the wooden, vaulted ceiling. Every nook and cranny had meaning, with the intricate stone work and biblical figures. Light coming in through the large windows that lined the walls cast the whole interior into a golden Eden. By the time they left Town Hall, both women were ready to sit and get something to eat. They picked one of the several cafes circling the square, which were covered with hunter green canvas awnings. Bistro tables outside were shaded with golden umbrellas and fenced in with black rot iron. They sat themselves at a table closest to the rail to get the best view of people walking by. The waiter eventually made it over, and Ruby ordered a bowl of mussels and lemonade. Retta ordered soup and water. Then they sat back and watched the show of people strolling through the square.

Six different tour groups were present, each huddled together, their guides holding differently colored flags. They moved as one unit from place to place, looking like they were attempting to set a world record for the largest three-legged race (or twelve-legged race, in this case). Ruby shrugged down in her chair and rested her head against the back, crossing both her arms and ankles. The sun felt so warm on her face that she could have fallen asleep had it not been for Retta's running commentary on the goings on around them.

"You should see this baby. I think she has the smallest feet I have ever seen. Okay, now you really need to see this. I think I just saw that man's whole butt when he bent down. Oh, he must have realized. He hiked his pants back up. What do you think that sculpture is? A boy? Or maybe a dog?"

Ruby kept her eyes closed but did, give the appropriate umms, aahhs, and ews as well as a mental shrug. She couldn't be bothered to move her shoulder.

"Hey, isn't that Fin from the hostel?"

That question needed more than a sound effect. Ruby

nearly fell backward in her chair. If her knees wouldn't have cracked into the underside of the table, she would have been prone on her back, and most likely in need of medical care. As it was, she would surely have bruises across both knees, and she would need a new set of silverware because hers were strewn on the cobble underneath and beside her.

Ruby's head twisted this way and that, and then fell on Retta, who simply said, "I knew you had seen him before."

Thank goodness the waiter came with lunch, because Ruby felt her hands mold to the exact dimensions of Retta's scrawny neck. Never having been a violent person, she felt a bit unnerved by the instinct to squeeze the smug smile off Retta's china doll face.

"Doesn't this look tasty, Ruby?" Retta smartly kept her eyes pointed down at her bowl, making figure eights with her spoon through the thick chowder. "I really worked up an appetite, what with the bike tour and the stairs. Well, and the walk from Prima Facie." Retta kept her head down, but raised her eyes to Ruby, looking guilty and apologetic at the same time. In a hushed voice, she asked Ruby about her knees.

Ruby stuck a not-so-real smile on her face. "They're throbbing. I'm sure it's just a mild contusion. Hopefully there's no swelling." Why not pile it on.

"I'm sorry. I didn't think you would react quite like that. You just seemed so strange after we saw him through the window. What happened, did you talk to him this morning?" She poured her water into the tall, narrow glass in front of her.

"I don't know what happened. It's so stupid. And no, I did not talk to him. I saw him when I was sitting with Chloris." Ruby sat up now, filled her cheeks with air, and let them pop like a balloon. She didn't even want to hear herself say the words out loud, but Retta looked so sincere and expectant that it came out in a fast string of words. "I saw him, and I felt tingly. There, that's it. I felt tingly. I'm sure everyone with eyes feels the same way when they see him, but I've just never had that happen before. How's your soup?"

Retta didn't seem to hear the last part, which was meant to change the subject. "He is something to look at, but I have to say, I did not feel . . ." she tilted her head, ". . . tingly." Retta must have known Ruby didn't want to say any more on the subject because she took a spoon of soup and held it over to Ruby. "You have to try this. I think it has curry."

"Thank you." They both knew the simple comment had a double meaning.

They continued on through lunch sharing the mussels and the soup, and then sat for a while after they were finished, simply enjoying the day and the company. They stopped at a park filled with trees and swans and at several more shops, making their way back to the hostel. It felt good to amble with no agenda and no pressing need to be anywhere. The clouds were now stretched out like pulled toffee, allowing blue to peek through only occasionally.

By the time they walked through the door, light sprinkles dotted the stones of the street. They glanced into the restaurant. There were two tables with people sitting around them having drinks. Ruby desperately needed to freshen up. Everything felt sticky, and a layer of fuzz was growing on her teeth. "I'm going to go back to the room and get my toothbrush. Are you staying here?"

"No. I'm coming with you. I need to lie down for just a minute. Don't let me fall asleep." Retta circled her shoulders, and Ruby heard them crackle as they made their way up the stairs and down the hallway.

Feeling meditative, Ruby took her time washing her hands and brushing her teeth. She ran a corner of her towel under hot water and held it over her face, letting the steam sink into her pores. When she emerged, she had a second wind. Ruby walked into the room, where Retta was sprawled across Ruby's lower bunk, looking like she had fallen asleep in the middle of creating a snow angel. Ruby decided to let her sleep for a bit and crawled up to the top bunk. She lay on her stomach, her head on her arms and watched the rain pelt the shack across the way.

* * *

Fin had worked all morning measuring, sanding, painting, and tearing the fascia from above the window in the front of Prima Facie. He now stood in the shower of the second floor, letting its hot water run in rivulets down his tired body. It had been hard work, and he loved it. Occasionally, he saw Ruby's blue eyes in his mind, and he had to smile at her startled look when he caught her staring at him.

It was refreshing to have something other than his family and his dodging of responsibilities to think about. His guilt had come in waves. He knew he would have to rejoin the Sinclair's soon and perform the duties his father had laid out, now that Ian was gone. For right now, in this moment, he wanted to be near Ruby. He had known many women, but never in his life had he felt an urgent need to be near someone. He had to know her. He sensed it in the air when she was in the room. He felt her. His awareness wasn't logical, and he did not even want to try and reason through the emotions. He couldn't explain the pull and, if asked to put the feeling into words, he wouldn't have been able to.

From Chloris he knew that she was staying another night, so he decided to make a point of being in the restaurant tonight, hoping that she would come for supper or a drink. What he would do when she came (and he knew she would) was where his plan became fuzzy. He had never felt so green. Fin had had dozens of women, and his body had enjoyed them, but he had never given his heart, and he had not thought beyond the pleasure of the moment.

There had been one, maybe two girls when he was younger that he had gotten to know, but they quickly realized his place in society, what doors he could open, what invitations were made, and how they looked on his arm. Status became more important to them than who he was. He developed a reputation as being engaging but aloof, and had quickly grown a thick skin with the fairer sex. It had served him well; he was never in peril of a broken heart. People were drawn to Fin, and when they were in his company, they saw him as a fun-loving, devil-may-care playboy who traveled the continent. He had impeccable manners, was never cruel, and had a joy for life that was contagious. Only with his family did all the walls he built around himself come down, and he felt real. He could breathe.

A conversation he had with Anne came back to him as he toweled himself off. She had been making fun of the fawning beauty that had been at his hip as well as his disinterested, hooded gazes at a party they had both been invited to. On the walk home, she looped her arm in his, squeezed his arm for a brief moment, and looked straight ahead. "There is a woman who will own your heart. You'll feel it to your toes and become lost. It's not really fair that we're the only ones that know you are more than a pretty face, Finey."

At the time, he had given her a hip check and told her that he could never find anyone that would measure up to her. The topic was then dropped. Now he wondered if the stirring he felt was what she had described. Had Anne been like this with Thomas? If memory served, they had announced their engagement shortly after that party. Who knew? Maybe they met at the party and she had been particularly introspective. He would ask when he saw her next.

CHAPTER FOURTEEN

By the time Ruby and Retta made it to the restaurant, Brian was sitting at a table in the middle of the room. Retta immediately launched in with the activities of the day, the sites they had seen, and the people they had met. She thanked him for his suggestions and, in return, he asked if they had seen a particular statue or gone into a certain shop. The conversation was easy, and Brian was funny and personable.

Retta sat next to him, facing the front of the hostel, and Ruby had her back to the door, looking at the kitchen and the back booth, which was occupied. Hans sat there with an older man and a younger looking woman. She could have been a wife or friend of the other man, who rested his hand on top of hers. It was still raining, but it was not the deluge of the previous night. People came in with umbrellas and wet jackets and made their way to empty tables or the bar, filling the room. Prima Facie seemed to be a popular place for backpackers and as well as a neighborhood gathering spot. It quickly became crowded.

After thirty minutes, they ordered some food. Retta compared notes with Brian about the view from the Belfry. Brian told them that they had indeed seen the Straight of Dover, which could be viewed from the belfry on a clear day. Retta was describing the town hall with her hands in the air, then she froze and her mouth clamped into a straight line. Her eyes went from the door to Ruby, and Ruby knew. It was him. She didn't know how she knew. Who was she kidding? Of course she knew. All she had to do was look at

Retta. Just like Retta, Ruby froze too—except for her heart. Her heart began to beat much faster than seemed safe.

Retta grabbed her hand and squeezed it. "Ruby, do not freak out but . . . Oh, you already know. Are you tingly?" Retta's eyes were wide and expectant.

Ruby tried giving her a scathing look, but her body didn't seem to move. Her chest felt heavy, and there was a building heat within her. She watched Retta's eyes watch him. She knew he was getting closer. She felt like she was holding her hand over a candle, and the pain of the flame was unbearable. There was a slight movement on the back of her chair. He walked inches from her, heading to the booth where Hans sat. When he passed, Ruby couldn't stop her eyes from following him.

His hair was wet, and glistening with droplets of rain. Even the back of him took her breath away. He shrugged off his black rain jacket, hung it on a hook attached to the wall, shook hands at the table, and slid gracefully into the bench next to Hans, which faced Ruby. She tried looking away, but Fin ran his fingers through his hair, and she was entranced. He smiled at the couple across from him, and then pinned his gaze directly at Ruby. It was the longest four seconds of her life.

At that moment, she realized that she had not known the color of his eyes. The room was too dim in the morning, and she had looked away too quickly. Now the lights were on, and he was closer than he had been before. They were grey, which seemed insignificant, but they were anything but ordinary. They reminded Ruby of thunderclouds right before they broke open, leaving nothing thirsty. Ruby loved storms—the smell right before the rain, the quiet right before the thunder, and the charged air—she did not think of grey as lifeless or cold. The color had depth and a heat that, at this moment, drove through her veins. With her finger, she touched her bottom lip absentmindedly.

Fin, who still watched her, arched one dark and perfectly shaped eyebrow and gave her a smoldering, lopsided grin. Her breath left her body. It was as if the air had just been sucked out of the room. *This is not happening. I must have seen wrong. He couldn't mean that look for me.* As if in a corny movie, Ruby glanced over her shoulder, wondering who or what was behind her which was the actual, lucky recipient of that look. She saw only a standing crowd. Someone stepped between them, and the hold was lost. She looked down at the table, where there were tiny drops of rain from when he had walked by. She dragged her fingers through them, making circles on the thick wood.

* * *

Even though he knew she would be there, Fin's heart jumped. He felt like he was walking through mud, slow and unsteady. He saw Hans, and was grateful that the table Ruby was seated at was in a direct line to the booth. As he got closer to her, Fin strained to keep his hand from gliding along her arm, which rested on the table. When he grazed her chair, he felt a bolt of electricity at the touch, but he kept his mind focused on getting to the booth where he could sit and observe from a safe distance. He needed to get control of his mind and his body and, for that, he apparently needed space.

Fin paid only half attention when Hans introduced his friends visiting from London. As he moved into the booth, he felt Ruby watching him. He could not resist looking at her, and there they were—those eyes that could hold his life captive. She kept her eyes on his and then, as if it had a life of its own, her finger touched her lower lip. He became unhinged. He felt that tiniest movement to his core. He shifted in his seat to make room for his libido, and smiled at the private joke. Then, someone cut off his view to her.

* * *

"Rruubby? Hello? Ruby? What do you think?" Retta and Brian looked at her like she was slow, and really she did feel a bit disjointed.

"What? I'm sorry. What did you say?" She blinked her eyes, trying to focus, but everything was a little fuzzy, as if she had been drugged.

"I said, you're coming to Greece with me, right? Then you can hit some other countries before you get up to Norway. Are they expecting you at a certain time? You know it will be light all night. How do they sleep? That would be so weird. Or, in the winter, all that darkness? No thank you. So what do you think?"

"What?" She was looking at Retta, but she still wasn't following.

Retta made a point of enunciating every word. "You. Are. Coming. To. Greece. Right?"

"Um." What else would she do, stay here and watch *him*? She had come to see as much of Europe as possible and to figure out who she was, to stretch herself. This journey was a time of self-discovery, not a time to latch onto a fantasy that had no future. It hit her then that she would not see him again and, strangely, she felt a prick of loneliness. Ruby mentally knocked herself in the head. *This is not a fairytale with a prince. Good lord, I don't even know what his voice sounds like. What am I doing?* "Yeah, I'll come with you. What're you going to do, Brian?"

"Well, thank you for asking, Ruby. I am going to join you. Think of me as your knight-errant. I want to make sure you both make it safely. It's quite a trip. That, and I need some sun. So, in reality, I'm only half a hero." He took a long drink from his glass. "I was telling Retta—while you were occupado—that we need to get the earliest train to Italy and, even with that, it will be an overnight through Germany and Austria before we get to the southeast of Italy for sailing. I think one leaves around seven. You up for it?"

A woman's high-pitched laughter made all three turn to the noise. A long-legged woman leaned over the top of the table where Fin was seated. She had both hands firmly planted on the edge, causing her breasts, which heaved out of her tight tank top, to smash together. She whipped her hair over one shoulder and continued tittering.

Why Ruby should be shocked, she had no idea. Chloris had all but spelled out that he was with a lot of women. Ruby wasn't even in the same league as this one. The woman's jeans fit her never-ending legs like paint, and her hair cascaded like a waterfall of amber. But really, who wears a tank top in this weather? Ruby took comfort in the fact that *she* at least had a brain. The woman touched Fin's arm in a seductive stroke that sent irrational flames of jealousy flaring through Ruby, or maybe it was envy. Before she turned back to the company at her table, she saw Fin gently but unmistakably remove the tart's hand from his arm. Good for him.

"I'm up for it." This was the exact kick in the head she had been looking for. She wrapped her arms around her waist, comforted by the heat that reached her skin.

Retta narrowed her black eyes at Ruby, in what appeared to be concern, and leaned in so that only Ruby could hear. "You okay? She looks like a bimbo, right?" She clamped her lips together.

Ruby didn't try to pretend she didn't know who she was talking about. "It's not a big deal. I don't even know him. I've never spoken to him, and I know absolutely nothing about him. Maybe he's a jerk, or better, maybe he has a huge growth protruding from his back." She laughed at Retta's screwed-up face. "Alright, that's a stretch, but I don't know him, and we're leaving tomorrow, so let's not talk about him anymore."

CHAPTER FIFTEEN

Bloody hell, hell, hell, hell! Why does she need to be here right now, or here at all? What was I thinking last night? Fin thought the obvious, of course, but now the whole mess made him want to pull out his hair. Fin knew Ruby had seen her pawing at him. Christ, the entire place heard her cackle. He looked to Hans for a lifeline, but his mouth was gaped—he looked like a big cat ready to pounce.

"I'm Hans. I own Prima Facie." He tilted his head to Fin for introductions, which would be impossible, for the mere fact that he could not conjure up a name even if a gun had been at his temple.

Fin felt like a huge cad. Anyone deserved better than this. Luckily, she extended her hand. "I'm Lisa. I'm a friend of Fin's." Lisa gave a coquettish smile. She may as well have rubbed her naked body up against his for all the discretion she showed. Lisa looked at the glass in front of Fin. "What are you drinking?"

He groaned inwardly. "Mineral water." His voice sounded tight and clipped. She simply stood, looking down at him with eyes that matched her brown hair. His upbringing kicked in, and he asked, "Can I get you something?" It was the last thing he wanted to do, but his options seemed limited at the moment.

"You weren't drinking water last night, were you?" She giggled and ran a finger along the back of his hand. He now knew how it was to feel dirty. He immediately took her hand off of his and placed his own in his lap. If she noticed the cut, she did not give any indication. Instead, she gave her order of Riesling to no one in particular. Hans raised his arm to a waiter and ordered for her, licking his lips as he looked back at her. Fin thought he might be sick.

Fin fixed his eyes onto Ruby between the mass of people now standing around the room. He saw her and the other two at the table lift glasses into the middle and cheer. She had a goofy grin on her face, and Fin wondered how many of those beers she had drunk. He felt instantly protective, and was so intent on not wanting to let her from his view that he hadn't noticed that Lisa was whispering something into his ear. He turned when she squeezed his leg much too close to his manhood.

"Fin, dance with me." She talked in a little girl voice and reached higher up on his leg. The band that came most evenings began playing, and the crowd created an impromptu dance floor. "Ooo, I love this song. Come dance."

He cursed under his breath, but took a different avenue and gave his best smile. "You go and I'll watch from here." She gave a shiver at the voyeuristic game she thought he was playing, took a swallow of her wine, and swayed her hips out to the floor. Fin rolled his eyes and looked back at Ruby.

* * *

Maybe she had too much to drink, but she was an adult, one who wanted to have her mind occupied by something other than the man across the room. Brian had told them that a band would play soon, and they saw equipment being hauled in and set up in a corner at the front of the room. They ordered another round of drinks, and Brian grabbed Ruby's untouched pizza. She had lost her appetite somewhere between the cackle and the boob flash. She felt less bitter after her second beer, and her third was going down slick as a whistle. She hardly even remembered Fin was across the room. *Ha! And I am funnier, too.*

Brian made some joke about yoga, and the three raised their glasses and cheered. Ruby didn't know why, but it was hilarious, and she didn't care. She slid a glance at Fin, who was entangled with his play thing. She looked to be eating his ear. She peeled herself off him and wiggled her butt, smiling over her shoulder before gliding out to the dance floor, her arms waving above her head. Ruby rolled her eyes and caught Fin doing the same. She couldn't stop her smile from forming.

Brian and Retta pulled at her arms and led her out to the dance floor. They gathered together, holding hands and started what could loosely be described as dancing. At any other time, Ruby would have been too self-conscious, but now she felt completely uninhibited. She bounced to the rhythm and swayed her head back and forth. She laughed at Retta's and Brian's hair. Retta's was a black lace veil swinging around her face, and Brian's crazy red curls looked like copper wire springing back and forth to the beat. He twirled Retta, and she became a figure atop a music box that spun around and around, laughing and smiling. Brian let her go, grabbed Ruby, and turned her around so that her back faced him. He lifted her arms and began to rock her back and forth. She closed her eyes to feel the music. Then his hands were gone, and she opened her eyes to a raging storm.

* * *

Fin watched Ruby as they headed out to the dance floor. All three held hands, his own involuntarily balled into fists in his lap. Her head moved to the music, and her loose curls skirted her shoulders as her neck curved back. She looked so carefree and happy that he found himself smiling just watching her. Fin guessed that she was a little tipsy, but not out of control, and he hoped they were finished. He would make sure she didn't get into any trouble. He told himself that he would do the same for anyone, but then realized that Lisa was also somewhere on the floor, and that he had all but forgotten about her. He made a note to check on her later.

The boy with the red hair looked to be okay. Fin vaguely remembered him sitting at the table with all of them last night. He spun the doll-girl, and Ruby laughed. When he took Ruby and pulled her against him, Fin had unconsciously moved to stand in front of her, a man possessed. The boy let go of her hands, as if he had been burned when he saw Fin loom over him. Ruby opened her eyes and stared straight into Fin's. He didn't know what she saw in them, but she seemed disoriented. She gasped and took a step back. She blinked as if she couldn't quite reconcile what was in front of her. Fin realized he must seem unbalanced. She had no idea he had been watching her, how much he wanted her, or, for that matter, who he was.

Not wanting her to run—not that he would let her get far—he tamped down his anger and jealousy. He laughed inwardly. *Maybe I am unbalanced.* He extended his hand to hers. "Dance with me." It was a statement, not a question. Fin's voice was low and direct. She bit her thumb nail with her front teeth and looked over to her friends, who stood like statues among the dancing throng. Fin looked over Ruby's head to the girl whose mouth hung open as if her jaw was disconnected. The boy with the crazy hair angled his head at Fin, but seemed more amused than anything. Fin raised his voice and looked at the girl behind Ruby. "Do you mind if I take her for a while?"

Retta looked at Ruby, who was still turned away from

him, and nudged her forward. "That would be fine. Bring her home by midnight."

Fin's arm rose as if he was on puppet stings and, with one finger, gently moved a curl from her damp forehead. Then, because her nail was still between her teeth, he couldn't help but run his finger along her lip to loosen the vice. As he knew she would, Ruby let go. He didn't know how long they stood watching each other, but each seemed reluctant to look away. He guessed that they had different reasons, his being that he simply liked to watch the emotions that played so openly on her face. Hers could have been that she thought he was unstable and didn't want to turn her back to him. He wanted to say something to put her at ease, so he said the first thing he could think of: "I'm friends with Chloris, I work here, for Hans, who is Chloris's father. He is right over there." He jerked his head to the table behind him, realizing that he was spewing from his mouth. She didn't move, and he was running out of options, save shaking her. He leaned in closer. "Do you want to get some air?"

* * *

So many things happened at once. She knew she was not making a good first impression, but her head spun and she needed a moment to sort out the situation. Fin stood in front of her. She knew that. He had been at the table with Hans, and then he was there, looking what, mad? No. Something else. It couldn't be jealous, but he looked crazed. *Did he really ask if he could take me? What does that even mean?* She still tasted the salt from her forehead, where he ran his finger along her lip. She felt like her legs would go out from under her. Luckily, he held her elbow. *Some air, yes.* "It's raining." *My god, was that the first thing I said?* He came to her rescue.

"I think it's let up. I'll get my jacket." Then, pinning her with a look, he said, "You stay right here, and I'll come and get you."

All she could do was nod. He tilted his head slightly and gave her a breathtaking half smile. He then zigzagged through the crowd. Ruby felt something hit her back. When she turned, Retta stood in front of her, her hand on hip, looking like a mother scolding a misbehaving child.

"Have you gone dumb? What are you doing? What did he say to you? Did you even say anything to him? Did he leave because he realized you were a little slow?" She nodded her head, answering her own question.

"Retta, you're funny, but what I need is a pep talk, not to be reprimanded. Slap me or something. No, I'm just kidding." She added that last part when she saw a glint in Retta's eyes. "He's coming back." Her insides trembled. "What do I do?"

Retta put her hands on Ruby's shoulders. "Okay, you are smart, relatively funny, pretty in a sort of way. You have a look."

Ruby's shoulders sagged. "That is the worst pep talk I've ever heard, and if I am not mistaken, a lot of that was insulting."

"Oh, Ruby, I'm joking. You're wonderful. The last couple of days have been so great, largely because of you. Be yourself. That's all you need to do. Did you hear the accent?" Her hand went to cover her heart, and she looked past Ruby. "He's back." She gave a little smile, bounced back to the dancing crowd, and was swallowed up.

Ruby felt the air behind her heat up. She knew he must be close. She took a breath and turned around. Too close. Her nose touched his chest. She looked up. An uncontrollable bubble of laughter came out of her mouth. He smiled down at her, stepped back, and held his jacket open for her. For such a simple gesture, it seemed incredibly intimate to Ruby. She could not wait to hold the material tightly around herself. She turned and slipped her arms into the sleeves. They hung well past her fingertips, so she pushed them up and held onto the edges with her balled fists.

Fin placed a hand on her lower back and applied just enough pressure for the two to move through the crowd, toward the door. The scent that surrounded her was intoxicating. His jacket smelled like motor oil, wood, and laundry that dried on a line. It was unique, and the essence was completely masculine. *I could breathe this in for a lifetime or*, she thought wryly, *at least for a night.*

The door was propped open, and they walked out onto the wide step in front of the hostel. Fin was right, the rain had let up. The air was cold, and drips fell from the trees branches that skimmed the roofline. Other people had the same idea, and small groups had formed along the sidewalk to take advantage of the now nearly clear night. The moon was full, causing the billowy clouds to glow in the dark sky. The stars were diamonds, and everything looked sharper, more brilliant. Out of habit, and because she needed something to ground her, Ruby lifted her head to find the Big Dipper. It was there, and she smiled with the familiarity. She felt Fin watch her. He then turned her face to him. He looked at her curiously. "I was looking for the Big Dipper. It's just something I like to do," she said.

He nodded his head. "We call it the Starry Plough." He dragged his gaze from Ruby and looked up at the sky. "My name is Finley, but I go by Fin. Chloris told me your name is Ruby. I hope I didn't scare you earlier."

Scared would have been the last description she'd give, but she couldn't tell him her heart was beating in triple time or that her whole body felt much too hot for the cool night.

Instead, she said nothing and, while he looked at the stars, she studied his profile. His hair was messy, but in such a way that she knew he didn't work to get it looking perfectly carefree. His nose was aristocratic, and coupled magnificently with his high cheek bones and sculpted lips, which she could now not drag her eyes from. They looked soft and pliable, like they would be quick with a smile or could easily brush up against hers.

He had defined features, and there was a strength about him that went beyond the physical. He gave off an air that he knew himself and was comfortable in his skin. Although she couldn't see his arms or back, his shirt hugged toned muscles. He was definitely someone who did things with his body. She wondered what his hands felt like. She had a sense they would be nothing like Scott's, which where smooth and soft from years of academia. She knew from being a recipient that the fire behind his slate eyes could sear equally with seduction or ire.

Thankfully, he did have a flaw. There was a light scar from the corner of his lip to his chin. *Ha!. He isn't perfect.* Then, two things happened: A huge drop of rain from a budding leaf above fell and hit her in the head and made its way down her cheek. Fin then looked at her and followed the path of the raindrop with his eyes as he brought his finger underneath her chin and tilted it up so that she had no choice but to look directly at him.

                                    * * *

"Ruby, I'm going to kiss you." Fin thought to give her a choice and be a gentleman but, in the end, he couldn't chance her saying no. His need had taken on a life of its own. Everything stopped—the talking, the car noise, the rain, the very air around them. They could have been crammed with millions of people or on a deserted beach, but it was only them. The moment was magic, and he knew she felt it, too. He saw it in her face, as if she had spoken the words out loud. She closed her eyes, her lips parted the slightest bit, and he was lost. He wanted to devour her. He cupped his hands around her face and leaned down to meet her. The second before he touched her lips, a warm sigh escaped her mouth and he inhaled it into his own, wanting to keep a piece of her. He glided over the smoothness of her lips with his, and she opened up wider, letting him explore with his tongue. She tasted like beer and cherries. He took one hand from her face and brought it down her back, drawing her body against his. He knew it was ill-mannered, but he wanted her to know just how much he wanted her. He felt her start, and then there was a slap on his back that felt like a horse whip.

"You bastard! You prick! What are you doing?" He turned around, Ruby now behind him. Lisa was screaming, and the people outside had inched closer to see the scene that would inevitably unfold. Her arm was back and her hand was open in mid-swing, ready to connect with his face.

Fin grabbed her wrist before she made contact. "Lisa, don't." His voice was steady and quiet with an inborn command to it.

* * *

Lisa yanked her hand out of his grip, still not ready to let go of her belligerent anger. "Are you joking? You're not with *her*." She looked with disgust at Ruby standing behind Fin, as if she were a piece of gum on someone's shoe. Ruby really couldn't fault her for asking, even if her question was rude. *What is he doing with me?* Albeit drunk and disheveled, Lisa stood like a model. Ruby felt suddenly small and uncomfortable.

She would have turned, but Lisa now hung over Fin's

shoulder, screaming at her. "You know he fucked me last night, don't you? Did he tell you that?" Spit flew from her mouth.

* * *

Fin would have been happier in an airplane that was in a death spiral, ready to plow into the ground or in the middle of a herd of stampeding hippos rather than in his present reality. He squeezed his eyes shut and tried escaping the train wreck that kept coming. What he needed to do was get Lisa out of here. He wanted to talk to Ruby and explain or apologize, but he would not be able to do that with Lisa yelling. He turned to tell Ruby that he would deal with the situation and find her later, but only faceless people stared back at him. He craned his neck to get a wider view, but she was gone.

CHAPTER SIXTEEN

Ruby knew exactly where she was going. She pushed through the crowd of people, and looked for Retta. She needed a friendly face, someone she could talk to. She really wanted to talk to Poppy, but didn't want to worry her. It would have been too loud in the hostel to hear anyway. Her mind was scattered. She needed to slow down for a second and think. She spied Retta pretending to drive as the band sang a pretty good rendition of Prince's "Little Red Corvette."

Retta met Ruby's eyes and waved her over. She leaned in and raised her voice so that she could be heard over the bass. "How was Mr. Wonderful? I can't believe you're already back. Is that his jacket?"

Ruby had forgotten the jacket in her haste to get the hell out of there. She'd figure out how to get it back to him later. "Retta, I need to talk to you. Can we leave?" Ruby usually worked problems out for herself but, when she needed more help, she always used Poppy, and occasionally Margie, as a sounding board. For her to ask Retta to listen to her and give her some perspective or advice seemed strange. At this moment, though, she didn't care. She wasn't thinking past the next few minutes.

True to her nature, Retta didn't blink. "Yeah, let's go." She weaved over to the reception room with Ruby trailing in her wake. As they passed the windows in the front of the hostel, Ruby lowered her head, just in case the lovers' spat was still in full swing. They made it to their room, but Retta didn't stop there. "From the look on your face, I would say you want to be somewhere other than here."

Retta grabbed her jacket that was lying on the bunk and opened the window by their bed. She then draped her legs over the sill and hopped out, onto the graveled yard. Ruby followed, closing the window as much as she could after herself. She knew that Fin was staying in the shack not thirty yards away, so she quickly skirted the building to the cobbled street.

Retta seemed to realize that Ruby needed some time, so she stayed quiet as they walked the twisted lanes, going nowhere in particular. After ten minutes, Ruby sat down on a bench to the right of an ivy-covered stone fountain. Water gurgled out of the mouth of a fish into a grey seashell below. The sound calmed her nerves. Ruby needed the quiet, and was grateful to have the company of Retta who, at the moment, was being uncommonly silent.

Ruby's body was bent, with her chest on her thighs, and her fingers grazed the rough inlayed stones of the small square. The stones were still wet from the rain, making the otherwise grey cobbles black. She dipped one finger into a puddle that had formed and flicked her finger against her thumb, sending mini jets of water a few inches away. Finally, she tilted her head sideways to look up at Retta. "Well, I am officially screwed. I kissed him—no, he kissed me. I didn't protest, and it felt different than anything I have ever experienced. The air shimmered. Good lord, I've turned into a walking dictionary of clichés, haven't I?" She tried to laugh, but the noise came out more like a choke.

Retta sat sideways on the bench, wrapped her arms around her knees, and faced Ruby. "So why are we here? Did you get scared? Did he say something idiotic? What happened?"

Ruby turned back to the puddle. She could smell him all

around her; she should have left his jacket on the steps to the hostel or on the hook where he had gotten it. As it was, she couldn't get away from him. "No. Lisa, the willowy brunette happened. She was hysterical, yelling at him, then at me that she had slept with him, and that is saying it way more pleasantly than she did." Ruby wrinkled her nose at the memory. "I felt like a stinkweed next to a perfect rose. Not that I like roses, they're too predictable, but you get what I mean. I couldn't even breathe. It was like someone drove a fist into my stomach. Then I'm thinking, 'I'm here for me.' All I did was kiss someone I wanted to. People do that all the time. We're leaving tomorrow. A measly kiss should be no big deal. But something just doesn't feel right, like the whole book just had one page. There was supposed to be a story, or at least a few chapters." Ruby straightened and leaned her head on the back of the bench.

"Let me tell you, you are no stinkweed. And you are way too unexpected to be a rose." Retta pointed a finger at Ruby. "You feel this way because you're not one of those people that take things lightly. You feel with your whole body, mind, heart, and soul. That's not a bad thing, it just makes life harder sometimes. You know what you are? You're Lily of the Valley." Ruby looked over at her and rolled her eyes.

"No, really. A Lilly of the Valley. You have to look for it to see it, but it's beautiful when you do find it. It looks delicate, but it is straightforward and resilient, making its way up through the snow in some pretty harsh environments."

For no reason, Ruby laughed. Then they both laughed. It felt good and slightly crazy. Although she hadn't said anything to Retta about her incident with Scott, she felt exactly that way—resilient. After a while, when they had caught their breath, Ruby stood up. "You're right. I need to think less and experience more. I'm going to suck this trip dry, dammit."

Retta unfolded herself. "Okay, that just sounds weird, but we need to jump in with both feet. Maybe we'll touch the bottom, and maybe we won't, but at least we jumped."

Ruby pinched up her face and held her hands up in question. "Well, that sounds just as weird. I was trying to sound like a badass, but you sounded like an oracle. I need something to eat. Brian ate my pizza. You want to split a waffle?"

Ruby felt lighter. She would be on her way to Greece tomorrow with two people she was excited to spend time with. They started walking toward the streetlights that lined the busy section of the village, in search of a warm, mouth-watering piece of Brugge. Ruby pulled Fin's jacket tighter around her and thought that maybe she would keep it as a souvenir. As souvenirs went, it was pretty great. She breathed deeply, bliss.

* * *

Christ, he wanted to punch something or, better yet, someone. Maybe they would hit back and put him out of his misery. He had gotten the raving lunatic away from the crowd and tried to talk some sense into her, for all the good it did. He got a slap in the face, which he probably deserved, and a screaming beauty telling him she could find a better lover in a trash dumpster. Unfortunately, she didn't like that his laugh boomed against the walls of the alley, but her comment was funny, and the next slap was just as deserved as the first.

He had looked in the restaurant and down a few streets for Ruby, but gave up after thirty minutes. She probably wouldn't want to see him anyway. Hans and his friends had gone up to the apartment that Hans kept. They asked if he wanted to join them, but he knew he wouldn't make good company and begged off, deciding instead to go back to his hovel and sulk. He forgot to stoop and slammed his head into the low ceiling, bringing him to his knees. For starting out rather well, the night had taken a distinct nosedive.

Now he lay on his stale mattress and, for the first time, thought about going home. It wasn't as if there was a future with Ruby; they were both transients in this country. What did he think was going to happen? She believed him to be a handyman living in a shack, and he knew nothing about her other than that she was American.

Fin looked out at the inky night and there, perfectly framed by his window, was the Big Dipper. He moaned and draped his arm over his eyes, now picturing her blue eyes looking up at him with a secret hope that he felt, too. When she had closed her eyes, giving herself over to him, in all of his life, Fin couldn't remember a time that felt so right. Thank goodness he was alone and not with Anne—she would squeal with giddy delight.

No, it was definitely time to go home and quit hiding. His father would not to be able to keep on at the pace required, and Fin needed to demonstrate to both his father and himself that he was not just the happy-go-lucky shmuck people thought he was. He wanted to prove himself—more than that, he would not let Ian or his family down. He closed his eyes and willed sleep to come. At some point it must have, because his next view was the first rays of light casting arms through his window.

CHAPTER SEVENTEEN

Ruby woke up to Retta and Brian both inches from her head, smiling down at her. She couldn't remember falling asleep. She had spent the majority of the night staring at the ceiling. The way his lips had touched hers and how his hands had felt wonderfully rough on the skin of her face chased in circles around her mind. Now, with her eyes open, it felt like she blinked with sandpaper eyelids. She had no idea what these two yahoos were doing.

Brian kissed her cheek. "Up-and-at 'em beautiful, perfect you." He beamed over at Retta, who gave a tight shake of her head.

It was all coming clear. She looked back and forth between them. "I'm fine. There was no permanent damage done. Now quit looking at me and, Retta, what did you tell him?" She threw the sheet back and sat up.

"Oh, Ruby, she just said you got verbally attacked by some amazon warrior, and before that, you were kissed senseless. I just want to know where I was when all this happened. I guess I need to work on my knighthood skills. I really botched it up." Brian shook his fingers through his hair.

Ruby looked over at his bed and noticed that the top bunk had not been slept in. Chloris must have slept somewhere else. Brian's sheets were balled up at the foot of his mattress, and his backpack leaned against the end of his bunk. He was completely dressed and ready to go. Ruby rubbed her eyes. "What time is it?" She could tell it was early. The sun had yet to make an appearance—the room was shrouded in a smoky glow from a light in the hall.

"It's just a few minutes after six. I thought we could grab something to eat before we walk to the train station. The staff said they could have some stuff out early for us. Then, Opa! Greece, here we come. Why don't I meet you lovelies in the restaurant? I don't want to offend your delicate sensibilities by ogling." He bowed, threw a kiss, and walked out the door.

Between Retta and Brian, she should be more than occupied, her mind not able to wander to unrealistic futures.

Retta pulled on a pair of bright red jeans. She already had on a grey turtleneck sweater. She turned to Ruby. "Sorry, I told Brian. You're not mad, are you?" She was now fastening the clasps on her backpack.

"No, I'm not mad, and thanks for walking with me last night. Are you excited to see your friends?" Ruby had had enough of the spotlight. She snagged the jeans she wore last night, threw on a black, long-sleeved crewneck, and twirled her favorite scarf around her neck. Rag wool socks and Tevas finished off the ensemble. She started yanking her sheets off the bed, and grabbed Fin's jacket, which was tangled in the cotton. *Oh brother, surely I didn't sleep with it. Eh, who am I trying to kid?* She tossed the jacket aside like it meant nothing, folded her sheets, and laid them at the end of her bed as Brian had done. She put the shirt she had worn to bed into her pack and pulled out her toiletry bag. "I'll be just a minute, and then we can go." She breezed out the door to the bathroom.

No matter where a person is, Ruby thought, bathrooms always have a funky smell. It's a combination of cleaner and people smell, old sweat and sour urine. Not a good mix. Luckily this bathroom had a small window high on the wall that someone was wise enough to keep propped open. Now, every time Ruby smelled the usual toilet scents mingled with fresh air and the chill of morning, she knew she would think of European lavatories.

She rubbed some toothpaste onto her brush, placed her hand on her hip, and started humming with the motion. She wet the hostel towel and used it like a washcloth, something the Europeans must not have, and wondered how they kept their skin so smooth and blemish-free. At their next stop, she decided she would take a shower but, right now, the thought of getting wet in the cold, tiled bathroom was more than unappealing. Besides, they needed to get a move on. Excuse made.

When Ruby got back to the room, Retta stood with her backpack on and hiked it up with a quick jump, as if it was a kid taking a piggyback ride. "It was so nice not to have to carry this beast for a while. At least we'll be on a train all day, so we won't have to lug them. I may have permanent back problems after this. I'm serious."

Ruby balled up her towel and added it to her pile of sheets. She hefted her pack onto her back and groaned. "You're right. It was nice." She looked at the bed, where Fin's jacket lay, and tried to decide what to do with it. Of course, I'm not really taking it, am I? She couldn't wait to touch it again. Is that weird? Yes, it is. She grabbed it like a beach towel or any other inanimate object and walked out the door, with Retta right behind. She had purpose. She would hang it back on the hook, she would eat food and guzzle some much needed coffee, and she would walk to the train. Adios!

They rounded the corner and, of course, there sat her bewilderment. She felt like she was being sucked into a vortex. Her body was not used to the carnival ride it had been on during the last forty-eight hours. The ups and downs and loop-de-loos left her stomach in knots, and her heart speeding up and slowing down like she was on the wildest of roller coasters.

Fin sat on a thick wooden chair pulled up to the corner booth. He had his back toward them, but she could have sworn his head rose slightly when she and Retta entered. Chloris sat on top of the backrest of the bench, her hands dangling between her knees. Hans was across from her, his elbows on the table and his chubby hands held his chubby cheeks, his glasses somehow secured to the very middle of his forehead. They were both listening intently to something Fin was saying.

Brian picked a table closest to the front, and already had three mugs of coffee and a plate piled with cheese and rolls on the table. Good man. She slid her pack off her shoulders, putting it down as quietly as possible, somehow thinking if she wasn't heard, she couldn't be seen. Retta took the opposite approach, dropping her backpack like a sack of rocks onto the wooden floor, making enough of a racket that the trio across the room turned. The scenario would have been funny if Ruby hadn't wanted to be invisible. The three could have been playing a game of "guess what the look on my face means" charades. Chloris: happy. Hans: grumpy. And Fin: sensually disinterested, like he was waging a war within himself.

Ruby had not yet sat down; she stood, facing them. She held the stupid jacket as if it was the wrong end of a branding iron. She wanted to fling it away, but her hand would not unclench. Brian broke the spell by kicking the chair over, straight into her shin. *Pop.* Spell broken. "Ruby, sit. Have some coffee. Sorry about the chair, but it was necessary."

Ruby gave a tight smile as a reply. She sat and grabbed

the cup, gaging how large her bruise would be. She faced the
window and concentrated on swallowing. Somehow she had
lost the ability innately known from birth. The coffee was
hot and sloshed like water in a fishbowl around her mouth.
The thought occurred to her that she might have to spit it
back into her mug. Then she felt a squeeze on her shoulder,
and down her gullet it went. Ruby looked up to a warm,
smiling wood nymph.

Chloris's dark hair was in a spiky disarray, and her
green eyes shown like sea glass washed ashore. "Hey, you're
leaving." It was a simple statement, made as she dragged a
heavy wooden chair over to the table, creating more loud
noise. The only people who looked this time were a pair of
what had to be twin brothers filling their plates with
breakfast. As she looked at them, Ruby wondered why, past
the age of five, they still had matching haircuts and wore
creepily similar clothes, but those were arbitrary thoughts
not meant for deep dissection.

"I'm Chloris." She tilted her head and smiled at Brian.

"Chloris, like the goddess of flowers?" Brian was
between bites and looking charmingly bright.

"Ha, I don't get that very often, but yeah."

"One of my many partial degrees is Greek divinities. I'm
Brian. The name fits you." He bit off another hunk of roll.
"You already know Ruby and Retta?"

"I do. So where are your travels taking you this
morning?" She looked at all three bags and then at Ruby.

"We're catching the seven o'clock train headed
ultimately to Brindisi, then the boat to Greece."

"Nice. Hey, there's a bus to the train station in . . . " she
looked at the coo-coo clock on the wall, ". . . about ten
minutes. It's faster than walking. Do you think you'll come
back this way?" She twisted a spike back and forth between

her fingers. "Everyone seems to be leaving. Fin was just telling us that he needs to go back home next week. My dad is wrecked—cheap labor, you know." She looked at Ruby expectantly.

Not sure what to say, Ruby looked out the window. "Huh, do you think you could give him his jacket? I forgot to give it back to him last night." She slid it off her lap and handed it to Chloris.

"You have time. You could go give it to him before you go." By the odd look on Chloris's face, Ruby was sure that she must be getting a vibe of some sort, but wasn't sure what to make of it.

Retta broke the silence. "They had an awkward, what would you say, incident, moment, well . . . " she fluttered her hands. ". . . Anyway, I don't think she wants to cross that bridge again. Right, Ruby?"

"It was nothing, and we really need to go." Ruby looked at her untouched plate, the Finley diet. All four chairs scraped back in unison. "I'll try to get back to Brugge. It would be fun to do something together." She had no idea if she would, but she genuinely liked Chloris and would make the effort.

"Just leave the plates and mugs. I'll get them. The bus stop is right outside the door." She stood with her hands on the back of the chair.

Ruby saw Fin's back still facing her. He looked motionless, like a marble statue. He had to have heard them. There were only the two brothers and them in the room. *Damn, he probably ended up with the goddess of legs and foul mouth last night. I must be one of hundreds of kissed lips, and here I am short of breath, for what?* She hiked up her pack, pulled some coins out of her pocket, and followed after her companions, smiling and giving a short wave to Chloris on the way out.

The morning was perfect. The air was fresh and cold against her face, and the day held the promise of sun. All three leaned against the sill outside Prima Facie and waited for the bus.

* * *

Fin knew the moment she entered the room. He was getting used to the charge in the air when she was near. It hummed. He had been telling Chloris and Hans that it was time for him to go. There were obligations to get back to. Then, it was as if a door had been opened, a movement, but it hadn't. He heard footfalls on the floor behind him, where he had seen the boy from last night sitting. He knew it was Ruby. He'd go on with his conversation, essentially ignoring everything else in the room. It would be easy, it just took focus.

Then, what sounded like a boulder falling from the sky messed up his whole plan. It would have been impossible not to look, and his head swung around instinctively. His eyes instantly locked on Ruby. She looked to be in pain, either from the noise or from being caught watching him again, the poor girl. The emotions he felt were like magnets repelling against each other. He wanted to stay detached, but made the mistake of zooming in on her like some sick homing device. He was flooded with the awareness he felt last night, when he had touched her. Desire, heat, wanting more than a touch—it was something he could not put his finger on. The sensations were on the fringes, but were not in focus. Then the red-headed, frizzy mop-top pushed a chair into Ruby. Fin wanted to smack him in the face. The problem was, he didn't know if he felt anger because the chair hit her or that the boy got to be close to her, sharing her time. With herculean effort, he turned back to the two at his table.

Hans sported his perpetual dire frown, but Chloris smiled and made her way over to Ruby's table. How could father and daughter be so different in temperament? Hans started to say something about projects Fin could finish in the few days he had left at Prima Facie. After that, his voice became white noise as Fin strained to hear what Chloris was saying. He heard the word "Greece," but not much else. He began formulating a crazy fantasy about following the three to Greece, and then had to mentally shake himself. *I am going home. I need to go home.*

His ears perked when he heard Chloris say his name, and he wondered how he had made it into the conversation. Maybe Ruby had said what a boorish ass he was last night. She must think he couldn't keep his dick in his pants, which, over the past weeks, would be more true than not, but it was supposed to be a dulling drug that had unfortunately lost its potency. He didn't know why he cared what she thought. He had never cared what people thought of him before but, for some reason, her leaving thinking ill of him rubbed him wrong.

Chairs scrapped the wooden floor, followed by a shuffling of feet. They were leaving, but he didn't turn. He would not do it. He was a flag staked into solid earth, not budging under any circumstance. Neither a gale-force wind nor Ruby could move him from this spot.

The restaurant seemed devoid of life when they left. It was quiet. Fin stared at the grains in the wood of the table. He heard the familiar groan of the bus engine coming down the street. *Ten more seconds.*

Then, Chloris dropped something on the table and, at the same time, cuffed him on the back of his head. How many times would he be hit by women in such a very short span of time? He looked up as she gave him a snotty sixteen-year-old girl glare. A lot of attitude lurked behind those eyes. His jacket was draped on the table like a deflated balloon. He picked it up and, before he knew what he was doing, he pressed it to his nose. Her smell clung to it, as if she had worn it all night. It was citrusy, like a fresh orange or a lemon, spiking his curiosity as to why. Had she eaten oranges? Did she use shampoo that smelled like lemons?

He stood up so quickly that his chair fell over backwards and hit the floor. He was now moving, and he didn't bother to pick it up. He saw the three of them walk awkwardly with their big packs down the narrow aisle through the bus windows. It would not have surprised him if the hostel door came off its hinges due to the force he used to swing it open. The bus pulled away from the curb as he pounded his fist on the accordion door. The driver swung it open and glared at Fin as if he had derailed his whole route by the disturbance.

Ruby was three rows back, sitting sideways in the tight seat. One hand was on the seat in front of her, her backpack against the window looking at him either with annoyance or joy. He wasn't sure which, but he would find out later. He smiled with anticipation and told the driver to wait for a moment. At the same time, he discretely handed him enough Belgium Francs that he would stay without question. He walked two steps and stood over her. Without hesitating, without even thinking, he uttered five simple words that he knew could change his life: "I think you should stay."

* * *

Ruby was befuddled. Her face heated, and she wiped her palms—which had instantly gotten clammy—against her jeans. She opened her mouth to talk, and then closed it. She gave her head a shake and opened her mouth again. "I'm," she said, looking at the two she was with, and then continuing, "*we're* going to Greece, I'm on the bus to the train to go to Greece." Her voice rose with every word, and her heart felt as if it could leap out of her chest. She knew that if she looked down, her shirt would be fluttering like a hummingbird's wings. The moment was just like a scene from a movie. She wanted to stay so badly it hurt, but that was crazy. She was on the frigging bus. Then, out of the blue, as if she were right next to her, she heard Margie: "*This is your life. You only have one. Well, that's debatable. Use it, stretch it, wring it dry, and then soak up all you can. It's your destiny, Ruby.*"

Fin leaned in closer, his voice a whisper. "Stay with me, give me three days. I'll get you to Greece with your friends." She was lost. His voice was steady, his grey eyes full of unwavering determination.

She gaped at Retta, who had tears in her eyes. "Oh, Ruby. Stay. You have to stay, and then you have to come to Greece." She ripped a piece of paper from the train schedule she held and frantically scribbled the number for the house in Greece. She held it out to Ruby.

Ruby was numb, without bones, jelly. Fin reached for the paper instead, and Retta balled it into his palm, boring her eyes into him, willing him to realize how important Ruby was and not to screw with her friend.

He gave her his best grin. Ruby figured it was his way of thanking Retta. After all, she had championed him. Fin reached over the seat and grabbed Ruby's pack like it weighed nothing. He took charge, and she loved it. He was the white knight (sans horse or armor), and though she was not a princess, the gesture still felt chivalrous and fairytale-esque. The bus driver mumbled words Ruby couldn't decipher, but she guessed it was something like "Get the hell off my bus."

Ruby walked up the aisle she had just come down and looked back at Brian and Retta, her face making some sort of distorted mishmash of apology and, "Crap, can you believe this is happening?" Brian gave her a thumbs-up. Did people still do that? The signal was very *Starsky and Hutch*. He then shouted that he would watch after Retta. *Two knights. Wow.*

CHAPTER EIGHTEEN

Ruby and Fin stood on the sidewalk as the bus pulled away. It was as if they were under the spell of a hypnotist—they both stared straight ahead at the street, into empty space, not knowing what to do now that the drama had passed.

In stressful situations, and always at inappropriate times—such as the quiet of a wedding or a prayer at a funeral—Ruby was given to uncontrollable laughter. At this particular moment, she felt it building in her stomach. She tried stopping it by pressing her fist under her ribcage and tightening her muscles, but it moved higher, closer to her mouth. Feeling the vibration behind her sternum, she tightened her throat muscles, but the flood was cracking the dam, and her tightened lips couldn't hold it back. What came out wasn't even close to a pretty, womanly laugh. It was a truck driver's yowl, sounding more like a belch than a giggle.

Fin looked down at her. His eyes held a spark of desire that made her breath catch. A slow, carnal grin spread across his face and absolute masculinity emanated from every inch of him. Ruby met his eyes. "So what now?"

* * *

Fin was pleasantly surprised by her directness, especially because he was accustomed to women on the hunt, who said things they thought he wanted to hear to try and snare something he was not willing to give. Now he felt like the hunter, a roll he much preferred, and his prey was exactly to his liking. He wondered why he had become so intensely attracted to her. He pondered if it was the timing. He'd had time to mourn his old life, his brother, and his family, and now he was ready to move on. Maybe, given his age, it was just time. No, the feeling went deeper than that. The next three days were his to figure out why, something he was very much looking forward to. He had three days to get his fill, and he told himself it would be enough. "I want you to go talk with Chloris for a bit while I get some things together. I'll come and get you in one hour. How does that sound Ruby?"

* * *

Another uncontrollable bubble of laughter spurt out because of the way Fin said her name. She needed to pull herself together, and coherent conversation was at the top of the list. It was as if she had lost all intellect, like she was in grade school and a boy had looked at her for the first time, *ugh*. She straightened her spine. "Okay. Here, let me take my bag." She reached for her bag, but he threw it over his right shoulder and opened the door with his left, holding it open for her.

"You go in, and I'll set this by the bar."

Chloris, who was walking out from the kitchen, stopped in mid-stride. "Ruby, what are you doing? I thought you were on the bus?"

Taking long strides and setting her backpack against the far end of the bar, Fin said, "I convinced Ruby to spend some time with me. I need to speak with your dad and do a couple of other things. Could you keep Ruby company until I come back?" He smiled at Ruby like he had a magical secret. She was floating, trying her best to stay on the ground. She attempted to smile calmly back at Chloris. If the casualness worked, she had no idea.

"Of course. I think Dad's in the kitchen." She waved her hand negligently in that general direction.

Fin looked at Ruby and said, "One hour, I promise." He drew one finger from her forehead to her jaw, leaving an electric path on her skin. She sucked in her breath and nodded. He disappeared from the room, and both women stood completely still.

Chloris turned her head in slow motion to look at Ruby. "I knew it. I knew he wasn't going to let you go. Did he tell you what he has planned?"

"Unh-unh, he just said he wanted me to stay. He got me off the bus. Retta and Brian are gone." It was a choppy run of words, spoken as if recalling a dream.

There were more people trickling into the restaurant in a variety of states—some freshly showered and raring to go, some still in nightclothes with hair in matted tangles, and others looked as if they were just coming in from the night. Chloris surveyed the room and turned. "Ruby, I'll get you some coffee. Did you eat already?"

Propping herself onto a bar stool, Ruby was about to say that she had eaten, but remembered her untouched plate. On cue, her stomach rumbled. "I guess I didn't eat. I'll get a plate."

She started to get down off her stool when Chloris put a hand on her shoulder. "Why don't you just sit? Do you want any meat or just cheese and a roll?"

"Yeah, some meat would be good, thanks." She sat back and swiveled around to look out on the room.

* * *

Fin still felt the softness and heat of Ruby's skin on his fingertip, and his chest sputtered in odd ways. He wanted to do so much more than a brief touch, but he didn't want to scare her, and standing in a room filling up with travelers was not the right place. He pushed his way through the kitchen door, gearing up for the gruff words he would undoubtedly hear from Hans when he told him his new change of plans.

Fin didn't know what made him rush to the bus. He was trying to stay away from her. He tried telling himself that he was leaving and that she was leaving, but she was a siren call he could not ignore. Three days. Three days and she would be out of his system. Then he could deposit her safely back to her friends, return to Stonehaven and his family, and begin where Ian had left off.

When they stood on the sidewalk, and after the bus had pulled away, Fin began mentally ticking off a list of preparations and formulating a plan to set in motion. The first item on the list was checked off. Hans had grumbled and cursed but, in the end, and after Fin reminded him that he had worked for him every day since his arrival, there was no argument that three days off was reasonable.

In response, Hans humphed. "The fuck you say? Well, you damn well will stay three more days to make up for it. Don't think you won't."

Fin snapped to attention and saluted. "Aye, aye, captain." A boyish grin that he could not wipe from his face since his plan was framed met Hans's flushed, brutish one.

"Oh, get the fuck outta here, and don't make a shit pie out of this." As an afterthought, Hans said, "Chloris likes her."

Hans turned, and to his back, Fin said, more serious than he intended, "I won't." Anyone who heard him would not have doubted the veracity behind the statement. Christ he was in trouble.

Fin walked back to the glorified shed and packed his small leather bag with essentials and, because what he had was meager, it took no time at all to check it off his list and go to his next destination. The information center was not far, which held a road map of the area he needed. Fin took the time to circle two places and run the pen along the route that was most logical. He stopped at a market, bought his favorite car food—Haribo tropi fruitti, gummy sour cherries and frogs—and then picked up some Guylian and two large bottles of mineral water. He placed it all in an insulated bag and, with his duffle and food, went to his next stop. He checked his watch: twenty-five minutes left.

Next on the list was getting out of Brugge. He was selfishly eager to have Ruby to himself, away from people he knew, and he wanted to avoid a possible repeat of last night's debacle. He walked a cobbled street fifteen minutes from Prima Facie to a home he had visited a handful of times since his arrival. Fin paid more than necessary to Harald, the owner of the hardware store, to garage his car for the time he would be in Brugge. After their initial awkward meeting, he and Harald had become friendly, and he and his wife even invited Fin to their home for dinner on more than one occasion. Fin paid him and, in return, Harald promised to run his car once a week for a few minutes to keep it in shape. Fin told him that he could take it out with his wife, Marget, but Harald said he did not want it on his head if some maniac ran into them. Fin punched in a code on the key pad and watched as the white wooden door creaked up slowly along its metal rollers.

Harald found a tarp, and lovingly covered the auto, saying that a thing of beauty should not be subjected to gathering dust. Fin laughed, but voiced his appreciation each time Harald brought it up, which was every time he saw him. Before he had come for the car, he had stopped by the hardware store, got the keys, and told them he would be out of town for a few days.

Marget, now a surrogate mother to him, patted his hand, saying, "Good for you, Finley. A change of scenery will be good for you." Her cheeks looked like healthy apples as she smiled up at him. Fin had charmed her with flattery and good humor the first time he had been to their home and, from that moment, her heart opened to him, her fondness palpable in her light blue eyes and motherly touch. Where such things could have rankled, he had found her warmth comforting.

Fin reached into his pocket and touched the keys—one more item checked off. He felt a nervous giddiness thrum through his limbs, which was ridiculous for a man his age, but he couldn't seem to squelch it. Instead, he rode it like a perfect wave.

Fin now rounded the corner and parked directly in front of the hostel door. He checked his watch again. *Two minutes. Perfect.* He got out and went through the door. Ruby sat at the bar, her head resting on her folded arms. Chloris spotted him and waved. He wondered if Ruby felt as carefree and happy as he did. Maybe it was that he was altering from his usual routine, but he realized that his feelings would be very different if Lisa were sitting on that stool.

Ruby's raised her head and turned to him, her face alight with joy. She lit up the room, and his heart leapt—she stunned him. The juxtaposition that hummed through him was odd, His head felt light, whereas the lower part of him felt very tight. He was exceedingly glad that his jacket covered that area of his body. Grinning, he made his way across the room. He felt like a green lad first experiencing a woman's attentions.

CHAPTER NINETEEN

Ruby saw Chloris wave, knowing it must be Fin. She was not remotely close to prepared for the sight she turned to. He was breathtaking. His hair was ruffled like he had been running, and his eyes shown with life. He dragged his fingers through his hair and smiled. He looked like he could have stepped off the pages of some men's magazine. He wore faded jeans, and a white crew neck peeked out from under a washed-out, red Henley that was covered by the jacket she wore the night before. The soft cotton hugged the contours of his chest. His jeans perfectly accentuated the outline of his trim waist and strong thighs. He had on the same heavy leather work boots she had seen before. They were obviously not a fashion statement, given the scuffs that marred them. She quivered. All of her nerves were alive. She was completely aware of him, her senses heightened by his mere presence. She smiled as he crossed the room.

He came to her side and held out his hand. "Are you ready?"

Ruby put her hand into his and bounced off the stool. An electric spark flew up her arm at the heated touch. She looked at him to see if he had the same reaction she did. Their eyes locked, and suddenly she could not wait to leave, wanting to find out more about him. She had thought to be cool and breezy, but she now wanted to be herself, to say what came into her mind without censoring. It would be difficult. Ruby had always been more of an observer—she kept herself well protected.

Ruby had an idyllic childhood; she spent her days with

her family, out of doors with her sister, or exploring alone. Even as a child, she hadn't been comfortable with a lot of people, and when she started school, she realized that she didn't fit the mold that most kids did. Her interests were not in popular sports or in fashion. A term teachers had forever said was "shy"—a description she loathed, but it stuck like a bad nickname. She was not outgoing or ready with answers. She liked to think in her own head. In a sense, being with Scott exaggerated her traits, but spit out the opposite. Now she wanted to put herself out there.

This trip was a chance to spread her wings and to grow into her skin. Nobody knew her. She could be anything she wanted, and quickly realized that being someone other than her true self was not the destination. It was experiencing new things, doing and saying things she might not have, but nevertheless thought or felt. There was no going back once she began unfurling. There was no putting the jack back into the box. Poppy had said that she was ballsy for traveling alone, that no one does that. At the time, Ruby didn't accept it as true, but she began to feel that Poppy was on to something. Ruby felt strong.

Thus far she loved the freedom she felt in letting people get know her. Bold and bashful was a funny combination. Ruby would never back down from something she was passionate about. She had distinct views and would argue her point *ad nauseam*, her mother might say. The friends Ruby had were few, but they were close and trusted. Putting herself completely out there for strangers was not second nature to her. This trip was exactly the shakeup and challenge she needed for herself.

Fin held her hand as he walked to the end of the bar, where she had propped her backpack. His hand was warm and strong in hers. She felt worn callouses his handy work had created, but there was still a masculine gentleness when he squeezed her hand before he let go to grab her bag. He caught her eyes in his, and stood almost as if he were going out into a storm and wasn't sure if he wanted to chance it. Just as quickly, the look disappeared. Fin tilted his head in the direction of the door.

Ruby said goodbye for a second time to Chloris, and moved toward the front of the hostel on auto pilot. Her wits, she thought, must be floating somewhere over her head, because they were no longer an attached part of her. Fin had a hand on the sway of her back, just as he had last night. She felt his warmth through her shirt, and his confidence calmed her stretched nerves. Ruby grappled within herself. *What is the worst that could happen? He could grow bored with me because, frankly, I cannot see the reverse happening. On the flip side, I could have a wonderful three days and be able to tell Poppy and Margie a magical story. They would eat it up.* A smile brightened her face as she walked outside, thinking of the two women literally on the edge of their seats.

* * *

Fin threw Ruby's bag into the back seat with more force than may have been necessary but, at the moment, he needed a surge of power to go somewhere. He was reluctant to let go of her hand, and now he wrestled with feelings he did not want to look too closely at. He told himself that these three days were like any other dalliance. Then he met her eyes, her clear blue blissful eyes, and was forced to admit that his feelings were completely foreign to him: his racing heart, his flashes of passion, his wanting all of her for himself.

Fin had always stayed at arm's length from women. They never wanted in the physical area, but he gave the bare minimum of emotion and took all he wanted before moving on. Admittedly, he was selfish—he never had an eye toward the future. If there was one thing that Ian's death had made him realize, it was that his time here, in this moment, was a gift and, if not cherished, became a slap in the face to those no longer able to sail the course they dreamed of. He ran his fingers through his hair and came back to the present. He looked over at Ruby. She stood, looking at her bag in his car. "Sorry. I didn't mean to throw it in that hard. You don't have any breakables do you?" Fin laughed, trying to lighten the mood. He opened the door for her, lifted her hair, and leaned in. "Cat got your tongue?" He couldn't help but touch her. He jumped on any excuse to guide her with his hand, to smooth a hair that was out of place, or to remove an invisible crumb that clung to her lip. Any excuse.

* * *

Ruby felt his breath like a warm hum across her skin and unconsciously moved into it. Thankfully, he was at her elbow. Otherwise, she would have been sprawled on the ground. Her legs were that unsteady beneath her. She melted into the passenger's seat and tried gathering her thoughts. "Is this your car?"

"It didn't look like this when I got it," he replied, giving her a side-long glance. "It's been a work in progress."

"I'm not a huge car person, but I love yours. What is it?" The simple dashboard and straight forward stick shift impressed her with its simplicity. She had always been a sucker for convertibles.

"It's a 60s Triumph. My brother and I worked on it together. It took a while, but it was worth it. It runs great. You ready?" He turned the key, and the car came to life. He deftly maneuvered through the streets, and they were quickly out of the village, speeding through the countryside.

The engine purred, and the tan leather seats had the

perfect give. They felt like velvet under Ruby's hands as she rubbed them. Ruby almost laughed out loud thinking about her ride—a white Trek mountain bike. She spiffied it up with a Norwegian sticker. Clearly, Fin's idea of fixing up a car meant something more robust. When Ruby looked out to the green fields, her eyes lit up. "I thought we were staying in Brugge. Where are you taking me?"

"I want to show you a place I think you'll like. We'll be gone for a couple of days. Is that alright?" He looked straight ahead at the road and held his breath, as if he thought she would tell him to turn around. Fat chance.

She simply looked straight ahead. Finally, she replied, "Well, I trust Chloris's opinion of you, and who could say no to spending time in this car?"

Fin hooted. "Very cheeky of you. Use me, will you? I may have to withhold treats."

Ruby feigned bemusement. "I didn't mean the car. I meant you. Who would not want to spend time with *you*? And what kind of treats are we talking?" Ruby's hair blew wildly as the landscape flew by in a green streak. Her scarf had loosened, flapping behind her like a steel blue eel gliding through water.

In one fluid movement, he grabbed both ends and pulled her closer. "Do you like sweet or sour?"

The nearness made her lightheaded. His scent got caught in the breeze and hit her straight on. It was subtle, earthy, and alive, like he had walked through a forest at dawn. She squeezed her eyes shut and then squinted through her lashes, somehow muting his effect on her, only able to eke out, "Both?"

* * *

He didn't let go of the scarf, but drew her closer. "Lucky for you, I have both." Then, because he was taking his new pact with himself literally, he reached for the proverbial gold ring, his mouth coming down on hers. He heard a small intake of breath and then a moan. Her lips were warm and soft as they opened for him to come in. His desire for her was raw and hungry. He felt outside himself, needing more—more of her taste, more of the heat she brought to him. He reached for the gear shift, pulled it down, and swerved to the side of the road in one smooth motion. Gravel crunched under the tires, and they came to an abrupt stop.

Fin felt Ruby's heart beat against his hand, which had brushed her chest. She reached to his nape and held him to her, her tongue playing with his. He left her lips and murmured her name into the softness of her neck. She shivered at his words.

Fin realized that all the kisses that had come before this were nothing compared to what he felt now. This is what a kiss is meant to be. He felt her heat race to meet his. His need became a living thing, something to be fed and tended. Their breathing became the same, raw desire, and he knew that he wanted every part of her right now. He moved his hand, unwinding the scarf from around her neck, and then, like a pitcher of cold water being thrown in his face, someone blared a horn as they passed. His hands stilled. "Christ, what was that?" Fin wasn't sure if he meant the horn or the uncontrollable passion that hummed in the confines of the car. Ruby touched her lips without answering. Fin knew that they would be warm and numb under her fingers.

Fin looked at her. To him, she was the definition of beauty. "Ruby, I'm . . ." He wasn't sorry—far from it—but he needed to say something. "I didn't mean for that to . . . don't think—Oh, hell. I don't . . . I mean, that doesn't happen all time."

Ruby snorted. "Yeah, I'm sure."

Fin couldn't let that comment pass. He held her eyes, "Not even close." He wanted her to see the truth behind his words and, at the same time, not put too much stock in them. The time he would spend with her was going to be light, a last hoorah before he went home. *Yeah, light.* He groaned inwardly.

In a daze, they both pressed themselves back into their seats. "Did you bring anything to drink? I'm suddenly really thirsty." Her eyes met his with a gleam of humor.

Shaking his head, he looked at her, thankful for her good nature. "In the bag, in the back seat."

He turned to get it, but Ruby stopped him. "You drive and I'll take care of this." She brought the bag to her lap and looked inside. She pulled out the water and twisted the metal top, letting out a hiss of air. Bubbles streamed up the side of the glass bottle. She put it to her mouth and tilted it back. "Aah, better. You want some?" Ruby held it to him as she looked into the bag. "I love these. I have to say, I have a bit of a sweet tooth." She lifted out the bag of gummy fruit and replaced the bag in the back seat.

Fin drank from the bottle and held it between his legs. Ruby ripped open the bag of candy. "Well, then it looks as if I hit the target. The bag is full of candy." Even that small thing, that he had gotten things that she liked, moved him, first because he knew one more little piece about her, and second because he made her smile again. The car was back on the road, and they fell into a comfortable silence. Most of the women he had been with could not be silent. They didn't know how. They needed to be heard, as if their prattling was a snare but, in most instances, it was poison. He quickly figured out that he did not much care what they were talking about, and that was the beginning of the end.

Things shifted with Ruby. He ached to hear her, waiting for her to reveal something of herself. Does she prefer showers or baths? Winter or summer? What books does she like? He knew he was in dangerous territory, walking on thin ice, reaching for something that he could not have, could not keep tucked away just for himself. He needed to stay detached. He also needed to enjoy, but to stay detached. Unfortunately, he seemed to gravitate to the role of moth to flame. Anne would most certainly find humor here, the self-proclaimed bachelor, forever mocking all those claiming the powers of love. His heart stopped. Love was not a word he wanted to use—he didn't even want to think about it. Spending time with Ruby was something, but it was not love.

He looked over at Ruby. Her head rested against the seat, and her face was tilted to the sun. She could have been on a beach. He grunted to himself, *She could be on a beach, in Greece with her friends*. He wondered if he had made a mistake in asking her to stay. Then she turned her head to him, giving him a serene smile, reminiscent of a Da Vinci painting. She held some private knowledge. He knew right then that he would have been a fool to have let her leave on that bus.

"Fin, did you say where we're going?" She had finished half the bag of Frutti and was working on the water.

He looked at her for two beats. "I don't think you've ever used my name. I like when you say it." He looked over at her, catching a rise in color on her cheeks. "Did I embarrass you?" He smiled, but kept his hands on the wheel, not wanting a repeat performance of earlier.

"No. I blush at the drop of a hat," Ruby grabbed onto her thumb nail with her teeth and quickly let it go. "Or at a compliment. It's a curse, really. I can't stand it."

"Well, I think it's charming. It makes me want to know more about what you're thinking." His eyes went back to the road. "We're going to an area south of here. It'll take about an hour. Have you seen much of Belgium?"

"No. I've only been traveling for a few days. I landed in Amsterdam and then went to Leiden and now Brugge. How about you? Chloris said that you had been at Prima Facie for a month. What did you do before that?"

On the tip of his tongue was, "Well, my brother and his family were killed in a senseless accident, my life imploded, and I couldn't stay. I knew I should, but I couldn't, so I ran away from home with nothing but my measly duffle." He didn't want to see pity in her eyes so, instead, he said, "It's actually been two months." He left it at that. "Where are you from, Ruby?" She paused and looked at him. He knew she must have questions and wanted to know more about him but, if she was curious, she didn't show it. She did not ask anything of him, for which he was infinitely grateful.

She let out a slow breath, seeming to have made a decision before responding, "Colorado. Do you know where that is? It's close to the middle of the United States. Lots of mountains."

They passed the time in easy conversation, with Ruby telling him about the funny experiences she had so far. They laughed together about the hotel in Leiden, the shower, and the boys in the alley. Fin had an unending string of questions about her family and where she grew up. Time flew.

CHAPTER TWENTY

They had gotten off the E19 and taken a left at a fork. They now wound their way through the lush countryside, turning at roads with long names that Ruby couldn't pronounce. Fin seemed to know exactly where he was. He made a left at a white barn and drove slowly for a mile down a narrow road that cut through a green field and ended at a small half-full parking lot.

"It's gorgeous," Ruby said, stepping out of the car and looking ahead at a path that made its way through a stand of narrow straight trees.

"The town we went through is called Hallerbos, which means 'the forest of Halle.' I'm going to put our bags in the trunk and put the top up. I came here with my family years ago, and I always remembered it." Fin bent into the backseat to get their luggage. "Do you need anything from your bag? It doesn't look like it will rain, but I'll take my jacket if you need it."

Ruby turned toward him, and was stunned at the sight. He had taken off his jacket, and his shirt stretched over his solid chest. He was not bulky, but his shoulders where broad, and he moved with an elegant confidence. She wondered what it would feel like to dance with him, something Old World, like the waltz—not that she knew how to waltz, but she was willing to bet that Fin did, and he would lead.

She drifted up from her reverie long enough to answer his question. "No. Not a thing, except maybe a piece of chocolate." She assumed that needing to see him in nothing but a smile was not included in his question but, to be truly accurate, that would have been a want and not a need. She wound her scarf back around her neck, trying not to think of the reason it had become undone. The sun made the leaves from the Beech trees glow like hundreds of tiny, neon green nightlights. It was still cool, and the scarf felt good against her skin.

"You do have a sweet tooth," he said, holding out his hand like a butler with a serving tray, revealing two of Belgium's finest on his palm. "Here you go."

Her fingers hovered for a moment and then plucked a marbleized, cream and milk chocolate seashell that quite literally made her mouth water. She knew that most people would take a dainty bite and then wait a reasonable time before taking another. Instead, she plopped the whole thing into her mouth and ran her tongue along the smooth ridges, letting it melt and coat her taste buds in thick cream. She couldn't hold back an appreciative, throaty groan at the sweet taste that played in her mouth. She closed her eyes and opened them to molten steel eyes gazing down at her, one brow arched in humor. Suddenly very self-conscious, Ruby bit down on the side of her bottom lip. "Those are really good. You should have the other one."

"Well, I can hardly deny myself after your reaction," he admitted, putting one into his mouth.

Ruby watched his gaze. It did not move from her lips. His eyes seemed to scorch her already heated skin. Then his lids closed tightly, and when they opened, they seemed clearer.

Fin fisted his jacket and clenched his jaw. "Shall we then?" He drew his arm in front of him, guiding her with his hand to go ahead. Ruby blinked twice before she moved her feet. He had an unreadable expression on his face. *Maybe its frustration or something else*? As if reading her mind, Fin ruffled her hair. "It's nothing, Ruby. Now I want to show you the forest." Like that, they were off. The trailhead lay twenty yards from the parking lot and was immediately swallowed by trees and underbrush.

The winding trail, covered in red wood chips, felt like a gymnasts mat under her feet. The smell was a mixture of wet dirt and moss, both floral and woody. The canopy became a natural aviary to what seemed to be hundreds of birds, each having its own song and wanting to be heard over others. The sound reminded Ruby of the round singing they did at summer camp, each person's voice rising and falling in a cacophony of sound. The Beech trees were tall and narrow, a grouping of seventeenth century soldiers standing guard over a magical kingdom, their foliage like feathers in their hats.

When they came over a rise, she knew why he would remember Hallerbros from childhood. A carpet of blue flowers stretched as far as she could see. The frequency that people used the word "awesome" had always annoyed Ruby—"That car is awesome"; "This sandwich is awesome"; "Your hair is awesome"—"awesome" needed to be saved for moments like this, ones that truly took one's breath away. The light coming through the leaves created a mosaic work of art on the forest floor. Some flowers became black in the shadows, while others were aglow in purple and blue, all coming together in the twining of green undergrowth. They stood silently on the path, looking down over the sight in front of them.

Fin stood behind Ruby and, just like the night before, she felt his heat envelope her. Without thinking, she leaned back into him, his stance steady under her weight. He was a safe haven, a port where she could rest. His arms encircled her,

and she had never before felt as right in her life as she did in
this moment. He held her like she was his, and she was
cherished. His arms both gentle and steel bindings from
which she could not escape had she been so inclined, which
she was not. Her head rested just below his shoulder, and
she felt his mouth stroke her hair back and forth. Then, in a
whisper as soft as a butterfly's wing, he said her name—or
maybe she imagined it. She turned her head and looked up
at him.

He squeezed once and released her. "A little further
there's a coffee house, or at least there used to be. Should we
go see?" His lips curved up slightly.

"Well, I definitely need something to kick start my heart.
I may as well be on my death bed for lack of excitement
around here." Ruby had already started walking the path, so
she talked to the air, but she heard Fin make his way to her.

"Very funny, sweeting. What do you think so far?"

"I've never seen anything like it. I wouldn't be surprised
if little brownies started flying around on dragonflies, tiny
twig spears in their hands. Did you come here a lot with
your family?" He hadn't said more than the bare minimum
about his family or about growing up, and Ruby's curiosity
was piqued.

* * *

Fin wasn't sure why he did not want to tell Ruby about
growing up with live-in help and elite schools, or about
going on vacations that included private charters and villas.
He was happy to take on the part of vagabond handy man.
No one had preconceived notions about him. He did not
want to see a change in Ruby, her thinking that she couldn't
belong to his exclusive world. He knew she would feel that
way.

The Sinclair family was tight-knit and well grounded.

His family was atypical in their privileged world. He and his siblings were held responsible for their life choices, and they were required to work alongside the help and learn from them. He, Ian, and Anne fought like any other kids, and played like them, too. Yet, he could not deny that they had privileges that many other people could not relate to. They spent summers on the Riviera and, at times, birthdays included well-known pieces of art or an Arabian.

He was not ashamed of his family, but he had seen first-hand the moment the light went on in people's eyes. Where many would take the information and try to worm their way in, he knew Ruby would backpedal, which was something he could not allow. It was best to give bits and gloss over others. He felt like a shmuck. He was deceiving her, and he knew it. He told himself that, with time and after she got to know him, he would tell her the truth, but there was no time. They had these few short days, so what was the point. Now he was justifying to himself, arguing in circles around in his head. He repeated his mantra: *Detached. Keep it light Detached. Keep it light.*

"No. We came here once when I was twelve. My brother and sister and I ran around the trails and played hide-and-seek, while my parents sat at the café. That's why I think it's close, maybe another kilometer." There, the truth, and he was still standing. Ruby, though, was inquisitive, and followed up her first question with another. He couldn't fault her; he wanted to know as much about her life as he could, to put puzzle pieces together to see the whole.

"I don't even know where you grew up. I would guess Ireland or Scotland. Am I right?" She ran her hand over a sapling that sprouted up next to the trail. It catapulted under her hand, springing back and forth, from shade to light, shade to light. He was being evasive, but couldn't figure out why he needed to be. Her imagination must have started running wild: He was an escapee, he had a wife he was hiding from, or maybe he was a highly trained, deadly assassin. Still, he didn't say anything, and she looked at him from the corner of her eye. "Okay, you want me to guess, or you don't want me to know anything about you, which is kind of weird, so I'll guess, Ireland."

Fin stopped and looked at Ruby. He ran both hands through his hair, gave a brilliant half smile, and looked down at his boots. "You'd be wrong. It's Scotland, and I do want you to know me. There are some things I don't want to talk about, but you can ask me anything. How about that, and I'll probably answer. I know it sounds strange. I'm not off my head, so you don't need to worry. There are just some things—very few, actually—that I don't want to think about."

She stayed silent for a time, her lips held in a tight line. When she let them go, they made the sound of a cork gun popping. "Okay, I am going to give you a list of questions, and you answer, okay?" She cast a sideways glance at him and held up her index finger. "Number one, have you been convicted of a crime?"

He laughed. "No. No crime, but I was warned with threat of expulsion not to urinate in public by our headmaster when I was in school."

"That must be a European thing. Growing up, I don't think I ever saw anyone pee in public. Well, I take that back. There was a crazy neighbor boy that pulled his pants down and ran after me, trying to spray me. Lucky for me, I was always a fast runner. Number two," she held up the next finger, "are you leading a double life? Do you have two wives and ten kids stashed in a Scottish castle in Limerick?"

His grin covered his face, and he shook his head slowly.

"No. No wife or kids, and it would be an Irish castle."

She looked at him as if he had asked her to solve an unworkable math problem. "What?"

"Limerick is in Ireland, so it would be an Irish castle, and I have no secret family in Ireland either. Not even a lass."

Ruby placed her hands on her hips and tilted her head. "Now, that I find very hard to believe." She gave the appearance of a Catholic nun talking to a student who tried to convince her that his dog ate his homework.

* * *

"And why is that, Ruby?" Fin's voice was like warm caramel. He had also taken a coil of her hair and was rolling it between his fingers. He was definitely less than the three comfortable feet apart that people stood when conversing. He took another step closer. Her head was stuffed with fuzz. *What did he say?*

Ruby put both palms on his chest, which was meant to give her some space, but he was hard and hot. She had meant to move him out of her bubble, but instead felt his shape underneath his shirt, and she was dazed. She closed her eyes and, with that sense gone, her other senses came alive. With just the tips of her fingers, she felt thin, billowy contours, rough hairs going this way and that beneath the soft cotton of his shirt. He smelled like the forest they stood in. His breath smelled fruity as it caressed her cheek. *He's a man witch, what are they called? A warlock. That's what he is. He's a warlock that jumbles up my brain and bewitches me.* With just enough force, she moved him away and, in a breathy voice said, "You have got to stop doing that." Her eyes were squinted, and circled her index finger at him like her own magic wand, fending off a powerful spell.

"What are you talking about?" His grey eyes appeared innocent, but his smirk told her otherwise.

"You know. You know what you do, with your perfect smile and your smoky eyes," she took a deep breath, "and your smell, your . . ."

She was cut off. Fin's brows arched. "I have a smell? That can't be a good thing."

She inhaled again. "God, but you have a smell. I can taste it on my tongue."

Fin still had her hair, his fingers moved slowly and methodically in circles. "What do you taste, Ruby?" With the lightest touch, his lips brushed hers.

"Huh?" It was the most she could say. In the back of her foggy mind, she was happy because Fin didn't seem to have any more luck than she. His breathing had sped up, he became more urgent, and his mouth now came down to hers with hungry need, not the soft, butterfly kisses from seconds ago. He had stopped playing with her hair, but he did not release it. Instead, he grabbed a handful and entwined his fingers, bringing her closer.

* * *

He needed to seize the reigns, get control of his out-of-control feelings. Fin had the ability to compartmentalize his feelings when he was with a woman. There was a box for everything: fun, sexy, flirty, droning, and annoying. These feelings, whatever they were, he did not have a container for, and it was throwing him off. Being with Ruby was like taking a sledge hammer to his symmetrical boxes—she couldn't be pigeon-holed. Rather than the realist life he had painted for himself, he was now dabbling in cubism, surrealism, and expressionism—they ran together in swirls of color.

His emotional state of mind reminded him of a book he used to read to Anne, *The Color Kittens*, making all the colors of the world. The hues were beautiful as they poured through the town, but the chaos of it all always drove Fin crazy. How did it happen that this person in his arms made him mix the colors of his life, blue with green and yellow with orange? He was having feelings he couldn't define. He didn't have words to describe the warmth and the waves or the heightening of his senses when around her. The awareness was crazy, which was ridiculous because he had known her for less time than it took to break in a pair of shoes.

To the world, he emitted a laissez faire attitude, which many mistook as being low on morals. The insolence came from people creating in their minds what they thought a Sinclair was. He had been sweet-talked, lied to, and schemed against, and all those things had taken a toll on who he thought he could trust. He was always fun to be around. He was confident and self-deprecating, humorous and intelligent. He was handsome without realizing or caring about outward appearance. All qualities that made others gravitate to him. However, his circle of confidants was very small, but those that new him best were the lucky ones. He wanted people to think he didn't care, but to the core, his values were entrenched in loyalty and tradition. He would slay dragons for those he loved, and if he were to let down his guard they would see a sense of honor and duty that would be hard to match. Now, as he never had before, he wanted to share himself with another person. He wanted to trust Ruby, and he wanted her to trust him with those special pieces she didn't show other people.

There was the rub. Why would he put himself out there when she was leaving, and he was going home? It was crazy, but he wanted the most intimate part of Ruby. He wanted to leave his stamp on her, and just thinking about what he wanted to do to her made him feel like a caveman dragging his woman back to the cave by the hair. He tried to push such thoughts out of his head, tried to let her leave with her friends, but he wasn't strong enough. So, now, here she was, and he knew she wanted him too. She couldn't hide the way her breath sped up, the rise in color of her cheeks, or the pulse on the side of her neck. The question was not if they would spend these days together—that was something he knew he wouldn't give up. Instead, the question was how they would spend them. Could he be satisfied with getting to know her, sharing space with her without having her body underneath his? Could he stop at hungry kisses and innocent touches?

The situation would be funny if it didn't feel like he was on the verge of a brain embolism because of his inner struggle. He knew he didn't want to hurt her, and if that meant being with her without sliding her shirt off her shoulders and taking her in . . . *Aaargh*. Surely he could do casual. He had always risen to such a challenge. For God's sake, he wasn't an adolescent boy, out of control of his emotions. Someone must be laughing somewhere, maybe even Ian.

Fin could not say how much time went by, but unless he was going to take her right there on the trail—which he had decided he would not—he needed some space. The evidence of his need was throbbing, almost painfully. Ruby had to have known, and when he took her shoulders and scooted her back, her eyes were drawn downward like a lightning strike to a flagpole (as it were).

Her face, the color of a juicy raspberry, met his with a perfectly formed "O" on her lips. Something sounding similar to a choked hiccup came from between her lips. "Sorry about that. It must be uncomfortable."

He stared at her with an unfathomable expression. He

loved her uninhibited laughter, not the perfectly orchestrated tinkling of crystal goblets tapping together that he was used to. Ruby's laughter was a gaggle of geese flapping their wings readying for flight. He couldn't pass up the opportunity to see if he could bring more color to her already rosy cheeks. "A wee bit, yes. I'm thinking about taking you under those trees to show you just how uncomfortable." He cocked his head toward the stand of trees.

* * *

The heat she felt was similar, she imagined, to a thermometer being dunked into a boiling pot, the mercury traveling in opposite directions. It was an odd sensation, since Ruby had always felt indifferent to sex. It was fine, like a bologna sandwich for lunch. She ate it, it was okay, and when she was finished, she went about her day without thinking about the sandwich again. The feeling she had now was very different, as if his eyes, his hands, and his mouth had a direct line to her clitoris.

She wanted to know what he would feel like. Would his body be a burning flame? Would she want more? Sex could be part of her self-discovery, right? Who was she with a different lover? She would consider the act an exercise, a study in body response. Ruby had a feeling that lying with Fin would beat Psych. 101, hands down.

Her eyes widened, her palms came together, and her mouth opened, gearing up to make her proposal, but Fin beat her. "I'm just jesting Ruby, I'm not a caveman," he said with a grunt.

Ruby's lips clamped shut. *Well crap, now I can't make my pitch.* If she did, she would come across as a loose, wanton hussy. She wondered how many different shades of red she could turn. Really, the situation was mortifying. Thank goodness he couldn't read her mind. She didn't know what to make of his comment. Had he wanted more than a kiss, or was he gently sparing her feelings because he did not want to ravage her?

Plainly he was affected, but was that an automatic response, like dogs sniffing each other? Given her options on how to answer, she went for light and breezy, rather than confused and disappointed—a good choice, she felt. "Pulling me under the trees in the blanket of flowers? Yeah, I know you were joking." She made an airy "fweet" sound and waved her hand in a mock slap. *Fraud, that sounds exactly like what I want.* Goose bumps sprang up on her arms thinking about it. Ruby gazed over to the shimmering bluebells and sighed, "Alright, find me this café you keep talking about."

CHAPTER TWENTY-ONE

They spent over an hour at the café and talked while they ate waffles dripping in butter and plopped homemade sugar cubes into strong espresso. It wasn't quite a café. It was more of a round hut that reminded Ruby of pictures she had seen in *National Geographic* of the rondavels of South Africa. The main structure was made of wood stained a rich maple, the roof thatched with patches of grass and moss. There was a window to place orders and four black, wrought-iron tables outside.

Clouds had gathered, and they felt an occasional drop of rain, but they were protected under the canopy of leaves above them. It was the perfect setting for a magical blue forest.

Fin seemed relaxed as he talked about growing up on the northern shores of Scotland. He sounded like he had had an adventuresome childhood, making homemade snares for rabbits and swimming in a pond near his house. He painted vivid pictures of riding his horse along the green fields with waves crashing below and of games he played with his siblings.

She discovered the story behind the scar. He had been racing with his brother, and the last hurdle to the finish line was a low stone fence. His brother smacked him in the arm to try to get ahead, and Fin lost his balance, hitting a stone on his way down. By the time they got back to his home, blood ran down his chin and ruined his shirt. They thought it would be funny to scare their sister, so Fin jumped out at her when they heard her coming down the hall. She saw the blood and fainted, right after she screamed the roof off the house. The brothers had to do without dessert for two weeks.

He laughed so hard tears filled his eyes at the memory. He wasn't censoring every word, as he had done before, letting Ruby glimpse the man he was behind his arresting face. It was as if she were a glass being filled with a favorite drink. His words flowed into her like a smooth liquid, and she felt lucky to have the chance to spend this time with him.

* * *

As time slipped by, Fin realized that he could pass all day watching and listening to Ruby. The rise and fall of her voice, and the mundane things that came out of her mouth were gifts to him. He was mesmerized when she absentmindedly touched a small scar near her eye or played with her hair. As he watched her, he tried pinpointing why he was so struck by her. Taken separately, he supposed her face may be called ordinary but the blue of her eyes, the petal pink hue of her unbalanced lips, and her hair, when taken together, made him crazy with want. When coupled with the sparkle of humor made her utterly intoxicating.

His mind started wandering what lay beneath those clothes that were lucky enough to caress her skin. Thankfully, she did not have a model's body, a body type he loathed and could never understand the draw to. She had feminine curves in places he could imagine holding onto as she arched beneath him. He smiled as she dug into her second waffle, her lips shiny with butter. He licked his own lips and continued watching.

They both laughed as Fin held his jacket above their heads and they ran down the trail back to his car. The rain was coming in sheets by the time they reached the parking lot, and Fin quickly opened the doors. He had laughed more in this one day with Ruby than in the last few months combined. Guilt from being happy never came, instead, he felt lighter, as if a weight had been lifted off his chest.

Somewhere in his head, he thought he needed to mourn for a lifetime over the loss of Ian. If he laughed or was happy, he believed he would forget or would not be honoring the memory of his brother and his family. Now, as he shared moments of his life that made him who he was with Ruby, they included Ian. He felt nothing but fortunate with the time he and his brother had together. He was letting go of the anger he felt because Ian had been ripped from his life. Guilt and fury were replaced with glimpses of the life he could have. It was as if the pressure that had been pushing down on him was slowly easing—there was weightlessness to it.

Ruby brought him out of his reverie. "Oh my god, I'm soaking, I'm getting your seats all wet." She tried keeping her body above the seat, and was not having much luck.

Fin was more concerned with getting the heat going so they could warm up. The temperature must have dropped ten degrees. When he was satisfied, he looked over at Ruby and burst out laughing. Her hair was plastered to her head, one piece stretched across her cheek like an albino worm, and her body was held at odd angles. "What are you doing?"

"I'm trying not to ruin your seats. Do you have a towel or something?" Her arms shook as she tried to keep herself up.

Fin pushed on her lower stomach, and she collapsed. "It's only a seat. Cows get wet all the time, right? They'll be just fine." His eyes moved to her shirt that was wet and clung to her like a second skin. Her hardened nipples were cherries on a sundae. He drew in a ragged breath. Ruby looked down, and both her hands flew to cover herself. Fin groaned. The way she clutched both breasts made him feel like he was losing his mind. His head thumped against the steering wheel, which he grasped as if his life depended on it. "Ruby, I'm going to get you a dry shirt as soon as the rain lets up but, for right now, I'm going to sit like this."

* * *

"Yeah, yeah. Okay, I'm not that cold." She heard another groan and realized that he knew exactly how cold she was. *Man, if it isn't the sweaty palms and involuntary blushing, it's the unruly nipples.*

"Oh Christ, forget it!" He yanked the door open. He could have been coming from behind a waterfall for the amount of rain falling from the roof of the car. A few curses involuntarily escaped his mouth, and then he returned into the now warm, confined space. Fin had her pack on his lap and was trying to squeeze it into the back without hitting Ruby in the face. It was just the outlet he must have needed. He pushed, swore, and pushed some more. He let out a guttural roar, and the backpack made it to the back seat. As the play was acted out, Ruby sat in stunned silence, there were no words.

Fin ran his hands threw his hair, and each finger became a tiny cloud that dripped rain. When he turned to her, he was completely composed. "You can get a shirt now."

"Thanks. I think I'll just go in the back and get it." She wiggled through the gap in the seats, and Fin took up his earlier pose, his knuckles white around the wheel. Ruby unclipped the buckles and dug down to find a shirt. Finally she reached a blue cotton, long-sleeved shirt. She unwound her scarf and put it on the floorboard. She then peeked to see if he was looking. For all the big talk in her head, she suddenly felt self-conscious with him seeing her undress. He had turned on some music, but was otherwise unmoved. She pulled the shirt over her head, but it was so wet that it wouldn't come off easily. She grunted, and it smacked against the window.

"You okay back there?" His voice was back to normal, making her stomach flutter.

"I'm fine." She debated changing her pants but decided not to, as it was only the cuffs that had gotten really wet. The heater would dry them off soon enough. When she made her way back to the front, she saw that he had changed into a dry t-shirt. "When did you change?"

He breathed evenly and looked over to Ruby. "I had a t-shirt on under my other shirt." He peered out the windshield. "It looks like it has let up. Shall we?"

With that, they drove through green countryside speckled by quaint towns with French names that oozed with history. The wipers kept time like a metronome, and the back and forth motion made Ruby's lids close, as if the sound was a lullaby.

* * *

Fin was happy she had fallen asleep. It gave him time to listen to nothing but the rain hit the glass, a soothing sound, familiar from growing up in rainy Scotland. He was also able watch Ruby. Her lips were slightly parted, her breathing slow and even. He felt a tenderness he hadn't known, but imagined it was similar to a father for his child. He chuckled to himself, hardly that. He moved a lock of hair that had fallen over her eye. No, hardly that.

Fin wanted Ruby to see the approach to the village that was coming up. He put his hand on her cheek and, while sleeping, she nuzzled into his warm hand and gave a humming sound. He took his hand away and said her name.

Her eyes moved under her lids and then fluttered open. She gave him a content smile and breathed deeply, bringing her shoulders up to stretch. She looked out her window. "Where are we? Did I sleep for long?" The car was stopped along the side of the road. "Tell me we didn't run out of gas."

"We did not run out of gas," he said, grinning. "We're coming into Dinant, the village we'll be staying in, and I wanted you to see it from a distance." He pulled back onto the road and went around a curve.

A grey, rocky cliff rose dramatically behind a village lined with tall, narrow buildings, each touching another. The only way to say where one started and the other stopped was by the deep colors: maroon, forest green, linen cream, and brown. The centerpiece was a church reaching above them, all in grey limestone with a black spire that looked like an onion balancing on top. They crossed the murky black water of the Meuse River and entered the town. Ruby stared up at the sheer rock in front of her. "What's that on the top?"

"It's the citadel. We can see it tomorrow if you'd like." Fin geared down as they made their way into Dinant.

* * *

The roads narrowed, and they had to wait their turn while another car passed them, heading the opposite direction. It occurred to Ruby that they would be staying overnight, something she must have known but had pushed out of her mind. Her mouth was suddenly very dry. Had he already made arrangements? Did he reserve one room? Surely, he wouldn't assume. She was at odds with herself about how she would feel. A part of her was tingly with the thought of sharing a room, but the other part was scared to death. What if he liked big boobs? After today's impromptu wet t-shirt contest, he knew her shortcomings in that area. What if he didn't like the way she did things? She and Scott had definitely not been experimental. Then the real zinger: What if she just didn't like it? Maybe she was fated to having average sex, something she knew she was supposed to do and went about it, like brushing her teeth. My god, she was working herself into a tizzy, overthinking what she didn't even know.

The car stopped outside a buttercream brick building. The color made Ruby want to dip her finger in and swirl it around, as if it was a heavily frosted birthday cake. As she looked at the hotel through the windshield, Fin came around and opened her door. She got out and stood on the sidewalk.

The hotel was similar to the other buildings in width. It was five stories, with four tall French doors spanning the length on every floor, delineating each room. Outside each window were three-foot Juliet balconies that could have been a quilling art project with all the black wrought-iron swirls making them up. The curtains were all open, and some of the doors were letting in the cool breeze, protected from the rain by brick outcroppings. Above the main door was a simple sign in black letters that read "Billet-doux." Ruby tilted her head and put a finger to her cheek. Fin's arm wrapped around her shoulder, and he leaned down to her ear, gently saying, "Love Letters," as if reading her mind. "Love Letters," she loved it.

"Why don't we get settled, and then I'll come and get our bags." He opened the door and held it for Ruby.

She immediately felt as if a stampede of horses were galloping over her chest. Her hand went to her throat, giving the appearance of person making it out of the desert after days without water. She walked through the beautiful wooden doors that were painted glossy black, with beveled panes from top to bottom. They walked across the floor, which was a small, hexagonal carpet of white tiles, bordered with a black and white basket weave. Greeting them inside the reception area was a large, round, heavy wooden pedestal table in the same shiny black.

Sitting on top was a lead crystal vase that was two feet tall with wide scalloped edges and holding a lovely bouquet of mixed flowers. Margie would drool onto the floor if she could see the kaleidoscope of texture and color. To Ruby, it was filled with the best of all flowers: purple hydrangea, Angelique tulips, white peonies, light green mums, and a sprinkling of mokara orchids and buttery yellow bupleurum. Ruby couldn't stop herself from leaning in and breathing in the heady fragrance.

When she looked up, Fin leaned against the Carrera marble counter with his usual, relaxed, self-assured posture. When she got closer, she realized that he was speaking French to the desk clerk. *Of course he is. He could probably ride a horse while standing on his hands reciting Shakespeare, in French.*

Ruby had taken the required three years of high school French, but was limited to "bonjour," "au revoir," and one she used daily in class, "je ne sais pas." He looked over his shoulder at her, straightened, started walking toward her, stopped in mid stride, and stood watching her. Everything stood still. Though her heart was beating, a calm had come over her. She felt like she could be the steam coming off a hot spring, weightless and hovering over the ground below.

CHAPTER TWENTY-TWO

Fin had asked Hans to make arrangements at Billet-doux before leaving. After grumbling an indistinguishable string of words, the older man said he would, but until Fin had keys in his hand, he wasn't sure Hans had come through. So far, all of his requests seemed to have been followed. Fin smiled when he thought about Hans making the reservations and about what the person on the other end of the line must have been put through. Fin spoke to the clerk, made further preparations, and turned to get Ruby.

She stood next to the flowers they had passed on the way in. His breath caught in his chest. The look she was giving him was ethereal, showing him the true meaning of being breathless. In front of him was a picture he wanted to keep, an old, faded photograph that he could pull out of his pocket, unfold, and cherish. Fin stood still so he could memorize everything—the colors, the glow of her face, her slightly parted lips with only a hint of a smile, and the breeze that ruffled her hair when someone opened the door behind her.

He felt as if he were on a moving sidewalk when he started toward her. Something mechanical propelled him forward, and his legs were gliding. He bent down and kissed the edge of her mouth. "Our rooms are ready. Let's get you up, and I'll get the bags in a bit." He smiled down at her, and she put her arm through his.

* * *

Fatigue from the climb up the four flights of stairs had

quelled her nerves. The hallway had the same, creamy white
of the exterior, and two iron and glass half-moon tables, each
with smaller versions of the arrangements in the reception
are, flanked the walls. The carpet was well-padded, short
diamond textured pile with the same cream color. Somehow,
it was without a single stain. Four doors ran the length of the
corridor, each in black lacquered paint with a brass oval
number plate.

Fin held a key that looked similar to a treasure box key
Ruby had while growing up. It was large, heavy, and very
old world—more like a toy. The door made a loud clink
when the lock slid back, and he opened the door.

If there were hotels in fairytales, this would be it. Ruby
walked across the room and pulled open the floor-to-ceiling
French doors. She had a spectacular view of the church, with
the Meuse River in the background. It very well could have
that been an old movie set had lowered this scenery as a
backdrop. It all looked so surreal. A break in the clouds
formed a spotlight on the river, and the few boats moored
there rocked back and forth with the current.

Ruby leaned against the rail, looked down to the road
below, and saw a handful of people braving the wet
weather. The rain had let up, and the clouds were not so
heavy. When she held her hand out, it was still raining, but
if felt more like the residual spray from a shower. She
realized that there was no sound behind her. Maybe Fin had
gone to his room. She turned. He had definitely not gone.

He rested a shoulder against the wood of the bedpost
with his arms crossed, watching her. He stood perfectly still,
his head slightly tilted with an unreadable expression on his
face. She would have given her left toe to know what he was
thinking. She walked back into the room, and he unfolded
himself and came toward her. He stopped inches from her

stilled body and glided his finger from her brow to her chin, and then put his finger into his mouth. "I see it's still raining."

Ruby reached up and touched her face. Droplets of moisture clung to her skin, giving the illusion that she had just come out of a steam room. He ran his finger along her eyelashes, catching the rainwater. She closed her eyes, not sure she could stop herself from dragging his lips down to hers. Her whole body shivered with his touch.

"Are you cold?" His voice was velvet.

Rather than tell him she was the farthest she had ever been from cold, she opened her eyes and met his. "A little. It must be the breeze."

He looked at her for five heartbeats. She knew this because her heart was thumping so loudly in her ears she thought people on the street could hear it. He moved toward the doors and quietly closed them. "Do you like your room?"

"Oh, my gosh. I was so amazed with the view I haven't even looked at the room." The room was absolutely lovely, not large but perfect for the setting. The walls were the color of an old battleship, and the floors were carpeted the same as in the hallway. The focal point was the bed, which was one of only three pieces of furniture in the room. It was a double, four-poster bed in the same black trim as around the windows. On each post was a tied swatch of white gossamer fabric that was as delicate as tissue paper. The bedding was also white, with a puffy feather-tic that looked like a big marshmallow on top, perfect for jumping into.

Ruby felt her face grow hot, so moved on to the bathroom. There was no door, just a large opening. The carpet ended, and continued with tile—the same as in the lobby. A large claw-foot tub with chrome feet was set at an angle with a view out the French doors and beyond. There was a plate rail at a ninety-degree angle in the corner above the bath, lined with cream, honeycomb pillar candles. Next to the tub was a pedestal sink with a rectangular, shiny nickel mirror above it. Behind a narrow door was a single toilet.

This hotel was worth the expense. Heck, she would eat only bread for a week to stay here for two nights. She walked back out to the main room. Fin sat on the edge of the bed and smiled. She then noticed the round night table. A silver, hourglass vase held five brilliant red poppies. Confused, she put her face closer and then looked at Fin. She had told him that she and Poppy had gotten their names when her dad had come to the door holding a bouquet of ruby red poppies on her parents' first date. "Did you do this?" She looked at him expectantly.

His hands rested on his knees. He looked up through his long lashes and gave her a lopsided grin. "It sounded like you really miss your sister, so I wanted to connect you two a bit." Before she could stop herself, she put her hands on his shoulders. Her weight made Fin fall back onto the bed, and she tumbled after. Her lips were on his, and he laughed against her mouth. "You like them then?"

"I love them. Thank you." She was propped up on her arms and looked down at his face. Fin held her wrists and tugged gently. She fell back onto his chest, her arms straight out like airplane wings. She felt his muscles tighten, and a lightning bolt traveled the length of her body.

* * *

The heat of Ruby's body on his was more than he could take. He needed to feel her underneath him. He rolled over, not letting her go. Her shocked face would have been comical if he wasn't fighting so hard not to rip her clothes off. His mouth came down on hers and gave little need to guess about his desire for her. His head spun as his tongue played with hers. He heard her breathing becoming ragged as his hand found the hem of her shirt. She jumped when he touched the warm skin of her stomach. It would have literally killed him if she told him to stop, but he wasn't the type to have someone come unwillingly. He was about to apologize for his forward behavior when she relaxed and moaned deep in her throat. That was all he needed. *It would be easier to stop the tide*, he thought. His hand slid up and cupped one breast. It fit perfectly in his palm, and he squeezed the puckered nipple underneath her bra. Her breath caught. With his own breath speeding, all he could say was her name. He felt every curve of her body under his weight, and nearly went up in flames. He wanted her.

Somewhere in his head, he heard a conversation he had had with himself, promising that this type of thing would not happen. A wicked laugh escaped his lips. He rose up to his forearms and looked down at her. "Ruby?" It was a question she needed to answer. Her eyes were the clearest blue he had ever seen, and they were wide with her own questions. He didn't know how experienced she was, but a fury ran in his blood as he thought of her with someone else. He wanted every part of her, and then wanted her again and again. He had never had such feelings before, a bone-deep need and possession.

It had always been sex for Fin—something he enjoyed— but these feelings were very different. He wanted everything to be perfect for her. He wanted her to writhe underneath him with complete abandon. He wanted her to have the emotions he was having—the searing heat, the crazy beating heart—and he wanted to hear her moan his name as he ravaged her. It was a good thing he was lying down, because his head spun with the passion that pulsated through him, all his blood pooling below his belt.

He looked up, saw the tub, and remembered his plans for her. This trip was to both spoil and to spend time with her, but he couldn't seem to keep his hands off her body. He felt like he was losing his mind. If he were, it was the best of all possible worlds. He had meant for her to luxuriate in a hot bath and walk along the river. He had already arranged for a late dinner to be sent up to the room so that they could enjoy the view, just the two of them.

With every ounce of willpower, he rolled onto his back, threw his arms above his head, and growled. "Ruby, I can't seem to keep my hands off you. I'd say I'm sorry, but I don't like to lie. I *will* say that my intention was to play the gentleman." He rolled his head over to look at her. She stared up at the ceiling, seeming dazed but happy. Happy was a good sign.

* * *

Ruby giggled because, in her wildest dreams, being in a hotel like this with a man like Fin should not have happened, but now that dream was real and lying next to her. She turned her head. Their noses almost touched, which made her laugh harder. "How were you going to play the gentleman?" Fin told her his plans. "Ooo, that does sound nice. I'd say it sounds better than what we were doing, but I'm not big on dishonesty either." She knew she had turned every possible color of red, but she didn't care.

"Okay, you stay here," Fin replied. "I'm going to start your bath, if I can get up. You're killing me, you know." He touched her nose and heaved himself up, groaning the whole way.

Ruby felt her body float above her, just like in the movies, when the recently deceased watch themselves from above. She could not stop smiling. Fin made her feel more in five minutes than she had ever felt with anyone else. Well, with the one other person she had been with, anyway. She rolled onto her stomach and buried her face in the feathers. She still felt his weight on her, his warmth, and the way he had kissed her. *My goodness, if he had more time, what else could he do?* She wanted that feeling again. As if the gods had listened, he was suddenly on top of her. His body ran the length of hers, and his breath was warm against her ear.

"Ruby, really you're killing me, Christ I want to feel you, bury myself in you." He pressed harder against her backside. "Okay, you need to get up right now, or you're not leaving this bed for the duration. Which one is it?" His voice took on an animal quality.

Ruby had never had anyone talk to her like that. She felt empowered that she could bring out those reactions in another person. She wiggled against him and was suddenly on her back, her hands pinned above her head.

"That's your answer?" His eyes were rolling clouds heated before a storm. His mouth left a trail of lightning from her jaw down to her collarbone.

She was about to combust into a pile of ashes. She arched her neck to let him have more of her. *What was it I was going to do?* She could barely remember her name. *Ah, the bath. Right.* She smelled lavender filling the room. In a groaned whisper, she managed to get out, "Did you, aaah, put lavender in the, ooh, water?"

He was on her ear and tickled her with, "Uh-huh."

It was then that she remembered she hadn't showered, and he was moving lower, past her collarbone. Before she became completely incoherent, she needed to decide what she was doing. He still had her wrists in one hand and was touching the sway of her back with the other, stoked and kneaded, bringing her closer.

She needed to soak and think. She pulled her arms, and he let go. "Are you okay?" He asked. There was no anger in his voice, but he asked it through clenched teeth, his jaw tight. He was propped on his elbow and moved a wavy strand of hair from her forehead.

Ruby scrunched up her face in a pained apology. "I think I will take a bath. Is that okay? I'm sorry."

He relaxed his mouth. "Ruby, its fine. Don't be sorry. I just want you to do what feels right. Don't worry that I'm about to explode. I'm sure I won't *really* explode. That doesn't actually happen, so don't worry your pretty head." He gave her a heart-stopping smile. He amazed her. He lightened the mood and put her at ease—he put her first. "I should probably check out my room anyway, right?" He made his way off the bed and held out a hand. "I'm right next to your room. You take your time and come and get me when you're ready. Does that sound good?"

Ruby stood next to him, still holding his hand. It felt amazing, capable of keeping her safe and taking her places she hadn't known existed. She wanted to kick herself for stopping him, but she needed some space to collect her thoughts. Everything swirled in her head, which wasn't necessarily a bad thing, but she just needed to settle herself down. "That sounds great. Thanks for getting my bath ready. I'll come and get you." She gave him an impish smile, stood on her toes, and kissed his soft lips.

Fin looked at the bed, which had an imprint of their bodies in the thick down, and then looked back at Ruby. He dragged his hands through his hair and groaned. "Okay, have a nice soak. See you in a bit."

CHAPTER TWENTY-THREE

Ruby walked into the bathroom, and her mouth dropped open. Fin had lit the candles, and with the sun lowering in the sky, the light shimmered with warmth. The claw-foot tub was deep, filled nearly to the top with lavender scented bubbles. He had placed a thick, white towel on a small black bamboo table within easy reach. Somewhere he had also found a white bath mat and laid it down next to the bath.

She peeled off her clothes, folded them, put them on the floor, and dipped one foot in. The water was hot, just how she liked it. There was nothing worse than trying to unwind and becoming grumpy in tepid water. This was a relaxing bath that she could spend a good hour in. She now stood in the tub and slowly lowered herself into the water. Her weight caused the bubbles to float up around her cheeks, making a snap, crackle, and pop sounds in her ears. She leaned her head back and rested it against a towel. Fin remembered everything. Her arms were weightless in the water and floated like two buoys anchored in the river outside. Intoxicated by the smell of lavender, she took a deep breath through her nose.

As the sun was angled to the side of the French doors, it turned the room golden, the clouds and the misty rain adding the dreamscape. Ruby closed her eyes and thought about the last few hours she had spent with Fin. There was an obvious physical attraction, of course. His face was gorgeous, but it was the easy comfortable way he held himself that made him so amazing. When he glided across a room, all eyes followed him just to see where he was going.

On top of that, he was funny, nice, cared about other people's feelings, and always seemed sincere.

Despite this, he seemed guarded—not that she though he was hiding something. Chloris said that he didn't talk about himself much, and the fact that he didn't divulge information was odd. Most people love to talk about themselves; they love to hear their own voice. Today he had given her glimpses of growing up, but there was something in his eyes that clouded over, and he turned the conversation back to her.

Ruby then thought back to when she first met Scott. There were never butterflies in her stomach, even on their first date. He made her comfortable, like a bowl of soup, but it had gone downhill from there. Yup, "soup" would best describe her feelings toward Scott. Fin, however, was like a swarm of bees that made her entire body vibrate. With Fin she felt volts of electricity at his touch and of his breath-catching looks. She couldn't wait to hear what he had to say next, make a funny joke, tell a story of the ocean, place a hand on her back, glue his eyes to hers when she talked, or experience the intense, fiery look he had when she caught him watching her. She wanted this and, even if she never saw him after these two days, she still wanted him. She never imagined a time in her life when she would feel like this again, and she was not going to pass it up. There was no more struggling back and forth with emotions or with what was right or wrong. Being with Fin was most definitely right. She closed her eyes and floated.

* * *

Fin had been down to the car to get their bags. He now sat on his bed and stared into space. He memorized the feel of Ruby, the heaving of her chest meeting his, and the way her neck fell back for him. He dredged up the taste of her lips, both sweet and salty and the soft noises she made when he touched a sensitive spot. He wanted to know all of her spots and to learn her body. What had he been doing all these years? The women he had been with before Ruby were mere bodies—they filled up space and time, and he used them to follow his instincts. Ruby, made him want to worship her. He wanted intimacy to be about her as much as he wanted it for himself. He never left a lover not reaching climax, but it was a rote exercise: put hand here, squeeze here, tongue goes here, pump, pump, pump, and done.

He would have to re-learn with Ruby. He wanted to start from the beginning—these feelings were what he was meant to have with another person. It stunned him that he had never realized, never had dreamt that there could be more, so much more. Beyond the physical, he was enthralled with the simple act of listening to her. When she talked about her sister, her face changed, and he knew by looking at her how much Poppy meant to her. The way she scrunched her pert nose or bit down on her thumb nail when she was nervous fascinated him. She had a subtle sense of humor that often caught him by surprise, and her laugh was genuine and organic. She had her own thoughts about the world, and she wasn't like the many others who said what they thought he wanted to hear. Something that had never happened to him before now was that he was content to simply to sit with her in complete silence.

He looked at her bag. He should probably take it to her room so she could change when she was done bathing. *I'll just put it inside the door and call to her that it's there*, he rationalized. *Then I'll leave . . . Right, I'll leave and wait for her to come to my room.* He put Ruby's bag over his shoulder and walked to her room. He lightly knocked, but heard nothing; no sound. *She must still be soaking.* He turned the key and eased the door open. *I may as well step in and put it by the bed.* "Ruby, I have your bag. I'll put it by the bed. Come and get me when you're ready."

* * *

Ruby thought she heard a knock, but it was so quiet in the room that it could have been a car outside. Then she heard the distinct hollow click of the lock sliding. She sat up, causing waves in the tub. Fin. She had hoped he would come back, but hadn't wanted to wish for too much. Then he called to her. She shivered, even though the water was still hot. "Stay." She could have been someone else in the room for the foreignness of her voice. It sounded shaky and airy, the same as her body felt. There was no sound from the other side of the wall. Maybe he had beaten it out of the room before she got the nerve up to say her one stupid word. *Aaargh, he would have heard if I had said it sooner, or maybe louder.*

She dunked her head under the water and screamed, opening her mouth wide. The water filled her mouth and then came out in a fast jet. When she ran out of breath, she popped up and felt bubbles melting down her face. She wiped them out of her eyes with her fingers. He was there, resting against the frame of the doorway. Her face went from warm to hot and then to something beyond—a sensation she could not put into words.

"You okay, Ruby?" With a sideways grin in place, he looked like a cat watching a mouse.

"I . . . I . . . " She blinked the water out of her eyes and couldn't string a coherent group of words together, even if she knew what she wanted to say, which she did not.

"You what?" He unfolded himself and slowly walked into the room. He was not a house cat—he was something more dangerous. He was prowling. His eyes were heated and his body was tense under the relaxed façade. "You what, Ruby?" His voice was molten lava, slow and hot.

Her head swam. She couldn't remember where she was. "I . . . I didn't think . . . I didn't think you heard me." Ruby's voice was a murmur that floated into the space between them.

He came forward until he towered above her. "I heard you. I think I would have heard you if I had been in another building." His voice was low. "Are you sure, Ruby, because I'm not going to be able to stop again."

The flicker of the candle cast dancing shadows across his face, making him seem even more predatory. She had already decided what she wanted—she wanted him, she just didn't know how to ask. "Yes." There, even though she had been reduced to single-word sentences, she got out an answer. "Yes, yes." She tried to smile.

Fin stood completely still and looked down at her, searching her face for something before he spoke. "Lean back," he said. She lowered back down to the towel as if a string was attached to her back. He ran a finger along the beads of her necklace and she broke. She had heard his words and knew she should answer, but couldn't conjure a single word. Her eyes were wide and looked up at him. He walked to the table where he had put the towel and grabbed a hotel shampoo that was on the shelf below. He knelt behind her and poured the thick liquid directly onto her hair. His hands massaged her scalp, lathering the shampoo. His fingers were heavenly, slow but firm. Her eyes closed, and her body melted. He reached for the nozzle. "Now sit up and I'll rinse the suds out. Keep your eyes closed." He fiddled with the temperature and then a waterfall cascaded over her head. He tilted her head back with one hand and ran the water through her hair with the other.

* * *

When Fin heard her single word, "stay," his world disappeared. Nothing else existed but that single word. He calmed himself for a moment before he went to her, and then all he could see was the tip of her head peaking above the bubbles in the tub. He thought she was yelling. The sound reminded him of when he and Anne and Ian guessed at what the other was saying underneath the water in the swimming pool. He would wait until she surfaced, unless he had to make a rescue. He smiled. She was absolutely captivating. When she finally did come up, he had to hold himself in place with some effort; otherwise, he would have dove into the tub with her.

Mini avalanches streamed down Ruby's face and covered her eyes when she popped out of the water. She had no idea that he stood so close or of the carnal thoughts going through his head. He needed to make sure she knew what he was asking, because he had only so much restraint. There would be no going back once he had his answer. Again, she said only one word, "yes," quietly but unwavering. It was the word he was holding his breath to hear.

As much as he wanted to scoop her up and bury himself in her, he needed to slow down. He wanted this night to be something she would remember every time she closed her eyes, smelled lavender, or heard the rain. "Lean back." Now that he knew she would be his, he could take his time. He ran his hand along her neck. "This is pretty. Where did you get it?" He examined the beads of her necklace.

Ruby's own hand came up to feel it. "Poppy gave it to me before I left on this trip. Each of the colors means something different, very new age." She smiled humorously.

"I like it. It suits you." He liked it even more knowing that her sister had given it to her, and not a boyfriend. He poured shampoo directly onto her head. His fingers felt wonderful in her hair. He had never washed a woman's hair, but he would do it again. It was a lover's touch, and it was erotic. Her eyes closed when he was about to rinse the soap. As the stream of water washed out the shampoo, it also washed the bubbles that clung to her body, bringing the water down, just touching the top of her pink nipples.

Fin touched the side of one breast with the backs of his fingers and then went deeper into the water, along her side. She opened her eyes, and they locked on his. His hands shook as he realized that he had never wanted anything to be so right in his life.

He took the towel he had put on the table and slowly ran it through her hair, making sure it didn't touch the water. Ruby's hair danced around her face in wet, messy waves. He put the towel over his shoulder and stood up, holding his hand out for her. Her eyes widened and she blinked like an owl, snapping her long lashes up and down. She looked at his hand and then back to his face, parting her lips with the smallest hint of a smile. She then took his hand as he eased her out of the water.

Fin couldn't keep his eyes from taking in her body. He watched bubbles slide down her breasts and stomach. They pooled in the tuft of light brown hair between her legs. He held her arm out. "My god you're beautiful Ruby." Her nipples stood out like ripe fruit he couldn't wait to taste. He wanted to run his hands down the curve of her hips and remove the suds that lingered here and there. She stepped out with one foot and then the other, dripping onto the lush white rug. Fin looked down at his hand as if he had never seen it before. "Well this is something new. My hands are shaking."

Ruby bit down on her thumb nail. "My whole body is."

"Christ, I'm sorry." He wrapped the towel around her and started drying her off. "Is that better?" He rubbed her arms and shoulders.

"I'm drier, but I'm still shivering. I don't think it's the water."

His eyes met hers. "Uh," she looked down. *That* he could not allow. He put a finger under her chin and brought her head back up. "I need you to look at me. You want to be with me, right?" He gave her one last chance. His heart burned in his chest, as if it were too full in there—as if something had to expand or it would break open.

"I do want you, but I . . . but I don't . . . "she clenched her jaw…"ummm, I haven't been with a lot of people. I'm nervous." His chest broke open, and he soared. He scooped her up behind the knees with his hand on her back and carried her into the bedroom.

* * *

When he held out his hand to her, all she could think is that she wanted to be in his arms. She felt no embarrassment standing in front of him, wearing only bubbles. He then said that she was beautiful. No one had ever told her that, and she knew his words went beyond her body, which his eyes were burning trails down. She didn't know how she knew, but she just did. When he said he was shaking, she realized he was nervous too, which somehow that made her feel better. He had to have had more experience than she, and yet, this was different for him, too. *He must have a lifetime more of experience. What am I doing?* That was the funny part, she had no idea. Well she should tell him, tell him she would be clumsy and awkward, great, she shook.

She looked down, but felt his finger bring her eyes back to his. "You want to be with me, right?" *Crap, he must think I'm crazy. Kissing, telling him to stop, pushing him down on the bed, stopping, telling him I'm going to take a bath. A bath? Who does that when they're being so thoroughly kissed that they can't remember their own name? Yep, he must think I'm crazy. I need to tell him before he runs.* She couldn't help but bumble through the reasons behind her hesitation.

Rather than laugh or poo-poo what she said, the sun absolutely shown on his face. His smile could have made the devil himself cry with how happy he looked. He swung her up into his arms and made his way to the bedroom. She was laid down where they had left off before, in a cloud of feathers. Then he was gone. Ruby watched as he came back, carrying a candle. He placed it on the table beside the bed. The sun was low, and the sky, now pink, outlined the silver, billowy clouds in oranges and yellows. If she hadn't been so awestruck by the scenery inside, she would have described it as breathtaking. Nothing could take her attention from Fin as he stood next to her. The towel was tangled around her waist, and he looked down at her with a mischievous grin. "Your skin is all flushed."

Ruby looked down and covered her breasts with her hand and arm. "It is? It must be the water."

He knelt on the bed beside her and sat back on his legs. He slid his hand along her cheek, his voice quiet, "Here," his hand stroked her neck, "and here." Ruby couldn't help but giggle behind her lips. He took her hand and set it next to her. "Leave that there." The room was cool, but she was heated from the inside. Waves of warmth touched her most intimate areas, and rolled with sensation. "And here." He circled her left nipple in slow rings, causing her hips to move and her breath to catch. He moved to the other one very diplomatically and began circling with his tongue. The sensation made it feel as if she would go through the bed. She arched up to meet him, putting her hands on his shoulders, trying to hold herself onto the bed. His hands wondered. He touched her calf, peeled back the towel, and squeezed her thigh. He then stroked between her legs while suckling and blowing on her breasts.

It was too much—there was nowhere for the heat to go. "Fin, Fin." What did she need to ask? "I can't, I don't . . . Oh, my god." She moaned and moved under his touch.

"What do you want, Ruby?" His lips slid back and forth along her stomach.

"I wa . . . I want . . . "

"This. Do you want this?" He slowly slid a finger into her slick opening. "Ahh Ruby, you're so wet. Does that feel good?"

Ruby grabbed at his hand. Her voice came out in a long breath, hitching at his name. "Oh my. Oh, Fin." He slid two more fingers in and stretched her wide, stroking in and out. He pushed gently on her stomach. She met his hand and moved her head to the side, certain she was about to explode or scream. She searched for something to bring some relief. There was a heat in her stomach that traveled down her legs, through her arms, and to her fingertips, with nowhere to go.

* * *

Fin watched her move and almost lost himself. She was so close, but he wanted more. He removed his fingers, bringing his mouth down on hers. "Not yet." He feasted. His movements were no longer tender, but hungry and wanton. He pulled his shirt over his head, barely broke contact, and threw it to the floor. Her hands clawed at his back as he made his way lower. He put his hand on the inside of her thigh and eased them wider. She pushed them together, and Fin chuckled. "Uh-uh. No you don't. Relax for me." His voice melted over her as he teased her legs open with a gentle caress. On a sigh, Ruby slowly let her legs fall open, but squeezed her eyes shut as if waiting for a shot from a doctor. He couldn't let that continue. He pushed himself up so he was directly at eye level, and kissed her jaw. "Ruby, open your eyes. Look at me."

Her face was still tense, scrunched, and her jaw was clenched, but her eyes opened a fraction. "Yeah?" she squeaked between her teeth.

His finger traced her bottom lip, causing her to relax her tortured jaw. "This isn't supposed to be painful. It won't be painful. Trust me." His hand traveled down her stomach and then further. His fingers began playing in her folds. They dipped in out and circled as he watched her with smoldering eyes. "That doesn't hurt, does it?"

A heat built where he lingered. Her breath came faster, her neck arched back. "No," she said on a whisper.

"Do you want me to stop?" There was a mischievous tone in his voice

Ruby snapped her eyes open. "No. No, don't stop. Oh my god, no . . . "

"I won't stop, Ruby. I'm not going to stop. I won't stop." His mouth kissed the bone at her hip, and his fingers still fondled. He replaced his hand with his mouth and, this time, her lids closed in a sensual moan.

* * *

She had never felt anything so exquisite. One hand grabbed at his hair while the other clung to the bedcovering underneath her as his tongue swirled and stroked. He found her most sensitive spot, and suckled. Ruby almost bucked off the bed. She needed to ask for something, ask for something because muscles tugged and everything got bigger in her head and the heat was more than heat—it was a brand, scorching hot. Fin didn't let her go, even though she moved either further away or closer, she didn't know. His strong hands on her hips brought her nearer. Her body was a bow string, taught with the tension. When she couldn't take anymore, when she wanted it to stop, and go on forever, there was a rush of release. She flew, shattering through the sky. As if from a distance, she heard something and realized it was her own voice crying out his name. She floated on waves of warmth that rolled through every part of her body.

Time ceased to exist. She wasn't sure how long it took her to come back to earth. Her body was soft and pliant, not the white hot it was before, but the glowing embers of a spent fire. Ruby felt Fin close, but he didn't touch her. Not able to open her eyes, her head snuggled into the puffy down. She thought she heard Fin move and slowly peeled back her eyelids. He had left the rest of his clothes on the floor and slid next to her. She was struck. Of course she had daydreamed about what he would look like, but her fantasy held nothing to the reality that snaked along her side. He was a Michelangelo sculpture in human form. His muscles were well used, long and lean, not what one got from pumping weights in a gym, but from working with his hands and legs. He kissed his way back up her body, slowly and softly. He nibbled at her neck. "That didn't hurt, did it?" There was a sly smile on his perfectly formed lips.

Ruby's mouth turned up at the corners. She felt giddy. "I've never felt anything quite like that. Can you do it again?" She stretched her shoulders, only half joking, though she laughed.

* * *

"I'm not quite done with you yet, and then we can do whatever you desire. I'm yours for as long as you want." It struck him then that what he said went beyond these two days. If he could ask for anything, it would be more time,

but he would never say those words to Ruby. He didn't
want to pressure her into changing the course she was on.
He knew how important this trip was to her.

Before he could think of more excuses to see her again,
her hand ran down his arm. Her fingers trembled, and she
seemed unsure as her eyes followed the path her hand took.
Her hesitancy made him want her even more, which he
thought impossible.

When she reached low on his stomach, her head came
back up and met his. "Can I?" She looked so innocent.

He put his hand on the back of hers and guided her to
his throbbing manhood. Her hand jumped when she
touched the smooth flesh under her fingers, and her eyes
and mouth opened in surprise. Now it was Fin's turn to
moan, "Ruby I need you, I need to feel you all around me,
taking me in." She shivered with his words as his hand
made another trip between her legs. She arched her back,
her breasts touching his chest. "Christ Ruby, I can't wait."

"I don't want you to wait"

He moved over her, covering her, his arms holding most
of his weight. Her knees came up and opened for him. He
couldn't wait. He had thought to go slow to let her adjust,
but he couldn't. He drove in completely. He heard her
breath catch, and he instantly stilled, didn't move one inch.
"Did I hurt you? Tell me if I hurt you." *Fuck, what am I
thinking?* He looked at her face. She seemed more surprised
than pained.

"No, I'm fine. I'm good. Just give me a second." Her
breath became more even, and her face glistened. He felt her
relax around him, and her hips moved up minutely.

"Are you okay?" He pulled out a fraction.

"No. I mean, yeah. It feels . . . Don't leave. Stay." She
moved her hips again. He completely filled her, and the heat

started.

"I'm right here, Ruby. Here." He came back to her.

"How do you . . . What are you . . . " Her voice became part of the still air around them.

Fin reached for a pillow and, as she curved her back, he slid it under her bottom, angling her up. He moved with her rhythm, following her lead. Ruby kneaded her fingers into his buttocks, her head thrown back. He felt completely out of control and at the same time amazed that he was stirred to this emotion

"Please, please, ooh." Fin knew from her voice that the world was falling around her.

He held himself back, clenched his teeth, and waited for Ruby. He wanted to see her shatter. "Ruby, look at me. I want to see you." She looked through her lashes just as she climaxed. She opened her mouth and let out a low moan from deep within her chest. He met her with one last thrust, and they fell together. He collapsed onto to her body, now dewy with spent desire.

They lay for minutes, their breath matching each other's. Neither said a word. Fin realized that he was probably crushing her under his weight, and rolled over onto his back. "Lord, Ruby." A rush of air blew from his filled cheeks.

She crawled onto his prone body, warm from their lovemaking. She smiled huge and wide down at him. "I think I made a good decision. I'm telling you, everyone should experience that."

Fin wanted to punch her previous boyfriend straight in the face. How could he have not brought her to climax? She had so much passion and gave herself wholly. *Idiot*. On the other hand, thinking of him with her, he would have wanted to do more than punch him. He tucked her head under his chin and wrapped his arms around her. "Are you cold?" His lips brushed against her hair, floral and wonderful.

She giggled as her fingers played in the wiry hair on his chest. "I am so far from cold. I don't even remember the feeling."

"I just need to say Ruby; it has never been like that for me. You're amazing," he said as he stroked her hair.

CHAPTER TWENTY-FOUR

When Ruby had told Fin that she had never experienced anything like their lovemaking, she did not mention that she didn't want anyone else but her to experience it with him. He would laugh her right out the door.

She didn't believe him. How could she? He must have had dozens of lovers, but the way he held her made her feel cherished. Even if the moment wouldn't last, at least she could pretend. She would take everything she could during her time with him.

"Uh-huh," Fin said as Ruby swirled around his nipple with her finger, watching it pucker. *Strange. What a weird body part.* Fin lifted his chest, which lifted her head. He put a finger under her chin and pierced her with his smoky eyes. "I'm not just saying that, Ruby. Before I was with you, I don't know what it was, but it wasn't anything like what just happened with you." She felt her cheeks becoming warm. He took the back of her head and drew her closer, his lips tenderly brushing hers. "I'll make you believe me."

Before she could make some snarky remark, there was a knock on the door and a male voice stated, *"Service en chambre."* Completely panicked, Ruby jumped back, underestimating her velocity. Her butt hit the floor first, and her legs flew out in a "V." She looked like part of a contortionist routine gone terribly wrong. Her head somehow managed to get halfway under the bed, as did one of her arms, while the other frantically grabbed for any kind of cover. She felt the feather tic and started to tug, which didn't do much good since Fin was still lying on it. "Move.

Move," Ruby said in a snarling whisper. "Who is that? Give me the sheets or the blanket or something." Her hand still yanked to no avail, and she tried pulling her head, which now seemed to be wedged between the bed frame and the carpet, from beneath the bed.

Another knock came, this one louder. *"Excusez-moi, service."* She pulled her head out, only to meet Fin, who regarded her with the most dumbstruck look a person could have. He howled, his booming laugh filling the room.

"Attensdez une minute!" Fin slid gracefully off the bed, wrapped a towel around his waist, and dragged the comforter down over Ruby. He was still laughing when he said, "Here, stay right there. I'll just be a minute." He stepped over her legs, and she wondered about her chance of injury if she were to dive over the railing outside the window. Instead, she covered her head and body with the comforter and pretended that she was Dorothy tapping her heals together and repeating "There's no place like home" in her head.

The door opened, and she heard something rattle into the room and stop next to her. Fin babbled something in French, which was followed by complete silence before two male voices roared with laughter. *Seriously, I am not coming out. Good luck prying the damn blanket off me.* Then, as to add insult to injury, a breeze from the hallway crossed over her feet, and she realized that they were sticking out from under the covers. She inched them underneath as inconspicuously as possible, but a whole other round of laughter bounced off the walls. The man eventually left, but she heard him chortle as he made his way down the corridor.

She lay there like a turtle in a shell. "Please go away." Underneath all the feathers, her voice sounded like her mouth was stuffed with marshmallows. The covers moved as Fin straddled her stomach with just enough weight so that she couldn't budge. He pulled at the material closest to her head, but she held on for dear life.

"Ruby," his voice crooned, "come out. I have food, and you could very well suffocate under there." She released the blanket, but didn't move. He slipped it down, and her face peeked out. His voice was smooth. "Did you get hurt during your tumbling routine?"

She could tell he was desperately holding back a laugh. She squinted belligerently, but couldn't quite pull it off while naked and under a puffy comforter, in an amazing hotel in Belgium, starring up at the most breathtaking man she had ever seen, after redefining her belief about what it means to make love. Still, she didn't want to let him off the hook completely. "I'll probably have a few bruises."

As if thinking, his lips puckered together, and his mock concern took a predatory turn. He slid the cover down a little more, exposing her shoulders. His mouth kissed along the small stones of her necklace and ended in the dip on her neck where the Chinese coin rested. "Right here?" His warm breath tickled.

Her mouth pulled up on one side. "No. Not there." *I am turning into a brazen hussy.*

Fin's eyes glinted, and he slowly drew the cover down further. Everything above her waist was exposed, and he scooted lower on her legs. She felt the fire behind his eyes as he bent to meet one of her rigid nipples. Nipping with his teeth, he asked "Are you hurt here?"

Both sides of her mouth turned up. "A little." *Yep, an absolute tramp.* He laughed against her flesh, now full of goose bumps. Her hips began moving against him, but before she could say, "Take me, you Scottish love god," well maybe not that, Fin asked her something.

* * *

His head was swimming, but as God was his witness, he wanted her again. She looked good enough to eat under all that billowy white, like whipped cream over the main desert. He was stiff as a board, and the towel wasn't doing much to cover him up. He came up to her ear. "Do you want to eat or do you want to do something else?"

Ruby's stomach rumbled, giving her away.

Fin's raised his eyebrows. "There's my answer. I see. Food it is." He covered himself with the towel and made his way to the bathroom. He came back wrapped in a white, plush terrycloth robe and had another draped over his arm. "Here we go." He held it out so she could back up into it. Ruby put her arms in, and he tucked it about her, tying the sash snugly around her middle.

He held her shoulders and scooted her over to the serving trolley. It was covered with a white, starched tablecloth and three silver covered dishes, a yellow Florentine tulip in the middle. Next to the table was a champagne bucket and stand, holding an iced bottle of Krug with a white linen towel wrapped around the neck. Fin looked around. There was one chair by the door, so he brought it over for Ruby. "I'll be right back. I'm going to get the chair from my room. When he came back, Ruby was peeking under the lids of the serving dishes.

"I wasn't sure what to order, but there should be something to suit your taste." For the next hour, they drank champagne and lingered over mussels in butter, rabbit with onion, potatoes covered with a brown sauce, and a soup with chunks of white fish, carrots, and leeks in a clear broth.

Their conversation flowed, and they both laughed and told stories of their lives. Fin still skirted around the edges, but he was relaxed and happy. He felt like a fraud, though, when Ruby asked him about how he got work as a handyman. He told her that it was part of his family business. He led her to believe that his family was manual laborers but, for some reason, he didn't want to confess the truth. She seemed comfortable with the false reality he wove, and didn't know how she would react if he told her his family owned multiple companies and huge tracts of land, along with stocks and houses.

When they couldn't eat another bite, Fin called for someone to get the cart. While they waited, they moved their chairs over to the opened French doors, propped their feet on the railing, and looked over the skyline. It was completely dark outside. The moon peered out from behind the high clouds and eerily lit the church spire in a bluish shadow. Fin was absolutely content.

When the staff came to get the cart, the server presented them with a small silver tray with four Belgium chocolates and a bottle of mineral water. Fin spoke to him in quick French as the man nodded and they walked to the door. Fin discretely handed him some bills; the man shallowly bowed and *mercied* his way out the door.

Fin stood in the center of the room. "Ruby, I've had a remarkable night. I'm going to let you get some rest, and I'll see you in the morning." He held her hand and brought it to his lips, kissing the inside of her palm. "Goodnight."

* * *

Ruby stayed were she was. She didn't want to beg him to stay, even though she screamed the thought in her head. Maybe he needed some time to himself. "Okay, see you in the morning." What else could she say? He brought the palm he had just kissed to his cheek and held it there. It seemed as if there was more he wanted to say, but he released her, picked up his clothes still on the floor, and went to the door. *"Bonsoir."* The door clicked behind him.

Ruby went and closed the French doors, suddenly chilled now that Fin wasn't next to her. She began tabulating how much this little adventure would cost her. The room alone must be a few hundred, but she decided to worry about it later. Hell, she had a credit card. Right now, she needed to relax and relive the last hours in her head. Her backpack leaned against the wall, and she retrieved her toiletries and made her way to the bathroom. There was a curtain that could be drawn around the tub, so she decided to shower and get ready for bed.

At one in the morning, Ruby stilled tossed and turned, wondering what Fin was doing. Was he asleep? Was he thinking about her? Not able to stand it any longer, she padded her way down the hall to his room. After a quiet knock, she heard a sound similar to a jackrabbit running through a field before the door swung open.

She saw him draw in a quick breath and, as he let it out, he mouthed what she thought was the word "beautiful."

She bit down on her nail. "Do you mind if I stay with you?"

Fin swept her up into his arms, but seemed undecided. "A sleepover, then?" He cocked his head as if deep in thought and spoke slowly with his query, "Huh. I guess that would be okay. Do you snore, because I cannot tolerate snoring?"

Ruby smiled. "Poppy says I grind my teeth, but I think it's only when I'm stressed."

"Well then, lass, we better make sure you're nice and relaxed before you fall asleep." A wolfish grin spread across his face. "I have a few ideas." He started ravishing her neck as she squealed in his arms. He laid her back on the bed, coming down on top of her. "I can't tell you how happy I am that you decided to pop over."

"So you weren't sleeping?" Her fingers made their way through his jet-black hair.

"No, I had other things on my mind." He untied the sash of her robe. When he spread the sides wide, he started to laugh. "Do you always sleep like this?"

Ruby had on her usual sleep attire: leggings, grey cotton long-sleeved CU shirt, and rag wool socks. "I got cold."

Fin's brows quirked, "Another thing I think I can remedy." He then brought Ruby to two more climaxes before they were both spent and lay prone on the bed. Ruby could have been an astronaut in space for how weightless she felt as they both snuggled under the covers. The last thing she remembered was Fin bringing her back into the curve of his body, and his arms wrapping around her in a lover's embrace.

CHAPTER TWENTY-FIVE

When Fin opened his eyes, a grey haze met him — the first light of dawn. He turned his head and admired his sleeping beauty. Ruby was on her side, facing him. Her pillow was turned sideways, and she had one hand under her cheek while the other hugged the pillow. Her pink lips were slightly parted, her breathing slow, and her hair was a mass of fluid sun rays on the pillow. All he wanted was to focus on her.

He thought back and realized that he had never spent an entire night with another woman. It was odd, but not incomprehensible. He always made sure he was at their place and was never without an exit plan. Now, ironically, he tried coming up with excuses to make Ruby stay. He inched closer to her and, without waking, she snuggled into his chest. She smelled sensual. Their love-making still lingered in the air, and the scent of lavender clung to her skin.

He closed his eyes and drifted back to sleep. When he woke up next, light streamed into the room and Ruby was gone. He threw back the covers, sat up, and ran his hands over his face and through his hair. There was a note on the bedside table: "Gone for a walk. Hope you slept well. R."

The clock read 9:20 AM. He decided to shave and shower before he went to look for her. It was a pleasant day, and it would be difficult to get lost in the small village.

Twenty minutes later, he had on a pair of khaki pants and a white t-shirt. He pulled on a navy blue Henley, tied his boots, and was out the door. He knocked on her door.

When there was no answer, he went down to the lobby. The women working the desk said she had seen Ruby leave an hour ago. He walked out and stood on the sidewalk, deciding which way to go. The air was fresh, and the sun that hit the damp walkway caused a fog to hover just above the ground. He figured Ruby would go explore, so he thought to make his way to the church. When he looked the opposite direction, there she was, radiating happiness. His heart became a hundred times larger, its beat sang throughout his body. She had on soft grey cargo pants and a bright yellow jacket. When she saw him, her face lit up, and she held up a paper cup to him.

* * *

Ruby stood on the step, and Fin stayed on the sidewalk, which raised her nearly to his eye level. She kissed his smiling lips. She looked at his damp hair. "Did you shower?"

"I thought I would give you time to get my coffee." He looked at her hand, "And I see that you did. Perfect." He took it from her hand and smiled as he sipped.

She playfully hit him in the chest. "Funny."

"But, because you got coffee, I'll figure out what we should eat. Did you shower yet?"

He ran his thumb against her cheek. It was cool on her warmed skin. Ruby felt her face heat up.

"What?" His voice sounded confused.

She looked down and shook her head. "Nothing. No, I haven't showered." Fin raised her face to his, not allowing her look away. She scrunched up her face and then mumbled a string of words that sounded like "ooi ksmwll uoi."

He dipped his head to meet her eyes and laughingly said, "I'll need a translation."

She looked at him defiantly. "I said, I could still smell you, and I didn't want to wash any bit of you off. There, and yes, I know it's gross." His hand dropped from her face, and he stood completely still. She was so embarrassed. She could have made up anything and he never would have known. "I couldn't get the water to work, or my key has gone missing, or I had to run after a cat that tried to take my shoes, anything."

Fin took a deep breath through his nose and blew it out slowly from his mouth. *Great,* she thought, *this would be the moment he'd say, "You're just a little too freaky for my taste, but it's been fun. Ciao Bella."*

"Ruby," she braced herself, "I'm finding it hard to move right now, but when I can, I'm going to need you up in that room, naked in my bed or anywhere else that suits you." He dangled his room key from his finger, and her face warmed even more. She licked her lips.

She stared at Fin's eyes, which watched Ruby's tongue moisten her lips. "Okay, that's it. Move." His voice had taken on a raspy, sexual growl. A heat instantly gripped her womanhood, but she was stuck in place, unable to move. "Ruby, I'm going to give you thirty seconds, and then I'm throwing you over my shoulder." His eyes were hungry and as dark as storm clouds. A bubble of laughter made it past her lips. "Twenty." He showed his teeth behind a slight grin. Ruby chucked her coffee into the trashcan on the street, snatched the key, and turned and ran into the hotel. She took the stairs two at a time.

She fumbled with the lock to Fin's room. Then she saw him reach the top of the stairs, and just like a bad movie, she was unable to get the key into the hole. He took his time walking down the hall, making her hands shake even more. The door finally clicked, and she flew into the room and threw herself onto the bed, laughing. She heard him come in and turn the lock. Over her shoulder, she watched him pull his shirt over his head, which left him in a snug t-shirt. She was about to explode.

His voice was quiet. "That was fast, Ruby." He glided toward her. "Do you trust me? Can I try something with you? You can say 'no.' It's okay, just tell me. Tell me what feels good or not, okay?"

He had a look in his eyes that she couldn't put her finger on but, honestly, she would have tried to swim the English Channel to find out what he was asking of her. "I do trust you." She sat on the edge of the bed. He took off her jacket and put it on the chair.

Fin pulled her shirt over her head. His brows rose when he saw that she wasn't wearing a bra. Her nipples were puckered, aching for his touch. "Nice." He circled both once with his finger. Gently, he pushed against her chest, and she lay back on the bed. He knelt on the floor in front of her and took off her shoes and socks. Then he slid her pants down, taking her underwear with them. She was completely exposed and, without thinking, started moving her hips in anticipation.

Fin's mouth curved up. "My god, you're amazing." He kept his eyes locked on hers and slid a finger into her tight opening. Her neck arched as she pushed against him "Christ, I've got to have more." His mouth found her clitoris and he sucked and licked as his fingers played.

Ruby's head spun with the exquisite feel of Fin's masterful mouth. Then, when she didn't think she could take any more, he tenderly turned her over onto her stomach. His hand trailed down the center of her body, over the gentle curve of her spine, and to the soft flesh of her butt, which she raised at his touch. She felt the wetness from herself on his fingers. Her head felt like it would explode. *What is he doing to me?* He continued down her legs with the back of his hand. Shivers ran along her body everywhere he touched.

He heeled his boots and left the rest of his clothes on the floor. Ruby's head was turned to the side, and she saw him come up behind her. He lowered himself onto her back and whispered into her hair, "Get up on your knees." He slid his hand along her side as she rose. He parted her legs further with his thighs and held himself over her with one arm. With his other, he stroked his hand up her back with just enough pressure, telling her to lay her head on the pillow. Then he reached between her legs from behind and ran his middle finger through her folds. She was slick and wet. "Christ Ruby, you're so ready." His fingers played with her and found her most sensitive spot, circling, circling, circling with his thumb while his fingers filled her again.

Ruby bit the pillow to stop from screaming out. She moved back into him, wanting something more. Her blood boiled. "Fin, my god." Everything throbbed as she pushed against his fingers. His thumb was magic. She was so close. He removed his fingers, placing the head of his penis at her opening. He grabbed onto her hips with both hands and buried himself in her. Then she did scream. It was too much and not enough. She panted heavily and arched her back, wanting to move, but he held a hand high on her back, keeping her in place. Through clenched teeth, he said her name over and over as they met each other. Suddenly, everything broke apart and, as if in a cave, she heard her voice calling out to him, and he came too.

* * *

Fin hovered over Ruby, not touching her skin, but aching to. He gently lowered her legs so she was stretched out, and then rolled next to her, finally spooning against her soft body. "Are you all right? I didn't hurt you, did I?"

Her lids were closed, but an angelic smile was on her face. "If that's what not showering gets me, I'll never shower again."

His laughter filled the room. "Ruby, I…." *Holy fuck, I almost said "I love you."* He had never said those words to anyone but family, and even then, never flippantly. *Okay, I need to get a grip.* He wasn't scared of love. In fact, he never thought about love or falling in to it at all. However, if he ever did fall in love, the falling would be electric, fireworks, a feeling that would smack him in the face like a freight train. Being with Ruby was a free-flowing stream without thought or reason. It was fluid and oozed from him like warm syrup, soothing and comfortable and definitely tasty. It occurred to him now, as he gazed at her, that before he had even spoken to Ruby or even saw her, that she had stirred something in him. When she entered a room, he felt her before he saw her. *Did* she electrify him?

He was conscious of her from the beginning, though he didn't name the feelings behind the awareness. *Oh Christ.* He had fallen in love with a woman who was leaving tomorrow, a woman from a whole different country who didn't really know who he was, a woman he had known for two days, and she was leaving. He felt as if he had been zapped by a stun gun.

Ruby turned to face him. "You what?" He focused on something over her shoulder, as if he hadn't clearly heard her. She thumped his cheek with a finger. "Hello . . . You what?"

His eyes met hers but, they were glazed over. And all he could get out was, "Huh?"

"You said, 'Ruby I,' and I asked what you were going to

say. You look kinda weird. Do you feel okay?" She sat up.

"Yeah, I'm fine." He shook his head to clear it, gave her his best smile, and ruffled her hair. "I was going to say, Ruby, I'm starving. Let's go eat our way through Dinant. What do you say?"

She tilted her head, her lips a straight line. Slowly, she responded, "I know that wasn't what you were going to say, but okay." She inched her way to the end of the bed and started picking up her clothes.

Fin was more than thankful that she left the non-coherent conversation where it stood, and didn't ask any more questions. He wasn't ready. Damn, he couldn't even say what he wasn't ready for.

Ruby smiled over at him. "Now I think I'll shower. Give me just a few minutes." She threw on her robe from last night and went to her room, carrying her clothes in a wad.

* * *

Forty minutes later, they sat at an outdoor table in front of a restaurant by the river. The day was cool but sunny, and everyone was out to enjoy it. They shared a bottle of mineral water and had a huge bowl of mussels in olive oil and white wine sauce. They also had an order of caprese, with big basil leaves as the vessels for olive oil and balsamic vinegar that gently lay over the reddest tomatoes Ruby had ever seen.

Fin wore aviator sunglasses and leaned back as he rested his head in his laced fingers. "What do you want to do today?"

Ruby looked up at him, a mussel halfway to her mouth, and said, "Let's walk along the river after eating, I want to go see some of the boats by the docks."

His eyes must have been closed behind his glasses. He seemed to be literally soaking up the sun. "Hmm, do you sail, Ruby?" His voice sounded sleepy.

She put another mussel in her mouth. They were so tender that she could eat the whole bowl by herself, and actually she probably was. "No, I've never sailed. You?"

He looked under his lenses at her, a small grin on his face. "A little." He leaned onto the table with his forearms. "Let's do that. Let's rent a boat at the docks." Now he was wide awake, his previous slight grin an all-out toothy smile. He looked like a ten-year-old boy on his way to Disneyland. Ruby nodded her head as she slurped some broth with an empty shell.

He watched with an impatient look on his face, "Okay, lady, shake a leg. Isn't that one of your sayings?"

"Yeah, sure. That's one of my sayings. Now, will you eat some of these? I'm about to grow shells for ears."

"But it's so fun to watch you. However, if it will get us out of here sooner, crack one open for me." Ruby rolled her eyes but plopped a mussel into his waiting mouth. He grabbed her finger between his lips before she could get it out, and lightly sucked. "Mm, sweet."

Ruby knew she had turned scarlet, so she hurriedly said, "Okay, I'm ready." She started to scoot back her chair.

"Are you sure you don't want some more, Ruby? I'll let you feed me." He waggled his brows.

Ruby humphed and heard him laugh as she walked toward the docks, trying to cool off the heat that had begun to build, again.

He caught up to her half way down the street and slung his arm over her shoulder. The gesture was playful and magnificent. When they reached the dock, the boat rental had one two-person kayak left—a good way to view the village. The Meuse River looked like glass as they fitted their life vests and talked to the man about the best parts of the river. The current was slow and the boat traffic was light. He suggested that they paddle up about a mile and then float back down. Fin reached up to help Ruby get into the boat, and the man handed them the paddles.

The last time Ruby had been in a kayak was during Girl Scout summer camp. She and her fellow camper had either gone in circles or were at a complete standstill. The girls never mastered the teamwork of paddling. After attempting to yell directions from the shore, a very grumpy mom waded out to make a water rescue as other campers tittered on the edge of the water.

Paddling with Fin was very different. He sliced easily through the water and kept time with Ruby's strokes. They went to the opposite side of the river and stayed close to its edge, looking for life under the water. Other than a couple small fish, there wasn't much to see. Ruby put the paddle across her thighs and dragged her hand through the water. It was cold and as dark as ink.

As they made their way up river, Fin pointed out landmarks that he remembered from the time he had been in Dinant with his family. As soon as the town ended, farm land took center stage. The fields had just started to turn green and came down and touched the water's edge. Fin explained how to tell the difference between flax and hemp, and they watched a flock of sheep being herded by two dogs. They turned around, and did more floating than paddling. They let the current take them where it wanted as they made their way back to the village.

Fin leaned up and ran his hand along her hair as he described what they saw. For her part, Ruby couldn't help but touch his leg as she turned to ask a question. Had they been in a more stable boat—one without the potential of flipping—she would have slid up his body and pressed her lips onto his. Instead, she changed the course of her thoughts before the boat did tip over.

Popcorn clouds drifted overhead, but there was no sign of rain, and the sun felt delightful. When they got near the docks, the same man who rented them the boat sat on a wooden chair and waved to them, a huge smile on his face. They pulled up alongside, and he tied them to a post. As they walked, he and Fin animatedly spoke of something Ruby couldn't understand. They left each other with pats on the back and more hand gestures. "What was he saying to you?"

Fin took her hand in his and rubbed his thumb back and forth against her skin. "He told me about a little café down a street not many tourists go to. He said they have the best cakes. Would you like to go?" They spent the rest of the day at the café, (which did have the best cakes), hiking up to the citadel, sitting in the church, and meandering through the streets. By the time they got back to the hotel, it was eight o'clock. Time really did fly.

Ruby tried to avoid talking about their last day together. She didn't know if he planned to go back to Brugge early, or if she would take the train from Dinant. If that was the case, she needed to figure out the train schedule. Maybe she should go back with him and leave from Brugge. Suddenly, an overwhelming melancholy overtook her. She was in her room, leaning back on two legs of the chair, her feet on the rail. The sun had set, but the sky still glowed in graduated degrees of blue, gold, and orange.

Fin had said he needed to do some things, so now she was alone with her thoughts. She remembered the reason she decided to make the trip. It wasn't the Scott thing, which had really started the whole thing, but it was the result—the strength she knew she had and that she had power over the way her life would go. The trip was meant to help her discover who she was, without family, a boyfriend, or anything else she was familiar with. It was to strip her life down and look to see what was underneath all the clutter. Who would have guessed that the first week into her adventure that the way she wanted to feel, things she had dreamt of—things she didn't even know—were standing in front of her. And now she was leaving.

A bubble of panic gripped her, and a burning in her chest that must have been connected to her tear ducts pricked her eyes. Certainly, she was not on the verge of tears. Did this experience with Fin need to be boxed up and packed away? Was this one of those jokes life pulled to see what you're made of? Maybe with space, these feelings would fade because, really, could a few days change her life? The funny part was that she didn't even know what he thought. Being with her could be one of many trysts, something he may or may not look back on and smile at over a cup of coffee, and then go feed the dog or paint the house. Would it be just another ordinary part of life? What if she hadn't gotten off the bus? She ran her fingers over the beads of her necklace, remembering what Poppy had told her: transform, inspire, empower, and luck. Was there anything about fate in there? There was a knock on the door.

The legs of the chair hit the carpet with a thud, and she went to the door. When she opened it, she felt transformed, inspired, empowered, and lucky—as if her life had a predetermined path she would follow, fate. Her breath felt shaky in her chest. Fin stood and watched her for a full five seconds. They both seemed to be in their own worlds. He took her hand and kissed the back of it, and all she could think was that was a gesture that should never have died away.

* * *

"Hi, Ruby. What did you do while I was away?" Fin felt like he was losing his mind. He had been gone all of an hour but, somehow, he felt disconnected. It was good that she was leaving. Maybe being away from her would give him some much-needed perspective. He had responsibilities to get back to, and none of them included the woman in front of him. Even as he rationalized in his head, he knew all of his reasons were lies. Something had shifted, and if he were to be honest with himself, the change was all because of her. He began to feel himself again, after drowning in the loss and the gut-wrenching sorrow and anger over Ian's death. How could his brother have let himself die? Ian had left Fin alone, and Fin hadn't known what to do. Now, rather than the resentfulness he felt for needing to do things he had never aspired to or wanted, he was ready to lead the Sinclair's. With Ruby he had laughed and loved without guilt. They had spoken of family, and now he was eager to see his again. She had given him a gift that he could never repay.

Ruby walked back into the room, making her way to the chair. "I was just thinking about tomorrow." She blinked her eyes.

Fin sat in the other chair. "That's what I was doing. I've made arrangements for you. You'll fly to Santorini from Brussels at ten tomorrow morning," His voice came out flat. "It should take us about an hour to get to the airport, and six hours for you to fly. Your friend Retta gave me the number where she'll be staying. It rang through, but no one answered. I would guess that you'll arrive at nearly the same time. There'll be a car waiting for you at the airport in Santorini. The driver's name is Dimitri. He'll take you to the house she and her friends rented." His arms rested on his legs as he looked at the floor.

From the corner of his eye, he saw Ruby's eyebrows rise. She spoke to his profile. "You know I have a Eurail Pass. I could have used that. I don't have to be in Norway for about three more weeks. How much was the ticket? I'm sure I can take a bus and get close to the house. I don't need a car. It's not a very big island, right?"

Confused, Fin turned his head to her. "It would take you at least two days to get there on the train and then the boat. I just want to know you got there close to the same time as Retta. It's what I had promised." He tried to smile, but the small gesture felt contrived.

Ruby's eyes widened and her nail went to her teeth, a child's pacifying blanket. "Yeah, but I really didn't budget for a plane ticket or a driver and then this hotel." He was still confused. "I mean, I have a certain amount of money I can spend on things, and I didn't plan on this." Her hand waved around the room. "I wouldn't change it for anything, but I don't know if I can swing a plane ticket. I have a thousand-dollar limit on my Visa. How much was it? Is it refundable? Maybe you can transfer it?"

A light bulb finally went on. Fin looked back to the pattern in the carpet. He shook his head and spoke quietly, "Ruby, everything is already paid for. You don't have to worry about any of it."

Ruby sprang from the chair, her voice louder than perhaps intended, "Of course I have to worry about it. I'm not letting you pay for my room or an airline ticket to Greece. Are you crazy? You've been working for weeks at Prima Facie. You're not spending your money on me!"

Fin thought through what he wanted to say before he rose to face her. "Ruby, the work I'm doing at the hostel is more like therapy for me. It isn't something I need to do. There were some things I needed time to think about, and the opportunity to work there presented itself." He put his hands in his pockets. "As far as you not worrying about anything, I asked you to get off that bus. I needed you to get off that bus, and these days have been some of the best I have ever had." He held her with his steel eyes. "I want to do this for you. Please let me do this." He held Ruby's arms that were limp at her sides. "Please." Fin didn't even know what he was pleading for any more. *Please let me do this. Please let time stand still. Please burn this into my memory. Please stay with me.*

* * *

Warmth spread to every part of her. His look was made for movies or sonnets. She couldn't have willed herself to look away. His eyes penetrated and were full of, if not love, then desperation to hear what he was saying.

She stared up at him. Her chest was heavy with words she wanted to say but didn't want to hear the answers to. Her nose started to burn, a tell-tale sign that tears were coming. She blinked and there they were, two thin streams making their way down both sides of her nose.

Fin didn't try to catch them. "Please let me do this." His voice was a whisper, and he skimmed his lips over hers, dragging the salty tears with them. He scooped her up and kissed her with an intensity that had never been there before—it was slow and deep. He gently laid her on the bed and looked at her as if she were a precious work of art. This moment wasn't the humorous hungry way they had played before. They memorized every detail, every line and curve and sound, because it was the last time they would be together. More silent tears pooled in her ears as he came down on her. They made love with reverence and openness, giving wholly. Fin never took his eyes off of Ruby. When she arched her neck and groaned, breaking apart in his arms, he filled her with everything in him. There was a connection neither wanted to let go of, something that couldn't be taken away. When she opened her eyes, he rolled off her and pulled her against his chest. Neither spoke. After a time, her breathing became slow and even. Ruby knew he wouldn't let go as she slept in his arms.

CHAPTER TWENTY-SIX

Morning broke with clouds and rain that captured the mood in the room. After minimal conversation, Ruby decided to take a shower and give herself a good talking to. *Jesus, I'm going to Greece, for Christ's sake. It's on my list of places I most want to see.* She faced directly into the stream of water and let it pound against her face. *I should be happy*, she told herself. *How many people can say that they are going to Greece after spending an unimaginable two days with a fairytale prince?* She tested a smile. Well, she would consider it a work in progress. She turned the water colder. It was what she needed to clear the fuzz from her head. She smiled again, and the action felt a little more natural. She would get to see Retta again, who would crap herself with the details she would pull from Ruby. She spit water out of her mouth and laughed at the picture of Retta in her head.

When she came out of the bathroom, Fin leaned against the rail as drops of rain hit the carpet at his feet. He didn't seem to notice or care that he was getting wet. He turned his head when he heard her, pushed away from the window and, in a voice that sounded foreign to her, said, "Are you ready then?" His tone was void of any feeling. He closed the doors and ran his fingers through his hair. To Ruby, he appeared like a brittle branch ready to snap. It made her body tighten with nerves.

Trying to read his face, Ruby looked at him blankly. "Yeah, I'm ready." There was a hard, remote look on his face and his eyes were flat, as if this was the last place he wanted to be. Yesterday he would have gotten her bag, but now he only watched as she hefted it up and made her way to the door. It may as well have been a slap in the face. She was in a daze as she walked down the stairs, feeling numb. At the same time, she had a heavy tightness in her chest.

Fin walked directly to the street, where his car waited at the curb. Ruby noticed that his bag was already in the backseat as he opened the door for her. He had been a busy bee while she was in the shower. He must be very eager to get out of here.

She sat in the passenger seat and stared straight ahead. She struggled to reconcile his earlier words that were filled with emotion with the chill that emanated from him now. He pulled onto the road. The rain came down harder now, sounding like someone throwing rocks onto the roof. The racket made it easy to keep quiet, as talking would have been impossible over the noise. Ruby glanced sideways at Fin. His heavy lids looked unemotionally out the windshield, and both hands tightly gripped the steering wheel. Ruby guessed that it wasn't the rain that made his knuckles white.

She leaned the side of her head against the headrest and held her thumb nail between her teeth in a vice grip. She probably looked relaxed from the outside, but her stomach muscles were so tight that they vibrated and wracked her body with uncontrollable tremors that came in waves. The tension was palpable, and she couldn't understand why he was acting so callous. She watched the rain hit her window and dance along the glass. There were no more tears behind her eyes. Now she was mad. He was being a complete ass, and the more time that went by, the angrier she got. *Does he think I'll break down, grab his ankles, and beg him to stay?* She grunted because that was what she wanted to do, but she was a grownup. She would say, "Thank you, I had a wonderful time," and then she would wait until she was on the plane to start bawling. *Such a grownup.*

* * *

Fin's hands hurt from trying to break the wheel in two. He knew he was being a prick, but his emotions were pulling him in opposite directions. Whatever this was with Ruby had nowhere to go, and he cursed himself for pretending that he thought it could. Once he got back home, his life would fall into place. He would start going to clubs and parties again. He would start where Ian left off, contribute to his family, and get back into the fold. His time with Ruby would become a pleasant memory. That was all. He looked over at her. He couldn't see her face because she was looking out the window, but her thumb nail was locked between her teeth, making the muscles flex in her jaw. *Yeah, I'm a complete prick*, he thought to himself. He desperately wanted to run his hand along her cheek, try to explain to her what she had made him feel, but to what end? *No, this is better. I'll play the bad guy.* He would hate it, he would feel like shit, but he would do it.

The airport exit came into view, and Fin took the turn for passenger drop-off. His insides were in knots, as if the devil was skipping up and down in his intestines. His throat was so tight that getting breath into his lungs took a feat of strength. He wanted so much to leave her with a good impression, but he needed to hold her at arm's length so she didn't expect anything and so that she could continue her trip with a clean slate. He was splitting inside. What he wanted was to brand his name into her skin so others knew she was his, place a "Do Not Touch" sign around her neck. Just thinking about her in someone else's arms made him want to rip the mirage's limbs from his make-believe body. The thought of violence was Vicodin, which for some reason he couldn't explain, numbed the barbarity flowing through his veins.

He slowed the car as the Lufthansa sign came into view. She would change planes in Athens and take Aegean Air to Santorini. He had booked the shortest, most direct flights he could find, hopefully causing minimal hassle for her. He stopped at the curb and looked over at Ruby, who still held onto her nail like a tenacious python. After seconds ticked by with neither moving, he got out of the car and came around to open her door, only to find her already out and trying to pull her backpack from the backseat. It must have been caught on something, because she cursed under her breath and violently tugged, trying to free it. He put his hand on her shoulder and moved her aside. She jumped as if a hot poker had touched her and snapped her shoulder away. Fin squeezed his eyes tight as he leaned in and freed one of the straps that had caught under the seat. Her reaction to his touch made him feel horrible, but he needed to keep up the charade. He smoothed his expression before he faced her, wearing a mask of indifference.

Ruby focused on a point down the walkway, leaving him with a moment to study her. She looked different, pale, nervous or scared, and completely alone. *Christ, I can't do this*. He put a finger under her chin and turned her face to his. "You okay?"

The look she gave killed him. Her jaw was locked to stop it from quivering, and her eyes were filled with unshed tears. "I'm not a huge fan of flying, that's all." Her voice was small and shaky. She looked away. Fin took a step closer, put his lips on the top of her head, and held them there. In a million lifetimes, he would never forget the smell of her. He backed up and met Ruby's closed eyes. It reminded Fin of when Ian's son would think he was hiding by merely shutting his eyes.

"Ruby." She didn't open her lids. "Ruby, look at me." He saw her drag in a breath, but she never let it go as her head reluctantly turned to him. He bent his knees so he was at her level. "Everything will be fine. You're going to have a great time." His voice was as smooth as a whisper.

Her head snapped up and locked on his. There was a fire behind her eyes. She nodded her head and looked at a watch that wasn't on her wrist. "I've got to go." She picked up her bag and put it over one shoulder. She didn't move. He took her ticket from his pocket and put it into her hand, running his fingers along her palm. "Thanks." She kept looking at him.

"I had a good time, Ruby."

Her eyes widened and her mouth dropped open. A gurgled breath escaped, "Yeah, me too." She turned and walked through the doors, never looking back.

Fin stood in place for a minute, or an hour, or five—he had no idea. The earth had opened up and sucked him in. He heard someone next to him, but he couldn't tell if they were talking to him. Then there was a tug on his shirt. He turned and saw a man in uniform wave his hands impatiently in the air and loudly say, *"Deplacer, Deplacer!"* Fin looked at him, jerked his head once, and made his way to his car. He lowered himself into the supple leather seat, gripped the wheel, commenced to pound his body into his seat over and over, and then changed to slapping the wheel and shouting into the dead, empty space.

When he came back from his psychotic episode, there was a small crowd that looked in his windows to see the demented man. He slumped against the seat, completely drained. He caught the eyes of a young boy, maybe nine years old, and they blankly stared back at him. His mother finally pulled him along, just in case whatever Fin had was contagious. He turned the key, put the car in gear, and squealed out of the airport, putting as much distance as he could between himself and the one woman who had touched his heart.

CHAPTER TWENTY-SEVEN

Ruby's legs had become tethered to iron balls. It took a conscious effort to put one foot in front of the other. Fin's last touch had burned her palm, which now itched like a healing scab. In a zombie-like haze, she made her way through the line of people checking baggage. She could hear his voice in her head: *"I had a good time, Ruby." I had a good time. "The soup is good, maybe a bit more salt." "The weather is rather gloomy." They're all interchangeable. "I have lint in my bellybutton." None had more significance than the other. "The light has turned green." I am a fucking idiot! I'd known from the start that he's a player. Christ, I saw the screaming result on the sidewalk outside of Prima Facie with my own eyes.* A crazy person's laugh, one she didn't recognize, came out of her mouth. The woman in front of her looked back, but Ruby blankly disregarded her. *Piss off.* The woman turned back around, and they all took a step forward.

She was ready to jump out of her skin by the time she made it through security. She scanned the concourse for a bathroom and practically ran when she finally found one. She banged into a stall and turned the lock. She didn't bother to lower her pants before she sat on the toilet and bent over, holding her head in both hands. A toilet flushed. Uncontrollable sobs shook her and snot dripped onto the linoleum floor. She was so far from caring that she simply watched it make a tiny, slimy pond at her feet. There was another whooshing flush.

After what seemed like hours, but must have been only minutes, her tears had run their course. She blew her nose in

some toilet paper and took more to wipe up the floor. She
stood up, took a few deep breaths, and swiped her hands
across her eyes. They felt tight and puffy, but it was nothing
that a cold paper towel couldn't help. She walked with her
head down over to the row of sinks and saw a hand reach
out toward her from the corner of her eye. Ruby looked to
the side. An attendant not much older than herself held out
a wet paper towel with a sheepish smile on her face. Ruby
scrunched up her face and said "Sorry." She took the towel
and held it over her eyes, continuing her explanation. "I'm
usually not like this. I'm not a crier. I know it's hard to
believe after that." She pointed her head to the stalls. The
girl looked at her blankly. "You have no idea what I'm
saying, do you? *Merci*." She held up the towel. The girl
nodded and squeezed Ruby's shoulder with an
understanding look. Ruby could have started crying again,
but instead turned the faucet on and splashed cold water
onto her face. She had a flight to catch. She shook her hair,
fished out the few coins she had, put them in the basket on
the sink, and walked to the gate.

They were seating first class when she arrived at the
boarding area. Her ticket was printed with "4A." She milled
about with the others who waited. There was an
announcement for first class passengers, rows one through
six, first in French and then in highly accented English. She
looked at her ticket again-4A." *No way, no flipping way*. She
walked up to the ticket agent and showed her ticket. The
woman smiled. "Please," she said, directing Ruby down the
ramp to the waiting plane.

When Ruby got to her seat, an attendant was at her side
saying, *"Je peux rien faire pour vous?"* He must have seen her
blank look. "May I get you anything? Water? Wine? A
magazine?"

Ruby tried to smile. "No. I'm fine, thank you."

"Very good." He moved on.

Fin has completely lost his mind. What was he thinking? How much did he spend on my ticket? He bought it at the last minute. Her head whirled. She watched as coach passengers began boarding. They looked at her the way she looked at first class ticket holders—a little curious and a lot resentful. Ruby pretended to study her fingernails as the passengers filed by, sure that they wondered how she had a first-class ticket. Hell, she wondered the same thing. It had been a long-standing tradition for her to make up stories about the people who flew in such coveted seats. An elderly, well-dressed couple occupied the seats in front of her. Their story was that they had both been in a concentration camp during the war. They vowed they would find each other, and they moved to Belgium and started a small business that grew, and now caters to a worldwide market. There was a scruffy looking man in his forties two rows up, on the aisle. He was at a flea market in France and bought a small drawing. He saw color underneath the paper and discovered a never seen Picasso, one worth millions. A small smile made it to her lips.

An attendant came on the intercom: "Welcome to Flight 771, bound for Athens, Greece. We are ready for takeoff. Please fasten your seatbelts and put tray tables up." Ruby's hands clenched onto the armrests, which instantly turned damp under her sweaty palms. *At least the thought of barrel-rolling into the ground will take my mind off the man I spent "a good time" with. I need to think of something else. Crap, I'm in first class. What does a person get in first class?*

She looked out the window and watched the landscape became a toy village. Cars looked like Matchbox trucks and sedans. Houses looked like dollhouses, and sheep were white dots against fields of green. She started counting down time. Someone had once told her that most planes, if they are going to crash, do so between zero and ten minutes from takeoff. A silent chant started in her head. *Please, please, please,* as if she could will the plane to stay in the sky.

Ruby rubbed the lucky coin at her neck and kept up her mantra: *Please, please, please.* She knew, without a doubt, that if she stopped rubbing, she would be personally responsible for the explosion that would surely result from the nose-dive the plane would take.

An announcement was made that the passengers could unbuckle—surely a good sign, but still not quite ten minutes. She hadn't realized, but her eyes must have squeezed shut at some point. There was a hand on her sleeve, and when she peeled back her lids, she looked up through a tight screen of lashes. The same man from earlier now held a silver tray that carried champagne flutes. "Champagne, Madame?" Ruby smiled and took one. *So this is what a person in first class gets, true glass.* Then came food, served on china plates. They served triopita, light and flaky, with feta and egg and a fig cut in two on the side. The coffee was thick and smooth, more like a not quite set pudding placed on top of a white cotton cloth.

Ruby decided that she loved Greece already, without ever having set foot on her soil. The attentive service made the time fly. She had never before been able to stomach airline food, which could be a combination of things. First, it sweated under plastic wrap. Second, airline food was always the same: rubbery chicken. Third, it was so cramped on planes that she didn't feel like constantly bumping into the person sitting next to her and try to cut said chicken. She had so much room now that she could flap her arms and not come close to anyone else. There was no one next to her, but if there had been, they could have shared one seat. By the time the plane started descending, which for some reason never caused her as much fear, she had watched a movie on her own personal screen and had more coffee and a shot of ouzo. Hot cloths were handed out, and she felt clean and energized rather than the usual stickiness after a flight.

Other than having to get her passport stamped and her bag from baggage claim, the transfer was uneventful. On the final leg into Santorini, the plane was smaller and the flight took only forty-five minutes. Below, the water looked a dark azure blue. Each island dotting the Aegean Sea had the whitish blue color of an opal as it got closer to land. None of them seemed to have much in the way of vegetation. From the plane, the earth looked beige and rocky, which was a distinct contrast to the sea they poked out of. Before she knew it, the plane touched down on the short runway. The airport was small, and the bags were waiting on the tarmac when they walked down the stairs out of the plane.

A handful of locals milled around outside the gate, asking tourists if they needed a taxi or a hotel. Ruby scanned the crowd and, toward the front, saw a man holding a piece of cardboard with her name on it. He appeared to be inspecting her, and she wondered if Fin had described what she looked like. He raised his hand, "Ruby?" His voice was a raspy hoot. Had he been smaller, he could have been sold as a traditional Greek doll.

She laughed. "Yes."

He dropped the sign into a trashcan and came toward her. He wore black pants that hung loosely on his thin frame and a tan dress shirt covered by a tan knit vest that buttoned up the middle. Salt and pepper hair was everywhere. His mustache was the same—it hung over his top lip and dripped down the sides. His eyes were dark mahogany and were set close together on a wrinkled, leathery canvas. He wore a traditional, black wool fishing hat that Ruby thought was only a prop in brochures for Greece.

He pulled an unlit pipe from between his teeth and held it in his hand as he took her in his arms. He squeezed tightly, as if she was a long-lost relative. Ruby felt the bones under his clothing and smelled pipe tobacco and garlic. With one last embrace, he held her at arm's length and looked her over. Ruby was so flabbergasted by the greeting that she did little but open her eyes wide and clench her teeth, forcing a smile.

"*Kalos Orisate*. Welcome, welcome." There was another hug. His whiskers somehow found their way to her nose and poked up her nostrils, tickling the hair. She blew out instinctively and twitched her face.

"I am Dimitri. Mr. Finley has hired me for your stay in Thera. Wherever you wish, we will go. I know Oia, where you will lodge with your friend. It is the most beautiful area in all of Thera. From here, it is twenty minutes. Would you like to go now?" Ruby knew there must be some miscommunication. Fin said there would be a driver to take her to the house, but surely it was not for her whole stay. "Have you been to Greece?" Ruby shook herself mentally and tuned into what Dimitri had said.

"Huh? Oh, no. This is my first time, but I've always wanted to come."

"Well, Miss Ruby, let me to show you my handsome island." Dimitri flung her pack onto his back as if he were a mule readying for a long trek.

Ruby's first instinct was to take it from him. She must be stronger than the five foot, ninety pound man next to her, who could be anywhere from sixty to ninety years old. Instead she thought better of it and let him lead her to the

outdoor parking lot. He opened the door of his white Nissan
Sunny, a boxy, four-door that looked old but well cared for.
She slid in, and worn, light brown vinyl material crunched
underneath her weight. Between her legs she saw crumbs
from crackers or a sandwich eaten long ago. They were
embedded into the seams, a now permanent part of the seat.
The interior smelled like Armor All or some other cleaner.
The dash was shiny—there wasn't a spec of trash to be seen.
Maybe he had cleaned it while he waited for the plane to
come in. His seat had a beaded cover that taxi drivers use for
air circulation or a massage. Ruby had no idea which, but
they always looked hard and unforgiving to her.

When he got in, he took a small notepad from his shirt
pocket and scanned it over. He had placed his pipe between
his teeth and mumbled to himself as he read over what must
have been notes about where they were going. After a bit, he
looked up and gave Ruby a crooked, stained, toothy grin.
"Let us go," he said. The car chugged to life.

"Miss Ruby, you have come at a very good time. It is
now nineteen hundred, and the sunset will be in one hour
thirty minutes. It is the best in all the world. I will tell you of
some things about my island as we go."

Ruby had yet to string two sentences together, for which
she was grateful. After her morning, all she wanted to do
was sit back and think of anything but the sick feeling she
got when she pictured Fin's face before she walked away
from him.

"Okay, long ago, Thera was a round island, but there
was a great eruption that sunk the center of the island. It is
called caldera, the only one there is in all the world, the only
one Ruby. Very special. You will see it from where you are
in Oia very well." He looked at ease as he maneuvered into
traffic. Although there wasn't much, the cars on the road

seemed to have their own agenda, and paid little attention to road rules.

Dimitri's voice had a raspy lilt from age, but was full of life at the same time. It comforted Ruby, as if she was listening to Santa Clause read his naughty and nice list. "Okay Ruby, now we will go to the west of Thera. We will pass many churches. If you wish to see them, I will take you. They are very old and very beautiful. Do you like wine, Ruby?" He plowed on, not waiting for a response. "We have very fine wine, very fine. And to eat, you like to eat, yes, the food?" He moaned, brought his fingertips to his lips, kissed them and let them fly—a very Italian gesture. "Okay, Ruby. My island is a volcano, so you will see many different beaches. You will have red, white, and black. Near Oia, they are very nice for swimming, or if you like, you can go to scuba. Okay, Ruby. Now you will see the sea. You see?" He pointed out the window.

They rode parallel to an indescribable expanse of the bluest water. "Yes, I see. It's amazing." When they had first started out, she wasn't sure what she thought of the landscape. It was harsh and rocky, with no vegetation except low thorny brush. Now, as they got closer to the water, the contrast between the red and ochre of the hills dotted with the white of the village and the azure water was like nothing she had ever seen. Though she hadn't thought it possible, she was becoming excited to be here.

"Okay, Ruby. Now you will see the famous blue dome churches of Oia. Do you see?" His eyes twinkled as he watched her look over the village.

A tingle of anticipation went through her body. Clinging to the tawny cliffs were bleach white, cave houses stacked one on top of the other and seeming to grow right out of the steep rock that reached down to the sea. It reminded her a little of Fred Flintstone's house in Bedrock, with no sharp angles or gaudy colors. The houses were crisp with monochromatic colors while, at the same time, tranquil with free-flowing shapes.

The car began going down the steep, curvy decent through narrow streets that felt more like sidewalks. Dimitri geared down and slowed to a crawl as the car went back and forth. He skirted around pedestrians and an occasional mule. "I telephoned Miss Retta. She is in the house and will wait for you there." It was funny to hear him say Retta's name, and she wondered what else Fin had told him. "Ah, here we are now." He pulled so close to the house that there was no way he could get out his door.

Ruby heard a familiar squeal and saw Retta's dancing body bound toward the passenger's side. "Ruby, Ruby!" Retta swung the door open and barely gave Ruby enough time to straighten before she was being rocked back and forth in a tight embrace. "Oh, Ruby. I've missed you. You're going to love this place. Come and look, hurry. Brian and I got here this morning. Look at the view. Can you believe it?"

Around a corner, she saw two crossed, bare feet propped up on a balcony wall. Brian's yelled to Ruby, "Hey, Ruby! So you flew in, huh? Nice. I'd get up, but I'm too comfortable."

Dimitri leaned across the seat and said, "Miss Ruby, okay. Miss Retta has the number of my telephone, and I will reach you tomorrow to see if you will go tour."

"Thank you for driving me. It was great. I appreciate it." She waved as Dimitri inched the car forward, made it back onto the street, and continued down the road.

Retta hooked her arm through Ruby's. "I cannot believe you have a driver. How'd that happen?"

They walked through the curved wooden front door. Instead of going into the details, Ruby stopped just inside the door. "Oh my gosh. This is amazing. Are your friends here?" It was just like entering a bright, airy cave. The walls were whitewashed, except for one, the sky-blue wall that led out to the patio. There was a small window and another wooden door, which was open. Through it, Ruby saw the rest of Brian along with more of the island peeking up through the still water.

"Go say hi to Brian, and then I'll show you around. And yeah, Jen and Marcie hiked down to the beach. They'll be back some time."

Ruby ambled onto the patio. The air was dry and felt like a whisper on her skin. Brian sat in a blue wooden chair, his feet still on the wall. His short-sleeved Cuban shirt was open, and his chest hair matched the springy copper curls on his head. "Rube." Mr. Cool flicked his head back to greet her. He had an amber colored drink in his hand, which he raised toward her and said, "Go get a drink and come out."

"I'm going to give her a tour, and then we'll be out. Come on, Ruby. You're going to love this place. By the way, I want the whole scoop on your last few days. You are so lucky you flew. The boat was awful. I'll tell you about it when Brian's with us. I'm sure he'll have things to add."

Ruby laughed when they entered the living space. There was an eclectic mix of furniture, most of it thick, wooden benches and chairs with red and orange cushions. Two washed-up pieces of drift wood placed on top of a chest created the coffee table. The kitchen was next to that. It was small, with a four-burner hotplate in an alcove, a miniature refrigerator, and a sink. Ruby poked her head into one of the two back-to-back bedrooms, each with a narrow door and two interior windows. The room Ruby peaked into had a set of twin beds, while the other had a double bed set into a curved niche painted the same sky-blue as the living room.

They were sparsely decorated—the only color came from bright, Florida orange bed coverings. The lone bathroom was also white, save for the dark terra cotta tile on the floor. The sink connected directly to the wall, where there was a shower head. The toilet was on the other side. It would have been average except for the window that opened out and had a stunning view of the Caldera. Who needed decoration when the scenery was so spectacular? Retta gave continual commentary throughout the tour. She and Ruby would share one of the twin rooms, and Brian was in the double.

"Ruby, you go outside and I'll bring our drinks out. Do *not* say anything until I'm out there." She wiggled a finger at her. Ruby smiled over her shoulder and drifted through the door. "I mean it!" she heard from the direction of the kitchen.

Brian turned his head. "Pull up a chair. I'd do it for you, but after these three days, I deserve to relax."

Ruby brought a chair over next to his. "So was it really terrible?"

His look was blank. In a drained voice, he said, "Damn, you have no idea." A grunt came out of his mouth right when Retta came out holding two glasses.

"Wait, wait. Let me get a chair. Let's toast to all getting here."

"Amen," both Ruby and Brian said in unison. They all clinked glasses. "Yasou!" It felt good to be with both of them again. Ruby took a generous gulp. The burn scorched its way down her throat. Her feet fell from the wall, and she started to cough. "You could have warned me. What is this?"

"It's a Greek mojito. You like it?" Brian showed his best sardonic grin. "You had a paid-for, six-hour airline flight and a hired car, is that right? Wow, Retta and I had three days of the closest thing to hell that I've ever experienced. Yasou!"

Ruby took another sip. The drink really was good, minty and tart with the lemon and lime. "Hey, I had no idea I was flying until this morning." She smiled right back. "Did I mention it was first class?"

"You are completely shitting me! Who is this guy?" After the words came out of Brian's mouth, Ruby wondered the same thing.

"All right, we'll tell you about our trip first." Retta's arms were already in motion, gearing up to tell the story. Her dark eyes were alight with excitement. She spun a crazy story of a night train filled with a soccer team, where fights and loutish things occurred, all in plain sight. The train was followed by a large boat where berths were unavailable, so they spent the night on the very cold and windy deck, huddled together and cursing. At three in the morning, two of five people disembarked, the only ones going on to Santorini.

They were told they could wait at the dock, which was locked up. There was a scary moment with a dog. Then a boat pulled up and they were waved aboard. At this point, Brian laughed and interjected that he was sure it was drug smugglers manning the boat. It fit only ten passengers, and they rode gut-heaving waves for hours with the seedy crew. Retta puked three times and lay prone on the floor, not caring any more about the filth, while Brian, who secretly thought they would die, turned five shades of green and looked for exit routes for when the shit went down.

Ruby held her stomach as tears spilled from her eyes, from laughing so hard. After they all caught their breaths, they looked out over the water. The sun was setting, and the oranges and yellows made the white buildings glow. They

could almost touch one of the blue domed churches that
dotted the steep hills of Oia, it was that close. Dimitri was
right when he said that the sunset was the best in the world.

"Okay, now for your story. What happened when we
left? I seriously thought my heart would stop when he asked
you to stay with him. I couldn't believe Fin held the bus and
then you got off. So, did you stay in Brugge or what? Where
did you go? Was he nice? Where is he now?"

Brian took another swig. "You had first class, and I had
that." He motioned his glass toward Retta.

Retta scrunched up her face and said, "I know you're
glad I was there."

Ruby struggled with what she wanted to tell them. *It was
magical until the carpet was pulled out from under me. I will
never experience anything close to the last few days ever again.*
No, it all sounded too hokey. Instead she decided to state the
facts without embellishing and be done. "We went to a
forest and walked around then went to Dinant, a small
town, and did some stuff there. Then I flew out today." She
took a sip and looked out at the water.

"Unh-unh. No way. I want details. What was the hotel
like? Did you stay in one room? Tell me you used protection.
My god, what did he look like under those clothes?"

Brian stretched and, with a gravely tone, said, "Okay,
time for me to take off. See you two later." He slipped into
his flip-flops and exited stage right.

Ruby's face had heated as she thought about the handful
of Margie's untouched gag condoms lying at the bottom of
her backpack. The timing was all wrong. Although she had
never been regular, it was still all wrong. Fin hadn't known
that however. *What the hell* had *they been thinking? Did he even
think about it?*

"Brian's gone, now tell me everything. Did you have

sex? Of course you did. You look all glowy. Was he amazing? When will you see him again? I have never seen a look like the one he had when he got on the bus. I thought we would all go up in flames."

Ruby blew out a deep breath. There was no way she was getting out of giving the details. "We had a great time, like nothing I've ever had before. He was funny and charming and incredible. He made everything perfect. There were flowers in the room when we got there. The hotel was amazing, and he had dinner delivered to the room that overlooked a river." She looked at Retta, whose eyes were wide and intent on Ruby's face. "He told me how much he liked spending time with me, and then he packed me up and may as well have dropkicked the plane across the water for as fast as he wanted to be on his way. So there's the story. Put a big 'S' on my head for 'sucker.' And I really don't want to talk about it anymore, okay?"

Retta shook her head confused. "No, Ruby. I saw his face when he got on the bus. He oozed for you."

Ruby bit down on her thumb nail, but felt her eyes burning. "I don't think so, but I don't want to talk about it. I'm not going to see him again, and I want to think about something else."

CHAPTER TWENTY-EIGHT

While on a ferry headed back to Stonehaven, Fin thought back over the last few days. He had somehow made it back to Brugge—but didn't remember any of the drive. He had turned up the music in his car during the drive, hoping to drown out the visions of Ruby that played like an old movie through his head and hit crazy speeds trying to run away from them. He finished odds and ends work in a day that normally would have taken three, and he told Hans that he needed to go back home. He listened to a string of colorful language thrown at him until Hans wore down and made him sit and have a drink with him. Hans told him that if he ever needed some work, Fin would be welcomed back. They left each other with Hans never asking anything about how he had spent the last few days, but instead with manly slaps on the back and chortles.

Then there was Chloris, who asked question after question about Ruby. Did she like the trip? What did they do? Was she coming back? Where she was now? Chloris's green eyes showed the depth of her displeasure when he didn't expound on the answers he gave her. Because he had a soft spot for Chloris, Fin wasn't about to tell her about the callous display he left Ruby with. He wanted her to think of him as someone to look up to and to count as a friend. He remained vague about Ruby's plans and, because he didn't know, being elusive was simple.

He gave Chloris the number and address where she could reach him. He no longer cared if she found out that his time spent in Brugge was a sham. He wasn't ashamed of where he came from or of the name his family carried. It was the people who changed or wanted things from him based solely on that name who made him so mistrustful. He knew that Chloris would never be in that category. In fact, as he told her before he left, he would love to show her around his favorite areas of Scotland.

The ferry had docked in Rosyth, and the clouds hung low and heavy for the two-hour drive to Stonehaven. After turning onto the lane that would take him to his parents, he realized that he was excited to see his family. He knew that they would not hold his "holiday" against him. The wheels of his car came to a stop on the gravel in front of the estate. He got out and looked at the house he always called home through an outsider's eyes. He couldn't help but think of what Ruby would think if he were to bring her to meet his family, which made his heart skip a beat. He wanted so much to bring her here. The appeal was a living, palpable force that grew inside of him. Would she think he had misled her or, after he told her how he couldn't live without her, would she forgive him all? The scenario was so absurd that he laughed out loud. His whole body jerked when he heard screams from a voice he knew very well. Ann's hair blew out behind her and she launched herself into his arms.

Fin caught his breath that had been knocked out him by his grown sister running into him, and she dragged him inside. Anne told him that their parents needed to check on one of the businesses in Birmingham, so they would be back in a week, and that she was there to check the mail.

Familiarity hit him when he entered the front room. It always smelled faintly of wood polish and dampness. As they walked to the library, they passed the carpeted stairway that, as kids, they had slid down, timing each other to see how fast they could go. He and Ian had always gone all out, and had gotten bruises to prove it. Although large, the house never felt excessive, and when they were not outside exploring or at school, it provided endless opportunities for young kids to get into trouble.

The outside was typical of nineteenth century Scottish estates. It held a bank of mullioned windows that ran along the large, grey, hand-chiseled stone blocks, all under the steep pitched roofs that were customary in the mid-1800s. The estate had been in their family for generations, and each added something new. The forty-acre grounds rolled with a large expanse of lawn in front of the estate and a circular pea gravel drive. The stables and tack room were always kept ready, although Anne and Fin were the only family members who rode lately. Further on was a stocked pond set in a stand of trees, where the siblings spent summer days swimming and fishing in its cold, deep waters.

A fire had been set in the library, and Anne folded her legs under her in one of the dark leather chairs. "Finey, start from the beginning. Are you all right? We were all so worried." She stopped and watched him, twirling her long dark hair around her finger—a childhood habit. "Your *very short* missives said you were in Belgium? What were you doing?"

Fin thought that his usual, devil-may-care attitude toward things had run its course. Losing Ian, his family, and the changes that happened inside him during his time away didn't seem to reconcile with his previous attitude any longer. He dragged his fingers through his jet-black hair and studied the thick Persian rug under his feet.

His voice was deep with emotion when he started in, "Christ, Anne, when Ian died, I thought the walls would crush me. I hate to think it, let alone say it, but I was so angry that he left me to pick up all his shit. Everyone knew I wasn't that person and, for the first time in my life, I didn't think I would be able to accomplish what was in front of me." His hands ran over his face. "I'm good at cavalier and ludic, but I've always watched at a distance with the business. My life was to have fun and give my two cents when it suited me. No one ever thought I would step into the family business. Hell, I never wanted it, and I felt completely alone."

Fin held up his hand to stop her protest. "I knew I could count on you, but it went beyond that. I can't even explain it. I left, and I apologize because I should have choked down my own selfish feelings and been the brother that Ian could be proud of, that you all could. All I can say is that I needed time, and I'm ready now."

When he looked up at her, Anne's delicate fingers covered her lips and tears streamed down her face. "Oh, Finey. I miss them so much, but you can run the business, you can step into his shoes, and he *would* be proud of you. I've never seen you be anything but perfect at whatever you do. I'm just so glad you're back."

They spent the next hour going over all that had happened since he left Stonehaven. His father had handed some smaller ventures over to a firm they hired in the interim, until Fin returned and could get up to speed with their holdings. But he still had his hands on the major assets, trusting only loyal employees that had been with the family for years.

His mother and Anne had the disheartening task of going through Ian's family's belongings and putting his home on the market—things Fin did not even think about. He inwardly winced at the pain they each were going through, all in different ways, but no one worse than the other. While there was nothing he could change, he knew he would go forward very differently.

Although it was misting, they decided to ride around the property—one of Fin's favorite pastimes. He loved the way the clouds hung as if they were a smokescreen and the smell of the peat and dirt when the horses kicked it up. It took them twenty minutes to get to his favorite place on the whole property, an outcropping where the land met the sea. Waves exploded against the rocky shore twenty feet below them with such force that the spray often made it up to Fin. He and Anne sat and watched the churning water. It was too loud to have a conversation. This spot had always been where Fin went when he needed to remember his place in the world, to remind him that there were things much bigger than him. When his life became caddish, exaggerated by the people around him, he came here and contemplated things important to him, things no one else, other than maybe Anne or Ian, knew of.

He gripped the horn, looked at the swirling greys and greens of the frigid North Sea, and remembered how easy it had been to talk to Ruby. He would gladly have told her anything she wanted to know. He also knew he would never tire of listening to her voice or watching her face play with every emotion. Being with her had been so easy, something he had never known before. At the time, he told himself he left to spare her any attachment she was forming. But now, in this place, where things were always clear, he realized he did what he did for him. He could not live through more heartbreak. After Ian and his family, he wouldn't be able to bear it, and it shook him to the core that she had filled a hole in him and then so easily walked away.

He ran his fingers through his hair and looked at Anne. She had a rascally grin on her dew-covered face as she raised her voice above the surf. "Race you home!" Her heels already pounded against her horse as she swung the reins around. She was a good forty feet ahead of him when he gave his horse full rein. Then he flew.

Anne was deep in the saddle, the braid she had loosely wound together before the ride flapped against the back of her jacket that billowed behind her. She looked over her shoulder and a black strand cut across her face. She looked just as she had as a child, happy and carefree.

Fin was at her heel as they rounded a curve toward the house. He squeezed his legs for the final sprint and won by a half a length. They all breathed hard as they slowed to a trot and made their way back to the stable. The horses blew small dragon smoke, their hides slick with sweat and rain. "That was what we needed, but you could have let me win, you know," Anne said.

Fin helped his sister down. "Now, what fun would that be?" They handed the reins over to the stableman, with whom they chatted briefly before moving indoors. Moisture beaded on the oilcloth of their jackets, as if they were a couple of ducks. They shook them out and hung them inside the front door and, although the layer of cloth had protected them, they decided to change and meet back in the library.

Anne had coffee brought in, and the fire had been stoked. They sat in the same chairs they had earlier, their cheeks still pink from the ride. Anne pulled a soft lamb's wool blanket around her shoulders and draped it over her legs that were tucked underneath her. Fin stared into the flame. He was a million miles away, with an American girl lying in his arms in a beautiful hotel in Belgium. He saw her sensual smile and felt her against his skin. He squeezed his eyes shut, trying to make the image disappear. He was in serious peril of losing his mind if he chose to go down that path.

There was a hand on his leg. "Who is she?" His face was unreadable when his eyes met Anne's. "Oh, please, Finey. I know you. Was it a model love fest in Belgium?" She had spent years watching one bimbo after another enter and quickly exit Fin's life. He never let anyone get too close. Of all people, she understood him. Before Thomas, Fin knew that she had felt the same as he did—jaded by people trying to seduce, only to find that it was the family name and not them that was the real seduction.

Fin looked away and didn't give one of his usual, flippant remarks that had become so common that they served as family jokes, like, "It's the price I have to pay," or "Life is rough for the beauties." Silly comments that didn't take into account the reasons behind his actions. He was a shining star, a comet that left stardust behind wherever he went. He had a magical aura. Because he was forever saying how he was more than content with his love life, everyone resigned themselves to the fact that he would forever be a bachelor.

"Fin?" Anne's question hung in the air. His expression was primal, an animal yet undecided to fight or flee when he pierced her with a pained, stormy gaze.

"Shit, shit, shit!" his voiced raised with each curse. He felt like tearing his face off. It would feel good. At least it would be different than the strangle hold that squeezed his chest the moment he left Ruby. He had to do something. He sprang from the chair. The innocuous piece of furniture suddenly felt like a cage keeping him in a false state of insouciance. Indifference was so far from the feelings that coursed through him. He started pacing while dragging both hands through his hair.

"Finley, sit down and talk to me. What is going on?" Anne tossed the blanket aside and reached her hand out to him.

Fin had never felt so out of control. He usually took on life as an amusing challenge, but this, whatever it was, was completely foreign. His voice held a tempest of emotion. "I don't want to sit down, Anne. I can't sit down." Then it exploded out of him, a dike giving way, crumbling under the pressure. "It was a girl, a stupid girl. We spent two days together. *Two* days. We talked about nothing and everything, and we could just sit, not a word said, and I felt more like myself than I ever have." He paced back and forth and stopped in front of the fireplace, gripping the thick stone mantel with both hands. "She made me laugh. God, it felt good. I could watch her forever, Anne, and now I am losing my mind. I taste her in the air. When I close my eyes, I can hear her say my name. I feel her touch." His forehead pressed against the mantel. "What happened?"

Anne fell back into the chair, apparently bowled over by what he said. Seconds passed. "Why, Finey, you've fallen in love." She sighed and put her hand on her chest.

"This is so far from humorous, Anne. What in the hell am I going to do?" His head was lowered looking at the flames dance back and forth.

"Go get her. Where is she? *Who* is she?" She had settled in again, getting ready to pull every last detail out of her brother.

Fin winced. "Her name is Ruby, and I don't know where she is. I don't know exactly where she's going. Christ, I don't even know where she lives. On top of that, she thinks I'm a handyman drifter."

Coffee sprayed out of Anne's mouth. "What? Why would she think that? What were you doing?"

He told his sister about meeting Hans and the work he had done while he was there, about the shack he called

home, and about some of the people he met, including
Chloris, Harald, and Marget. He skipped over that he was
drunk most nights and had a revolving door of
unremembered sexual debauchery. He ended with the time
he spent with Ruby, the freedom she had given him to be
himself without worrying if she was with him for reasons
other than wanting to be in his company. He talked about
how he wanted to make sure she was okay and the almost
inherent instinct he had to protect and care for her. When he
finished he felt drained, as if he had finished a footrace and
was now bent over to catch his breath.

Anne let an amount of time go by, and the silence hung
in the air. When he finally looked at her, she said, "It doesn't
matter that she is from America, Fin. If you don't try and
find her and tell her how you feel, you'll hate yourself. You
may pass up something that comes around once in a
lifetime. She would be an idiot not to marry you and, from
what you've said, she doesn't sound like an idiot. I already
love her because you do. She loves you for you, and it won't
matter what she thought before."

"Marry her?" When she said those words, his heart
skipped a beat. Those were two words he never thought
would make it into his vocabulary. Now he swirled them
around, tasting them like a good wine. Of course he would
marry her. It seemed so natural. Rather than his usual
distaste he had toward the whole concept, an electric shock
that he repelled away from, he felt light as air and giddy
with thought that she would be his forever.

Now that he knew his course, he needed a plan.
Together, he and Anne talked about his responsibilities
toward the family. Although she wanted him to find Ruby
immediately, he was not going to leave without fulfilling
obligations and discussing them with his father. They had a

close relationship, even if it was strained at times, especially when Fin was growing up. His father had seen the unfulfilled potential that Finley had. Later, his father accepted that his youngest son had chosen differently than Ian and, although there were still heated arguments about what path he would take, at this point, any would suit his father. The conversation should prove interesting when his parents returned.

After he spent time with his parents, Fin would call Chloris at Prima Facie. Maybe she knew Ruby's information. She might still be in Greece. She'd be traveling for weeks anyway, a thought that sent every type of emotion surging through his body. She would meet so many people, and it was impossible not to be drawn to her. Maybe it was like she had said: the draw was unique to him. He smiled when she had said that. She had no idea. If anyone did touch her, though, he would happily rip them apart. Then there were all the dangers of a woman traveling alone. Maybe he still would go crazy. Mentally, he marked off the time until he could be with her again.

CHAPTER TWENTY-NINE

Ruby wriggled into the smooth black stones that made up Kolumbo beach. She was becoming a beach connoisseur, and loved each day's adventures. Dimitri called at nine o'clock every morning to see where she wanted to go. By nine-thirty he was in front of their house with a picnic basket filled with water and some kind of Greek dish his wife had made for them. As much as he tried selling her on visiting churches and museums, Ruby wanted to visit the different beaches of Santorini. He had become tricky, however; on the way to the beach of the day, his car had an uncanny way of acting up right in front of a museum or church or one of the many wineries that dotted the island. He would feign aggravation by kicking a tire and letting out a frustrated growl. He'd then raise his hands in defeat saying, "Okay, Ruby. You and Retta go into the Folk Museum. It is very nice. I will fix my car, no problem." Retta and Ruby were now used to the routine and found it rather charming—they had seen things they had no intention of seeing before.

She and Retta had wandered the narrow, curving streets of Oia. On their second day, they purchased a few gauzy dresses that fit the feel of the island more so than the clothes they had for the wet, cool weather of mainland Europe. Dimitri told them that the weather was unusually warm for the time of year, which suited them just fine. Brian often joined them later in the day. They would write a note that told him the beach they were going to and, around noon, when he woke up, he hitchhiked or walked to meet them.

They would spend the afternoon swimming or seeing who could skip stones the furthest, all while eating the food in the basket: baklava, grape leaves, figs, or other regional foods. In other words, Santorini was a beach paradise.

Retta asked more about Ruby's time with Fin and now, given some distance, it was easier for Ruby to tell her more details, including that she had never felt anything even close to what she did with Fin the whole time she had dated Scott. She told her how that Fin would simply look at her and make her melt and about how right it felt to be with him. Now the three days she spent with him seemed like a dream. She wasn't sure what she was exaggerating about and what she wasn't.

Retta kept saying that he had probably freaked out and that she needed to call him. The funny thing was that Ruby didn't even know how to contact him, even if she wanted to. Although she desperately wanted to talk to Fin, she didn't want to be that girl—the chaser, the needy one. Still, she couldn't stop from wishing that he would track her down, declare his love, and whisk her off into the sunset, but she kept that wish to herself. She was embarrassed to even think it in her own head, so she decided that her time with Fin was only a memory, the best memory, one she could look back to when she was eighty and realized that only a handful of people must be so lucky. Still, that he let her go was a bitter pill.

One sundrenched day faded into the next as they jumped off cliffs and got used to lying topless on the rocks. The nakedness felt liberating, and after some initial modesty, she didn't care. When Brian occasionally turned onto his stomach and moaned as he shook his lions' mane, she didn't care about that either. They hiked from one village to the next just for a glass of local wine. They took a snorkeling

tour and saw the lava formations and colorful fish under the
clear blue water. They laughed so hard that she was sure she
saw signs of stomach muscles.

As ideal as Santorini was, she often found herself
playing the "what if" game. *What if he would have asked me to
stay? What if I had told him what I was feeling? What if he was
standing here now?* It was pathetic, she knew, but oh well.
Her dreams, which she truly could not control, had also
become strange. She often drifted off on the beach as the sun
warmed her skin and the ocean lulled her peacefully to
sleep. In one dream, she floated on her back in the cool
water when a fish bit down on her hair and started dragging
her through swelling waves. She saw Fin on the beach and
tried screaming to him, but all he did was smile and raise his
hand. Then she woke up, mad all over again.

Now she, Retta, and Brian sat on their veranda that
overlooked the crystal water below. Dimitri left them at the
house, like he did every day, with kisses on both cheeks
saying, "Okay, Ruby. I will telephone you at nine." She felt
so guilty when he first started this routine, but he seemed
genuinely happy every day, thinking that he was pulling the
wool over their eyes with his sly detours and hearing their
adventures of the day. Soon the ritual felt normal.

They were browned from days of sun, and dried salt
from the water clung in patches to their skin. "Ruby, do you
want some more dip?" Brian sunk some bread into a bowl of
eggplant humus that Dimitri's wife had made and handed it
over to her.

"Ruby, Ruuubby. Are you asleep?" He nudged her with
his foot.

"Wha." Her eyes came half-way open, and her voice was
lazy. "I am just completely relaxed. My body's weightless."
She grabbed the bowl and dipped her finger into it. "This is

so good. I'm going to miss seeing what's inside that basket every day."

Retta came twirling out and stopped on a dime, carrying their nightly Mojitos balanced on a bar tray. "What do you mean you're going to miss? Where are you going?" She put the tray on the table and hooked her hair behind her ears.

"I've been here for over two weeks. I thought I was going to stay for three days. You knew I was going to Norway. It's going to take me forever. Jen and Marcie are still here. Maybe you can spend time with them."

It had been so weird. The girls were friendly, but they were never at the house. They had met some locals and often stayed with them. In the time Ruby had been in Santorini, she had seen them twice—once coming out of the shower and they all had dinner one night at a fish restaurant in Amoundi. "Of course, Brian is here. By the way, what are *you* doing?"

Brian flashed his straight white teeth. "I'm goin' with the flow, sister. I may hang here awhile longer, then jump on over to Turkey to see what's goin' on there. Who knows."

Ruby looked at Retta, and they burst out laughing, "How very seventies, Haight Ashbury of you, 'goin' with the flow,' 'hangin'' and 'jumpin''." Ruby flicked him in the thigh.

"That's right, mama." He leaned back, grabbed his drink, and passed one to Retta. "When are you taking off?"

"I think the day after tomorrow sounds good. I want to make some stops on the way." Ruby cocked her head. "Isn't it strange not to have any agenda?"

All three of them nodded silently, until Retta broke the silence. "I can't believe you're leaving. We have to go to the beach tomorrow, something special."

"Ret, babe, we go to the beach every day." Brian made

crazy eyes at Ruby.

"I know, but maybe we could rent kayaks, or we could jump off the cliff. What do you want to do Ruby?"

"You know what I want to do? I want to get Demitri's call, find what surprises are in the basket, then go to the beach and lay all the live-long day. I can't think of anything better." Ruby hoped Retta couldn't see the slight tenseness around the corners of her eyes at her last comment. *There is one thing that could be better.*

"You know what you should do? You should have Dimitri call and make a reservation for a berth for the trip back to Italy. Or better yet, get a flight."

Brian shook his head. "I really don't want to do that trip again."

Retta looked at him, her face scrunched in thought. "Was it really that bad? Maybe we wanted it to be a better story, so we embellished a bit."

"Was you sprawled like a fish on land with spit and puke dripping out the side of your mouth an embellishment? You've got to be kidding me. If anything, we skipped over some things." His fingers caught in his springy curls.

"Okay, you're right. It was awful. Try to get a cabin or fly, that's exactly what you should do. Did Fin get you a roundtrip? That'd be great. Are you going to stay in Italy? Oh, you should go to Venice. My god, I'm going to miss you." Per usual, no comment was needed for the long string of jumbled sentences. Ruby smiled. She would miss Retta, too.

* * *

Ruby sat at a café at St. Mark's Square. She couldn't remember most of the trip that got her to Venice. Luckily, she listened to Brian and got a boat cabin to Italy. Dimitri insisted that it was part of what Fin stipulated in his instructions about her stay in Greece. In other words, he told Dimitri to "Give her anything she wanted." She knew she should feel warm and fuzzy about his concern, but really after he left her like a toy he had gotten bored with, she was more baffled than anything. She forced herself to stop thinking about him every minute of every day. In fact, hours went by that she thought about the places she wanted to go and things to see. She was nearly back on track, but Fin was center stage again.

She screamed inside her head, realizing that no good would come from kicking a chair or pounding a fist on the table. Americans were not well-liked already, and she didn't need to toss a flaming log onto the fire. Instead, Ruby sat back and watched tour groups follow their designated, umbrella-toting guides. She willed herself to stay in the present rather than relive the mystification of the past. The café was a perfect spot to look over the entire square. Saint Marks was an intricate stone rectangle that could very well have felt claustrophobic had it not been for the opened end looking out to the sea. The arched windows and entries made it feel like a thousand eyes were staring at her. She had come to love the whole concept of a square—it was a gathering place in the heart of the village, where locals and tourist could walk to, sit, and talk for hours.

America didn't have cities like this. Everyone drove to their destination, did their business, and drove back home. Walking had become obsolete. To a European, a thirty-minute walk was merely something you did. The same walk in America became an outing one would need to prepare for, perhaps with a water bottle, for sure a snack, suntan lotion, hat, and well a backpack really. Here, outdoor cafes were everywhere, both in small farming communities and in large cities. Being a people watcher, Ruby loved the communal atmosphere.

She remembered Pearl Street in Boulder, Colorado, which was lined with outdoor seating—something unusual in most small towns. *Maybe I could live someplace like this, but what would I do? Work at a hostel? Maybe rent mopeds? Okay, I'm having mental diarrhea. Back to my tea.* Ruby still felt queasy after the three days it had taken to get to Venice. The boat ride was just like Retta and Brian had described. She hadn't gotten sick, but when she got on solid ground, kissing it wouldn't have seemed crazy. The larger boat to Italy was better; she shared a room, but her body was just now getting back to feeling as though it wasn't swaying when she walked. She then took an eleven-hour night train from Brindisi to Venice. She thought it would be the most efficient way to spend her time, but never again. Sitting upright, listening to drunken revelers—which must be standard on all night trains—was worse than getting a filling without Novocain.

She had settled into a room for let by a woman who approached her at the train station. It was small and basic, but it had a small window that overlooked a canal, and it was private. After so many days with people, it felt good to have space to herself. She walked the maze of stone streets for hours, looked in glass shops, shops filled with Carnival masks, and some with cheese and sausage.

* * *

Ruby now sat and watched kids feed the millions of pigeons in St. Mark's Square, only to scream and start to cry when the dirty birds chomped down on their little fingers. She needed a shower just watching the birds land en masse when grown people covered their bodies in seed for a corny photo op.

"Do you mind?" Ruby looked up at two Barbie dolls; they were Ken and Barbie come to life. They were both tanned, toned, and very blonde.

Ruby lowered the cup from her mouth. "Excuse me?"

"You're American, right?" Barbie said in an eighties, Valley girl, perky voice. Ruby tried a genuine smile and nodded her head. She may as well have been wearing a "Proud to be an American" t-shirt, and here she thought she looked native. Silly girl.

"Oh . . . my . . . god. All we want to do is talk to someone from home. Can we sit with you?"

Well, hell, what could she say, except, "Yeah, of course."

"I'm Mindy, and this is Andy. How long have you been traveling?" Andy pulled a chair from another table.

"A few weeks. I'm Ruby, by the way." She needed to see if she was right about them, "Where are you from?"

"Long Beach." *Eureka! Dang, I'm good.* "Andy wanted to surf Cantabria, but he promised I could see Venice. I swear I am, like, so tired of no one understanding us, aren't you?" Mindy actually whooshed her long, sun-bleached hair over her shoulder.

Ruby looked from one to the other. Andy still had yet to say a word, and she guessed he may be quite stoned from the blank, glassy way he stared at the sugar cubes they brought for her tea. "No, I think it's pretty much par for the course when you're in Europe," Ruby said. Well, that got a snort from Andy. "Anyway, I need to go, but nice meeting you." Already paid up, she made a quick exit and started wandering again.

Venice was truly a maze. Streets ended at the green water of a canal, and Ruby would have to backtrack and do it all over again. Ruby finally made it to an area where gondolas were docked and watched how the gondoliers prepared them. By the time she found her way back to her room, it was dusk. She was exhausted. Even though it was only nine o'clock, she called it a day. One more day in Venice would be enough and then make her way to Hallstat, Austria.

* * *

Ruby leaned her head back against the train seat. It would take a bit of a crazy route, but she was on her way to Hallstat. Her thoughts turned to how funny it was, the lengths people go to make a train compartment seem full so they didn't have to share. She now did the same; her pack was on the seat across from her, and she tossed her pullover onto the seat next to her. Of course, that was no deterrent for Rambo, who first looked in the window and then threw the door open. No kidding, it was John Rambo—he held a beer in one hand, a cigarette in the other, was dressed head-to-toe in camouflage, and even had a band in his hair. What are the odds?

"I won't speak English. You Americans think all countries bow to you. I bought this watch. Look."

Ruby looked. Its face showed an American flag.

"An American flag. You like it? America, bah." For the next hour, she was forced to listen to Rambo talk about how he wouldn't speak English because he was German, which was a tad odd, given that he rambled on and on, his watch had a big American flag, and he showed pictures of his American car, but who was she to question a fictional soldier? Never having had a migraine, she couldn't be sure that's what was happening to her head, but her ears felt like they would bleed at any time if she listened to one more word. Rambo was one of many in a string of interesting characters she met during her travels.

In the next two weeks, Ruby's Eurail pass more than

paid for itself. She was in constant motion. She moved across Austria and up to Czech, where an old man, Rudolf, got off the train with Ruby and gave her a tour of Prague and spent three hours showing her the city he had grown up in. Prague with Rudolf was amazing and could never be reproduced in a lifetime. He told her about growing up under Communist rule and that parents needed to lie to their children, telling them that east was paradise. If they didn't, they'd receive a house call from the government. He held her elbow every time they crossed the street and said "Watch yourself" in a gentlemanly, old world way.

From Prague, Ruby went into Germany. She first stopped in Nurnberg, where she spent two days with a woman from Austria. Then on to Munich, where she walked for hours in the Deutsches museum with its amazing exhibits that people are encouraged to fiddle with. She asked questions of a museum worker and ended up being invited for a beer after he got off work. In all her traveling, Ruby came to realize that she didn't have to be alone unless she wanted to, and she admitted that she enjoyed the hodgepodge of company she had been with.

From Germany she went down to Switzerland and, in the youth hostel in Interlaken, met two men, one from South Africa and the other from Australia. They spent a beautiful, sunny day on a boat tour and hiking to a waterfall. On the way back, when she desperately needed to find a toilet, they mistook a Hari-Krishna compound for an ordinary building. It wasn't until they clued into the posters and pamphlets that they ran out laughing so hard she no longer needed the toilet, but a change of clothes.

One of the most memorable moments took place in Italy, when she tried getting to the Cinque Terre. She was thumbing through a guide book when a man in the train car with her asked where she wanted to go. As it happened, he and a friend were taking a sailboat near her destination and invited her to come. After the man saw her hesitate, he promised he wasn't crazy, and that she could do as she wished. *Think, think, think.* Okay maybe it was stupid, but Ruby ended up spending two days on a boat skirting along the Italian Riviera.

One night they docked in a village and wound their way through unbelievably small alleys to the best food Ruby had ever had. The cook, who looked to be in her nineties and wore an apron pinned with safety pins, came out to chat with her two friends, Ruby's shipmates. Wow, the whole evening was surreal and magical.

Names and faces came and went. It was strange to Ruby to spend days with someone and then to leave, knowing she would never see them again. She felt alive, and each experience brought her closer to knowing who she was and how much she could do.

On the fringes of her mind, hanging like a fuzzy dream, was the time she spent with Fin. Although she didn't really have a plan, she felt pulled to go back to Brugge. She told herself it was to see Chloris, and she wanted to, of course, but it also meant returning to where Fin had lived. A sick part of her wanted to walk where he did and be with someone he had been close to, even though he would have left weeks ago. She cringed at this last part, but maybe he left something, anything she could touch and hold. God, she felt pathetic. So she crisscrossed Europe and inched her way closer to where she knew she would eventually go. When she got to Luxemburg, she knew it would have been crazy to not make the short, two-hour trip to Brugge. She had held out as long as she could. She was a druggy who needed one last fix before she quit cold-turkey. What would adding one more little crack in her heart hurt?

Everything was familiar when Ruby got off the bus and walked to Prima Facie. The closer she got, the more she consciously had to make her feet slow down. Her heart beat in double-time, and her stomach was in knots. *My gosh, if this is the way I feel when he isn't here, I can't imagine what I would be like if he was.* It had been a little over a month since she had been in Brugge, and now the colors were more vibrant, with flowers in full bloom and the grass a carpet of summer green. She stood outside the hostel window and warily looked inside, hoping that Fin would come out through the kitchen or round the corner, and at the same time hoping he wouldn't. The only person she saw was a pert forest sprite. Chloris was behind the bar, hair in spikey disarray. Her head bobbed, as if she was singing a song. Ruby tapped on the window.

CHAPTER THIRTY

Chloris looked up when Ruby tapped and did a genuine double take, her eyes as wide open as her mouth. Ruby heard a squeal, and then Chloris launched herself across the room. As Ruby opened the door, she missed everything Chloris asked except the two words, "get here." The meaning was clear, though. Ruby couldn't help but smile at the sight of Chloris; she dropped her backpack to the floor and said, "I just got off the bus from the train station. I wouldn't have been in Brugge without being right here, would I?"

"It is so weird that you would come today." She shook her head, "Come and sit down and tell me what you've been doing." It was afternoon, so most of the tourists were already out for the day. The restaurant was empty, except for an older man reading a paper at a center table. They made their way back to the corner booth.

Quick snapshots of her last time here popped up. Fin sat at this booth the night he first kissed her. This was where she danced when he came behind her and changed her life. *Maybe coming back wasn't such a good idea.* She saw him everywhere and wanted him more than anything she had wanted in her life. The need physically hurt. *No. Not a good idea at all.*

"Did you go to Greece? Oh, I can't wait to hear everything."

Thankful to have something else to think about, Ruby started in on Greece. She skipped over the days spent with Fin in Dinant, which, surprisingly, Chloris didn't complain or ask about. Maybe Fin had told her they had a good time and that he was moving on. She promised herself she wouldn't ask. Now, she needed to threaten herself with something good, like no more chocolate, to keep her from reneging.

Chloris laughed about the Rambo character when Ruby paused and thought about something Chloris had said earlier. "Hey, what did you mean that it was weird I came today?" Her lungs seemed to collapsed, as if her body knew something her mind didn't and she needed to brace herself for what was coming.

Chloris's green eyes darted to the table and then back up at Ruby. She pursed her pink lips together. "Fin called this morning, asking if you had been back. He told me, after I pulled it out of him, how he was quite an ass when he left you. He wanted to know if I knew how to get in touch with you."

It was a good thing Ruby was sitting. Her face felt like it was on fire and, although her eyes were open, everything went black. *This must be what it's like to drown*, she said to herself, thinking of one of her biggest fears, because she couldn't get any air into her lungs. They felt as if they had shut down. She picked up the glass of water in front of her and tried to get her bearings. Small ripples played across the surface from the tremors that surged through her limbs. Finally, the gulp painfully slid down her constricted esophagus in one big water bubble. She put her glass down before it broke and pretended to pick something off the table with her fingernail. She wanted her voice to be nonchalant, calm. Instead, it came out in a strangled whisper, "What'd you say?"

"I told him I hadn't seen you and that I didn't know how to get in touch with you, which is true. I didn't get your postal information, because I thought I would see you before you went back to America. Then I completely lit into him about how I thought I knew him and why would he have been like he was to you." Her face scrunched up in apology. "Sorry, but I couldn't help it. I saw him when he watched you. Fin had been here long enough for me to know the way he acted with you was not typical. My god, he was with so many women it was a joke." Her face looked pained. "Ruby, what I'm saying is that I saw him with them, and it was like he used them to forget something else. More often than not he was drunk and his eyes were blank. Then you came, and I saw when he first looked at you. His whole body changed. I don't know. I can't explain it, but something happened. Then he asked you to go away with him. He had never done that—not even close. He had always completely withdrawn from those other women after he had been with them. He wasn't mean about it, but they knew." She took a breath and touched Ruby's finger that had worked so hard it had started to gouge the wood.

When Ruby looked up, her eyes brimmed with unshed tears. She didn't want to cry, she hated tears, but it seemed that she no longer had control over her body. Because she couldn't stop them, she ignored them. She looked at Chloris as one unruly droplet slid down her cheek. "Thanks for saying that, but it was pretty apparent that I was exactly like every other woman. I had thought there was something, but there wasn't. You're right, I knew. There was no question he was done." Ruby gave a half-hearted smile. "I'm sure he loved you reading him the riot act." *As long as I'm being gutted, may as well twist the knife.* She had some irrational need to hear something, anything about him.

"Actually, he maybe didn't enjoy it, but it seemed like he knew he deserved it. He said he had made a mistake and that he would find you. He gave me a number to reach him at." Her green eyes sharpened as she continued, "Do you want it?" She held the paper in her hand.

Ruby realized that if she would have come an hour earlier, he could have been on the phone with Chloris when she walked in. Her stomach roiled and her feet started sweating. *Crap, I'm going to get sick.* To a sixteen year old, Fin saying he would find her probably seemed romantic, but Ruby knew that he had been pacifying Chloris and most likely his conscience at the same time. She jumped from the booth and ran to the bathroom down the hall. Thankfully it was empty, because she barely made it to the toilet before she spewed the roll she had eaten on the train into the water-stained porcelain.

After she had puked more than humanly possible, Ruby became aware that nothing matched the feeling of bile burning her nose. Her unwashed hair stuck to her sweaty forehead, and her eyes watered from the force. When the nausea left, she went to the faucet, stuck her mouth under the stream, and spit like she was at a dentist: swish and spit, swish and spit. She splashed water over her face and looked into the mirror. *Man, I look awful.* It seemed like she had done pretty well with her feelings, but as she looked at her face, she saw telltale signs of gloom. Her eyes had lost their luster and were three shades lighter. Dark rings looked like nearly healed bruises on her face. She pinched her cheeks, a hint her grandmother had given her to appear sprightly. She tried smiling, but it felt forced and looked awkward but, with practice, it would get better.

When she opened the door, Chloris leaned against the wall, her arms crossed over her stomach and her eyes slits. "You're pregnant, aren't you?"

Ruby felt like she had swallowed her tongue, if a thing

like that was possible. There were no words, so she blinked repeatedly, waking from a nightmare.

"Why were you sick?" Chloris's thin arms were planted on her boyish hips. She looked like Tinker Bell reprimanding Peter.

A laugh burst out of Ruby's lips. She mirrored Chloris's stance. "I am not pregnant. I've been moving non-stop and eating some food I'm not used to, and when you were talking about …him," she couldn't choke out the name, "it threw me over the top. It's nothing. Let me get my toothbrush before I really offend you." Her second attempt at a smile didn't hurt so much. "Are there any rooms open?"

Chloris tried reading Ruby's face. After a bit she, must have decided she believed her, because she pushed away from the wall. "We have a private available, but both mom and dad are gone—some weekend thing—so you can stay in the apartment with me." She smiled up at Ruby. "How long are you staying?"

"I need to get up to Norway. I think I'll check out flights. A guy I met said it was pretty cheap, so I'll stay all of tomorrow, and then I need to go. I'm already later than I told my relatives I would be. Do you think you could call the airline for me?"

"Yeah, of course. No problem. I wish you could stay longer. With my parents gone, I have to stay here all day." Her shoulders slouched.

"I feel like I've been running a race since I left Greece. It'll feel good to have a day to relax. I'll stay with you and keep you company." Even though she knew she would see Fin everywhere, she wanted to spend time with Chloris. She wasn't about to stick her head in the sand over an apparition.

* * *

Chloris showed Ruby the apartment and told her that she should take a bath and relax. She said it innocently enough, but it had been a few days since Ruby had showered and, after the events of the day, she knew she was in desperate need. She soaked for nearly an hour, using the bath soap she had gotten with Retta and added hot water twice. She felt much more like herself as she made it back down to the restaurant.

More people had trickled in from their day spent exploring. Ruby thought she recognized a couple of girls she had met in Germany, which was strange. She was part of an underground society of world travelers. There should be some secret handshake. Ruby had never been part of any kind of group, not quite making it into any one category — not sports, not arts, and not academics. She took nibbles of each, but never sat at the table. It felt good to belong to something, even if it was more abstract. She nodded to the girls and moved to where Chloris poured beer at the bar.

The rest of that day and the next, Ruby sat in one chair or another in the restaurant and thumbed through magazines left behind by people, or she helped Chloris behind the bar. She did her laundry in a washing machine instead of a sink, and even used the drier at the hostel. The thought of a boat and another night train compelled her to buy an airline ticket to Oslo. The rolling waves and no sleep had become more than unappealing. Besides, the flight would save days of travel.

She had been sick again right after she woke up. She really *must* have eaten something that didn't sit well. Chloris gave her the nymph's eye, but let it go after Ruby told her that she had eaten clams and mussels in Luxemburg that even at the time tasted a little off. Instead of using the "P" word again, Chloris made some peppermint tea, which seemed to do the trick. The night before Ruby left, Chloris brought some soup up to the apartment, and they sat and talked about where they both planned to go next. "I think I'm going to go to Scotla…" Chloris's hand clamped over her mouth.

Ruby pretended that she didn't know what Chloris was about to say. They both seemed to intuit that any topic related to Fin or romance or, really, anything male, was off limits. So they stuck to telling funny stories about traveling.

Chloris was more worldly, so she told stories of snakes falling from trees in Thailand and of hot spring baths in Chili. Ruby got to tell of a girl bitten by bedbugs in a hostel in Austria and how, as a result, she looked like a leper. They traded information and both extended open invitations for visits. Chloris didn't know where her mom would be next, but she told Ruby she would write to her. Maybe they could meet, wherever it ended up being.

When Ruby woke up the next day, she felt better. She had slept well and her stomach wasn't queasy. She needed to catch the eight o'clock train to make it to the airport on time, so she was up early with Chloris having tea and toast—she wasn't quite ready for coffee yet. They left each other at the door. Ruby actually felt a lump in her throat when they said good-bye, although she was sure that they would see each other again.

* * *

Between the flight and the train ride it took eight hours, but Ruby stood outside the station in Kristiansand, waiting for Borghild, the best friend of her paternal grandmother. They had grown up together in Norway and then came to the United States to work as maids in New York when they were just sixteen. Ruby listened to stories of how they couldn't speak English when they first arrived and of the

unbelievable adventures they had when they were together.
She couldn't wait to meet the lady about whom she had
heard so much over the years. When she walked out of the
station, a handful of people were there to pick up or drop off
passengers. She spotted Borghild right away because of the
pictures in their grandmother's photo albums she and
Poppy pored over as kids. Borghild had aged in the sixty
years, but her face was very familiar. Ruby felt an instant
connection.

"Oh, Ruby. You look just like your pictures. Esther wrote
and sent a photo of you at her birthday in April. You all
looked so good." She held the picture out to Ruby, who took
it from the older woman's hand and looked at it. The photo
was taken at her parents' house a few days before Ruby left
for Europe. They all stood around her grandmother, who sat
in the center like a queen.

Ruby remembered that the day had been beautiful. She
had always loved April in Colorado. Spring was completely
unpredictable. The weather could either be seventy and
sunny or thirty with a foot of snow. What she loved most
were unexpected hints of the change in season, especially
the purple and yellow crocus that poked through the winter-
hardened soil and the cool, sweet smell in the air. These
were always welcomed changes. There were slight traces of
spring green tickling the trees. Even the clouds had a
different look—billowy with rain, rather than heavy with
snow.

For some reason, the picture made her want to cry. She
had not been homesick on this trip once. She had missed
Poppy, but had been so busy that she hadn't had time to be
homesick, until now. Looking at all of them smiling into the
lens, she blinked back the stinging in her eyes and wondered
when she had become such a maudlin sap.

Either ignoring or unaware of Ruby's tear-filled eyes, Borghild changed the subject. Ruby was grateful for it. "How was your trip here? I think it was a smart idea of yours to fly. It would have taken quite a while to make that trip from Belgium." Her accent was funny—a little East Coast with a Scandinavian sing-song lilt.

They were in the parking lot before Ruby said her first words to Borghild. "It was really good, thank you for coming to pick me up. Grandma has told me so much about you. I'm to report back everything we say and do."

Borghild smiled and opened the car door. "I miss Esther so much. If I was younger..." The words hung in the air. Ruby looked over the roof of the car at her. She was shorter than Ruby by a few inches and wore a tight cap of straight, grey hair on top of her round, wrinkled face. Her eyes were the watery blue that seemed to come with age. There was something else that Ruby couldn't put into words: She was wizened, comfortable, and happy. She had warmth that radiated from every pore. Ruby felt a pull toward her, as if she had known her in several lifetimes before today.

Borghild continued her thought. "Well, if I was younger I would have to start all over living my life, now wouldn't I?" Her eyes were a mix of reverie and mischief. She patted Ruby's thigh. "We're going to my home. I have a light snack for us, and Ragnar is waiting for us there. I usually stay with him, but I got a nurse to come in while you are here so we can go out when we'd like." As she spoke, she tapped Ruby's leg with her warm hand. Ragnar was her husband of many years. There had always been a bit of a mystery that surrounded the couple. Grandma told her that he was becoming hard to care for but, beyond that, she hadn't said much, so Ruby wasn't sure what to expect.

It took forty minutes of slow driving to reach Borghild's

house, which sat close to the street on a large lot. Typical of other houses they drove by, it was a white, shiny, wooden Cape Cod two story with a rounded, black-tiled roof. She loved the look. It was clean, different from anything in the United States.

When they walked up the short path to the door, Ruby breathed in deeply. The scent of lilac was carried on the cool breeze, filling her lungs with its sweet perfume. A row of large bushes in a patchwork of purples and whites ran along a short wooden fence that was once painted white, but had weathered over the years to reveal areas of grey, sun-bleached wood underneath. Unlike the perfectly mowed lush lawns in the States, Borghild's was completely natural. Dandelions spotted the reedy, knee-high lawn and, rather than being the gardener's nemesis, they became a bright accent to the tawny, green and straw colors where they shared the space. The windows of her house were perfectly symmetrical across the front of its white exterior, two sat side-by-side on the upper left, another two sat side-by-side on the upper right, and two large grated windows sat on either side of the entrance.

Walking through the front door, Ruby quickly realized that apart from the outside, elderly people's houses were the same everywhere. They stood in a living room filled with thickly upholstered, well-worm chairs in drab brown colors and a couch against a wall. A low oval coffee table sat in front of the couch, and on each piece of furniture was an indentation from years of people sitting in the exact same spot.

What was unexpected was the scenery out the huge picture window at the rear of the house. The view was of a long stretch of green lawn that butted up to a dune of reed grasses with a crisscross of worn paths through the white sandy knolls to the water's edge. "That's an amazing view," Ruby said, still carrying her pack on her shoulders. She stood motionless, looking out at the water in the distance.

"It's so nice today. We'll take our coffee on the deck. Ragnar will like that. We've had a lot of rain lately, and he doesn't like to be cooped up. Ruby, I'll take you to your room, and then we'll have a snack. Astrid, that's the nurse, is here somewhere, and Ragnar will love to see you." She set her purse on the couch and started up the stairs that were inside the front door.

Ruby followed Borghild's slow pace up the steep, narrow stairway to the second floor. The walls were white with wooden slats and, rather than looking stark, the decor was airy and beachy. Her room was the back bedroom that looked out to the sea. The window was open and without a screen, so the white, gauzy curtains billowed out the window in the breeze. "I hope this will be okay, Ruby. It's a small room, but I thought you would like the view."

"It's beautiful. I love it." She put her bag onto the floor inside the door and walked to the window. She stuck her head out and looked down. She saw a very sparse head of white hair attached to a thin, wiry figure sitting, legs crossed, on a black wrought-iron chair. By deduction, she assumed the man was Ragnar. He sat still, except for the slight tremor in his tanned hand that rested on a round table next to him. For some reason, Ruby was transfixed watching him. It may have been the way he sat or the veins in his hands—she wasn't quite sure.

Borghild spoke, bringing her attention back to the room. "I'll let you get settled. Come down when you're ready. We'll sit outside and you can tell me all about Esther." She had a sparkle to her voice.

"Okay, that sounds good. I'll be down in a minute."

Borghild quietly closed the door, and Ruby was left in the small space by herself. She surveyed the room, deciding that if she could create her own space, this would be it. The ceiling came down at an angle to one side of the room that her twin bed was pushed up against. A small, white side table sat next to the bed with a lacy doily on top and a vase of light and dark purple lilacs, which filled the room with their sweet scent. The floor was a thin, planks that were oak in color, and there was a large round rug that came from under the bed, covering half the floor. The bedding was white, with a feather tic folded at the foot.

Two pictures hung on the walls and, as she got closer, she realized that they were very familiar. Her grandfather had drawn since she could remember, and these were two of his sketches. One was a pencil drawing of a lighthouse on a rocky shore, and the other was a ship in colored pencil with a Norwegian flag flapping in the wind of a dark, white-capped sea. He never thought he was good, but Ruby had always loved to watch as he created a work of art from a blank canvas. He was her favorite artist.

She sat on the bed and closed her eyes, drinking in the smells and sounds around her. Unwillingly, she wondered what Fin was doing at this exact moment.

CHAPTER THIRTY-ONE

Ruby had thrown the good impression she wanted to give to Borghild straight out the window. She might as well have stomped on it. On her first day in Kristiansand, she came down for a snack and looked at the shrimps suspended in a reddish aspic mold and immediately ran out to the deck, not sure where the bathroom was, and proceeded to heave her guts out onto the lawn below. She apologized over and over to Borghild and then did the same with Ragnar, who had had a front row seat.

She told Borghild that she'd been fighting off a stomach bug, but inwardly she felt shaky and uncertain. It was five weeks since she had last seen Fin, and she calculated and recalculated, coming up with nothing. She had not gotten her period, but she had always been all over the place with that, so paid little attention, figuring it would happen when it happened. With traveling, time changes, different food, and stress, she thought that not having her period wasn't unusual.

Borghild gave her some crackers and peppermint schnapps, told her not to worry about a thing and that she was glad Ruby was with her rather than at a hostel. Ruby agreed. When the nurse got Ragnar settled for a nap, Ruby and Borghild sat outside and talked about her grandmother, sharing stories from years ago, when they were young. Ruby sat and listened to Borghild's soothing voice, trying to push the thoughts she was having from her head. *If I don't think it, it isn't, right?* Borghild told Ruby that Ragnar had been very vibrant up until two years ago, when he was diagnosed with

Alzheimer's, but now he was deteriorating quickly. She didn't make her life a sad story, but was rather thankful for the days she had been given with him.

The next day, Ruby took the bus to the center of Kristiansand. She walked in and out of shops, not really seeing anything. In fact, if asked, she could not have recalled a single one. Her mind wasn't in a haze; rather, it was moving too fast, creating a jittering frenzy of unending scenarios. At least now she could explain away the vomit. *It is because of stress. There.*

Borghild hadn't wanted to be away from Ragnar too long and told Ruby that the day after tomorrow was all theirs. The nurse would be there all day, so planned to take a drive in the countryside. The next morning, Ruby stretched when she woke up and lay still for ten minutes, gauging her stomach. She felt good. There was no queasiness to ignore. She stood up, and the room spun, but that sensation could be just getting up too fast. Ruby had an overwhelming need to talk to Poppy. She thought she was being crazy, and Poppy was always the voice of reason. She got dressed in layers: her Tencel pants that she was ready to burn, a long-sleeved, robin-egg blue cotton shirt, and a pull-over. Add the Teva's and she looked like she had every other day on this trip.

Ruby made her way downstairs and found Ragnar in a chair by the window, gazing out at the sea. She could spend days watching at his face. At one time, he must have been very handsome, but Ruby liked his face now. He still had a strong, squared jaw, and his blue eyes, looking at nothing in particular, were pools of history. The wrinkles in his face were deep and crisscrossed in what seemed a random pattern. Most likely they followed a worn path from the emotions of a lifetime of laughing, smiling, crying, and loving. His long bony hand was on the table, where he tapped a finger, as he had done yesterday. A blood bank would give hundreds to tap those veins that stuck up like steel-grey earthworms under his thin, tissue-paper skin.

This time as she watched him, his lips were moving, but he didn't seem to notice that she was there. She moved in closer to hear what he was saying. She took the chair next to his, and he continued looking out the window. She heard him now, and knew what he was saying. He repeated Borghild's name over and over as if it were a talisman, a rope he clutched to keep the shred of remaining sanity he had. As she looked at his vacant eyes, she wondered if he knew it was his wife's name he repeated.

Without realizing, tears began making two steady streams down Ruby's cheeks, dripping onto her pants. She was overcome with the knowledge of the love that Ragnar must have for his wife, realizing at that moment she would never settle for less. As sick as it was, she wanted her husband, after they had lived a long, happy life together, to repeat *her* name as his mind slipped. Maybe that was why she cried; she could not imagine ever feeling for someone else the way she did for Fin. She put her hand to her stomach, and more tears came. She quaked from the inside.

Looking to the right and then to the left, she scanned the room for a telephone. Poppy would say something to calm her. She saw a cordless phone cradled in a stand on the kitchen counter. She held her calling card and made her way to the phone. She wiped her eyes as she entered the room that smelled of coffee and cakes, spicy with yeast and cardamom. Her stomach soured with the smell of the coffee, a scent she had always loved, but now brought bile up her throat.

Borghild stood by the sink and turned toward Ruby. Her

eyes became concerned, probably at the dried tears and the blotchiness that speckled her face. Ruby swallowed hard, willing herself not to heave onto the floor.

"Ruby, what's wrong?" Her voice was rushed as she came closer.

Ruby swallowed again. "It's nothing. I was just thinking about Poppy. I have a calling card. Would you mind if I used your telephone?"

"No, you go right ahead. Take it outside or up in your room for some privacy. When you're done, we'll have some cake and I'll get you the bus schedule."

Ruby took the phone and went past Ragnar, out onto the deck. The air was cold from the morning breeze coming off the water, and she hoped the fresh air would lessen the nausea she still felt. She breathed in through her nose to stop her shaking and dialed the string of numbers. She hadn't even considered the time difference, and quickly counted back eight hours. It was midnight in Boulder.

The phone rang once, twice, three times. A soft, groggy voice came through, "Hello." At first, Ruby didn't answer, her throat had constricted. Poppy's voice came through again, but now it was a question. "Hello?"

"Poppy, it's me. Did I wake you up?" Her voice was tight, like it had always been when she tried talking while trying not to cry. There was a moment of silence, and she heard rustling, probably sheets being ripped from her sister's prone body.

Her sister was now wide awake, and her voice sounded authoritarian. "Ruby, what's wrong? Are you crying? Are you okay? Where are you?"

A snot bubble flew out of Ruby's nose as a half laugh, half cry gusted out her mouth. She sniffed and wiped her nose on her shirt. "I'm fine. I'm with Borghild in Norway."

She paused. "I just miss you. I wanted to talk."

"It sounds like you're crying. Are you okay?" Poppy sounded a little calmer, but still worried.

"I need to tell you something, and I just want you to listen." In a very short time, she told Poppy about meeting Fin, the time they had spent together, the way they left each other, and how she was now frantic with how her mind was jumping to conclusions.

Poppy spoke in lawyer mode. "You're right. You're jumping to conclusions. You've never been regular, so let's not freak out." The way she used the word "let's," like they were in this together, made Ruby want to cry again. "Can you get a pregnancy test there?"

"I'm sure I can. I don't know. I'm going into town this morning. They have pharmacies. I'll go look." She wiped her nose again. "What am I going to do?"

"Ruby. stop. Until we know anything for sure, which we will today, let's not go crazy."

Ruby's voice rose, below hysterical, but on the verge. "Why would I be throwing up if I'm not…" *God, I can't even say the word.*

"I want you to go get a test and call me back before you take it, okay? Promise you'll call before."

"Okay, I'm going to go. I'll call you in a few hours. Thanks. I'll call you. Bye." Tremors had laid claim to her body, her stomach was tight, and she had to fist her hands to make them stop shaking.

* * *

Ruby walked along Markensgata, the pedestrian area in the center of Kristiansand, where people bustled in the sunny weather. She had left Borghild's holding a bus schedule and a promise to eat the pastry in her hand. She scanned the signs above the shops for one that might carry a home pregnancy test. Yo-yoing between cursing and being scared to death, she found a shop that had an "Apotek" sign above the door on a green background with a white pharmacy cross.

She walked through the door and meandered up and down the aisles. After a couple minutes, she came to the women's hygiene lane. There, on the third shelf up, were the boxes with pictures of a stick with a plus sign. She looked around as though she was stealing the Hope diamond, rolled her eyes at herself, snagged the test off the shelf, and made for the register. The look the checker gave her was quizzical, not sure if Ruby was happy or not. Ruby chose to look at a non-existent spot on the counter, take her bag, and run.

When she got back to the house, Borghild and Ragnar were eating their noon meal. Ruby said hello and that she would be back after she freshened up. She took the stairs two at a time, clutching the bag in one hand and the telephone in the other. She ran to the bathroom and shut the door. Sitting on the toilet, she pulled the card out of her pocket and dialed. It would be four in the morning in Boulder. She opened the bag and looked at the box.

The phone was picked up before the first ring ended. "Ruby? Did you get the test?" Poppy had obviously had a pot of coffee. "Are you okay?" She sounded like the Energizer Bunny.

"I have the test. God, my hands are shaking. I can't make them stop." The box looked like it might jump out of her hand and hit the wall.

"I'm right here. Take the test. Don't worry. Are you taking it?" Ruby imagined Poppy tapping her foot a million miles a minute.

"I'm going to throw up." She heard an intake of breath

on the other end. "No, not really throw up. Okay, I'm getting it out." She pulled her pants down, squeezing the phone between her ear and her shoulder. "Okay, I'm peeing." She looked down. "Oh crap, I forgot to take the wrapper off. Oh my god. Hold on."

She put the phone down and, at the same time, tried stopping her stream of pee. She ripped open the dripping white plastic. *I'm an idiot.* She returned the phone to its place. "I don't even know if I can pee anymore." She heard what she thought was a choked giggle. "Poppy, this is so not funny."

"I know, I know. I'm just hyped up, I'm sorry. Okay, are you ready?"

"I'm going. How long do I wait?" Ruby's eyes were closed.

"Maybe a couple of minutes? What does it look like?"

Ruby looked down at the window on the end of the stick. Instantly a purple plus sign appeared. All the blood seemed to drain from her body. She couldn't feel or hear anything except for a whooshing deep in her head. Her shoulder must have relaxed, because she saw the phone drop to the floor in slow motion, bouncing twice before rolling onto its side.

She heard noise coming from the phone and assumed it was Poppy. Of course it was Poppy, probably panicked on the other end. Who else could it be? Still, she simply stared at the phone. She looked back at the purple plus sign she held in her right hand and put her left on her stomach, her heartbeat wild against her rib cage. She picked up the telephone.

"Ruby? RUBY? Answer me, RUBY!"

Her voice was quiet when she answered, but she felt utterly calm. "I'm pregnant, Poppy." A tear slid down her cheek. She wasn't completely sure it wasn't a happy tear, which meant she was perilously close to joining Ragnar, sitting in a chair, staring out to sea.

There was silence for three heartbeats, and then Poppy the lawyer started in. "You need to come home. Give me the airline, and I'll call and change your departure city to Kristiansand and change your date. It won't be a problem. I'll make a doctor's appointment for you. Oh my god, Ruby. Are you okay?"

"Yeah, I'm fine." She thought it strange that no mention of Fin was made, he was a non-entity. All of her sister's energies were devoted solely to her.

"I don't want to leave yet. Can you see if you can change it for two days from now? Borghild got a nurse to stay with Ragnar just for my visit." She was having an out-of-body experience. She felt as if she were discussing a second cousin or, closer, a stranger. How could she be sitting on a toilet in Norway, discussing a pregnancy she had never anticipated with a man she was in love with but had no idea where he was, and a future she could not begin to imagine?

"All right, this is Tuesday. I'll have you on the Friday flight. When I get to work today, I'll make the calls and I'll get back to you at Borghild's later tonight with times." Poppy paused. Her next words had shed her controlled voice and sounded like a concerned sister. "I wish I could be there with you, but everything is going to be fine. It's going to be fine. We'll figure everything out when you get here. I'll call you in a few hours. I love you."

"I love you, too. Thanks for taking care of everything. I'll talk to you later, bye." Ruby pushed the button, disconnecting the call. Her mind was a maelstrom of snippets of thoughts. Her shoulders slumped and she stared at a square of tile on the floor. She threw the box into the trash, methodically wrapped the test in toilet paper, and held her hand over the can, but she couldn't drop it in. She went back to her room across the hall and, unable to explain why, tucked the test into a pocket in her backpack and made her way downstairs.

* * *

Poppy called, just like she said she would, with the times. Ruby would have two stops—one in Amsterdam and the other in Detroit, getting to Denver nineteen hours after she left Kristiansand. They talked for a while, and Poppy hung up telling her that she would be at baggage claim when she got to Denver.

Ruby spent the hours prior to her sister's call walking through the low dunes to the water. Borghild joined her in the garden. She hadn't asked any questions, although she must have known something was different. Most likely she didn't want to pry, for which Ruby was grateful. Borghild left her saying that she needed to check on Ragnar and told her of nice places for a walk. Ruby made it to the water and spent the next hour sitting on a flat rock that just reached the water. She saw tiny fish swimming and, as this was not a wavy area, she didn't have to worry about getting wet.

She started coming to terms with everything and with the fact that she was already desperately protective of holding onto a moment in time that she was lucky to have had. She would forever get to keep a part of Fin and, whatever else happened, that was a quantity that wouldn't change. A small smile made it to her lips as she crossed both arms around her middle.

Beyond these thoughts, she didn't want to go there. Her parents would cry and be disappointed—she really didn't know. She also knew she should try to contact Fin, but every time she thought about him, she hyperventilated. She would call Chloris, sure that she would have his information. She remembered when Chloris had said that Fin told her he would find her, and heat surged through her body. *Why would he say that? He's so beyond me. I am a wallflower, I keep to the background. He is a lightning bolt that you can't help but look at.* She decided to stick with her original thoughts. He was simply pacifying a young girl so he didn't need to get into an uncomfortable conversation. But, if she could, she would wish for it to be true.

Ruby knew she should feel like a trollop. Crap, she didn't even have an address or phone number of the man's baby she carried, but she couldn't conjure up those feelings. Nothing in her life had ever felt so right, and she wasn't going to belittle the time they spent together.

She went to bed early, which should have been difficult given that it stayed light until almost eleven o'clock. Somehow, though, she fell asleep immediately and didn't wake until morning. It was so warm under the covers that she snuggled down and looked out of the window. So many things went through her head that they became white noise. She heard talking coming from below her and figured that it was the nurse coming to stay with Ragnar. She and Borghild would leave for their day together after breakfast. Ruby looked forward to having something else to think about.

CHAPTER THIRTY-TWO

When Fin's parents had returned, and after his mother had gushed tears of joy, he asked for a meeting with his father. Behind closed doors, Fin did not apologize—he didn't feel that he should apologize for who he was and what had brought him to this place. However, he did outline where he was going from this point on. Rightly so, his father was wary to embrace his son's words immediately. Nonetheless, one thing he knew about Finley was that whatever he did, he did one hundred percent. Though, he did not agree with where his efforts were directed in the past. After hours of going over spreadsheets and ledgers, predictions, acquisitions and losses, they were both more comfortable with what the future held. During the next weeks, Fin was relentless in learning as much as possible. He met with key employees, who seemed genuinely pleased that he was taking the reins, often commenting that Ian would be proud with the direction he was going.

Fin stayed close to home since returning from Belgium. He went on daily rides around the property and had dinner with Anne and Thomas, but he had no desire to go beyond the boundaries of his family's borders.

Unfortunately, Stonehaven was a typical small village, and word got out that he had come home. Gregory and Peter, friends of Fin's since boyhood, all but threw him over their shoulders and spirited him away to start where they had left off months ago. They ended up at The King's House, a tavern by the water where they had been regulars since they were young. Familiarity hit Fin the minute he walked through the red door. The low ceiling comprised of pressed tin with a nondescript pattern, and the rest of the intimate bar was filled with wood: wooden floors, bar, bar stools, and tables. The stale smell of alcohol mingled with meat and fish brought floods of memories of drunken nights that he half remembered, the other half of which he wished he could forget. The trio, all handsome and wealthy, had a reputation for being the center of attention. They were fun, rakish, and cared little for what others thought.

Before they even sat down, a tray of whisky was brought to them by a buxom, black-haired barmaid. Her name was Katie, and if he wasn't mistaken, each of the boys had partaken of her goods at one time or another. She leaned down and rubbed her overflowing breasts against Fin's arm, purring in his ear, "I heard you were back." Fin pretended not to notice and brought the glass to his lips, in turn, causing Katie to straighten.

Peter leaned forward, probably trying to get a feel as well. His wavy red hair fell over his brow. "Yeah, he's back. Just keep these coming." His mouth turned up in a sideways grin. "He's been locked up in the big house, and we're going to make sure he has a good time." He jerked his head toward Gregory.

Gregory's eyes were locked on the swell of pale flesh oozing out of Katie's low-cut shirt. Because he had a few drinks under his belt, it wouldn't have surprised Fin if spittle had dripped from Gregory's mouth. Fin rolled his eyes, wondering if they had always acted like thirteen-year-old boys, and realized that yes, they had.

The night continued in a haze. By the time they were on their third round, Fin was foggy headed and wondered why he hadn't come out earlier. People pulled up chairs, and he was buying rounds for who knew how many. Storytelling and laughter was the order of the night, and before long, Katherine, a blonde beauty, was stationed on his lap. He and Katherine had a long-standing arrangement that if either was so inclined, they often left together, no questions asked, and better, no attachment, just straight-forward sex.

He tried telling his mates earlier about Ruby, about how being with her felt different, but he was met with guffaws and another round. He now wondered if it was crazy to think that he was a changed man and, with his head swimming, he told himself that Ruby could be with anyone at this point. He started to get mad, blaming her when he knew, if he had been sober, these would not be the feelings he would be having. But right now, and very much not sober, he could blame her for his behaviors.

Katherine's tongue had made it into his ear, and she was running a hand up his thigh. Fin closed his eyes and saw a picture of Ruby ruffled and lying in twisted sheets, smiling at him. He actually growled, thinking this would be a good way to banish an apparition. "Christ!" he howled at the air, nearly throwing Katherine from his lap. Between clenched teeth, he turned toward her. "Are you ready?" He stood and took her with him.

"Oh, I'm ready." She ran a finger from temple to jaw, and Fin turned his head to get away from it.

Gregory looked up at Fin through half-lidded eyes. "Leaving us Fin? I assume you can make it home, if you go home." He blew a drunken half laugh, half grunt through loose lips. Fin didn't bother replying; instead, he made his way out the door.

Katherine lived three blocks from the tavern. On the walk there, she tried to do typical sexy, womanly things—a giggle, a well-placed hand—but Fin just wanted to get on with it. His feet slid against the ground, and the term "drunken sailor" planted itself in his head. He would have started whistling if his lips didn't feel like two jellyfish bouncing off each other.

She had a two-story apartment in a typical stone building a block back from the water, and they hastily made their way past the living room to the stairs that led to her bedroom. Fin leaned heavily on the rail, and Katherine leaned heavily on Fin, so it was slow going.

She wrapped both arms around his neck when they reached the landing and started walking backward, pulling him into her room. She fell laughing onto the bed, dragging him with her as he pushed onto her body. "Fin, I've missed you. Have you missed me?" Her voice was whiny and completely unattractive to him. Ruby would never sound like that.

He closed his eyes and plunged his tongue into her mouth. The stale taste of whisky and beer met his messy kiss. Ruby always tasted sweet, like oranges or mint. He grabbed her arm and slid his hands down to her hips. They were bony, as if she was starving herself and thought that men found emaciation attractive. Ruby had curve to her body. He could still feel her under his touch and in her response to him as she arched her back to get closer. She had a wonderful combination of strength and softness.

"Fuck, I can't do this. I've got to get out of here." Fin stood and was buttoning the buttons Katherine had worked on. He all but ran as she sat open-mouthed on the bed.

A week later, Fin remembered the incident with Katherine as he looked out the window of the library, waiting for Chloris to arrive. Chloris had phoned three days before, asking if she could visit. He would be happy to see her—more than that, she said that Ruby had come to Prima Facie, but she wouldn't tell him more until she saw him.

Sneaky little elf. She knew I'd drop everything for information about Ruby. He had stopped pacing and now stood with one hand against the window frame, watching the rain hit the drive, waiting.

CHAPTER THIRTY-THREE

Chloris sat cross-legged on a high wooden, black lacquered stool that fit under the large dark grey soapstone island in the Sinclair's kitchen. Fin was chopping a pile of vegetables that were going into a salad he was making. Chloris was over the shock of Finley Sinclair's real identity. Fin knew that for Chloris, his station had changed nothing about the way she was with him. He knew it would be like that with her, but still he was thankful. He told her everything that brought him to Prima Facie—about Ian and about the way he had become jaded and cynical, a person he wasn't proud of or wanted to continue being. She merely waved a hand and, in a voice much older than her years, said something to the effect that life brings things our way by many different means, and it's what we do with them that ultimately makes us who we are. *Amen, sister.*

Chloris ran a finger over the cool, smooth surface of the counter and watched it make dips and swirls over the stone. Her unearthly green eyes looked from underneath her lashes. "Are you wondering about Ruby?"

Fin almost jumped out of his skin to ask about Ruby, but he didn't want Chloris to think he wasn't interested in *her*. Now, though, he was ready to wring her neck at the sly smile she taunted him with. He played along, lifting a shoulder negligently. "Yeah, you did say she came back, right?" The hair on the nape of his neck stood at attention, and he had to concentrate to breathe evenly. Chop, chop, chop. "How was she?" When Chloris didn't answer, he stopped chopping and looked up. "What?"

"I know she wouldn't want me to tell you this, but she wasn't good." With her elbow resting on the stone, she twirled a black spike of hair between her fingers, making the point stand straight out.

Fin's heart, which he thought was already at maximum beats per minute, went into overdrive. "What do you mean she wasn't good? Was she hurt? Did something happen? God, tell me nothing happened to her. Chloris, tell me what it was!" He was no longer "tranquil Fin." He was "irascible Fin," who was about to jump across the island and man handle a wood nymph if she didn't tell him something in the next half a second.

She let go of her hair and scrunched her face up, apparently at odds with what to say now that she had started. "No, she's fine. Nothing happened to her." Fin loosened his death grip on the knife in his hand as she went on. "Except you broke her heart." Spoken like a true sixteen-year-old girl. As he planned to remedy that, he gave her his best sideways smile, but she wasn't quite done. "She got absolutely sick everywhere, though. Twice." She narrowed her eyes.

The knife, poised to decapitate a stalk of asparagus, dropped from his hand and clanged against the polished wooden floor. He felt like he was in a movie where the person stands still, but everything around him speeds past. His voice was low when he spoke. "What do you mean, 'she got sick'?" *I know. Of course, I bloody know.* He thought she was on birth control. She didn't say a thing, and he wanted her so badly that it never occurred to him to ask. *Christ, I didn't even care.*

He heard blood pumping in his ears. He reached deep to feel regret or anger, but all he came up with was concern for the woman who would now, without question, become his wife. "Where is she Chloris? Tell me she's not still traveling while she's pregnant." His heart swelled at the word. He could see Ruby's face. He wanted to strangle himself for the way he had left her. She must be so scared. "Where is she?"

Chloris blinked. "No, she said she was sick from mussels she…ate…in…Luxemburg." Her voice got quieter and slower the longer she spoke. "Could she be pregnant?" Now her eyes were mere slits.

"I don't know, but I need to find her." He wasn't about to go into details about Dinant.

"Fin."

"Chloris, I really just want to find her."

She must have seen something when she looked at him and softened. "She went to Norway to see a friend of her grandmother. I have the number. The women's name is Borghild." She started digging through her bag at her feet. She handed him the number on a folded napkin.

Fin was already walking to the phone. He would be with her in a few hours. His heart was beating out of his chest. He dialed the number, letting it ring five times before someone answered.

"Hallo."

The voice was definitely an older woman. "Hello, I'm trying to contact Ruby Larson. I believe she is staying with you." His voice sounded in control, which was completely the opposite of his emotions.

"Who is this?"

"I'm sorry. My name is Finley Sinclair. I'm a friend of Ruby's. Is she there?"

"Ruby told me about you, but I'm sorry. She left this morning back to America."

CHAPTER THIRTY-FOUR

Ruby looked out of the small oval window and began performing her pre-flight routine. She held the lucky coin and started her mantra. After twenty minutes, she was able to release her left hand from the armrest and lean her head back. She replayed her conversation with Borghild from two days ago. She had taken Ruby out of the city to Lillisand, a picturesque small harbor village. There they sat at a café at the water's edge, and Borghild spun a magical yarn of her own personal love story.

Borghild and Ragnar grew up together in Kristiansand. They spent time with their families every summer at a cabin in Risor, on the Skagerrak Gulf. As kids, it was their wide open playground. They fished, ran through the woods playing hide-and-seek, swam, and took canoes through inlets.

Borghild was the older of two sisters and thought of Ragnar as an older brother. He was seven years her senior, and the last summer they had at the cabin was when he turned eighteen and had joined the Norwegian Army. Borghild was eleven then, and swore that she would write while he was away. She had written schoolgirl letters with hand-drawn pictures of places he would know. He wrote back sporadically, keeping his missives basic and funny.

When the war began, she kept writing, never knowing where he was or if he received her letters. The years went on, and so did her life. She and Esther had a year of escapades in America. She had boyfriends and went to dances. She had her first kiss and giggled with her girlfriends about the strangeness of the changes in their lives. Borghild always heard about Ragnar through her parents and aunts, and she always held her breath until she knew he was okay. He was shot once, was in the hospital, but had returned to his company a week later. That was when Borghild was sixteen; she could no longer write about schoolgirl things. Instead, she wrote about her feelings and important things that were happening, giving rich descriptions that, if he closed his eyes, could hopefully transport him.

During the summer of her eighteenth year, she was at the cabin in Risor with Esther and two other girlfriends from school. They were picnicking at the water when a man came walking on the rocky beach toward them. As he got closer, Borchild could make out Ragnar's familiar shape. Although he had filled out and gotten taller, she knew it was Ragnar. She bounded up and ran into his arms, which wrapped instinctively around her.

Borghild told Ruby that she would never forget that day. She could still smell his musky scent and feel his strong arms. It was at that moment that he stopped being a brother figure, and they fell completely in love. He had kept all of her letters and told her how much they had meant to him. He often read them by flashlight when he was about to give up hope that he would return home.

Ruby listened, enthralled by the romantic story. Borghild, seeing Ruby forming a question, held up her hand. "Ruby, sometimes we have to make choices in life. We made our choice, but it came with a great price. You see, Ragnar was my cousin and because of that, we lost our families. They could not condone our marriage, and we haven't spoken to them since that time. We also knew that we could never have children—something I don't regret but often think about. When I was younger, I wanted a baby so much I could feel him in my arms, but I *needed* Ragnar, so my choice was made, and we've been happy."

She looked at Ruby with penetrating eyes and continued, "I have a feeling you need to make choices in your life, Ruby. From what you've told me about your Fin, you could have it all. That isn't something that comes along very often and, as scary as it may be to put your heart in someone else's hands, the rewards might be worth it." Borghild put her hand on top of Ruby's, which had unconsciously gone to her stomach. Ruby told her bits and pieces of her time with Fin, and Borghild must have guessed the rest, given Ruby's perpetually queasiness.

Ruby looked down at their hands together. "I'm scared. I don't know what to do, and nothing is the way it's supposed to be."

"Ruby, dear, life has a way of preparing us for the unexpected. I've always believed that it's in those murky times, those times that aren't so clear to us, that magic happens. Your job is to grab the brass ring when you see it and not pass it by, thinking it's too hard to reach."

Ruby spent her last day at Borghild's house sitting on the deck, watching Ragnar roll homemade cigarettes and murmur Borghild's name over and over, the paper getting shorter and the ash hanging like a spent sparkler on the fourth of July. She promised Borghild she would write and tell her what happened, even though she couldn't begin to imagine her ending would be quite like Borghild's. Did an unemployed, broke, pregnant single women trump a women who lost her family for love?

The plane touched down at DIA at four-thirty. Twenty minutes later, Ruby was heading to baggage claim. She had already gone through customs in Detroit, so she only needed

to make her way to the train that would take her to the
terminal. As she descended on the escalator, she saw Poppy
checking her watch and looking around. If she wouldn't
have caused a hubbub, Ruby would have pushed the elderly
couple in front of her aside and ran to her sister. As it was,
she drummed her hands on her thighs impatiently, willing
Poppy to look up. She tried wedging between the two but,
for a slender couple, they took up an inordinate amount of
space, and she couldn't get through without causing a
possible hip break if one of them should take a misstep.

Poppy looked up right as Ruby took her first step off the
escalator. She was in work clothes, so must have come
straight from the office. Her blouse was out of her pencil
skirt, and her hair spilled down her back in waves from
being in her signature chignon. "Oh my god, Ruby." Poppy
ran toward Ruby, arms already open. Ruby ended up with
her arms pinned to her sides as Poppy held her in a
deceptively strong embrace and rocked back and forth.

Ruby felt comforted, like a child being held after a
traumatic event. She couldn't believe she was home and
how many things had changed in such a short amount of
time. They stood without moving for minutes before Poppy
eased up and looked down at her. "Are you okay?"

"Well, aside from having the button of your blouse
permanently imprinted into my cheek, I'm good." Ruby
wanted to be strong rather than break down in her arms.
Lord knew she'd had enough time to get used to the "P"
word, but maybe not. All of her barriers came down with
her sister, and her eyes began to sting.

Ruby waved her hand in front of her face. "I'm fine. I'm
sappy." she started laughing, and tears sprung from her
eyes. "I mean, I'm so happy; not sappy." More tears.

Poppy wiped the tears from her own eyes. Even as kids,

if one cried, the other was close behind. She grabbed Ruby's hand. "Let's get your bag and get out of here." The baggage from her flight was already coming down the shoot. Ruby's was one of the first bags out.

It took no time to get to the parking garage, and Ruby clicked her seatbelt in place just as something in her peripheral vision caught her eye. She screamed bloody murder and threw herself against the belt as a figure popped out of the back seat. "Holy shit. Crap, what are you doing?" The burn from the strap stung her neck.

Poppy had her door open. "Oh, crap. I forgot to tell you, Margie insisted on coming. Sorry."

Margie leaned forward, her grey curls flat against the right side of her head. "Ruby, I'm sorry. I fell asleep waiting for you guys. Did I scare you?" Her arms circled around the headrest as she leaned into the front seat.

"Yeah, Margie. I almost took my damn head off trying to get out of the car. My heart is beating out of my chest." She stretched her neck to gauge the damage.

Margie and Poppy looked at each other. "Are you okay? Is everything okay?" Margie asked.

Ruby looked at them both with a blank stare, closed her eyes, and blew out a long, steady breath. "I'm not going to break. You just scared the shit out of me. She looked sideways at Margie before giving her a huge smile. "It's good to see you."

Margie touched her shoulder and said, "You didn't get much use out of my going away gift, did you?" The car was completely quiet for four beats, and then they all laughed so hard that the little car shook. It felt so good to be back. If they could laugh at Ruby being pregnant, she knew everything would be fine.

Chapter Thirty-Five

Fin hung up the telephone and turned to face Chloris. She stood on the balls of her feet, something he noticed she did when she was anxious, her green eyes wide with anticipation. "What did she say? Is Ruby there?"

Fin ran his fingers through his hair. "She left this morning back to America." He kept his eyes on the girl in front of him, mentally planning his next move. "Chloris, I need her information in the States. It will take me a few days to get things in order here so I can be away, but I'll go and find her." It was silly, but he wanted to be the person Chloris had imagined he was before he screwed up so badly. "I'm going to be busy for a while. This would be a perfect time for you to meet my sister, Anne. She works at a small gallery. I think you'll like it, and I know Anne would love to show you around."

As he suspected, Chloris and Anne hit it off instantly. He left them together while he worked on the logistics for his trip. Several times he held the telephone to call Ruby in Colorado, but he never punched the numbers. He needed to see her in person. He kept telling himself that in three days, he would be with her.

He arranged for Jon, his secretary, to keep him apprised of emergencies but, other than that, to pass anything off to Bruce, a man who was up to speed with the changes Fin had made. His father was not to be involved in anything. It was past time that he should enjoy complete retirement. Jon made flight arrangements and placed some calls to Boulder, per Fin's instructions. By that evening, most everything was in order.

As the sun set, Fin sat in a tavern with Anne and Chloris being bombarded with everything he needed to say and everything he should not say to Ruby when he saw her. His mind was spinning with female insight, and after what he felt was an acceptable amount of time he threw his hand up in surrender, saying he couldn't take another suggestion.

Anne and Chloris looked at each other and folded their arms over their chests. Anne pierced him with a glare. "Okay, just don't mess it up. I really like her, and I want her to be a part of our family."

Fin gave her a lopsided grin and said, "Anne, you've never even met Ruby."

"I may not have met her, but I feel like I know her. Given that I have never seen you like this with a woman—not even close—I know she must be very special. I also had Chloris to fill me in today."

Fin gave Chloris a pointed look. He had made her promise to not say anything about Ruby's possible pregnancy until he had a chance to see her. The look she returned told him that she hadn't said anything. When he spoke, his voice was filled with emotion. "You're right. I've never felt like I do when I'm with Ruby. Now I just need to make her believe me."

CHAPTER THIRTY-SIX

It had been three days since she returned home. As Ruby walked to Whimsy, she thought about her time home so far. She called her parents the first day to reassure them that she cut her trip short because she was homesick. Because they knew her, they didn't really believe her reason, but there wasn't much they could do. She ended the conversation saying she would come to see them after settling in. She didn't know what it meant to be "settled in," but it sounded good, and they were placated.

The day after she returned, she sat with Poppy and Margie on Poppy's front porch and told them everything about her trip. She told them about meeting Retta, how she was a geyser of energy and enthusiasm, and how she had come to really like her. She described Chloris and her flitting like a pixie sprite, as well as her engaging presence for such a young girl. She described the places she saw and the funny things that happened along the way, like Brian the morning after they had first come to Prima Facie, and about Borghild and the feeling that she had known her all her life. Then she talked about Fin.

She thought to skim over most of her time with him and just touch on the highlights, but when she started, it was as if a dam had given way—she couldn't stop the words from rushing out. By the time she finished, everyone's eyes glistened and Ruby's heart felt like it was splitting open.

Poppy leaned forward. "Are you sure you don't want to call him? After everything you said, the way he left just doesn't make sense. Something else must be going on. And now…well, I think you need to tell him."

"It still doesn't seem real." She took another pregnancy test that Poppy had bought, and yep, there was still a plus sign. For good measure, she took a third, and it was also positive, so she supposed there was no question. Now the morning sickness was a regular part of her day: Wake up, puke and, two hours later, puke again, and so on.

"I'll call Chloris next week and see if she has a number for Fin, okay? What am I supposed to say, 'Hey, sorry it appeared you never wanted to see me again, but I'm cooking your bun in my oven?' He doesn't even live in the states. What do you think he's going to do, drop everything for me? He has some handyman business with his dad and, for all I know, he has little Fins all over the world?" The thought made her next words come out thick. "I don't know if I can do this. What if he doesn't want to see me or want a baby? I swear, I don't know what I would do if he said he just didn't care. I only want to remember the time we had together, and if I don't call him, I'll never have to hear that he doesn't."

Margie stood in front of Ruby, her hands planted on her hips. "Do you hear yourself? 'I can't do this.' 'I don't know that.' Well, it's not just about you anymore. I agree with Poppy, something doesn't seem right with the way he left. There's a piece missing. You're going to call him because you're not a coward. You're an incredible woman who very well may be at the pinnacle of her destiny and, by god, I'll push you off if I have to."

Ruby blinked to bring Margie into focus through the tears that had pooled but hadn't fallen from her eyes. "How did I end up with so many amazing people around me? You're right. I'll call him because it's the right thing to do." That night, she went to bed curled up next to her sister after promising that she would be at Whimsy tomorrow to help Margie with the delivery and arranging for the shop.

CHAPTER THIRTY-SEVEN

Fin tried to make it three days but, in the end, if he had to wait any longer, he didn't know what he would do. He was already biting everyone's heads off, including Chloris's. She finally told him that he should leave early, which was all he needed to hear. He chartered a jet so that he didn't need to make the stops that commercial airlines do. He left in the evening of the second day, and would be in Denver by early morning.

Chloris knew the address for Ruby's parents, but said that Ruby had told her that she planned to stay in Boulder with her sister until she figured out what to do. Chloris didn't have that address. Fin and Chloris knew about the flower shop, so he thought he would start there. Her friend that owned it would surely know how he could find her.

Fin planned to sleep through the flight, but he couldn't turn off his head. For the first time, he began thinking about the worst possible scenarios. *What if Ruby doesn't want to see me? What if I have completely blown it? What if she's met someone else while traveling? What if she got back together with the man she spoke about in Dinant?*

Fin had always been a glass half full person for a reason—things always worked out for him. Losing Ian was the first tragedy to touch his life, and it shook him to his core. It was the reason he pushed Ruby away. He didn't even recognize himself after his brother's accident. He had lived a charmed life; he sucked everything he could out of it and spit out the seeds. Then, with Ian, he realized what could happen when someone he deeply cared about was taken. He wasn't sure what he would do with another loss.

When Fin landed in Denver, he was so wired that his insides buzzed, as if an electrical current was pumping through his veins. Jon had arranged for a car to be waiting for him with a map on the passenger's seat, the address to the flower shop circled, and hand-written directions next to it. Fin made a mental note to give Jon a week off when he got back. With his nerves the way they were, he didn't know if he could have done it himself.

The sky was a color blue that he had never seen. It almost looked black, and the mountains, even in the summer, were snowcapped. He headed toward them, estimating the drive time at about an hour, from what it looked like on the map. It was eight-fifteen in the morning, which meant that he should arrive in Boulder at around nine-fifteen or nine-thirty. *Breathe.* He went through what Anne and Chloris had told him and tried it out loud in the car. He sounded like an actor trying out for a part in a bad movie; his voice sounded choppy and rehearsed. *Breathe.* After thirty minutes, Fin turned on the radio and started going through the programmed stations, stopping when he found a song he knew. He turned it up and sang, "...these are days to remember..." and pushed the pedal down, trying to relax and clear his head.

CHAPTER THIRTY-EIGHT

Ruby decided to walk to the shop. It would take her twenty minutes, but the air was fresh and already warm. She wore a dress she had bought in Greece. It was sleeveless and came up high on her collarbone. The color was a gauzy mix of the blues that surrounded them on Santorini—the azure of the church domes, the airy blue of the sky, and the deep blue colors of the ocean. She and Retta had found the dress on a rack set up on a narrow side street. She smiled at the memory. The feeling of the dress against her bare legs as she made her way to Pearl Street made her feel somehow free and happy—something she would have thought impossible.

It was eight forty-five by the time she walked through the door of Whimsy and the bell tinkled above her head. Margie had unlocked the door so that she could set the buckets of flowers out to the walk in front of the shop before she opened. There were three buckets of daisies and tulips inside, ready to go out, so Ruby placed them in a cluster just outside the door as she took in their earth scent. She walked back in and saw Margie bringing up another bucket. Margie stopped with the suspended container of flowers. "Oh my god, Ruby. You are absolutely glowing. How are you today?" She wrinkled her nose. "I hope I wasn't too hard on you yesterday, but I love you so much and that namby-pamby stuff just isn't you."

Ruby held the door as Margie set down a bunch of pink peonies. "No, I needed to hear it." They stood looking at the arrangement and then walked back in the shop, the door closing behind them.

"Something wonderful is going to happen, Ruby. I can feel it, can't you? It's in the air, on my tongue."

"Maybe it's the pastry you have on the table." Ruby smiled.

"Don't be a smart ass. I'm telling you, it's in the air. Hey, turn up the radio, I love this song." She cupped Ruby's cheek and walked on, swaying her head and singing, "You know it's true that you are blessed and lucky..."

Ruby had been anxious all morning. When she woke, she knew that she had dreamed of Fin. She could feel his arms around her as they had been when she was in his bed. She opened her eyes, smiling, until she realized that it was the comforter around her and not his arms. Even now she felt nervous, like little sparks were popping all around her. She chalked them up to the residual effects of her dream.

Margie looked at Ruby with concern and said, "You okay? You look a little shaky? Here, come and sit down. I had a special delivery this morning I need to get ready. We'll sit at the table and get it arranged together."

"I don't know. I just feel weird, nervous or something." Ruby tousled her hair with her fingers and rubbed her hands over her face. "What was the special order?" She sat down facing the back of the shop at the mosaic table and cradled her chin on her intertwined fingers.

"It was a rush from Holland, really specific. I'll go get the bucket and bring you a glass of water. You eat that pastry." Margie made her way to the back of the shop.

Ruby tore a piece of flaky bread from the cheese Danish. She had come to realize that even if she felt queasy, eating something helped. She sat wondering what type of tulip had been ordered. They had a supplier in Washington, but occasionally someone wanted tulips directly from Holland.

Ruby thought that spending that much on flowers was pretentious, but Margie liked the price she could tack on merely for their origin.

"Here they are. Absolutely beautiful. They remind me of a fairy forest. The color is so vibrant, don't you love them?" She set the bucket at Ruby's feet.

Ruby put another chunk of pastry into her mouth and looked down. Her breath caught, and her whole body went numb. The blood completely drained from her and, at the same time, her heart pounded like a bass drum against her ribs. When she finally found her voice, it was nothing more than a whisper. "Who ordered these?"

"Ruby, what's wrong? Do you feel sick? Is it your stomach?" Margie kneeled in front of Ruby, clasping her hands.

"Who ordered them, Margie?"

"I don't know. Let me go get the slip." She must have read something in Ruby's tone. "Here, here it is. Let's see. It was a Jon Ashcroft, why?"

She let out a fast breath, her head buzzing. "Where did it originate, the order?"

"He ordered from Scotland to have them delivered here overnight." She looked up. All of Ruby's questions started coming together. "Ruby…?"

"Who's the order for?" She hadn't taken her eyes off the smaller version of the carpet of blue bells that covered the forest in Dinant.

"They're for pick-up this morning. No name." The bell tinkled above the door.

Ruby went completely still, and shivers ran up her back. Her head was down, but when Margie didn't say anything to the person who walked through the door, she looked up through her lashes to see what she already knew. Margie looked toward the door with her mouth open, as if she was about to speak but had turned to stone. Suddenly, Ruby was on fire and shaking uncontrollably. She didn't want to turn, and there was no sound indicating what the person was doing behind her.

* * *

Fin had no problem finding Spruce Street. He could picture Ruby living in Boulder perfectly. It was beautiful and natural with an eclectic mix of people walking and riding bicycles. His nerves were stretched when he got closer to his destination. He thought about what Margie would say. Surely Ruby had contacted her since she had returned. She was one of Ruby's closest friends. *Would she have mentioned me? Would my name conjure up fond memories, or resentment and anger?* He thought about the flowers he had Jon order and wondered if they had arrived. He speculated if she lived close. Maybe he had passed Poppy's house and didn't even know it.

There was one more block to go to arrive at the flower shop. Although it most likely wasn't open yet, Fin was prepared to wait until it was. Looking at the addresses above the doors as he drove, he knew he was close. He parked the rented silver Audi against the curb. He sat two doors down from Whimsy and watched the front of the shop for five minutes, drumming his fingers on the steering wheel. Staying in the car was not an option. He felt like a caged lion, so he decided to get out and walk to release some of the nervous energy that was pent up.

Four five-gallon buckets filled with flowers were placed on the walk in front of the large windows, so he knew that Margie was there, even though the store didn't appear to be open. He wanted to talk to her before customers came, maybe get an idea of where Ruby's mind was before he went to find her.

He eased out of the seat and stretched his arms above his head. It had been over twenty-four hours since he slept but, rather than being tired, he was edgy. He was running on adrenalin. He was sure his surroundings were great, but he was focused only on the building he was walking to. He looked through the leaded glass windows and saw his own reflection and the distant mountains behind him. He turned the knob and walked through the door. The bell chimed as it opened. He froze, his hand still gripping the handle.

She sat like a statue in front of him, her head down. Everything else disappeared. He couldn't say if other people were in the shop or even what was around him. He also couldn't move. He had never been nervous in his life but, at this moment, he found it hard to breathe. He couldn't mess this up, but everything he had rehearsed left his head the moment he walked through the door. He looked at where her eyes were still glued. She stared at the bucket of bluebells he had sent to Margie's. Her head came up slightly to look at the woman standing next to her. Fin took his eyes off Ruby and looked at the short, vibrant woman he assumed was Margie. Her mouth was open, but no words had come out, he was sure of it. She stared at him with an unjustified look of awe.

* * *

It felt like minutes, although it must have been only seconds that they all were frozen.

"Ruby." His voice was so familiar to her, and her mere name had so much emotion. It sounded the same as when he made love to her. Her body felt like it would break into a million pieces. She turned her head, closing her eyes as she looked over her shoulder opening them as slowly as a dream. He was there. It wasn't a dream. Her breath that she didn't know she was holding came out in a gust, and tears streamed down her face. Before she could register what was happening, he was at her side and scooping her up. He sat where she had been and cradled her in his arms.

"God, Ruby, I am so sorry." He kissed her hair and her cheek, rubbing her arm and saying her name over and over. Her head was against his chest so that she could feel his heart beat almost as fast as hers. All she wanted was to be lost in this feeling forever. She didn't care about the reason he was here or if and when he would leave. She didn't want to think at all. Then he stilled and, when she didn't look up at him, he put a finger under her chin and tilted her head up. She had nowhere else to look, except at him. His eyes were the grey of summer rain clouds and were filled with as much intensity.

* * *

The emotion was palpable when Fin spoke, and his voice was velvet. "I need you to look at me, Ruby." He paused, making sure she was listening, "I can't tell you how sorry I am about the way I left you. There are some things I need to tell you about why I pushed you away, but I need you to know something before another minute goes by. I love you, I love you, and I'm not leaving without you. Do you understand what I'm saying?" His heart was beating out of his chest. He tried to slow it by concentrating on breathing in and out, but as he looked at her, he was struck by his own words. *No, I could never leave her. I have never wanted anything with the force that I want her.* He didn't know what she would say. Hell, he didn't even know if she knew what he was asking.

Two things happened simultaneously: Fin spoke the most important words of his life at the same time that the bell chimed above the door. There was a loud intake of breath, which could have come from any of the three women that now occupied the flower shop, but Poppy was the first to speak. Her voice was controlled but short, "What?" Her eyes locked on the scene in front of her.

It was thirty seconds before Fin took his eyes off Ruby and turned to Poppy, whose mouth now also gaped open. He gave a lopsided grin. "You must be Poppy. I've asked your sister to marry me, but I think she may be in a slight state of shock." He stroked Ruby's hair and kissed her forehead. His grey t-shirt was soaked from her tears that still streamed down her face in quiet rivulets.

Poppy took two steps closer. "Ruby?"

Ruby looked up at her sister. "I can't…" The rest was cut short as she sprang away from Fin and ran to the back of the shop. They all heard a door shut and then the very familiar sound of puking.

They looked from one to the other. Fin got up and followed the path that Ruby had taken. His legs felt detached, and he heard only "I can't" before she leapt from his lap. *I'm going to lose my mind.* He knocked on the door of the now silent room.

"Ruby, are you okay? I'm coming in if you don't open the door." No sound came. He turned the knob, thankful it was unlocked so that he wouldn't have to force his way in. She stood looking at him, tears mixing with snot and spit. She looked so scared. "Ruby…"

In a guttural sob she choked out the words, "I'm pregnant."

He hadn't known what his reaction would be if his presumption was right, but his heart soared. "I know Ruby, and I am so happy. I love you, and I'm so happy."

She sucked in a huge glob of mucus through her nose. "How did you…" She went on, changing her words, "…I don't want you to marry me because I'm pregnant." She now choked on sobs, her breath catching.

Fin looked down at her and took both of her hands in his. He smiled. He knew he had an audience behind him, but he didn't care. These words were meant only for the woman standing in front of him. "Ruby, fate brought us together. I felt you the first time you stepped through the door of Prima Facie. Without even seeing you, I felt you. The air was electric."

He paused and took an even breath. "I've lived my whole life thinking only about myself and what I wanted. Then there was you, and all those things I lived for meant nothing any more. I see you in everything around me — the blue of the sky, a laugh, even a breeze. I close my eyes and I see you. I love *you,* and we're having a baby and, if it's possible, I love you even more. I want to marry you, and though I didn't put words to it, I knew it the night I first kissed you. Will you marry me?" He sucked in a breath and held it, waiting.

Without hesitating, she was his arms, her head in his neck. "I love you. I'll marry you!" There were more choking sobs, but they now came from the doorway.

"Ruby, I think you just found your true self." Margie's voice was quiet but happy. The words came from the day that they had given her a bon voyage: "We thought we should celebrate the beginning of your journey in finding your true self."

Fin opened his arms, and then they were all standing in the tiny bathroom holding each other. He looked at Poppy over Margie's head and, in a voice that held all of his emotions, said, "I love your sister, and I'll do everything I can to make her happy." Poppy only nodded her head; there was no way she could speak. Eventually, Ruby loosened her grip and slid back to the floor. Fin, however, was not quite ready to let her go, so held her to his body. She sniffed in again and started laughing into his chest.

Fin looked down. "I believe it's time for a new shirt." He beamed at Ruby. "I need to talk to you. Is there some place we can go?" He looked at the protective women next to Ruby. "Do you mind if I steal her for a bit?" They bobbed their heads in unison.

Ruby caught a glimpse of herself in the mirror. "Oh my god!" She covered her face. It looked like she'd been run over by a trash truck, its contents dumped on her face.

Fin laughed as he came up to her and hugged her from behind. "As crazy as this sounds, I don't think you've ever looked more beautiful."

Ruby's eyes looked up to the ceiling and back to him with an incredulous expression. "Are you insane? Go, go, and do something while I try and wash my face."

He turned her around and came down onto her lips, kissing with more passion than he ever had. His head swam as he released her mouth. "I love you. I'll be right back." He looked down at his shirt and said, "I'll go change my shirt." He tapped her nose. "You have five minutes." He squeezed through the doorway that Poppy and Margie filled and walked into the main shop.

* * *

Ruby looked at the mirror again. "I swear I will not go out like this." She wiped her nose with the back of her hand. Saying she would be back, Margie flitted out of the room.

Poppy looked at Ruby. "He was right, Ruby. You have never looked more beautiful. You're glowing from the inside out." They looked at each other in the mirror. "I've got so many questions that I don't even know where to start."

Margie came back in with a cloth from the shop. "Poppy,

I'll fill you in, but right now we have to make her look human again. No offense Ruby, but beautiful is a bit of a stretch right now. Geez, let's at least get the slime off you." She ran the cloth under cold water and laid it over Ruby's face.

Ruby took hold of it. "I can take it." She rubbed it over her eyes and nose, and when she looked out, Margie was gone again. Poppy was talking.

"What happened? I want to hear everything. My gosh, you're getting married." Her eyes welled up.

Margie was back. "Christ, Poppy, don't start that. Ruby will start all over again. Here, take this and start brushing. I told you I would tell you and, when they get back, we'll get more of the scoop." Margie handed Ruby a disposable toothbrush with paste already on it. Ruby looked at it and then at Margie. "I have them in my purse. You never know." She ran a brush through Ruby's hair as Ruby swished and spit into the blue glass sink.

When she looked up, Fin was resting one shoulder on the door frame. He had exchanged his grey t-shirt for a faded blue one, and he took her breath away. He held a bluebell up to his nose and smiled. "You ready, lass?" They all exited the cramped bathroom as one. Poppy and Margie fanned out when the space opened up, but Fin never left Ruby's side. "We'll be back." Holding the small of her back, he guided her out the door.

CHAPTER THIRTY-NINE

Fin needed to be touching her in some way. He was holding her hand, but it wasn't enough. He needed so much more. He looked to the side. The car was parked near an alley by the flower shop, and he pulled her in that direction. "We need to make a quick stop before we make it to my rental." He took a few steps into the shadowed ally and held her against the brick of the building. His voice was ragged, "Ruby, I'm sorry if this offends you, but I cannot take another step without it."

His hands cupped her face and, at the same time, her hands grabbed at his shoulders. The need coming from both of them was powerful. As he descended onto her mouth, he moaned her name as she opened hers for him. It could have been one minute or ten—all Fin wanted was to melt into the woman that had changed his life and that now he would never have to be without. He was dizzy with the force of that realization.

He broke from her, his voice fast and forceful, "I have a room not far from here. We can go there, or I'm afraid I'm going to compromise you against this wall."

Ruby laughed uncontrollably and asked, "Where're you staying?"

He looked at her with smoldering eyes. "Ruby, I swear I am about to explode for wanting you. Christ, I haven't even checked in yet. I came right from the airport." He raked his fingers through his hair. "It's on Walnut and Tenth Street. Is that far? Do I need the car?"

She was still laughing, and said, "If we drive, we can be

there in less than five minutes."

He slapped her butt playfully. "Then we definitely drive." He fished the keys out of his pocket as they walked to where he was parked. He went around and opened the passenger door for Ruby.

She eased in to the soft leather interior and waited for Fin to get in. "Nice rental."

He looked around, as if he was seeing the car for the first time. His lips came together in a straight line, and he nodded absently. "Yeah, I guess it is." He slowly brushed away a strand of hair that had fallen over her eye. "Lead the way."

* * *

A shudder ran the length of her body with his touch, and heat pooled between her legs. She gave the most direct route to the Hotel Josephine and, as promised, the drive took four minutes. Fin popped the trunk. His luggage was brought to him by the valet, who traded places with Fin and went to park the car. He threw his leather bag over one shoulder and put an arm around Ruby. He looked at her and smiled. "I've cooled down a little. I can check in, and we can go for a walk if you'd like."

Ruby felt the warmth of his arm around her. With complete candor, she grinned and shook her head. "Actually, if you don't mind, I only want to be with you with no one else around."

Fin moved his arm lower on her back and scooped her up into his arms. "Well then, my lady; that is what you will have." He brushed her lips with his and walked through the glass doors of the hotel.

Ruby searched for the embarrassment she should be feeling being carried into a hotel, but felt only pure joy. He set her on her feet when they reached the counter. Ruby looked at the woman behind the desk as she ogled Fin, but Fin was focused only on Ruby. She felt the intensity of his gaze without even looking. His finger was making circles on her bare shoulder, and goose bumps sprouted in seconds.

"Finley Sinclair."

The girl, who couldn't have been more than eighteen, opened her mouth and finally found her voice. "Huh? Oh, yes. Are you having a good day?" She began typing onto the keyboard.

Fin took his eyes off Ruby and looked at the girl. "I have a feeling it's going to get better in the next ten minutes." Ruby felt her face heat up and looked at the stone floor.

The girl snickered. "Alright. We have you in the suite overlooking the Flatirons." As she produced the key card, she told them about the amenities the hotel offered. Ruby didn't hear a thing. Fin's hand was around her waist, causing sparks to fly. She had to use all of her concentration to breath.

* * *

"This is Rodney. He'll show you to your room, Mr. Sinclair." They made it up to the room. Fin handed some bills to Rodney and then proceeded to hang the "Do Not Disturb" sign on the door.

Fin turned and walked slowly toward Ruby. Her eyes were so blue. He was mesmerized. His heart felt like had just been shocked by a defibrillator, and he was sure that Ruby could hear it beating. She licked her lips and looked over her shoulder, past the sitting area and into the bedroom. He kept walking until he was inches from her. He then came even closer, putting his hands on her shoulders and leading her backward through the door, until the backs of her legs butted up to the bed. He looked at the dress she wore, gauging.

She seemed able to read his mind. "It goes over my head."

"It's pretty. I like it."

Ruby shivered as his hands glided down her arms. "I got it in Greece with Retta." Her voice was a whisper.

"Did you?" He smiled and gathered up the material at the same time. Ruby nodded and lifted her arms. The gauzy cotton grazed her skin as it went over her head. She was left in nothing but her aqua, bikini underwear. Fin suck in a breath. "Ruby, you are so beautiful." His hand went to her stomach. "Does anything hurt? Is this okay?"

She touched his chest. "My boobs are tender." She giggled.

"I'll be gentle with them." He bent and ran his tongue around one erect nipple and paid the same attention to the other. "Does that hurt?" He reached around, pulled the puffy comforter down, and pushed down gently on her shoulders, easing her to the soft cotton sheets. He took his clothes off and joined her under the covers. They spent the next hour indulging in each other's bodies, Ruby crying out his name as she shattered in his arms.

Fin drew a bath, filling the deep tub with the hotel's jasmine bubble bath. Ruby sat against one end, and Fin the other. He bombarded her with questions about the time they were apart, about the countries she saw, the people she met, what she saw, and what she liked and disliked. He finished with the pregnancy. He told her about Chloris coming to Stonehaven, telling him that she had seen Ruby, and about her hunch. He apologized again and again and, staring at the bubbles, said in a sure voice, "Well, I have a lifetime to make it up to you."

Ruby rolled her eyes. She had told him repeatedly that yes, he had been an ass, but she didn't care about any of that now. She just wanted to go on from here and be happy. They spoke about the baby. Fin was so excited and optimistic that the feeling seemed to rub off on Ruby. Her face became more relaxed and animated the more they talked of their future.

He helped her dry off and wrapped the hotel robe around her pink skin. "I'm going to order room service. You go sit on the terrace and I'll be out in a bit. I still need to talk to you about some things."

* * *

Ruby wiped her hands on the robe as she walked out through the French doors, knowing that Fin wouldn't say anything until he was ready. She had felt that he wasn't being completely honest with her, so she mentally went through a list of possibilities. *He is in trouble with the law and is on the lamb. He's in a relationship with a psycho who won't let him go. He has a child he has never seen.* While the options were endless, she stopped herself—none of those made sense with the man she knew. She leaned her head back and looked at the sheer rock walls of the Flatirons in the distance. She had heard Fin ordering something on the telephone, and he was now probably getting dressed. In her head, she pictured Fin standing in the doorway of Whimsy—it still seemed like a dream. How many times had she willed him to come to her? Now he was here, and the reality was better than anything she could have imagined. She pulled her legs up and tucked the robe around herself. Then, as she sat still in the silence, the force of what was happening struck her.

Two months. Two months. She had wanted to find out who she was. She had dumped a boyfriend, traveled to Europe, met some extraordinary people, fallen in love, and became pregnant. Her throat burned and, at the same time, constricted to the size of a thin straw. If she hadn't started crying, she would be laughing at how insane her life sounded.

She felt Fin's hands on her shoulders and hoped he wouldn't come around and see her crying again. As much as she hated crying, a person surely wouldn't know it spending any time with her. She was an annoying bathroom sink — drip, drip, drip.

He kissed her neck. "You smell good." He kissed her cheek, damn. He came around and kneeled in front of her. "Ruby, what's wrong? Do you feel okay?" He brushed a rogue tear from her chin.

A bubble of laughter came up her throat. "I haven't had a lot of time to sit and think. Poppy or Margie have been with me, filling my time, and I was just sitting here wondering, 'What the hell are we going to do? Where are we going to go?' I work part time in a flower shop and, oh my god, I don't even know what you do. You live in Scotland. Okay, I am officially freaking out. I feel like I can't breathe."

She tried taking in air through her nose and blowing it out her mouth, but it kept catching in her chest. "I'm having a baby. How am I going to take care of a baby?" She started rocking back and forth, something that was supposed to be soothing, but now she shook so hard that nothing less than a morphine drip would calm her.

* * *

Fin placed both his hands on the side of Ruby's face. True, there were some logistics that needed to be worked out, but he needed to reassure her that there was nothing else to worry about before she went off the deep end. He kept his voice level and held her gaze. "Ruby, the first thing is that *we* are having a baby. The next is what I wanted to talk…"

His words were cut off by a knock on the door. Fin

growled an unintelligible expletive under his breath and stood. "I'll be right back. Take a deep breath." His finger traced her bottom lip. He stopped at the veranda door and looked at her. "Hey, I love you." Ruby shook, looking at him blankly. A grunt came out of her mouth.

He came back carrying two glasses of orange juice and set them on a small table. He had been going over in his head what he wanted to tell Ruby, but now that the moment was here, he didn't want to cause her more stress. Fin pulled the other chair across the concrete of the balcony and faced Ruby. His knees touched her chair, and he rested his arms on his thighs. He took a gulp of air and held it in his cheeks before blowing it out in a big whoosh.

He ran his fingers through his hair. "I'm a little nervous. I knew exactly how I wanted to say this, but it seems to have flown out of my head." Ruby clenched her jaw so tightly that he thought her molars might explode. He decided to get on with it before they had to make a dental visit. "I guess I'll start with my childhood."

He described a privileged upbringing, private schools, tutors, and lessons—things that, as a boy, he thought everyone had access to. He told of the closeness of his family and that when they got older, as siblings, they became the closest of friends, being burned by others that only wanted things from them. He gave her a brief synopsis of his family's business. He told of how, until recently, he had been, perhaps not the black sheep, but something close to it. He told of how he lived only for himself, became cynical and jaded and, in turn, probably used people in his own right.

The night of the winter party came flooding back. He felt the icy road through his pants and the cutting wind on his face as he looked at his nephew. His voice was ragged as he described the brother he idolized and how his world had dropped out from underneath him when Ian was killed. With some shame, he told her that he had, in essence, run away to Brugge and had ingratiated himself to Hans. He skipped over the revolving door of women that never helped him forget anything, but did tell her that he spent most days laboring and all nights drunk, trying to forget his grief and the responsibilities he shirked.

He then told Ruby that the instant he saw her, a kind of awareness hit him like a thunderclap. He couldn't explain the emotions that she brought out in him and how he wanted to be the best person he could be with her. He had never felt anything close to the sensations he had when he was with Ruby, and he knew that he would never be able to be without it. Ruby's eyes filled with tears at his pain. She stopped him to ask questions a few times, but mainly let him talk without interruption. Fin picked up her hand and ran circles around the back of it with his thumb. "So now you know everything." He gave a lopsided grin as he continued, "You already said you would marry me. You aren't going to back out, are you?" His voice was deceptively light, but the strain he felt was palpable. His heart skipped a beat when she didn't answer right away.

* * *

Ruby watched his thumb as it made its way around her hand. Everything about him made her feel safe and loved. She slowly looked up at him and could tell that he was waiting for her next words. "You know, when I went to Europe I went to find out who I was on my own." She paused, and his hand stilled. "But, what I found was that the person I was, and everything I can be, is intertwined with you. It's kismet." She touched his lips. "I love you."

He looked at her reverently. "I love you, too." She smiled at him with her whole heart. They both sat without saying anything, looking at each other with smiles that resembled a cat after a good nap.

Fin pulled her hand and brought her into his lap. Ruby curled into his strong frame and breathed in his scent. "Ruby, we're having a baby." He brushed a strand of hair from her eye. "I never thought those words would make me feel so happy." He chuckled, and she playfully punched his shoulder. "I would venture a guess that your sister is climbing the walls, wondering what's going on. Why don't you call her and we can meet her somewhere." He ran his mouth along her silky hair. "Chances are great that it is going to resemble the inquisition, correct?"

Ruby cocked her head and nodded. "I would say the chances are high." She started wriggling off his lap. "I'm going to go call her."

His arms tightened. "Tell her I have some questions for her, too." He raised one brow mysteriously.

She blew out a puff of air. "Yeah? Okay." She took one last deep breath in, filling herself with his smell—a combination of jasmine from the bath and fresh air—and made her way inside to make the call.

CHAPTER FORTY

They met Poppy at a café on Pearl Street with a small outdoor eating area. Poppy was already seated at a square table with a croissant and a soup-bowl sized cappuccino, her finger playing in the frothy milk. She looked up as they approached and wiped her finger on a napkin. Standing, she took Ruby into a big hug. "Are you okay?" She held her out to look at her, and pulled her back into another embrace.

"I'm good." Her voice was muffled, having to make its way through a think bunch of hair, a shirt, and a shoulder, but the message was received. Ruby eased into the chair by the rail, and Fin languidly sat next to her.

"I've been going crazy wondering what you were doing." She looked at the sly smile playing on Fin's lips and the color that had risen on Ruby's cheeks. Her eyes narrowed. "What *have* you been doing?"

Before Fin could say anything, Ruby piped up, "We were at the hotel, talking." She pierced Fin with a "Don't even think about it" look. In return, he smiled angelically and bit his tongue.

She looked at Poppy, happy to change the subject. "Did you take the day off?" She had just noticed that Poppy's skirt had been replaced with faded jeans and that her hair was loose down her back.

Poppy looked from one to the other. "Huh, okay." She wasn't convinced that her sister was being honest about what they had been doing, but went on. "Yeah, I took a sick day so I could spend time with both of you. Sam is coming to meet us."

Right on cue, the sinewy man made his entrance and placed both hands on the rail. "So, we're all playing hooky?" His smile was natural and relaxed. He made his way to the table in perfect hooky attire: faded red cargo shorts, flip-flops, and a "Off My Cloud" t-shirt. His hand shot out. "Hi. I'm Sam."

Fin stood up and shook his hand, "Finley. Ruby's told me a lot about you."

The waiter came to their table and took their order. Then they spent the next two hours in lively conversation. Poppy ran through all of her questions in lawyerly fashion—the how's, logistics, intentions, and his background.

Fin gave information freely, telling them about his upbringing. He made Poppy and Sam laugh so hard at some of his stories that tears rolled from everyone's eyes. He described his family's business, telling Poppy that he would need to spend time in Scotland, but that he should be able to do most of his work over the phone, allowing himself and Ruby to have the flexibility to share their time between Colorado and Scotland.

He even recruited Sam to draw up some plans for a house and guest house he wanted to build on his family land for Ruby, himself, and the little one on the way. Mentioning the baby gave way to a whole other conversation of names and shopping trips.

The only thing that came close to breaking the magic spell was Sam reminding them that Fin and Ruby still needed to break the news of the shotgun wedding to her parents. This time it was Poppy who waved her hand in the air, as if the pregnancy and a wedding were mere flies that needed swatting. "They are going to be so happy. They belong together. Hell, I already love him."

By the time they stood to leave, it was if they had all been friends and family for years. The joy and excitement of life was a physical presence all around them. Ruby and Poppy walked ahead, making plans for Poppy to come to Scotland, while Sam tried to convince Fin to come and play soccer with some men he played with two nights a week.

Ruby looked over her shoulder just as Fin's eyes met hers. His smile made her catch her breath, and everything seemed to stand still for that moment. She reached down and stroked her stomach. To her depths, she knew she was ready to begin their destiny.

THANK YOU

The inspiration for this book was formed over twenty years ago, when I put on a backpack and decided to discover Europe and myself. I met amazing people and experienced a magical time. There were parts of that trip that I couldn't put away on a shelf and that tickled at the back of my mind. I'd like to thank those people who made my book come alive.

My editor, Jeff Ludwig, who never stopped encouraging me and bounced ideas with me to shape this manuscript into something I am proud of. You are more than editor—you are a friend.

My sister, Karen who read endless versions of pages, paragraphs, and chapters. You've been my champion throughout this process and never let me put it away.

My parents, who have always let me spread my wings without discouraging outrageous ideas.

Lisa Fender and the rest of the writers group who gave me much needed guidance.

To my sister's book club, who were my first non-family readers and my friends who read along the way: Robin, Jane, and Jennifer.

Lastly my family, for your support.

ABOUT THE AUTHOR

Becki Alfsen spent four years traveling in twenty-four countries around the world—two of those teaching English in Japan. She is a graduate of the University of Colorado, Boulder and lives in Denver with her family, where she works with special needs children. She wrote this book while at home raising her two sons. *Wandress* was a finalist in the Romance Writers of Denver Molly contest. This is her first novel.